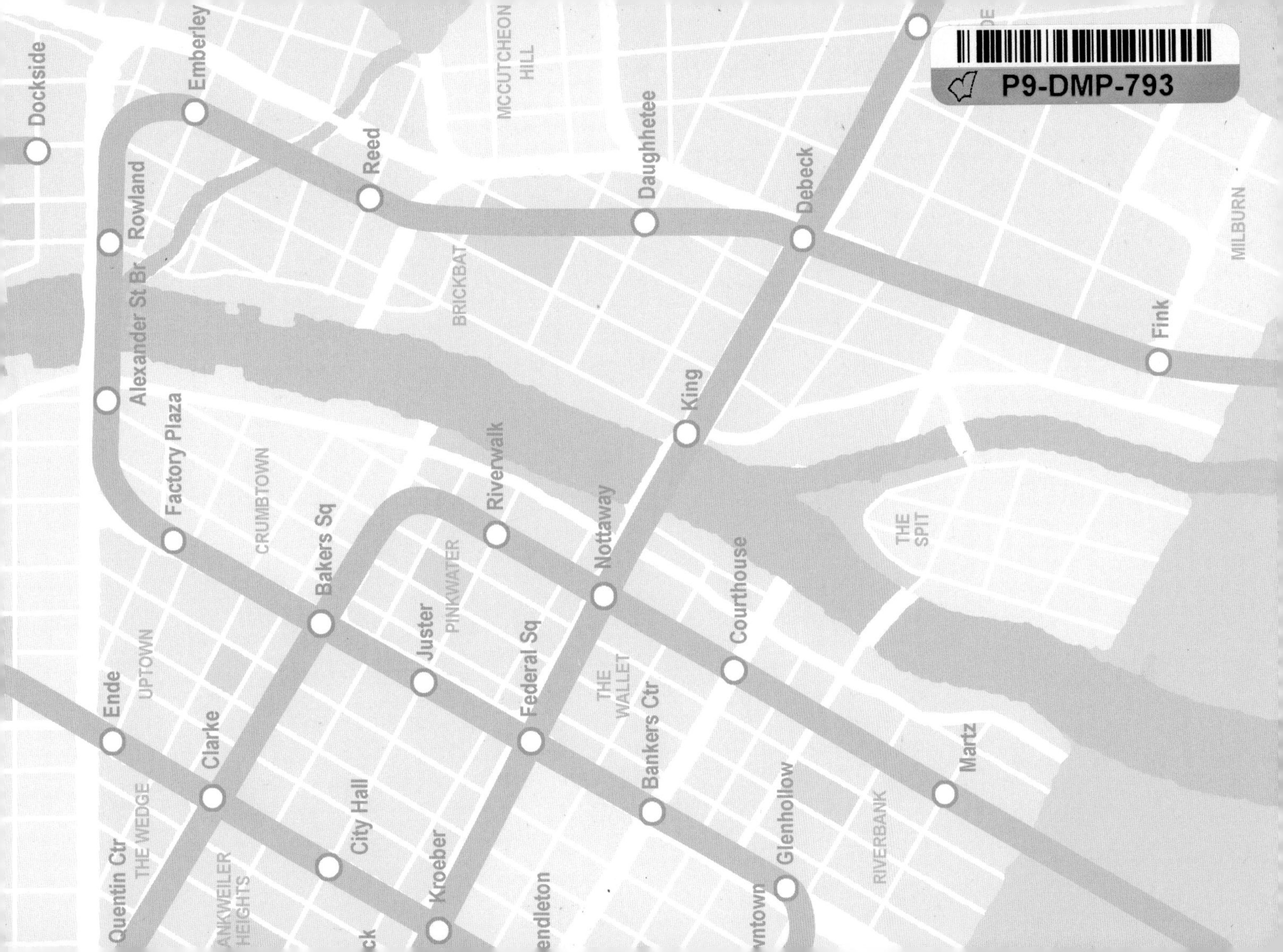
Dockside
Emberley
MCCUTCHEON HILL
Reed
Daughhetee
Debeck
Rowland
MILBURN
Alexander St Br
BRICKBAT
Fink
King
Factory Plaza
Riverwalk
CRUMBTOWN
THE SPIT
Bakers Sq
Nottaway
Courthouse
PINKWATER
Juster
Federal Sq
THE WALLET
UPTOWN
Ende
Bankers Ctr
Clarke
Martz
City Hall
Glenhollow
RIVERBANK
THE WEDGE
Quentin Ctr
ANKWEILER HEIGHTS
Kroeber

THE CREEPY CASE FILES OF

MARGO MALOO

THE MONSTER MALL

DREW WEING

:01

First Second

NEW YORK

First Second

Margo Maloo was co-created by Drew Weing and Eleanor Davis

Published by First Second
First Second is an imprint of Roaring Brook Press, a division of Holtzbrinck Publishing
Holdings Limited Partnership
175 Fifth Avenue, New York, NY 10010

Library of Congress Control Number: 2017957141

ISBN: 978-1-62672-492-1

Our books may be purchased in bulk for promotional, educational, or business use. Please contact your local bookseller or the Macmillan Corporate and Premium Sales Department at (800) 221-7945 ext. 5442 or by e-mail at MacmillanSpecialMarkets@macmillan.com.

FIRST EDITION

First edition, 2018
Book design by Drew Weing and Molly Johanson

Printed in China by Toppan Leefung Printing Ltd., Dongguan City, Guangdong Province
10 9 8 7 6 5 4 3 2 1

Drawn with a Zebra .05mm mechanical pencil, inked with a Platinum Carbon fountain pen, Platinum Carbon Ink Cartridges, PH Martin Bombay Ink, any old cheap brush for areas of black, and Deleter White for corrections. Drawn on Strathmore 400 series smooth bristol. Colored with Photoshop, a Cintiq Pen Display, and a lot of scribbling.

BY ART WE LIVE

FOR MY MOM, WHO ALWAYS BELIEVED ME WHEN
I TOLD HER THERE WAS SOMETHING UNDER THE BED.

Greetings, loyal readers! Charles Thompson here, bringing you the news and making the world a little safer for kids everywhere.

As you'll remember, I've recently relocated to Echo City (not MY idea—thanks, Mom and Dad). My new home base is a creepy old apartment building called the Bellwether. My instincts told me something was not normal about this new home, and I was right! On the very first night, I was rudely awakened by an enormous troll!

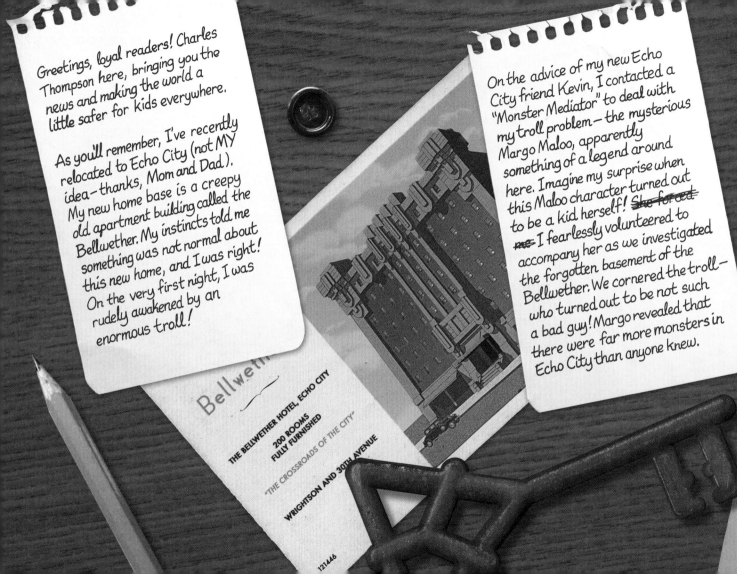

Bellwether

THE BELLWETHER HOTEL, ECHO CITY
200 ROOMS
FULLY FURNISHED
"THE CROSSROADS OF THE CITY"
WRIGHTSON AND 30TH AVENUE

121446

On the advice of my new Echo City friend Kevin, I contacted a "Monster Mediator" to deal with my troll problem—the mysterious Margo Maloo, apparently something of a legend around here. Imagine my surprise when this Maloo character turned out to be a kid herself! ~~She forced me~~ I fearlessly volunteered to accompany her as we investigated the forgotten basement of the Bellwether. We cornered the troll—who turned out to be not such a bad guy! Margo revealed that there were far more monsters in Echo City than anyone knew.

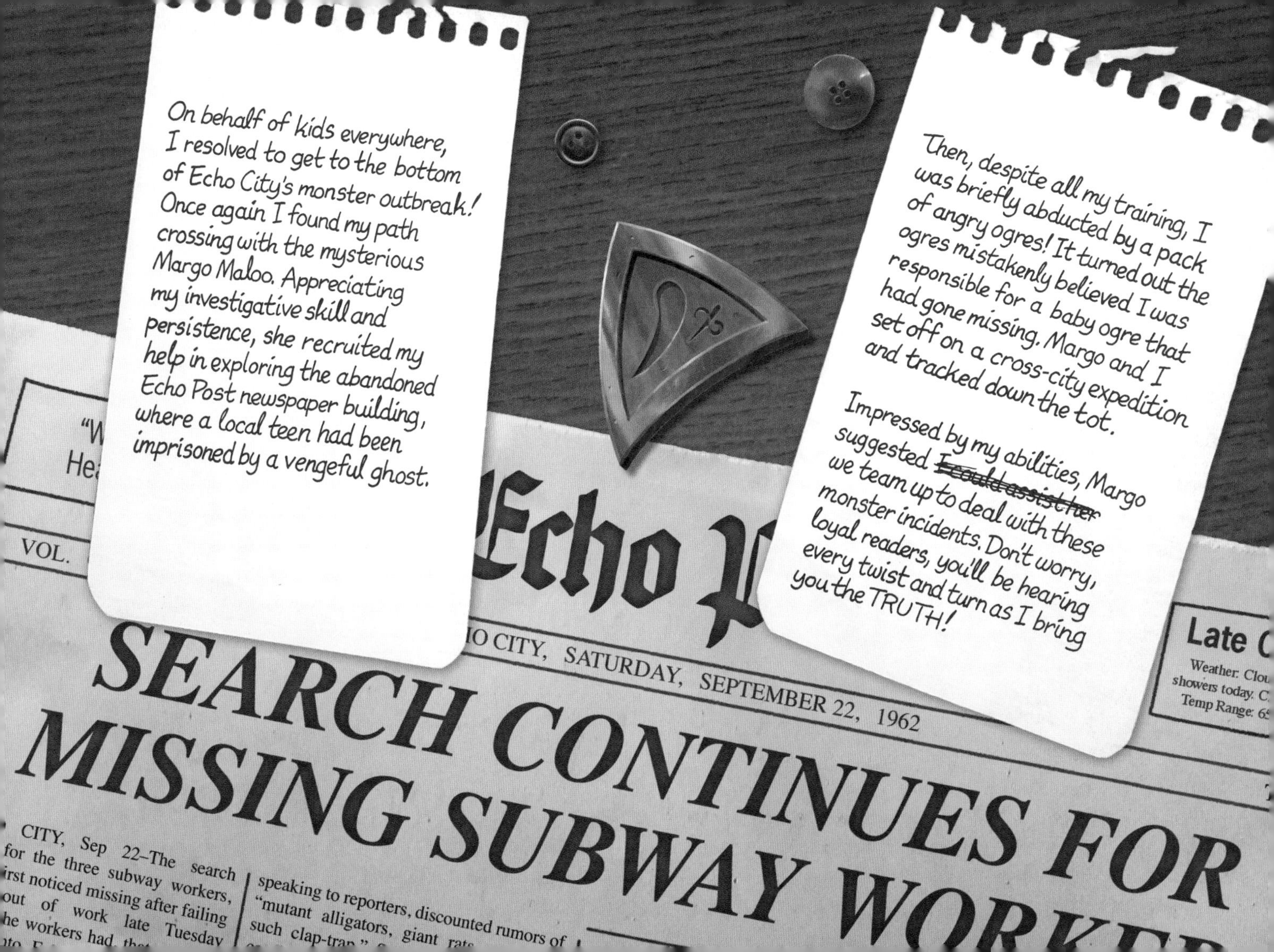
On behalf of kids everywhere, I resolved to get to the bottom of Echo City's monster outbreak! Once again I found my path crossing with the mysterious Margo Maloo. Appreciating my investigative skill and persistence, she recruited my help in exploring the abandoned Echo Post newspaper building, where a local teen had been imprisoned by a vengeful ghost.
Then, despite all my training, I was briefly abducted by a pack of angry ogres! It turned out the ogres mistakenly believed I was responsible for a baby ogre that had gone missing. Margo and I set off on a cross-city expedition and tracked down the tot.
Impressed by my abilities, Margo suggested ~~I could assist her~~ we team up to deal with these monster incidents. Don't worry, loyal readers, you'll be hearing every twist and turn as I bring you the TRUTH!
Echo P
VOL.
O CITY, SATURDAY, SEPTEMBER 22, 1962
Late C
Weather: Clou
showers today. C
Temp Range: 65
SEARCH CONTINUES FOR MISSING SUBWAY WORKER
CITY, Sep 22–The search for the three subway workers, first noticed missing after failing out of work late Tuesday he workers had
speaking to reporters, discounted rumors of "mutant alligators, giant rats such clap-trap."

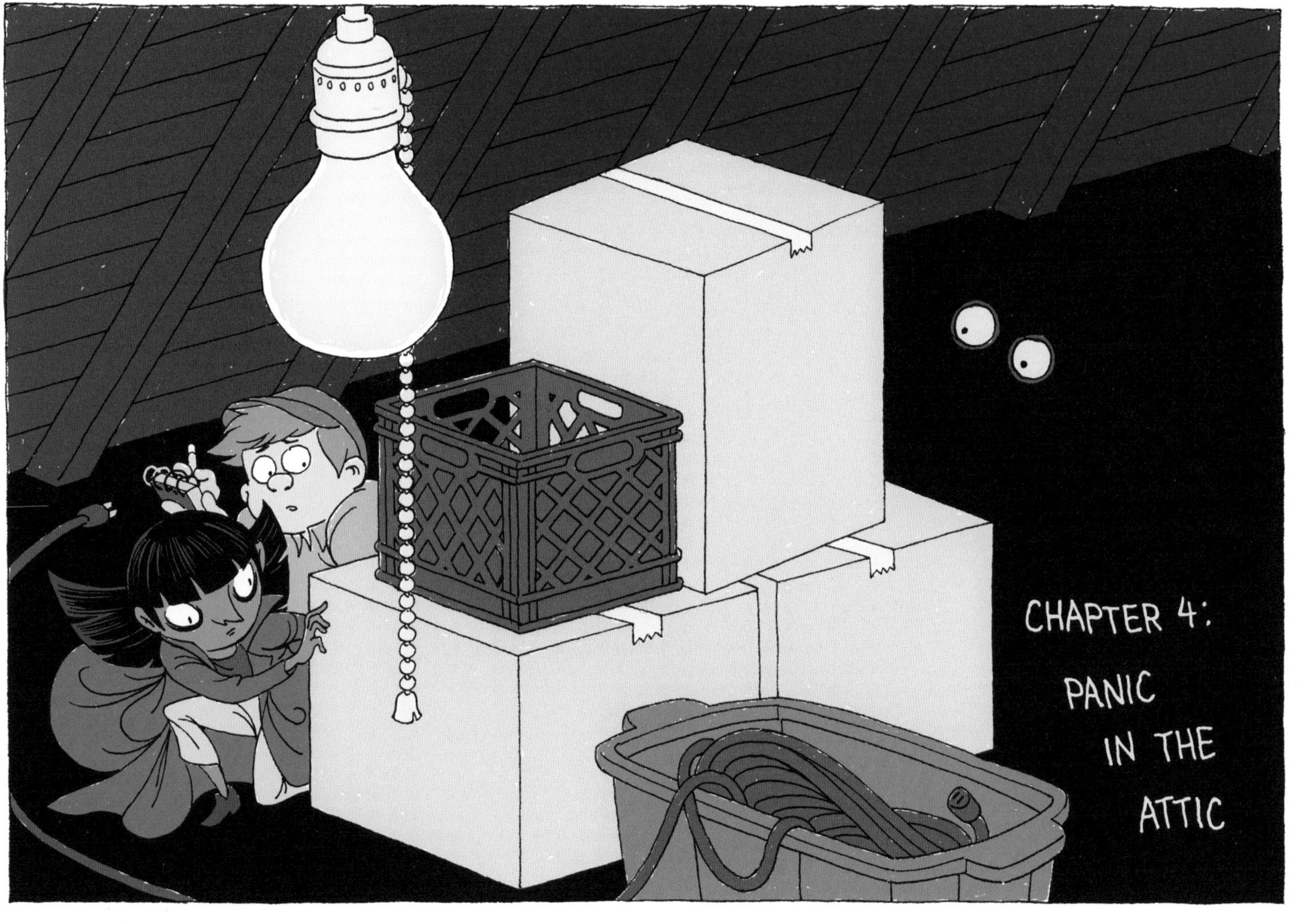
CHAPTER 4:
PANIC
IN THE
ATTIC

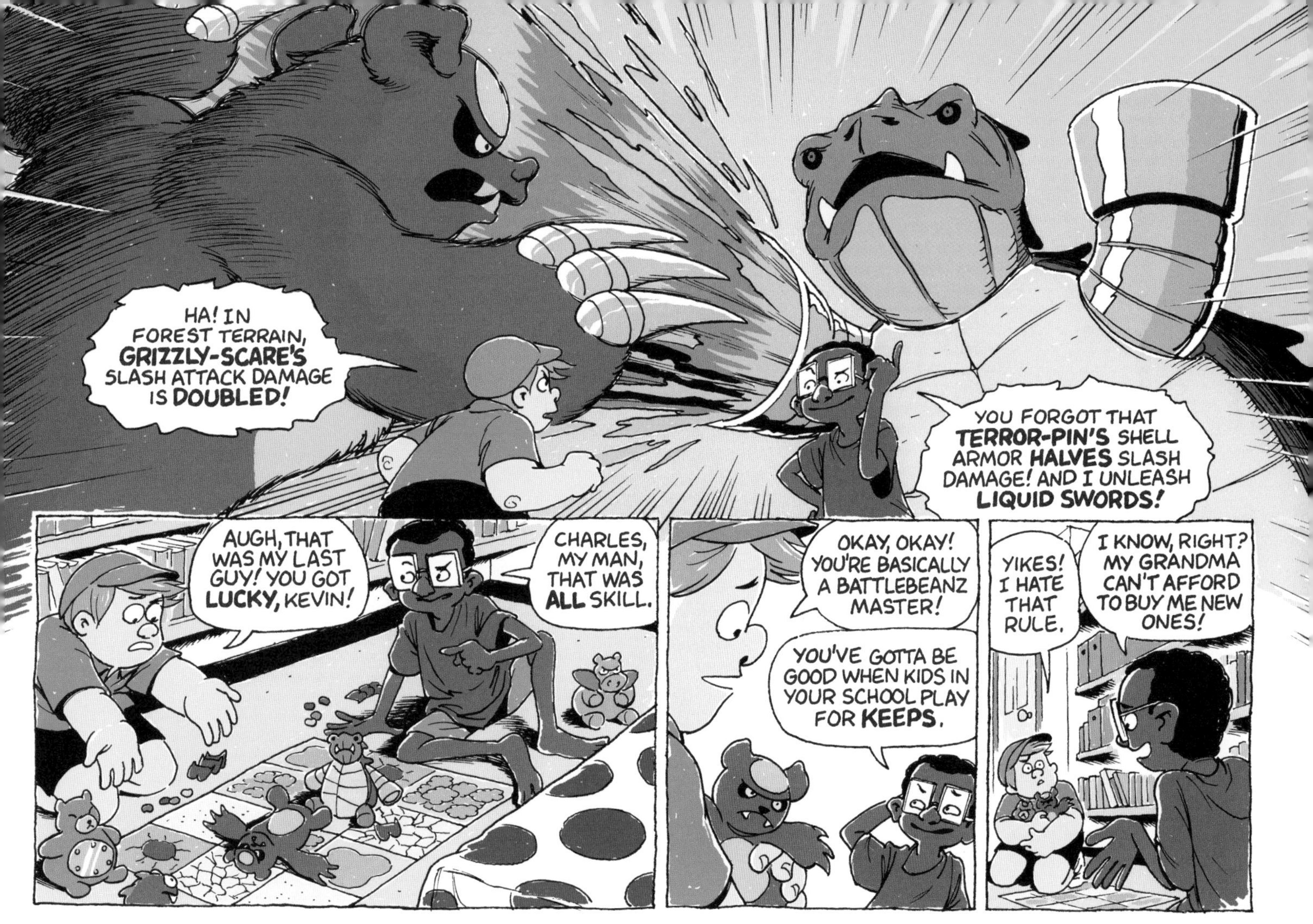

HA! IN FOREST TERRAIN, GRIZZLY-SCARE'S SLASH ATTACK DAMAGE IS DOUBLED!
YOU FORGOT THAT TERROR-PIN'S SHELL ARMOR HALVES SLASH DAMAGE! AND I UNLEASH LIQUID SWORDS!
AUGH, THAT WAS MY LAST GUY! YOU GOT LUCKY, KEVIN!
CHARLES, MY MAN, THAT WAS ALL SKILL.
OKAY, OKAY! YOU'RE BASICALLY A BATTLEBEANZ MASTER!
YOU'VE GOTTA BE GOOD WHEN KIDS IN YOUR SCHOOL PLAY FOR KEEPS.
YIKES! I HATE THAT RULE.
I KNOW, RIGHT? MY GRANDMA CAN'T AFFORD TO BUY ME NEW ONES!

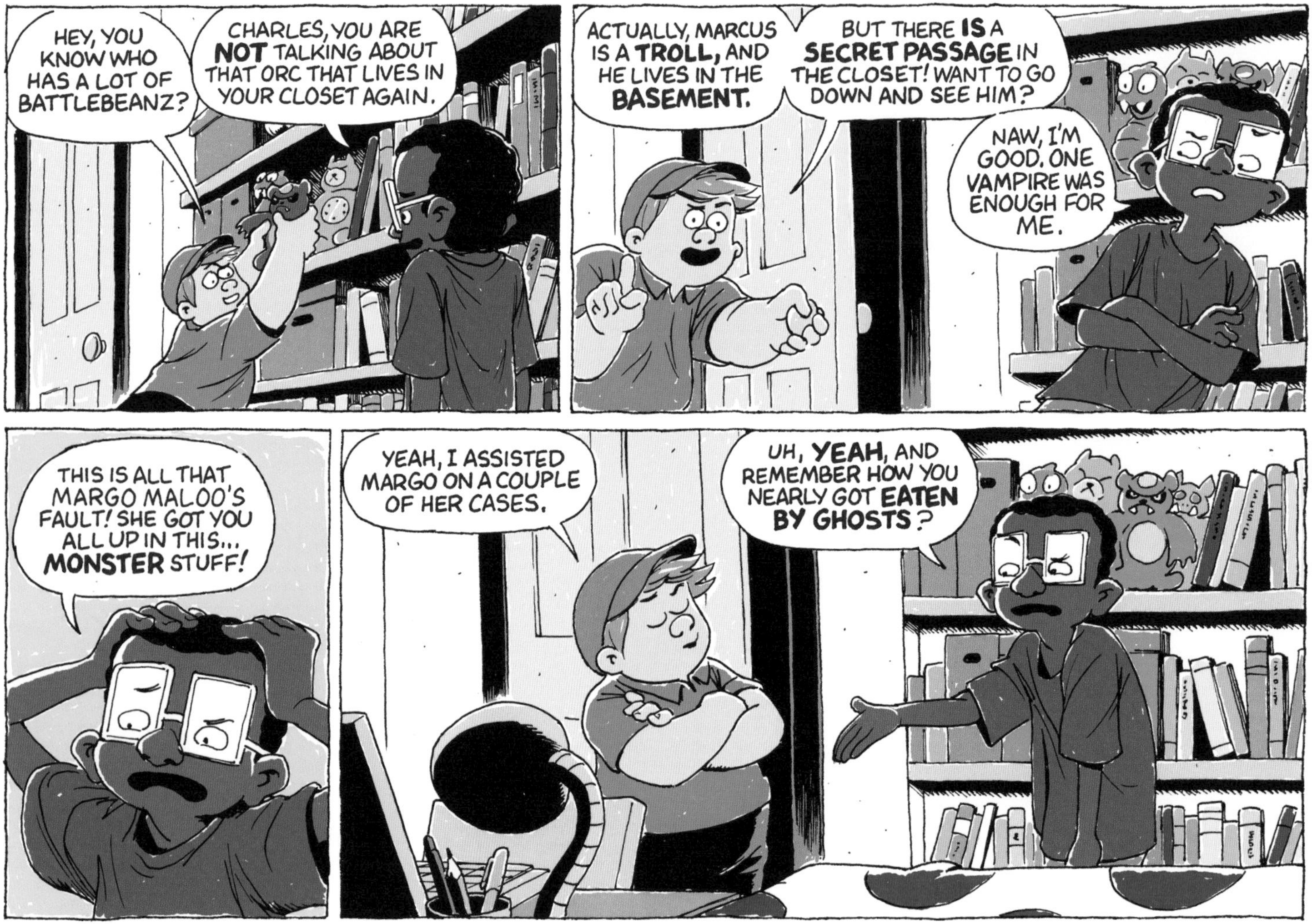
HEY, YOU KNOW WHO HAS A LOT OF BATTLEBEANZ?
CHARLES, YOU ARE **NOT** TALKING ABOUT THAT ORC THAT LIVES IN YOUR CLOSET AGAIN.
ACTUALLY, MARCUS IS A **TROLL,** AND HE LIVES IN THE **BASEMENT.**
BUT THERE **IS** A **SECRET PASSAGE** IN THE CLOSET! WANT TO GO DOWN AND SEE HIM?
NAW, I'M GOOD. ONE VAMPIRE WAS ENOUGH FOR ME.
THIS IS ALL THAT MARGO MALOO'S FAULT! SHE GOT YOU ALL UP IN THIS... **MONSTER** STUFF!
YEAH, I ASSISTED MARGO ON A COUPLE OF HER CASES.
UH, **YEAH,** AND REMEMBER HOW YOU NEARLY GOT **EATEN BY GHOSTS**?

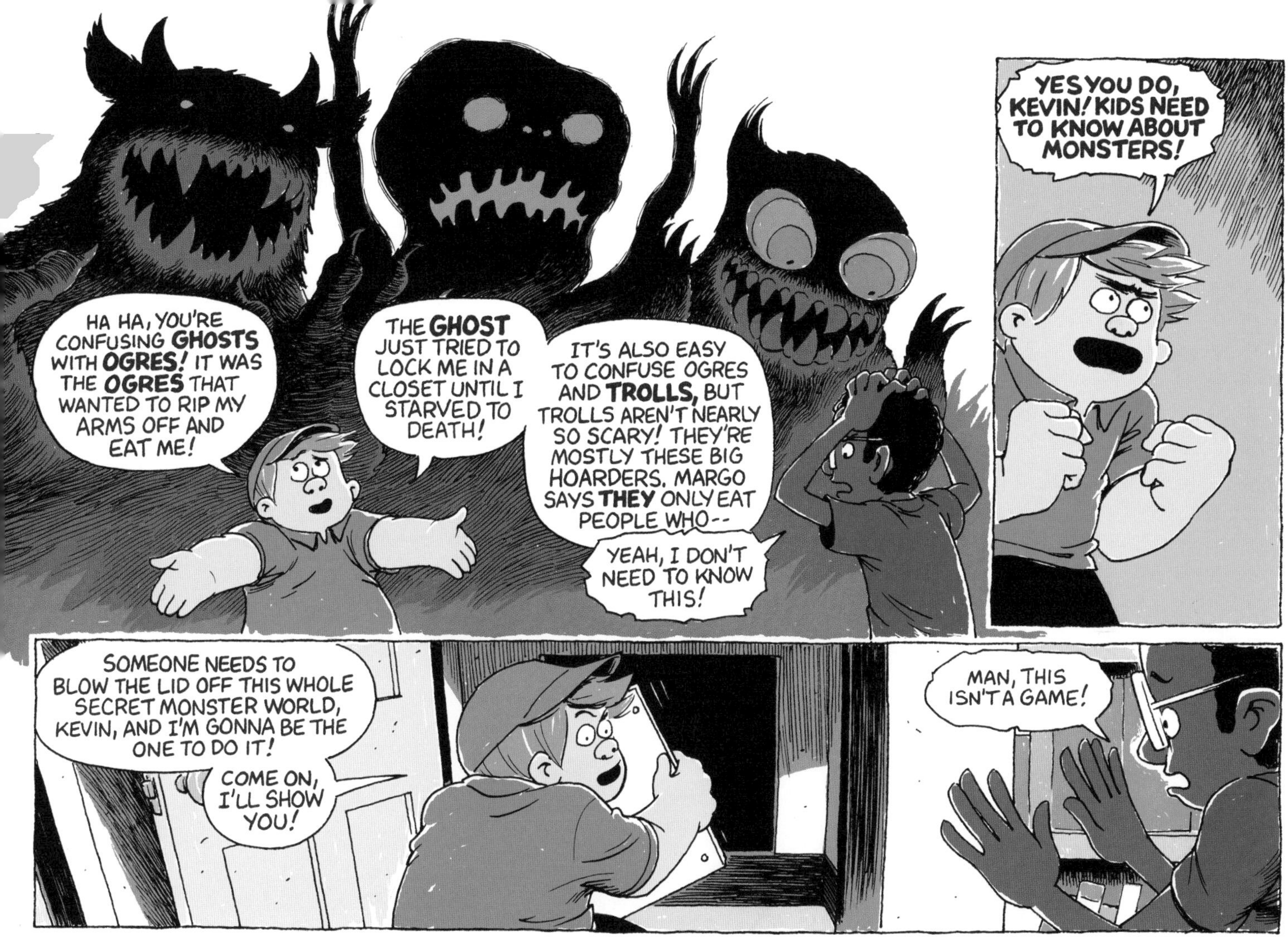
HA HA, YOU'RE CONFUSING **GHOSTS** WITH **OGRES!** IT WAS THE **OGRES** THAT WANTED TO RIP MY ARMS OFF AND EAT ME!
THE **GHOST** JUST TRIED TO LOCK ME IN A CLOSET UNTIL I STARVED TO DEATH!
IT'S ALSO EASY TO CONFUSE OGRES AND **TROLLS,** BUT TROLLS AREN'T NEARLY SO SCARY! THEY'RE MOSTLY THESE BIG HOARDERS. MARGO SAYS **THEY** ONLY EAT PEOPLE WHO--
YEAH, I DON'T NEED TO KNOW THIS!
YES YOU DO, KEVIN! KIDS NEED TO KNOW ABOUT MONSTERS!
SOMEONE NEEDS TO BLOW THE LID OFF THIS WHOLE SECRET MONSTER WORLD, KEVIN, AND I'M GONNA BE THE ONE TO DO IT!
COME ON, I'LL SHOW YOU!
MAN, THIS ISN'T A GAME!

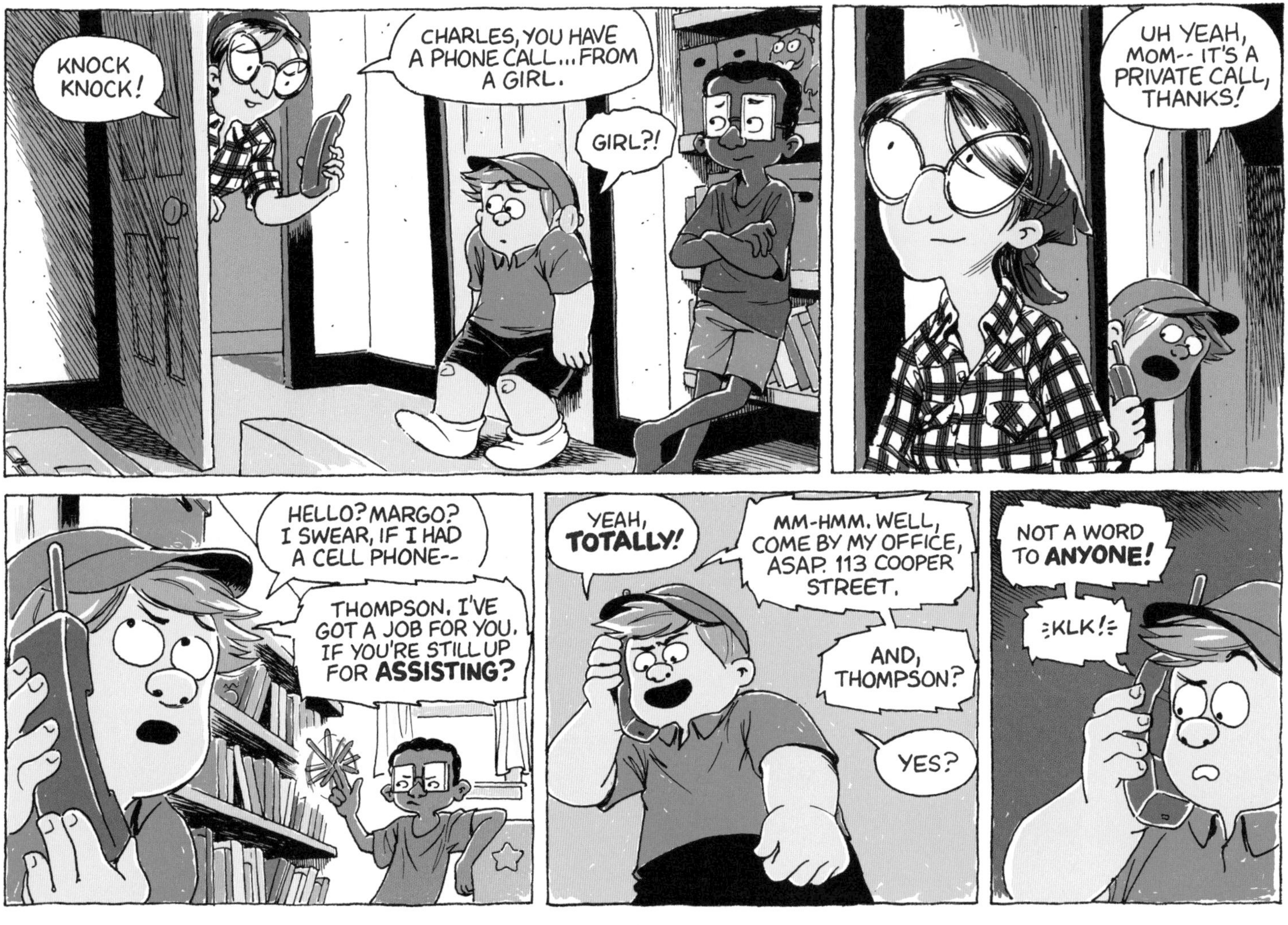
KNOCK KNOCK!
CHARLES, YOU HAVE A PHONE CALL... FROM A GIRL.
GIRL?!
UH YEAH, MOM-- IT'S A PRIVATE CALL, THANKS!
HELLO? MARGO? I SWEAR, IF I HAD A CELL PHONE--
THOMPSON. I'VE GOT A JOB FOR YOU. IF YOU'RE STILL UP FOR **ASSISTING**?
YEAH, **TOTALLY!**
MM-HMM. WELL, COME BY MY OFFICE, ASAP. 113 COOPER STREET.
AND, THOMPSON?
YES?
NOT A WORD TO **ANYONE!**
KLK!

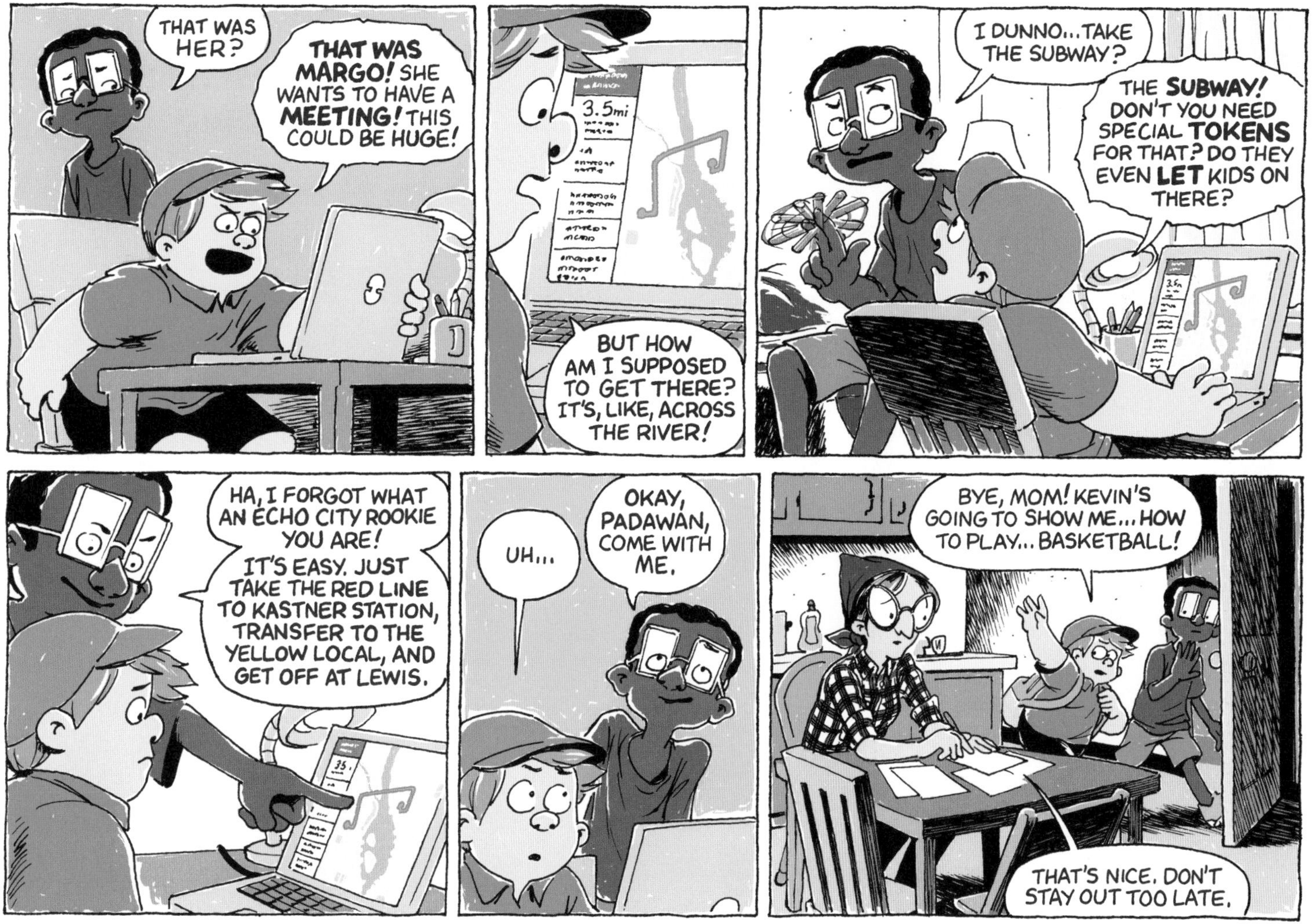
THAT WAS HER?
THAT WAS MARGO! SHE WANTS TO HAVE A MEETING! THIS COULD BE HUGE!
3.5mi
BUT HOW AM I SUPPOSED TO GET THERE? IT'S, LIKE, ACROSS THE RIVER!
I DUNNO... TAKE THE SUBWAY?
THE SUBWAY! DON'T YOU NEED SPECIAL TOKENS FOR THAT? DO THEY EVEN LET KIDS ON THERE?
HA, I FORGOT WHAT AN ECHO CITY ROOKIE YOU ARE!
IT'S EASY. JUST TAKE THE RED LINE TO KASTNER STATION, TRANSFER TO THE YELLOW LOCAL, AND GET OFF AT LEWIS.
UH...
OKAY, PADAWAN, COME WITH ME.
BYE, MOM! KEVIN'S GOING TO SHOW ME... HOW TO PLAY... BASKETBALL!
THAT'S NICE. DON'T STAY OUT TOO LATE.

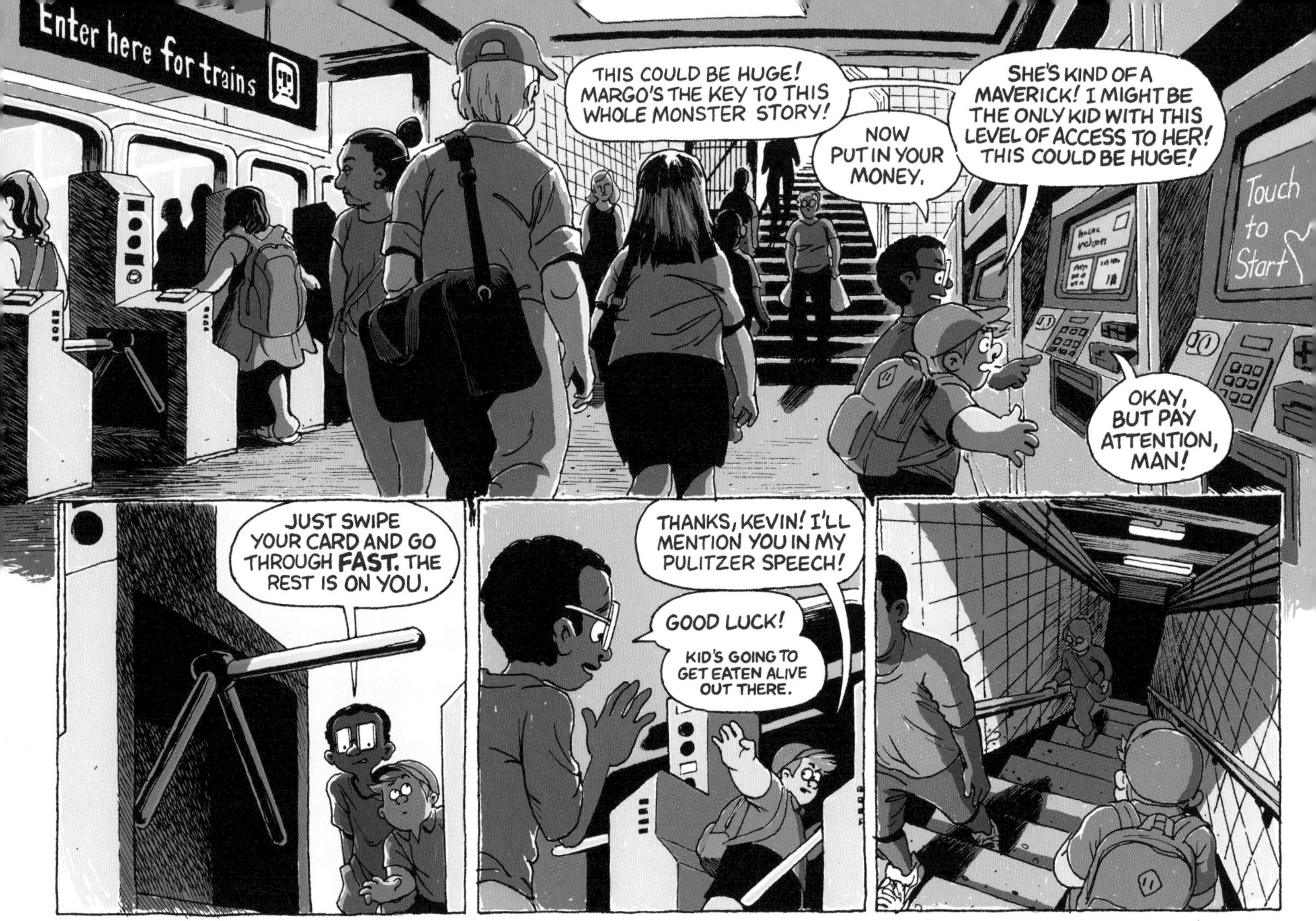
Enter here for trains
THIS COULD BE HUGE! MARGO'S THE KEY TO THIS WHOLE MONSTER STORY!
SHE'S KIND OF A MAVERICK! I MIGHT BE THE ONLY KID WITH THIS LEVEL OF ACCESS TO HER! THIS COULD BE HUGE!
NOW PUT IN YOUR MONEY.
OKAY, BUT PAY ATTENTION, MAN!
Touch to Start
JUST SWIPE YOUR CARD AND GO THROUGH **FAST.** THE REST IS ON YOU.
THANKS, KEVIN! I'LL MENTION YOU IN MY PULITZER SPEECH!
GOOD LUCK!
KID'S GOING TO GET EATEN ALIVE OUT THERE.

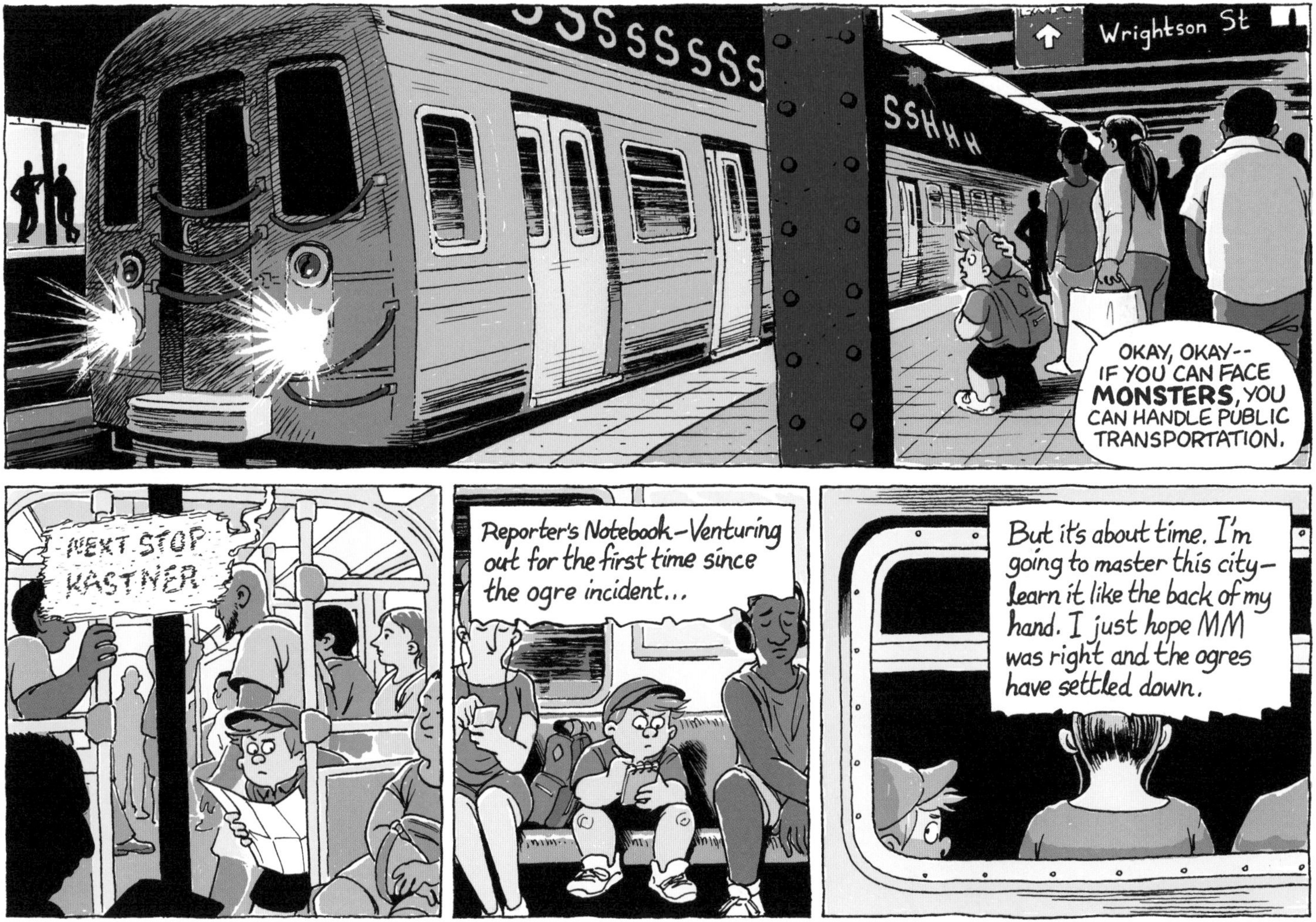
SSSSSSSSS
Wrightson St
SSHHH
OKAY, OKAY-- IF YOU CAN FACE **MONSTERS**, YOU CAN HANDLE PUBLIC TRANSPORTATION.
NEXT STOP KASTNER
Reporter's Notebook–Venturing out for the first time since the ogre incident...
But it's about time. I'm going to master this city–learn it like the back of my hand. I just hope MM was right and the ogres have settled down.

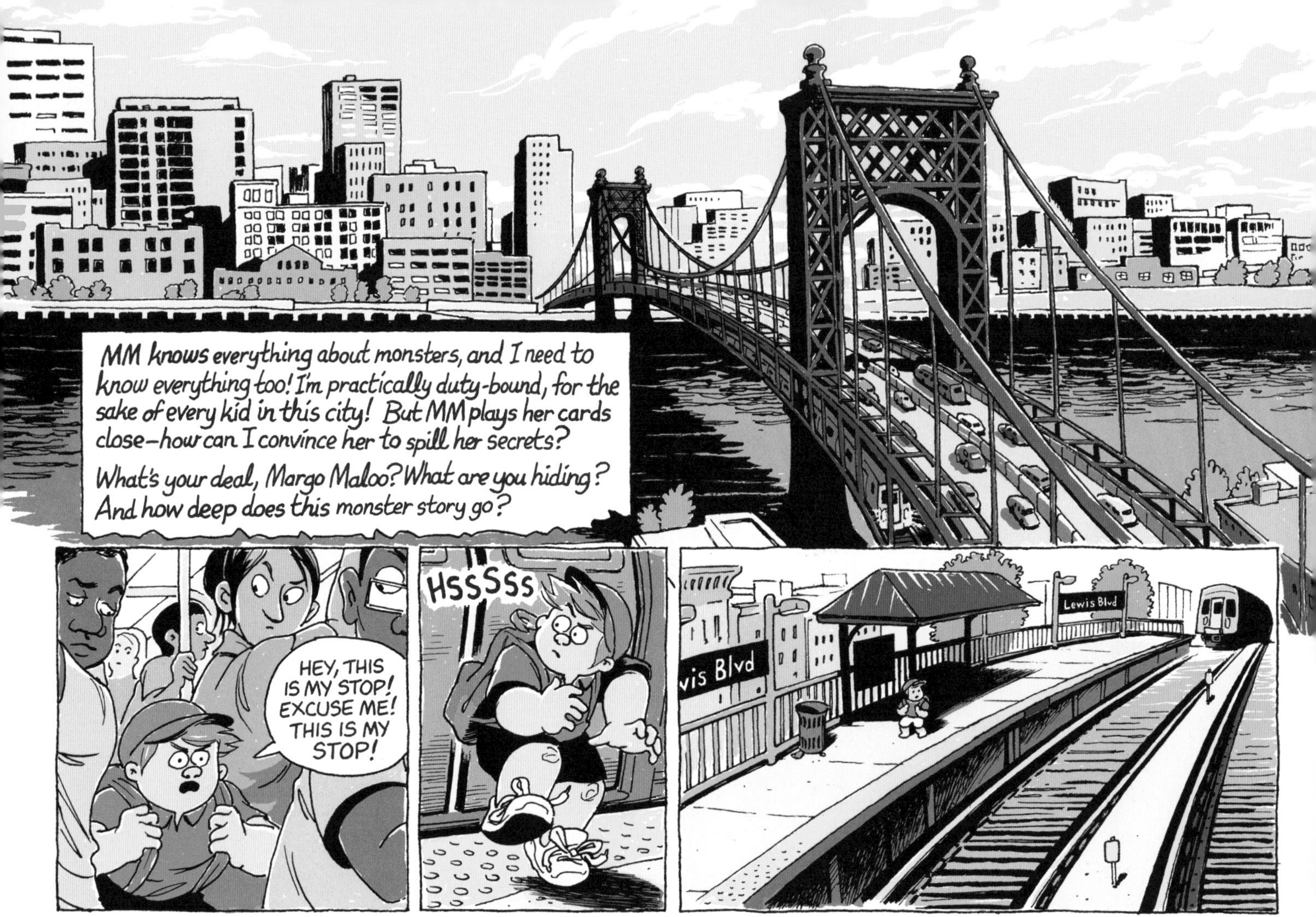
MM knows everything about monsters, and I need to know everything too! I'm practically duty-bound, for the sake of every kid in this city! But MM plays her cards close—how can I convince her to spill her secrets?
What's your deal, Margo Maloo? What are you hiding? And how deep does this monster story go?
HEY, THIS IS MY STOP! EXCUSE ME! THIS IS MY STOP!
HSSSSS
Lewis Blvd
vis Blvd

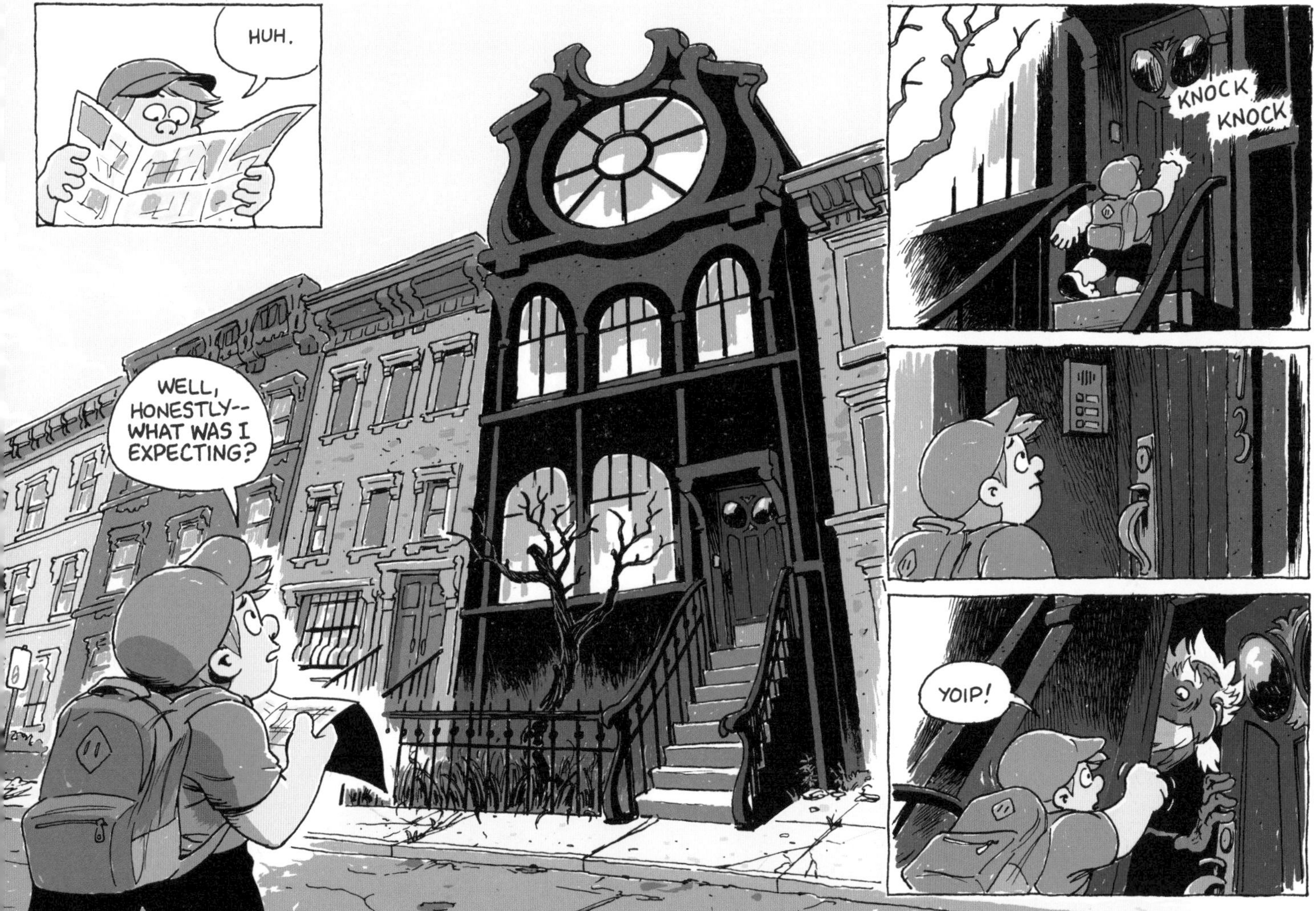
HUH.
WELL, HONESTLY-- WHAT WAS I EXPECTING?
KNOCK KNOCK
YOIP!

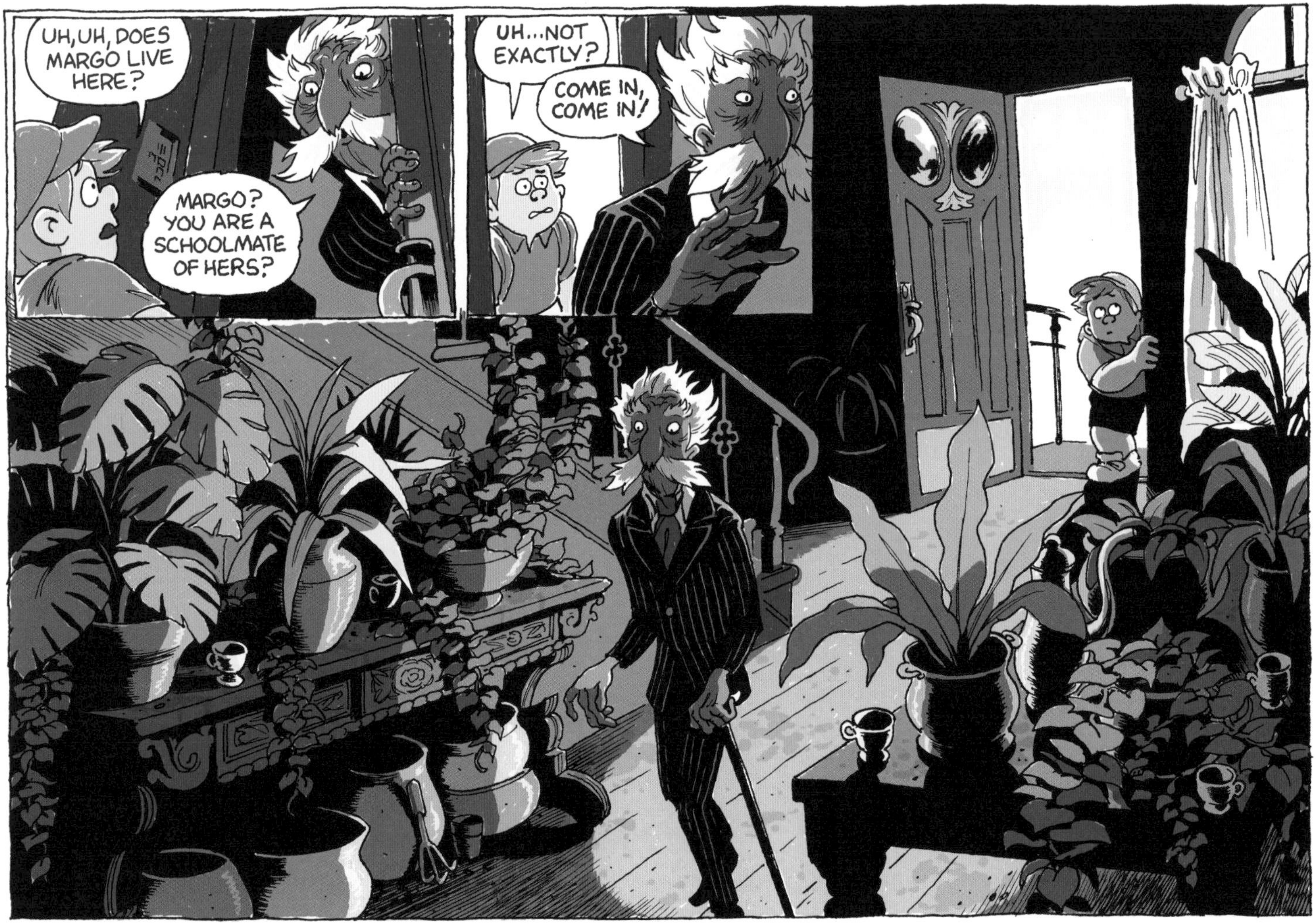
UH, UH, DOES MARGO LIVE HERE?
MARGO? YOU ARE A SCHOOLMATE OF HERS?
UH...NOT EXACTLY?
COME IN, COME IN!

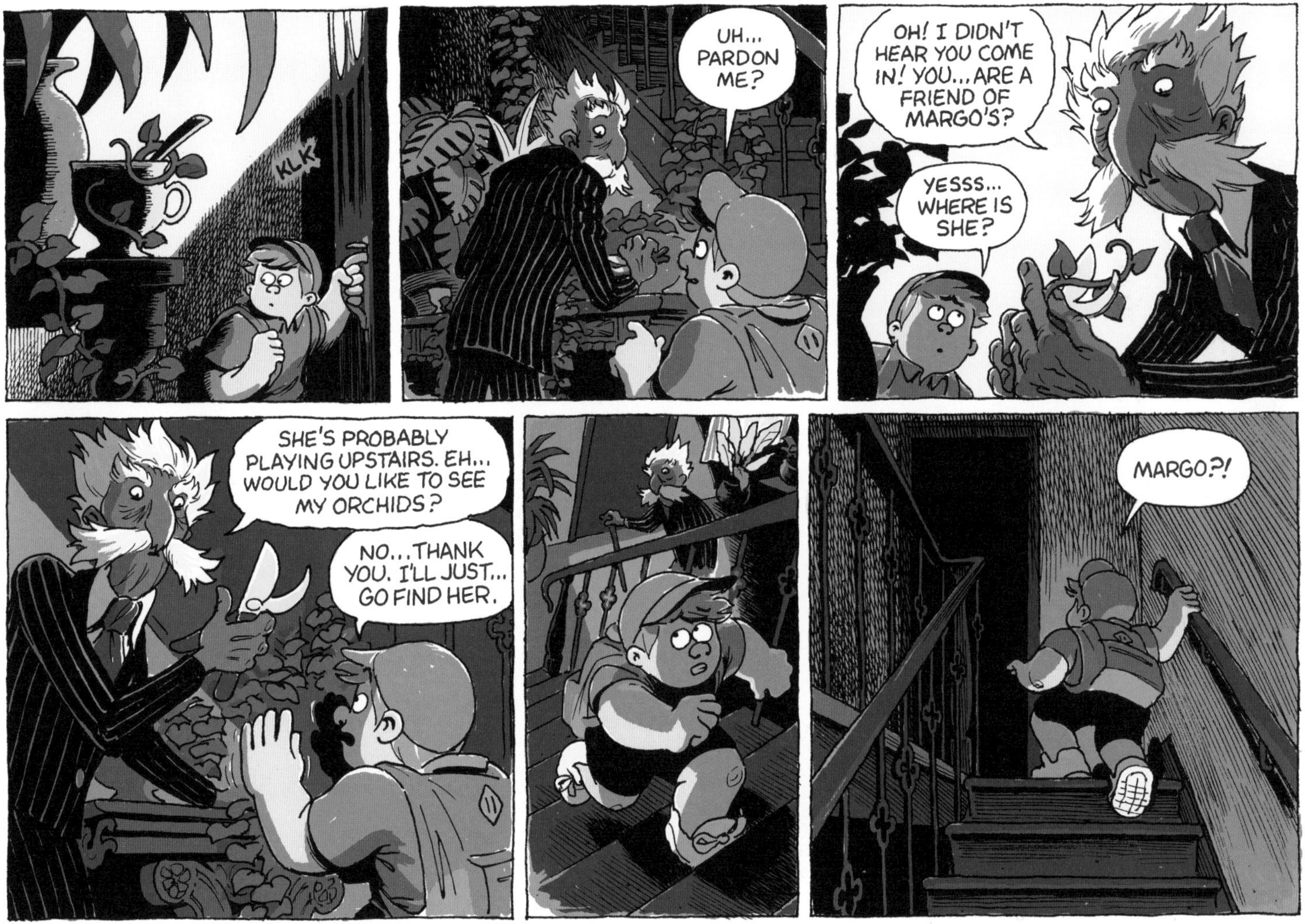
KLK
UH... PARDON ME?
OH! I DIDN'T HEAR YOU COME IN! YOU...ARE A FRIEND OF MARGO'S?
YESSS... WHERE IS SHE?
SHE'S PROBABLY PLAYING UPSTAIRS. EH... WOULD YOU LIKE TO SEE MY ORCHIDS?
NO...THANK YOU. I'LL JUST... GO FIND HER.
MARGO?!

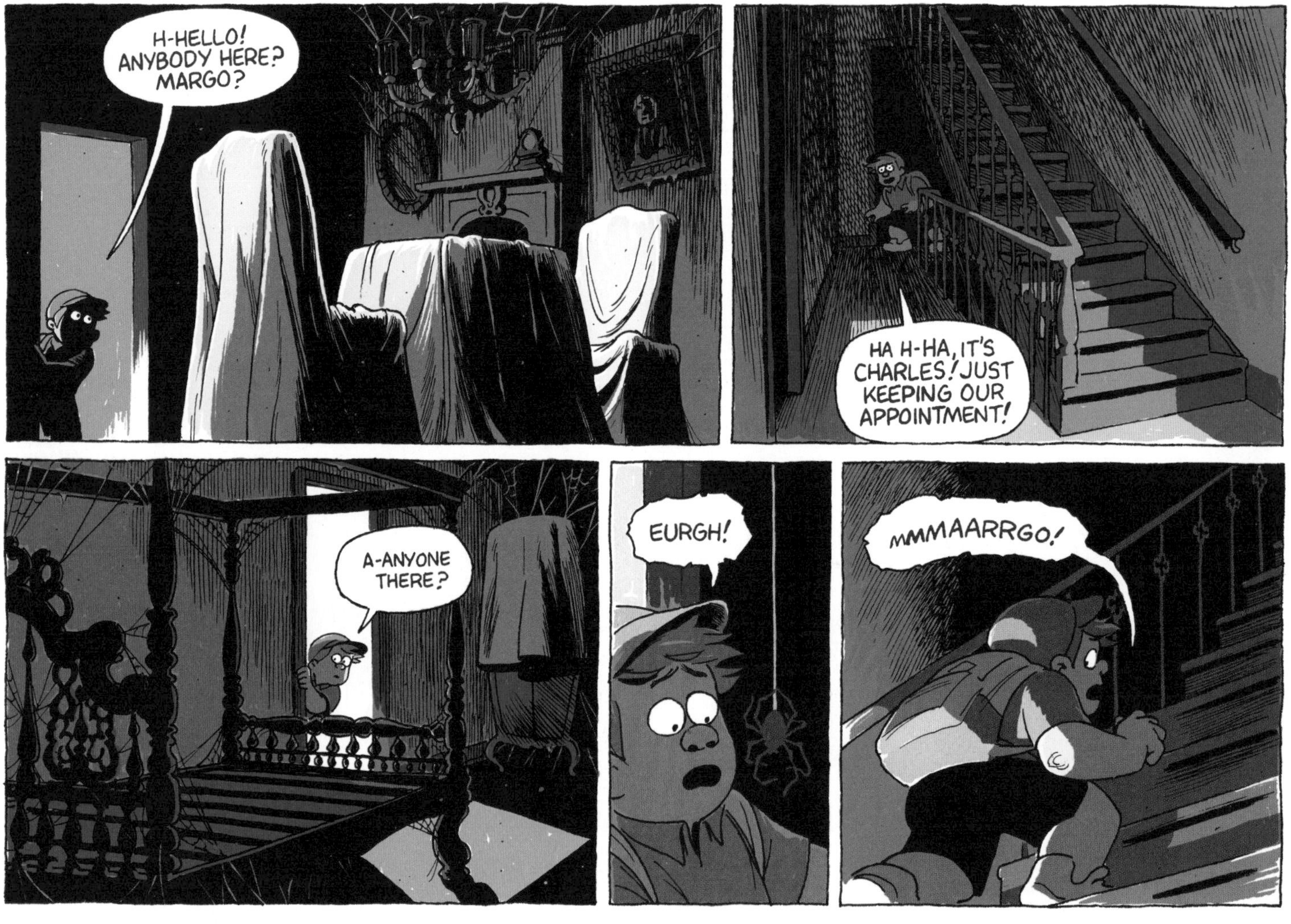
H-HELLO! ANYBODY HERE? MARGO?
HA H-HA, IT'S CHARLES! JUST KEEPING OUR APPOINTMENT!
A-ANYONE THERE?
EURGH!
MMMAARRGO!

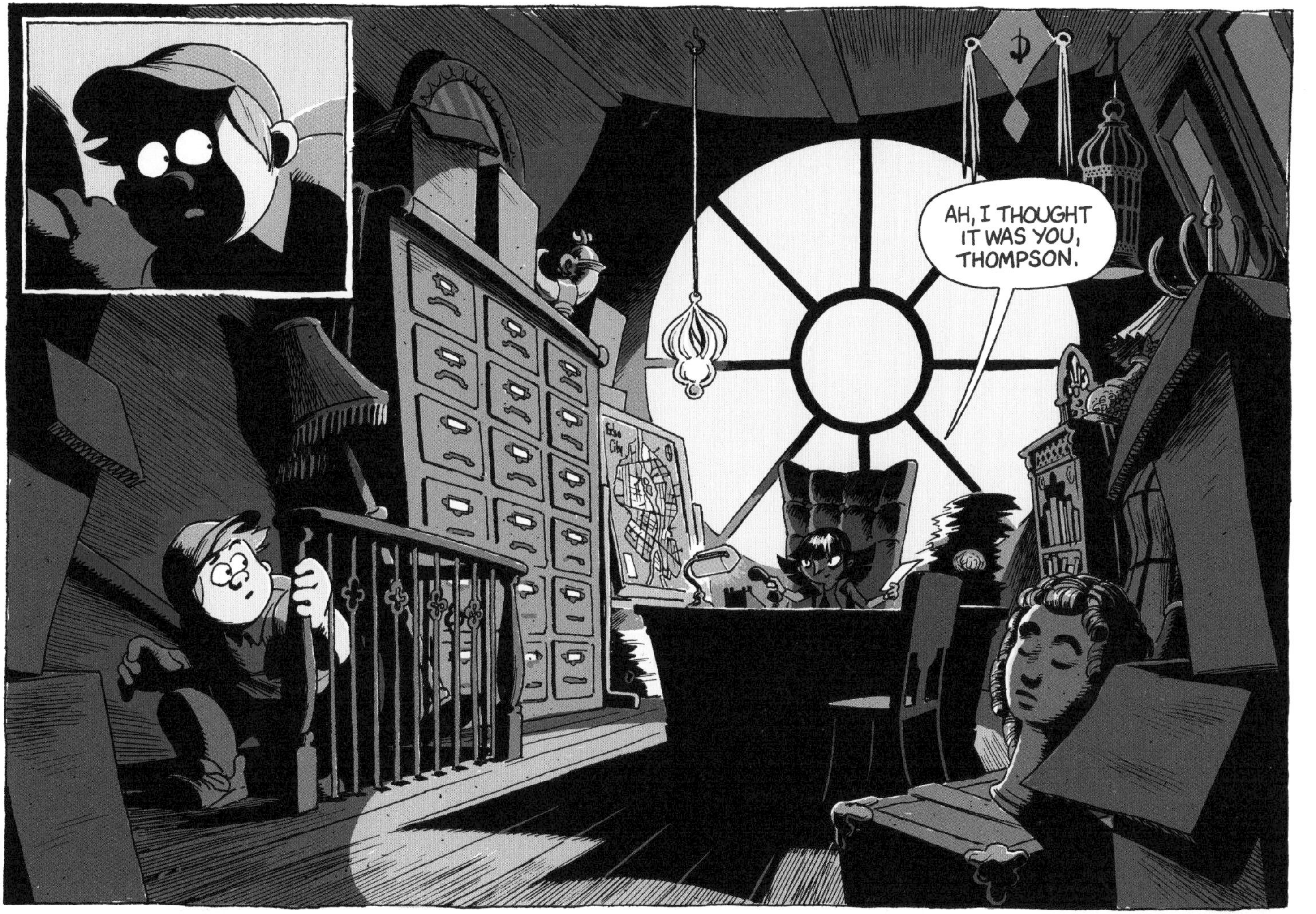
AH, I THOUGHT IT WAS YOU, THOMPSON.

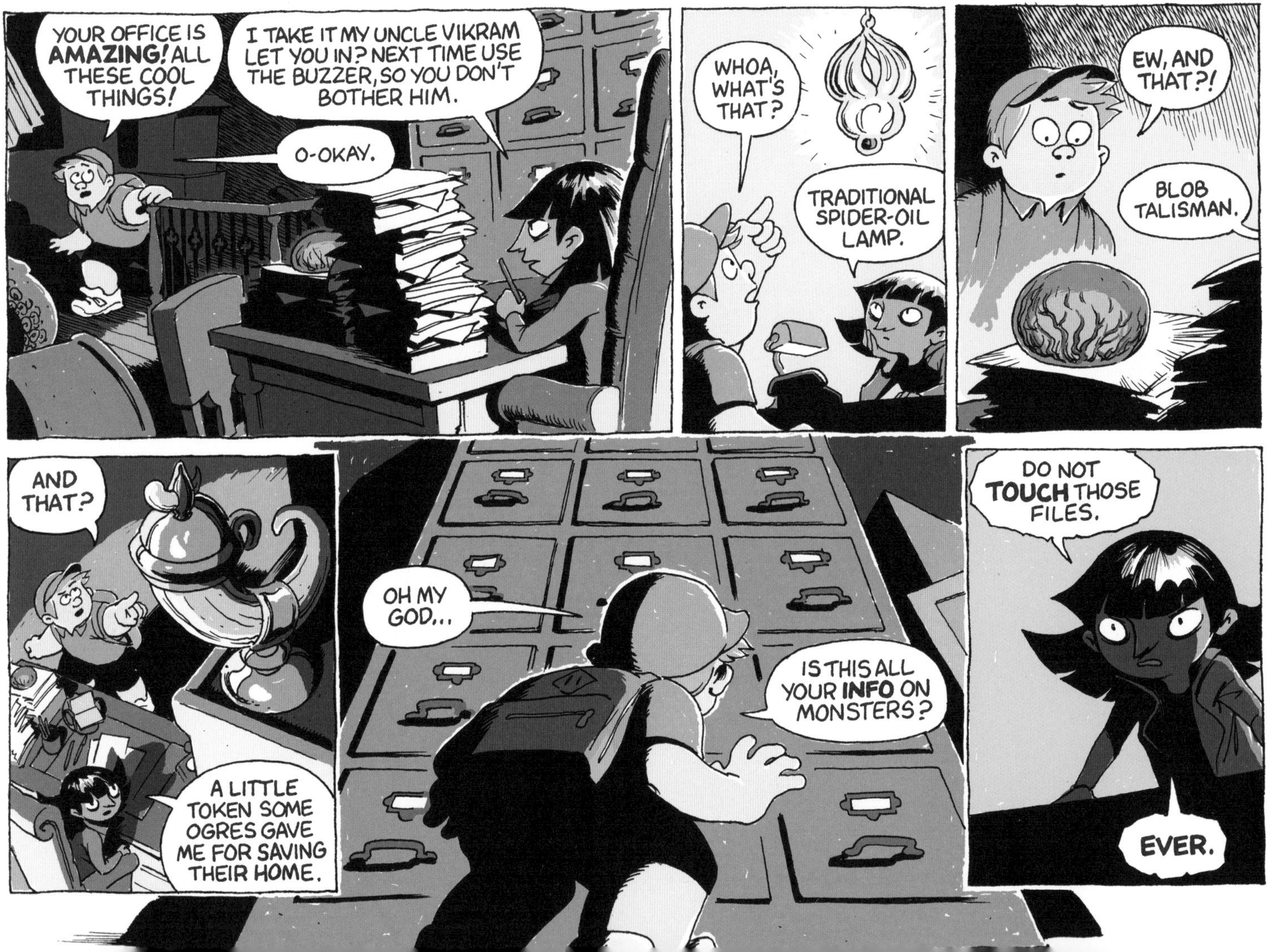
YOUR OFFICE IS AMAZING! ALL THESE COOL THINGS!
I TAKE IT MY UNCLE VIKRAM LET YOU IN? NEXT TIME USE THE BUZZER, SO YOU DON'T BOTHER HIM.
O-OKAY.
WHOA, WHAT'S THAT?
TRADITIONAL SPIDER-OIL LAMP.
EW, AND THAT?!
BLOB TALISMAN.
AND THAT?
A LITTLE TOKEN SOME OGRES GAVE ME FOR SAVING THEIR HOME.
OH MY GOD...
IS THIS ALL YOUR INFO ON MONSTERS?
DO NOT TOUCH THOSE FILES.
EVER.

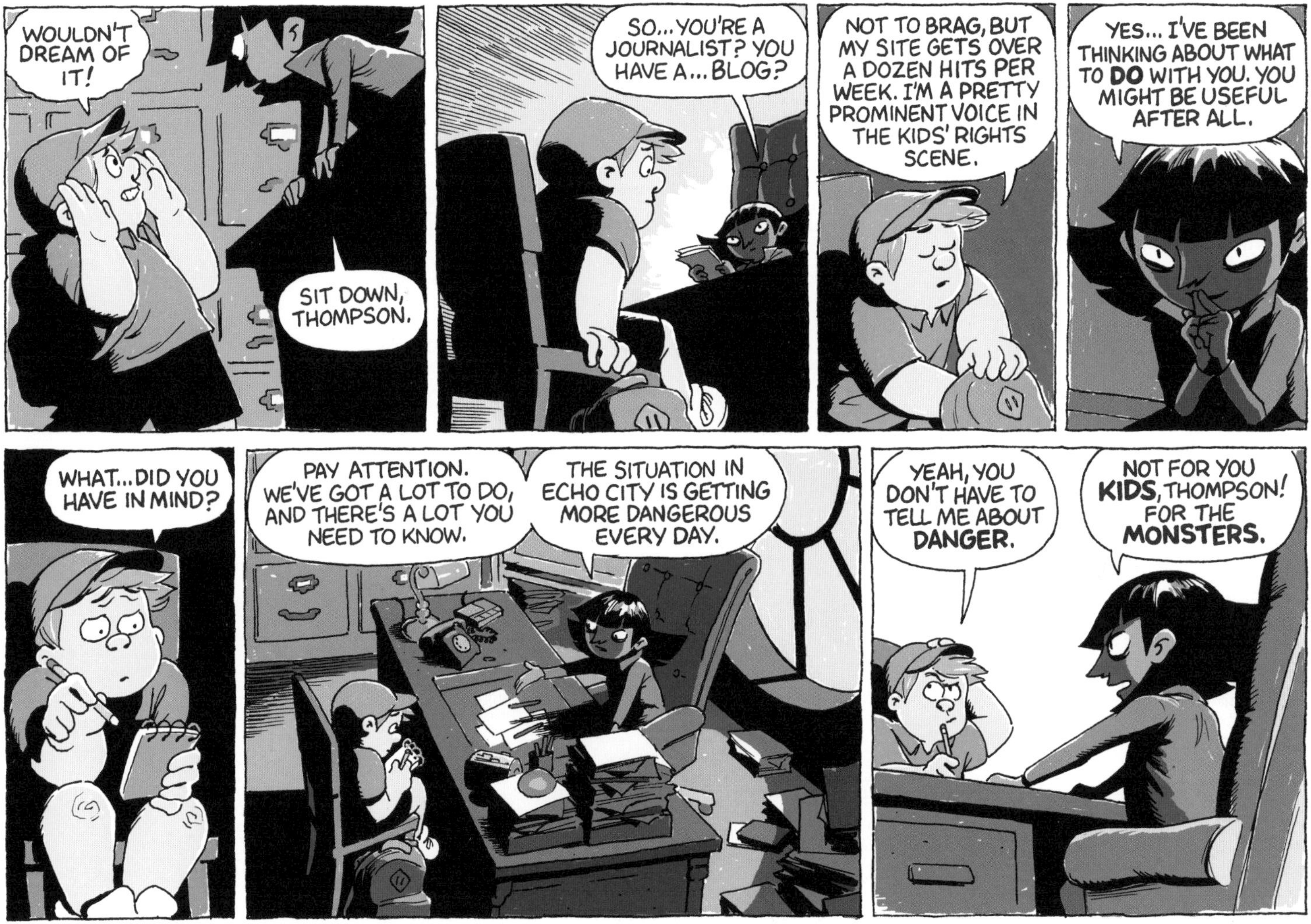
WOULDN'T DREAM OF IT!
SIT DOWN, THOMPSON.
SO... YOU'RE A JOURNALIST? YOU HAVE A... BLOG?
NOT TO BRAG, BUT MY SITE GETS OVER A DOZEN HITS PER WEEK. I'M A PRETTY PROMINENT VOICE IN THE KIDS' RIGHTS SCENE.
YES... I'VE BEEN THINKING ABOUT WHAT TO **DO** WITH YOU. YOU MIGHT BE USEFUL AFTER ALL.
WHAT... DID YOU HAVE IN MIND?
PAY ATTENTION. WE'VE GOT A LOT TO DO, AND THERE'S A LOT YOU NEED TO KNOW.
THE SITUATION IN ECHO CITY IS GETTING MORE DANGEROUS EVERY DAY.
YEAH, YOU DON'T HAVE TO TELL ME ABOUT **DANGER**.
NOT FOR YOU **KIDS**, THOMPSON! FOR THE **MONSTERS**.

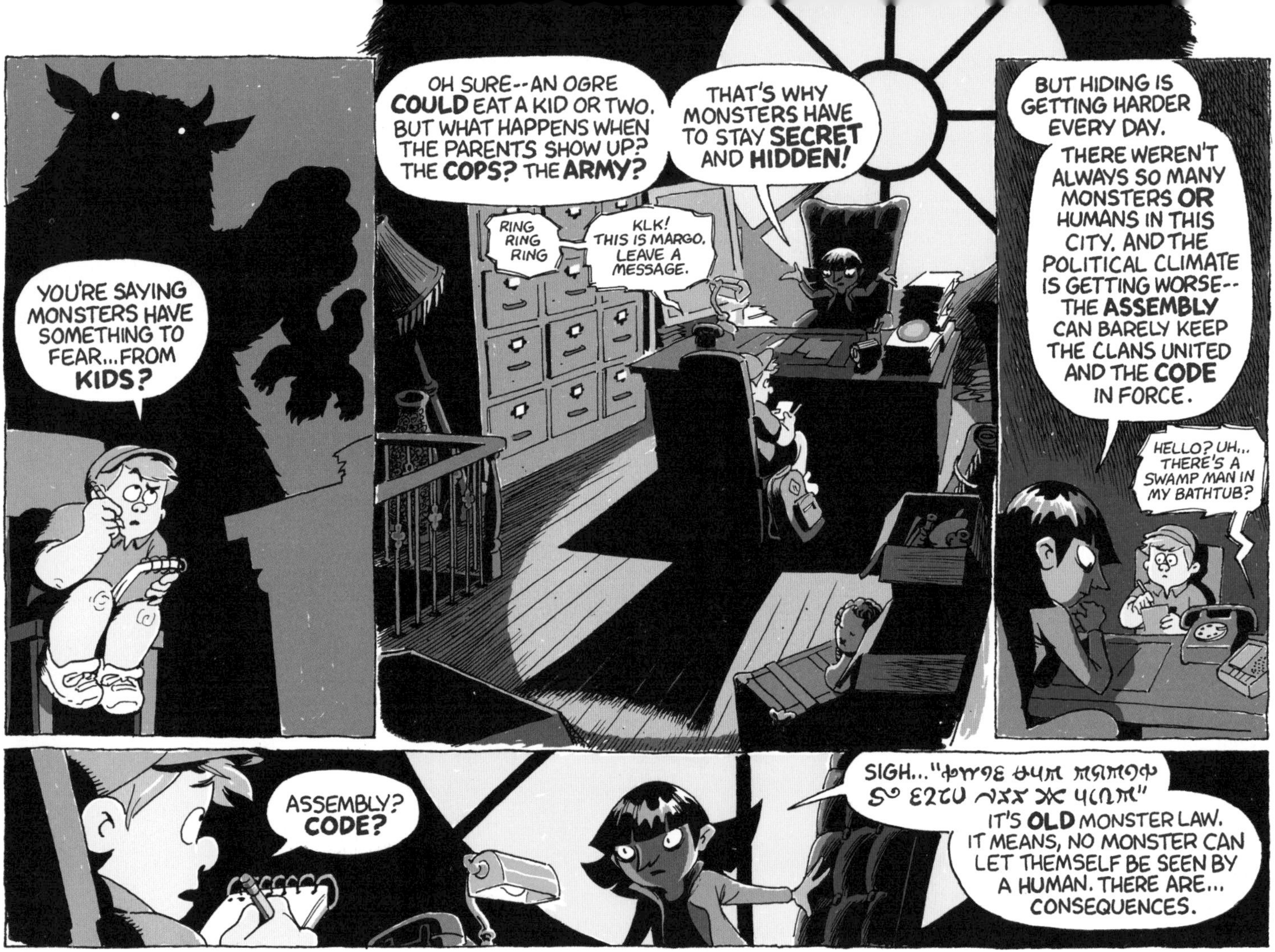
YOU'RE SAYING MONSTERS HAVE SOMETHING TO FEAR...FROM KIDS?
OH SURE--AN OGRE COULD EAT A KID OR TWO. BUT WHAT HAPPENS WHEN THE PARENTS SHOW UP? THE COPS? THE ARMY?
THAT'S WHY MONSTERS HAVE TO STAY SECRET AND HIDDEN!
RING RING RING
KLK! THIS IS MARGO. LEAVE A MESSAGE.
BUT HIDING IS GETTING HARDER EVERY DAY.
THERE WEREN'T ALWAYS SO MANY MONSTERS OR HUMANS IN THIS CITY. AND THE POLITICAL CLIMATE IS GETTING WORSE-- THE ASSEMBLY CAN BARELY KEEP THE CLANS UNITED AND THE CODE IN FORCE.
HELLO? UH... THERE'S A SWAMP MAN IN MY BATHTUB?
ASSEMBLY? CODE?
SIGH...
IT'S OLD MONSTER LAW. IT MEANS, NO MONSTER CAN LET THEMSELF BE SEEN BY A HUMAN. THERE ARE... CONSEQUENCES.

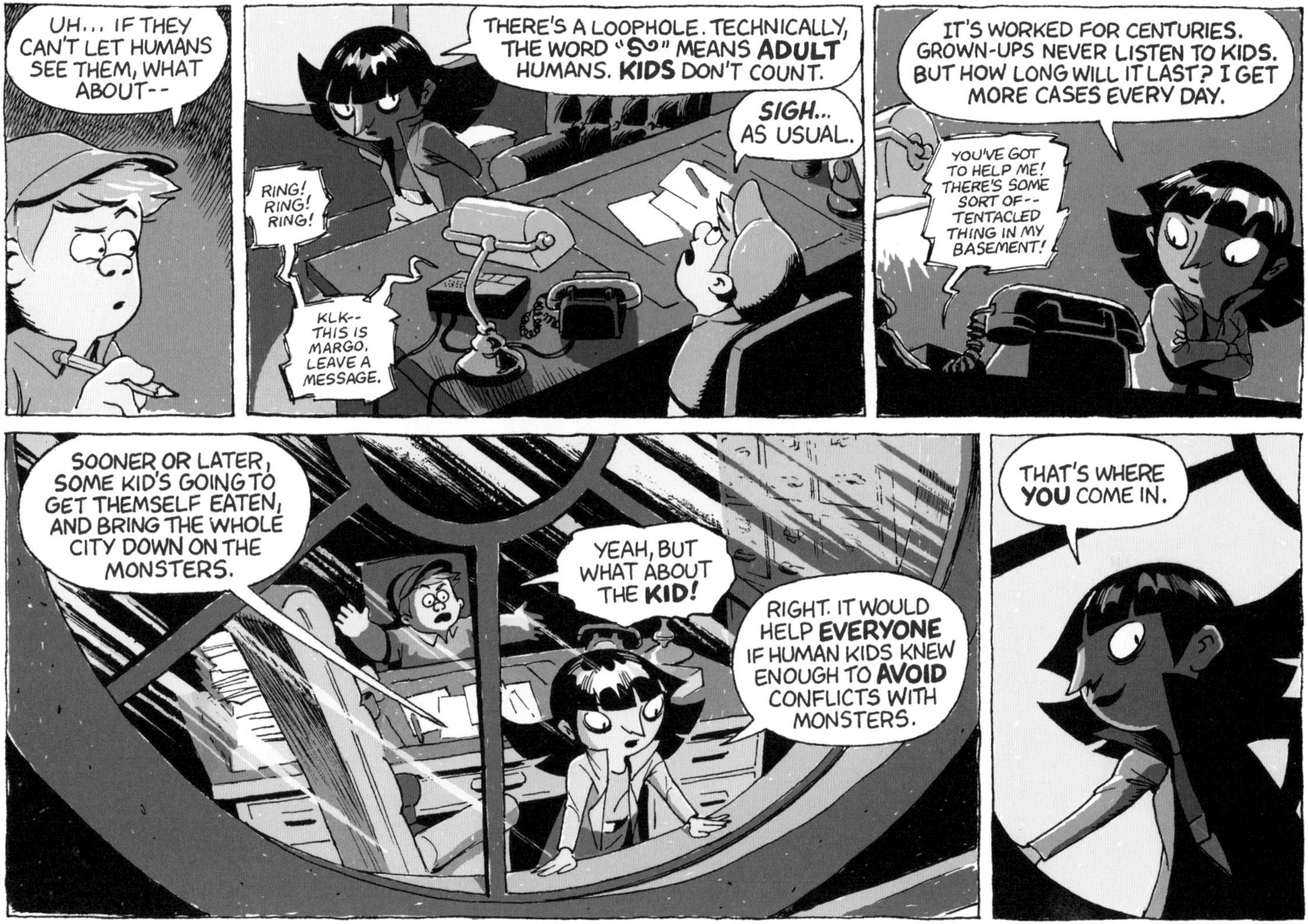
UH... IF THEY CAN'T LET HUMANS SEE THEM, WHAT ABOUT--
THERE'S A LOOPHOLE. TECHNICALLY, THE WORD "S~" MEANS ADULT HUMANS. KIDS DON'T COUNT.
RING! RING! RING!
SIGH... AS USUAL.
KLK-- THIS IS MARGO, LEAVE A MESSAGE.
IT'S WORKED FOR CENTURIES. GROWN-UPS NEVER LISTEN TO KIDS. BUT HOW LONG WILL IT LAST? I GET MORE CASES EVERY DAY.
YOU'VE GOT TO HELP ME! THERE'S SOME SORT OF-- TENTACLED THING IN MY BASEMENT!
SOONER OR LATER, SOME KID'S GOING TO GET THEMSELF EATEN, AND BRING THE WHOLE CITY DOWN ON THE MONSTERS.
YEAH, BUT WHAT ABOUT THE KID!
RIGHT. IT WOULD HELP EVERYONE IF HUMAN KIDS KNEW ENOUGH TO AVOID CONFLICTS WITH MONSTERS.
THAT'S WHERE YOU COME IN.

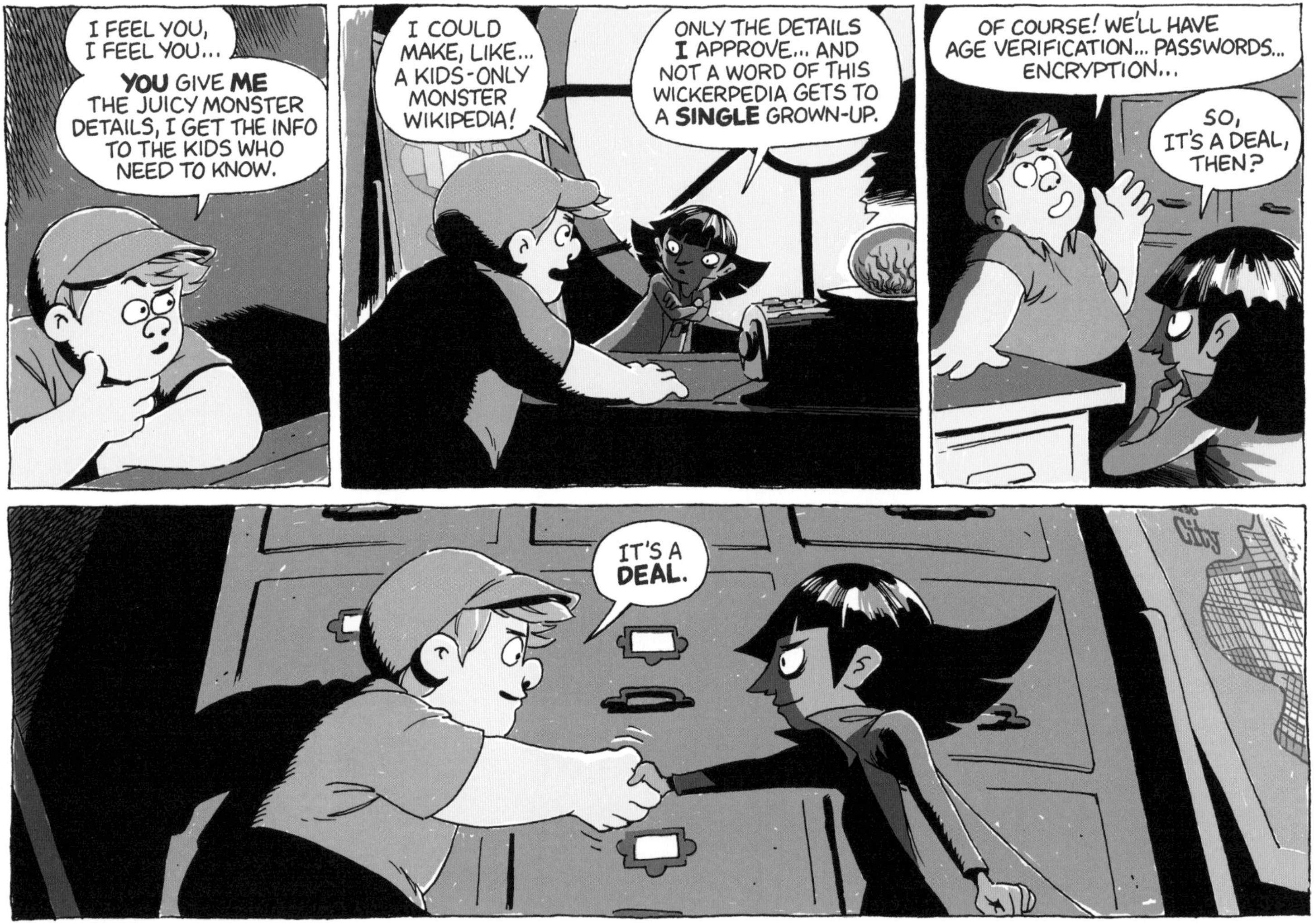
I FEEL YOU, I FEEL YOU...
YOU GIVE ME THE JUICY MONSTER DETAILS, I GET THE INFO TO THE KIDS WHO NEED TO KNOW.
I COULD MAKE, LIKE... A KIDS-ONLY MONSTER WIKIPEDIA!
ONLY THE DETAILS I APPROVE... AND NOT A WORD OF THIS WICKERPEDIA GETS TO A SINGLE GROWN-UP.
OF COURSE! WE'LL HAVE AGE VERIFICATION... PASSWORDS... ENCRYPTION...
SO, IT'S A DEAL, THEN?
IT'S A DEAL.

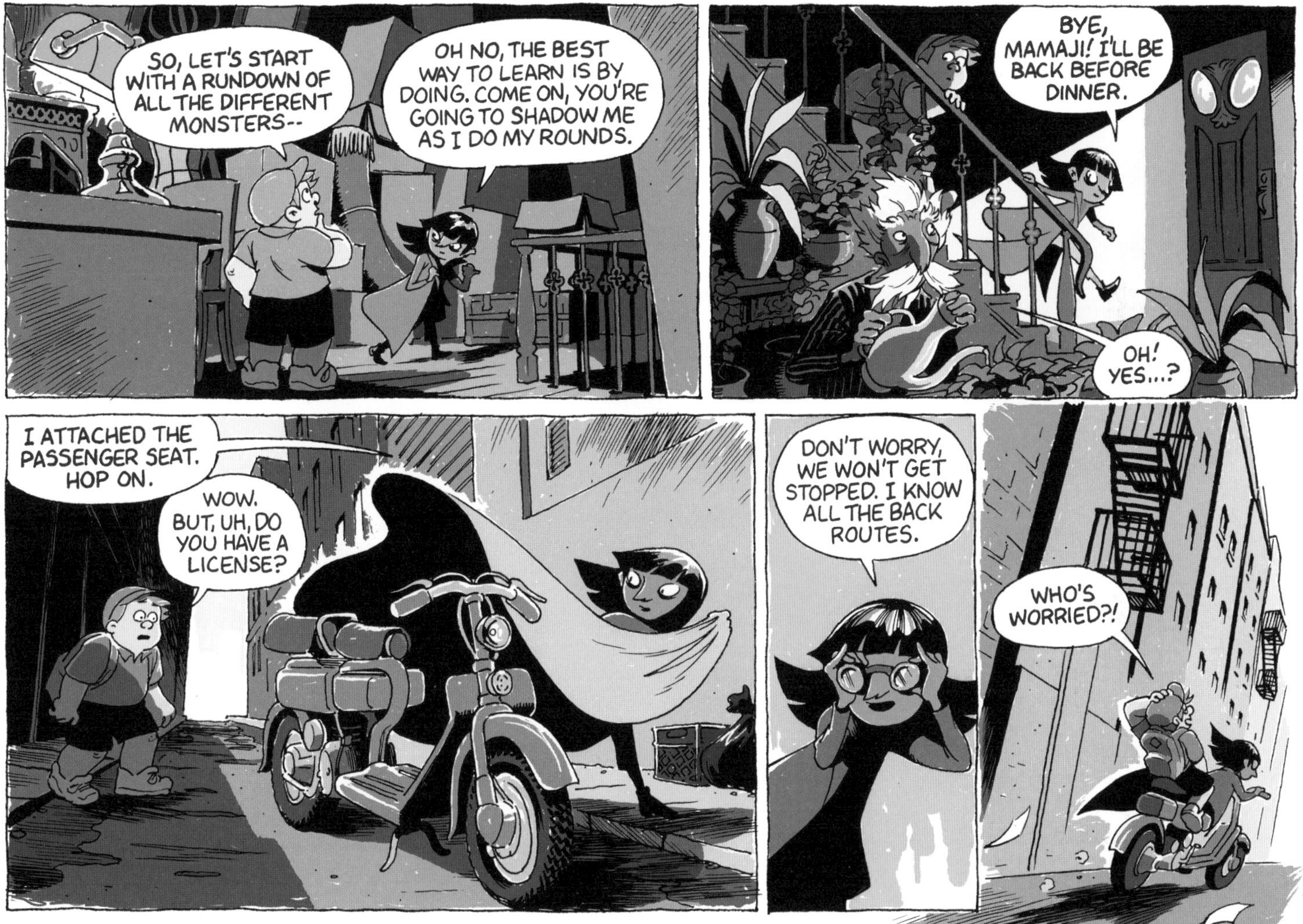
SO, LET'S START WITH A RUNDOWN OF ALL THE DIFFERENT MONSTERS--
OH NO, THE BEST WAY TO LEARN IS BY DOING. COME ON, YOU'RE GOING TO SHADOW ME AS I DO MY ROUNDS.
BYE, MAMAJI! I'LL BE BACK BEFORE DINNER.
OH! YES...?
I ATTACHED THE PASSENGER SEAT. HOP ON.
WOW. BUT, UH, DO YOU HAVE A LICENSE?
DON'T WORRY, WE WON'T GET STOPPED. I KNOW ALL THE BACK ROUTES.
WHO'S WORRIED?!

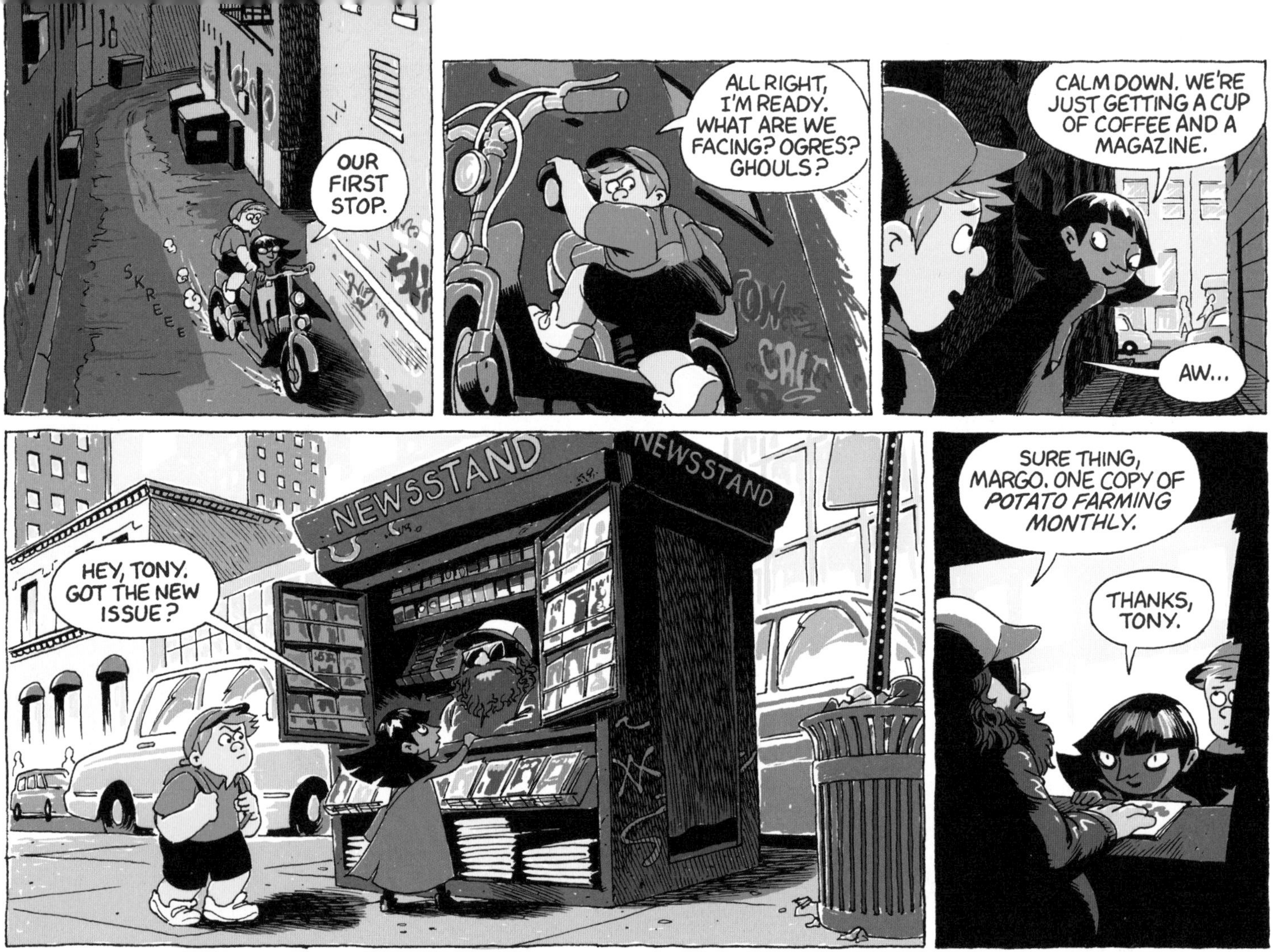
OUR FIRST STOP.
SKREEEE
ALL RIGHT, I'M READY. WHAT ARE WE FACING? OGRES? GHOULS?
CALM DOWN. WE'RE JUST GETTING A CUP OF COFFEE AND A MAGAZINE.
AW...
NEWSSTAND
NEWSSTAND
HEY, TONY. GOT THE NEW ISSUE?
SURE THING, MARGO. ONE COPY OF *POTATO FARMING MONTHLY.*
THANKS, TONY.

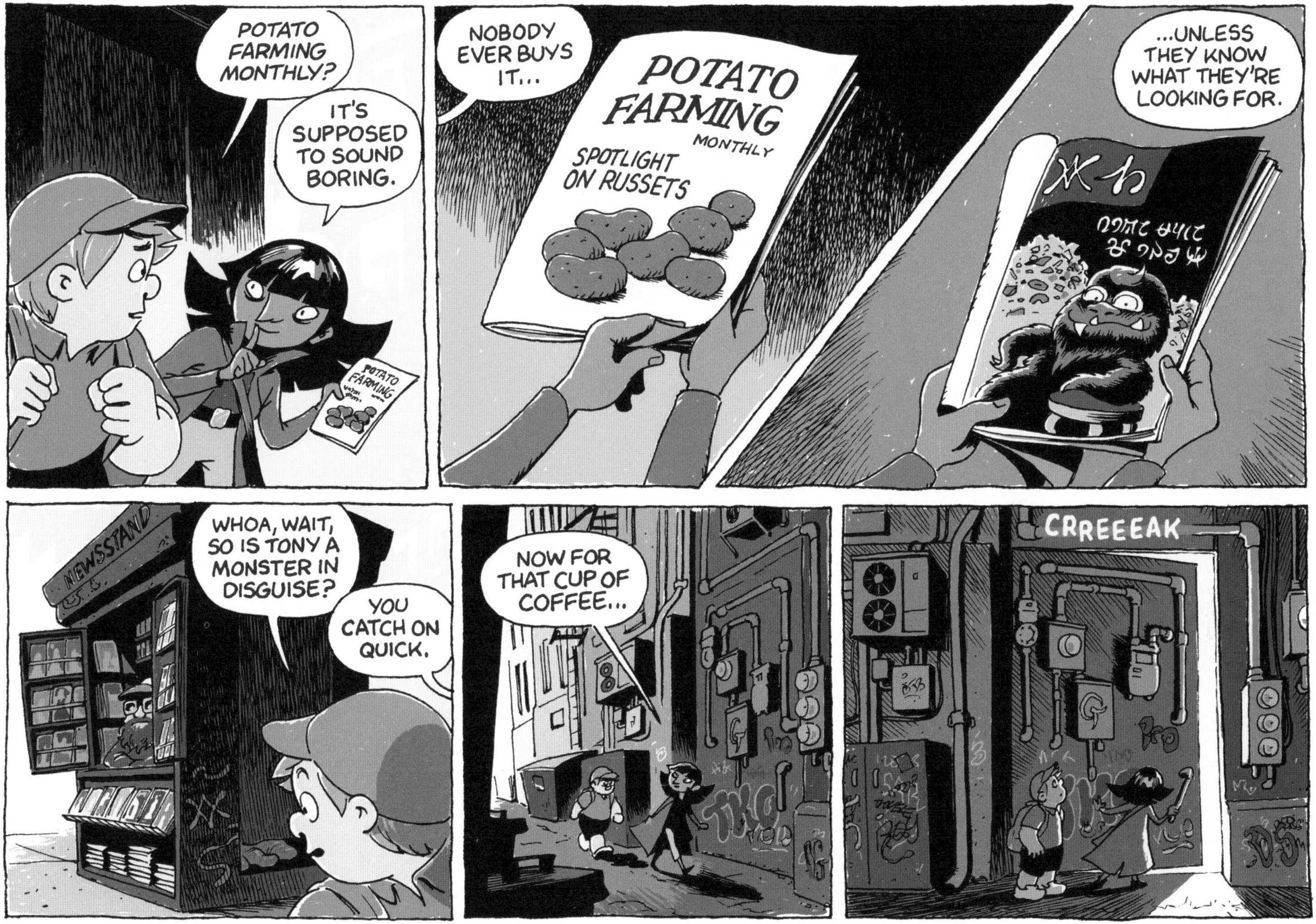
POTATO FARMING MONTHLY?
IT'S SUPPOSED TO SOUND BORING.
POTATO FARMING
NOBODY EVER BUYS IT...
POTATO FARMING MONTHLY
SPOTLIGHT ON RUSSETS
...UNLESS THEY KNOW WHAT THEY'RE LOOKING FOR.
NEWSSTAND
WHOA, WAIT, SO IS TONY A MONSTER IN DISGUISE?
YOU CATCH ON QUICK.
NOW FOR THAT CUP OF COFFEE...
CRREEEAK

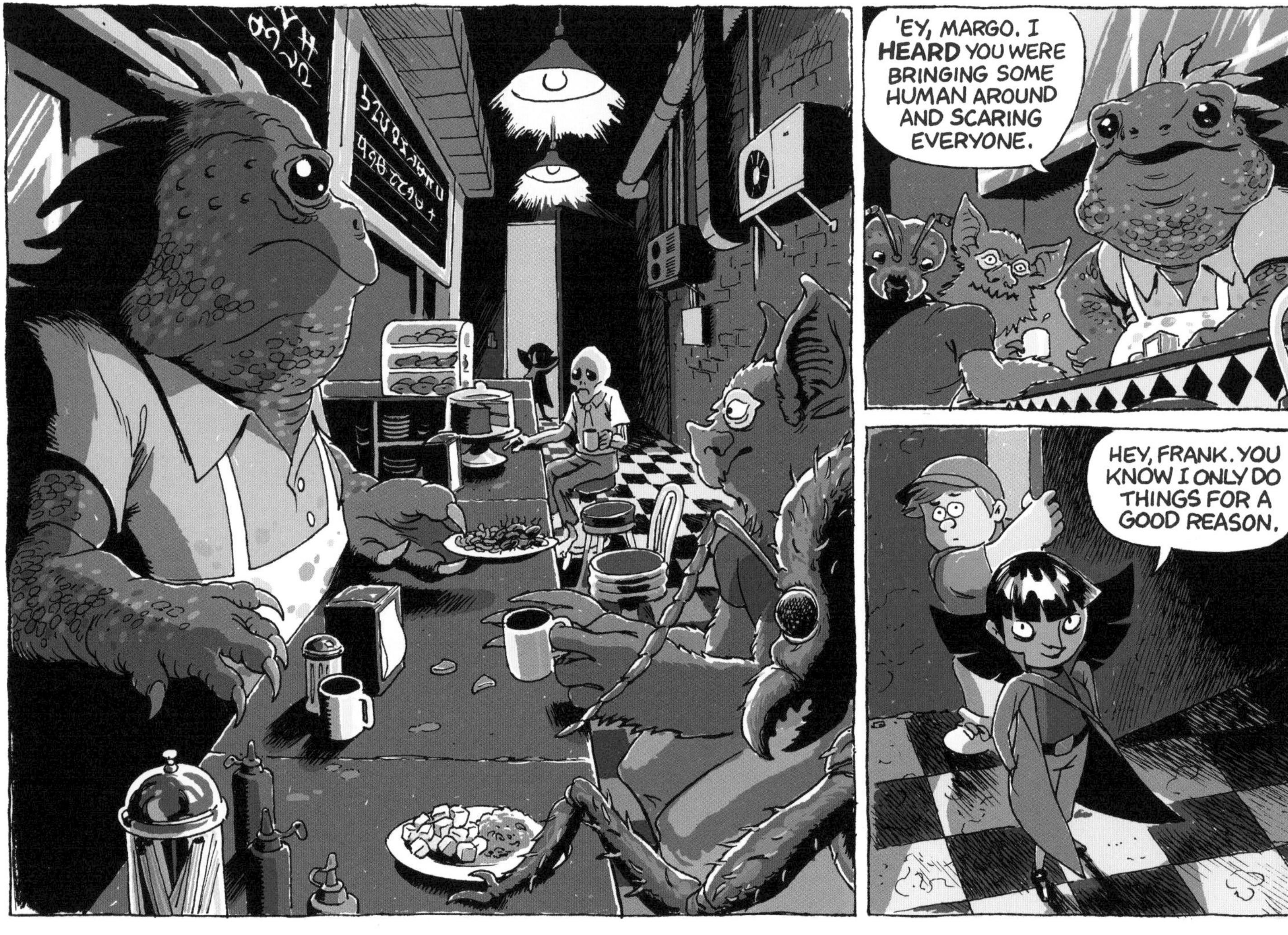
'EY, MARGO. I **HEARD** YOU WERE BRINGING SOME HUMAN AROUND AND SCARING EVERYONE.
HEY, FRANK. YOU KNOW I ONLY DO THINGS FOR A GOOD REASON.

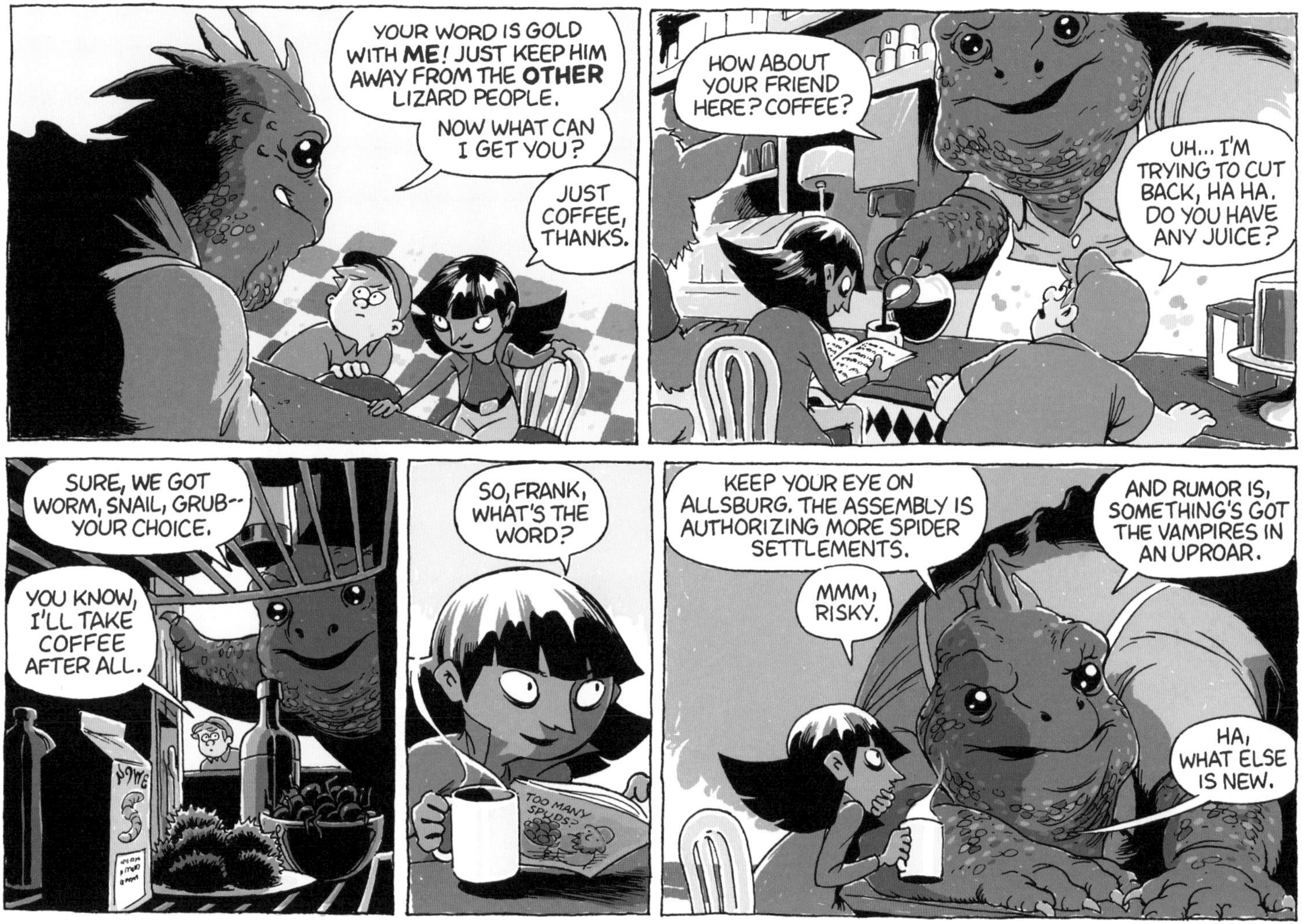
YOUR WORD IS GOLD WITH **ME**! JUST KEEP HIM AWAY FROM THE **OTHER** LIZARD PEOPLE.
NOW WHAT CAN I GET YOU?
JUST COFFEE, THANKS.
HOW ABOUT YOUR FRIEND HERE? COFFEE?
UH... I'M TRYING TO CUT BACK, HA HA. DO YOU HAVE ANY JUICE?
SURE, WE GOT WORM, SNAIL, GRUB-- YOUR CHOICE.
YOU KNOW, I'LL TAKE COFFEE AFTER ALL.
SO, FRANK, WHAT'S THE WORD?
TOO MANY SPUDS?
KEEP YOUR EYE ON ALLSBURG. THE ASSEMBLY IS AUTHORIZING MORE SPIDER SETTLEMENTS.
MMM, RISKY.
AND RUMOR IS, SOMETHING'S GOT THE VAMPIRES IN AN UPROAR.
HA, WHAT ELSE IS NEW.

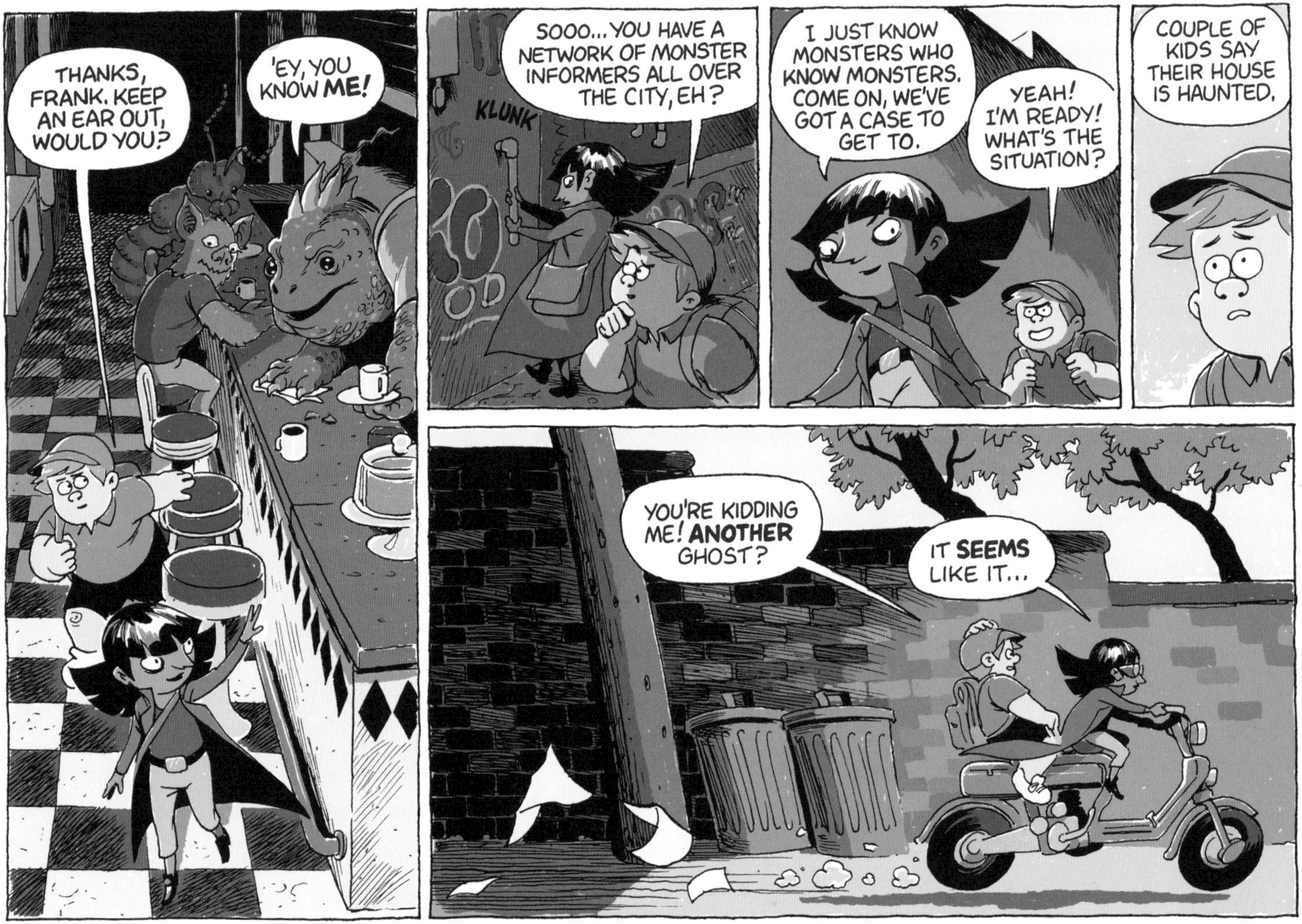
THANKS, FRANK. KEEP AN EAR OUT, WOULD YOU?
'EY, YOU KNOW **ME!**
KLUNK
SOOO... YOU HAVE A NETWORK OF MONSTER INFORMERS ALL OVER THE CITY, EH?
I JUST KNOW MONSTERS WHO KNOW MONSTERS. COME ON, WE'VE GOT A CASE TO GET TO.
YEAH! I'M READY! WHAT'S THE SITUATION?
COUPLE OF KIDS SAY THEIR HOUSE IS HAUNTED.
YOU'RE KIDDING ME! **ANOTHER** GHOST?
IT **SEEMS** LIKE IT...

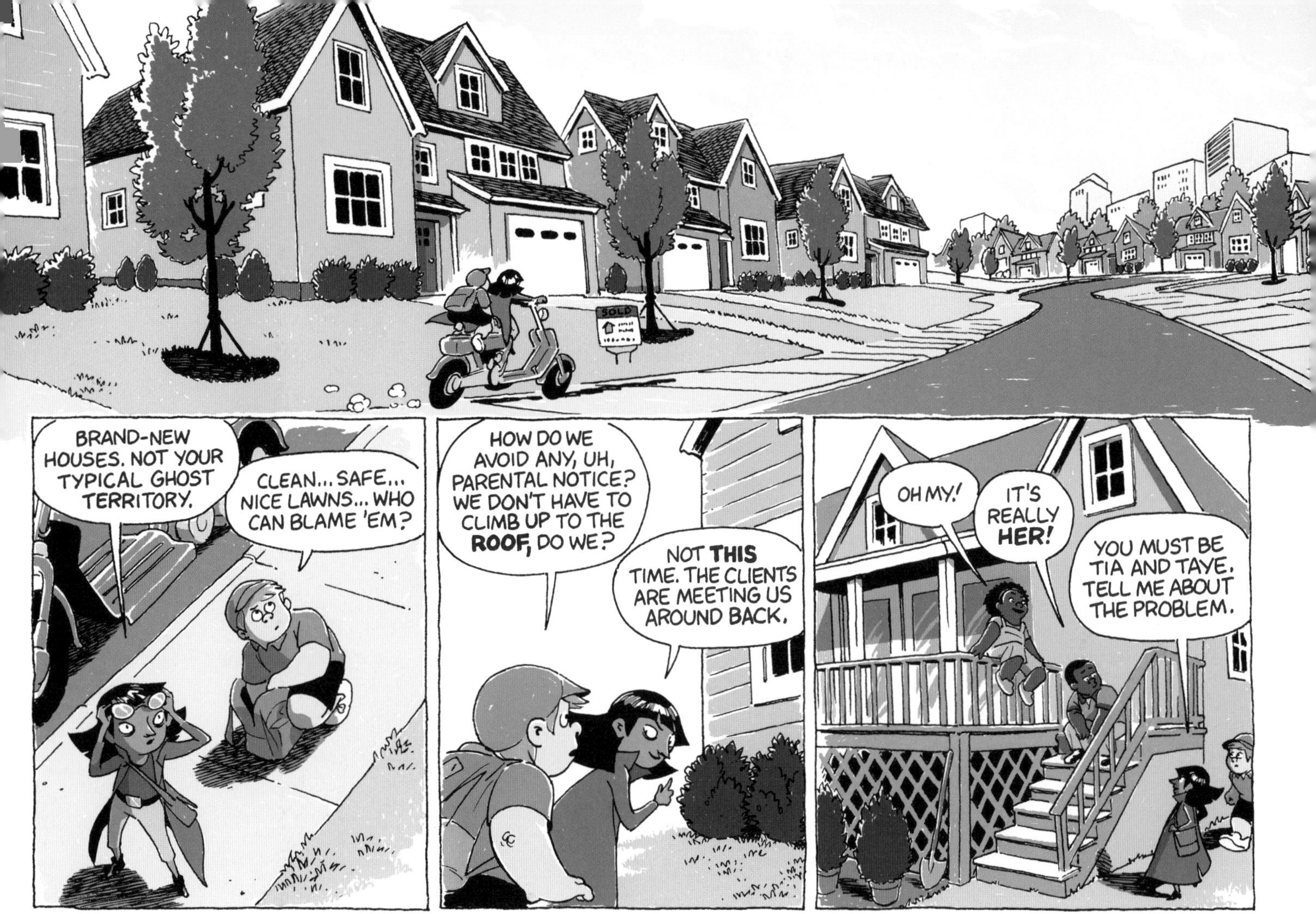
SOLD
BRAND-NEW HOUSES. NOT YOUR TYPICAL GHOST TERRITORY.
CLEAN... SAFE... NICE LAWNS... WHO CAN BLAME 'EM?
HOW DO WE AVOID ANY, UH, PARENTAL NOTICE? WE DON'T HAVE TO CLIMB UP TO THE **ROOF,** DO WE?
NOT **THIS** TIME. THE CLIENTS ARE MEETING US AROUND BACK.
OH MY!
IT'S REALLY **HER!**
YOU MUST BE TIA AND TAYE. TELL ME ABOUT THE PROBLEM.

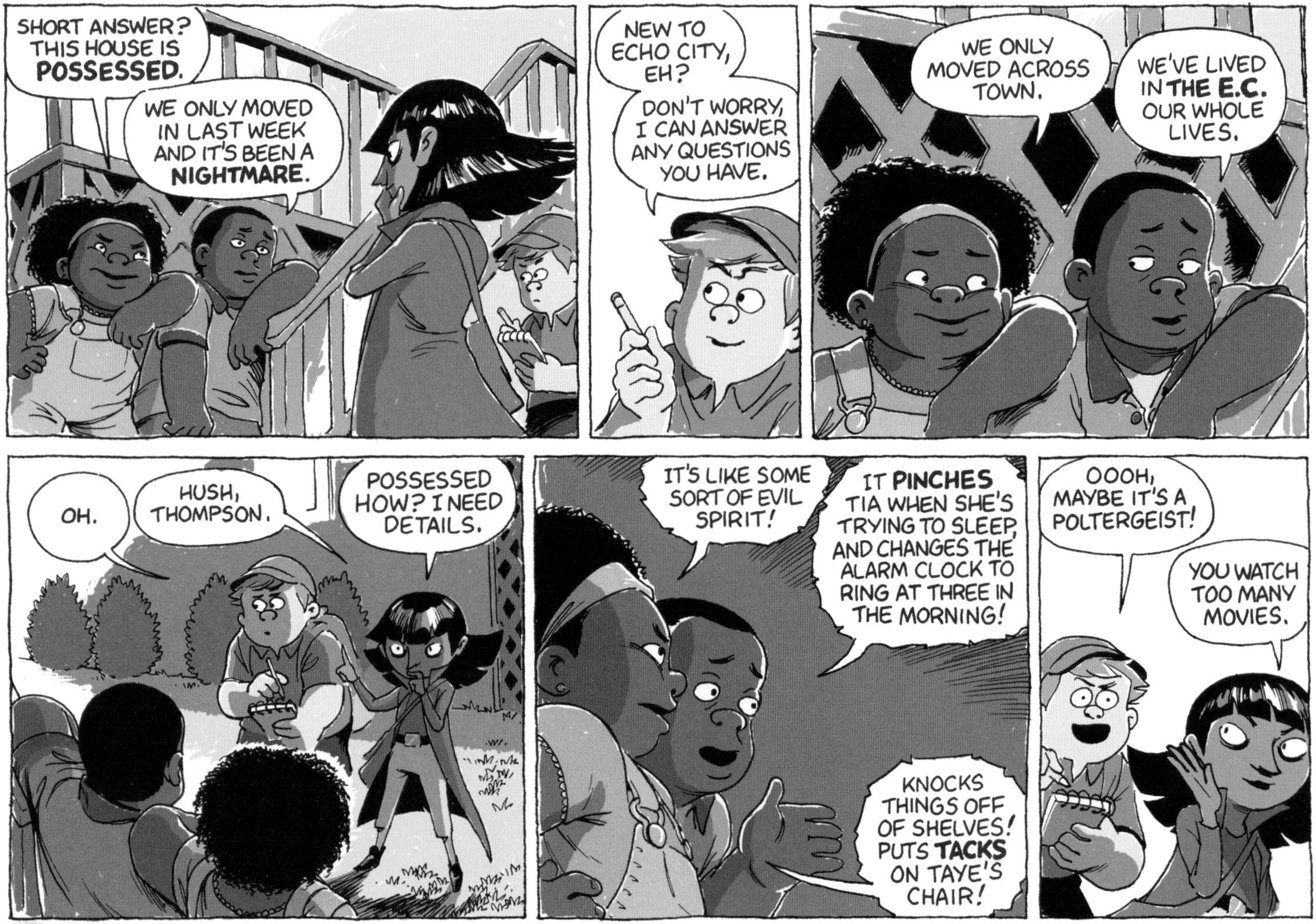
SHORT ANSWER? THIS HOUSE IS **POSSESSED**.
WE ONLY MOVED IN LAST WEEK AND IT'S BEEN A **NIGHTMARE**.
NEW TO ECHO CITY, EH?
DON'T WORRY, I CAN ANSWER ANY QUESTIONS YOU HAVE.
WE ONLY MOVED ACROSS TOWN.
WE'VE LIVED IN **THE E.C.** OUR WHOLE LIVES.
OH.
HUSH, THOMPSON.
POSSESSED HOW? I NEED DETAILS.
IT'S LIKE SOME SORT OF EVIL SPIRIT!
IT **PINCHES** TIA WHEN SHE'S TRYING TO SLEEP, AND CHANGES THE ALARM CLOCK TO RING AT THREE IN THE MORNING!
KNOCKS THINGS OFF OF SHELVES! PUTS **TACKS** ON TAYE'S CHAIR!
OOOH, MAYBE IT'S A POLTERGEIST!
YOU WATCH TOO MANY MOVIES.

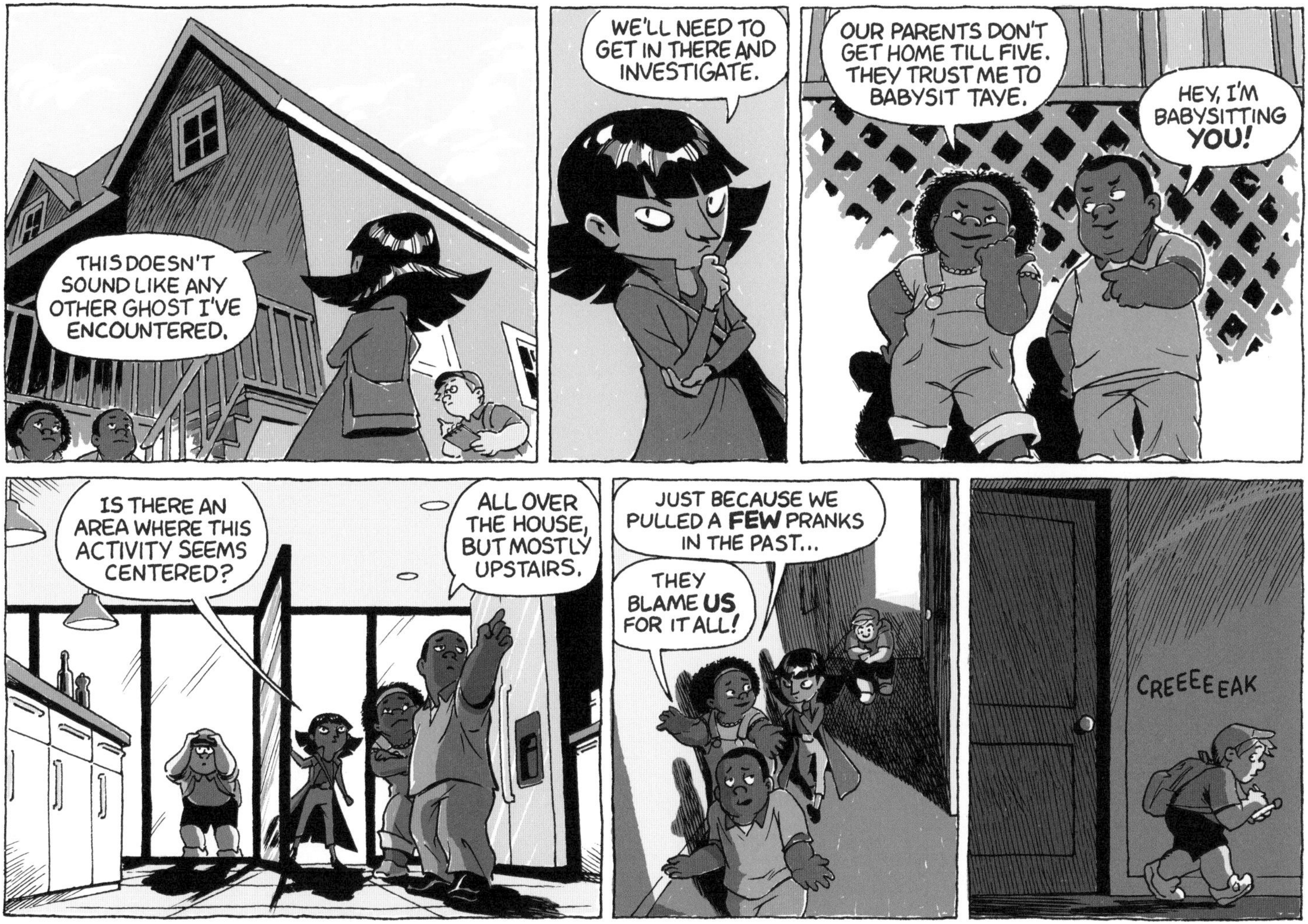
THIS DOESN'T SOUND LIKE ANY OTHER GHOST I'VE ENCOUNTERED.
WE'LL NEED TO GET IN THERE AND INVESTIGATE.
OUR PARENTS DON'T GET HOME TILL FIVE. THEY TRUST ME TO BABYSIT TAYE.
HEY, I'M BABYSITTING **YOU!**
IS THERE AN AREA WHERE THIS ACTIVITY SEEMS CENTERED?
ALL OVER THE HOUSE, BUT MOSTLY UPSTAIRS.
JUST BECAUSE WE PULLED A **FEW** PRANKS IN THE PAST...
THEY BLAME **US** FOR IT ALL!
CREEEEEAK

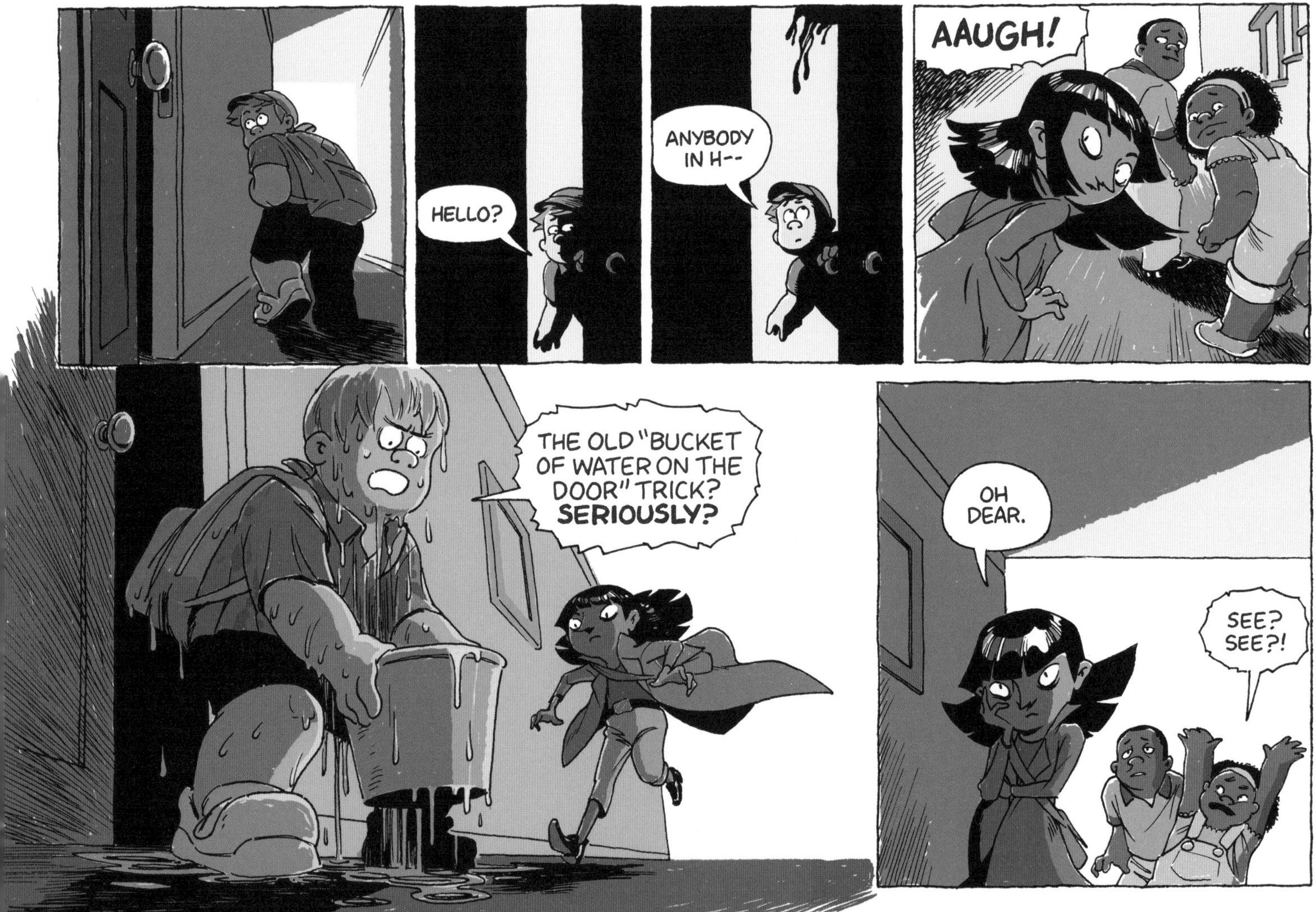
HELLO?
ANYBODY IN H--
AAUGH!
THE OLD "BUCKET OF WATER ON THE DOOR" TRICK? **SERIOUSLY?**
OH DEAR.
SEE? SEE?!

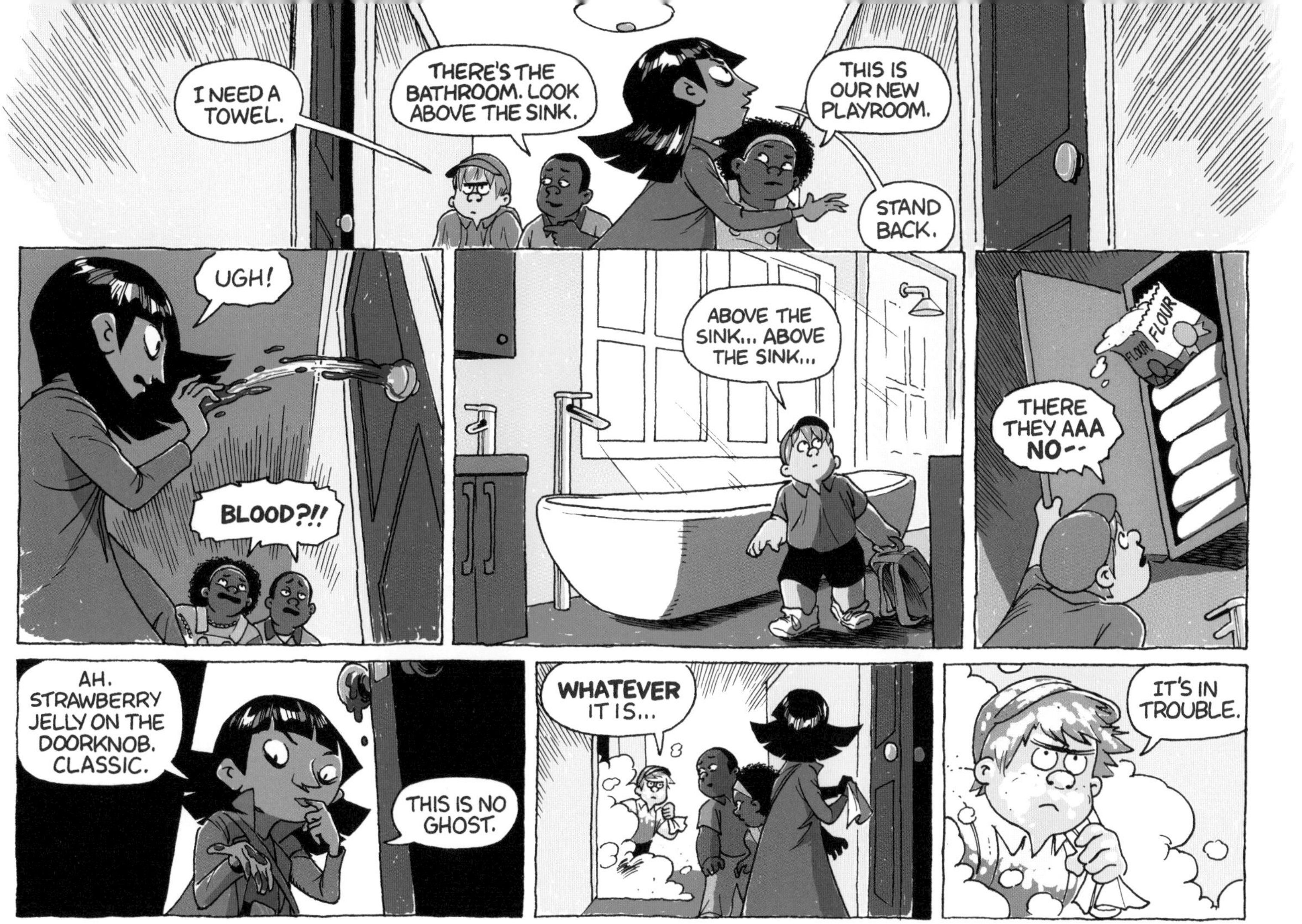
I NEED A TOWEL.
THERE'S THE BATHROOM. LOOK ABOVE THE SINK.
THIS IS OUR NEW PLAYROOM.
STAND BACK.
UGH!
BLOOD?!!
ABOVE THE SINK... ABOVE THE SINK...
FLOUR
FLOUR
THERE THEY AAA NO--
AH. STRAWBERRY JELLY ON THE DOORKNOB. CLASSIC.
THIS IS NO GHOST.
WHATEVER IT IS...
IT'S IN TROUBLE.

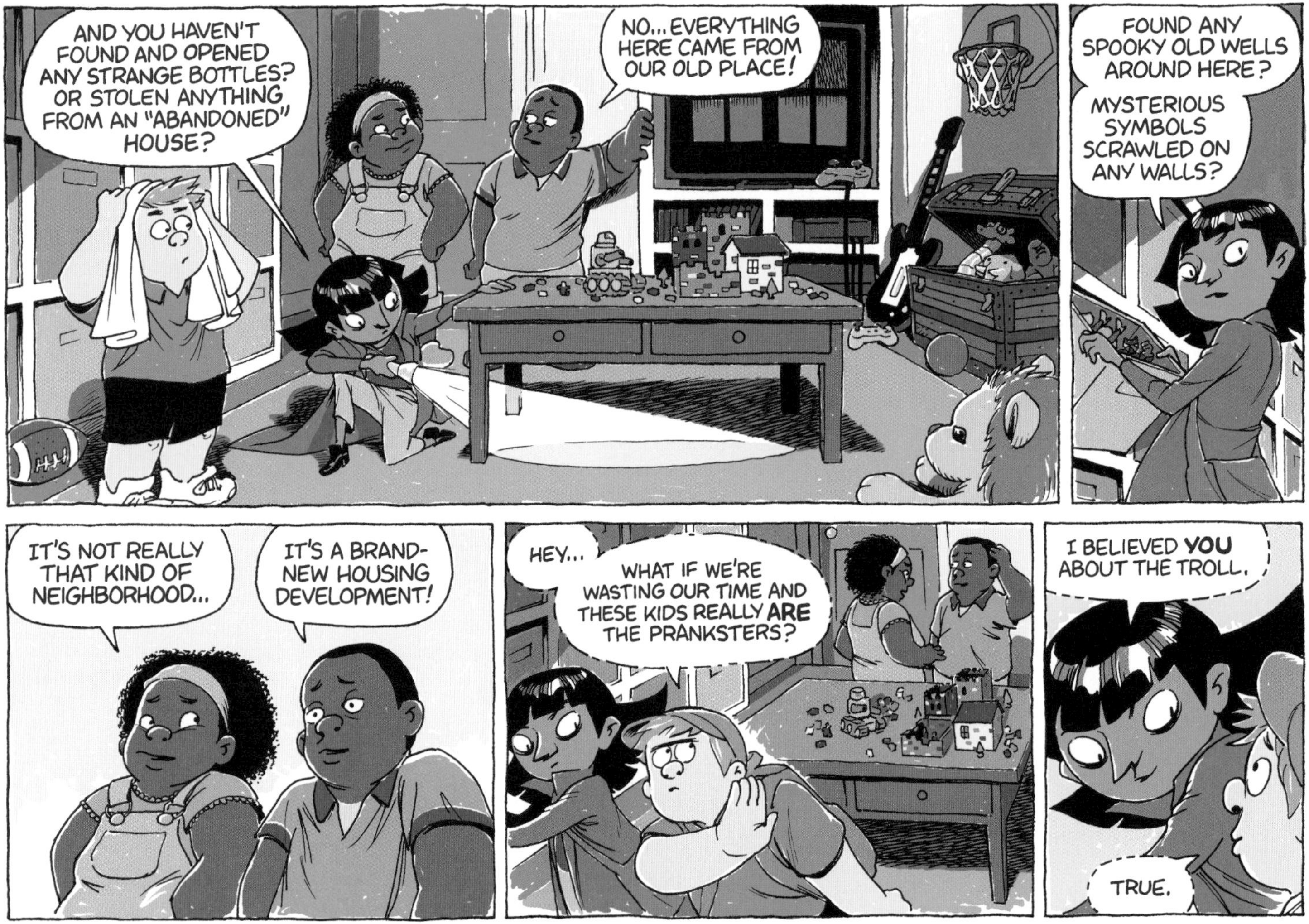
AND YOU HAVEN'T FOUND AND OPENED ANY STRANGE BOTTLES? OR STOLEN ANYTHING FROM AN "ABANDONED" HOUSE?
NO... EVERYTHING HERE CAME FROM OUR OLD PLACE!
FOUND ANY SPOOKY OLD WELLS AROUND HERE?
MYSTERIOUS SYMBOLS SCRAWLED ON ANY WALLS?
IT'S NOT REALLY THAT KIND OF NEIGHBORHOOD...
IT'S A BRAND-NEW HOUSING DEVELOPMENT!
HEY...
WHAT IF WE'RE WASTING OUR TIME AND THESE KIDS REALLY **ARE** THE PRANKSTERS?
I BELIEVED **YOU** ABOUT THE TROLL.
TRUE.

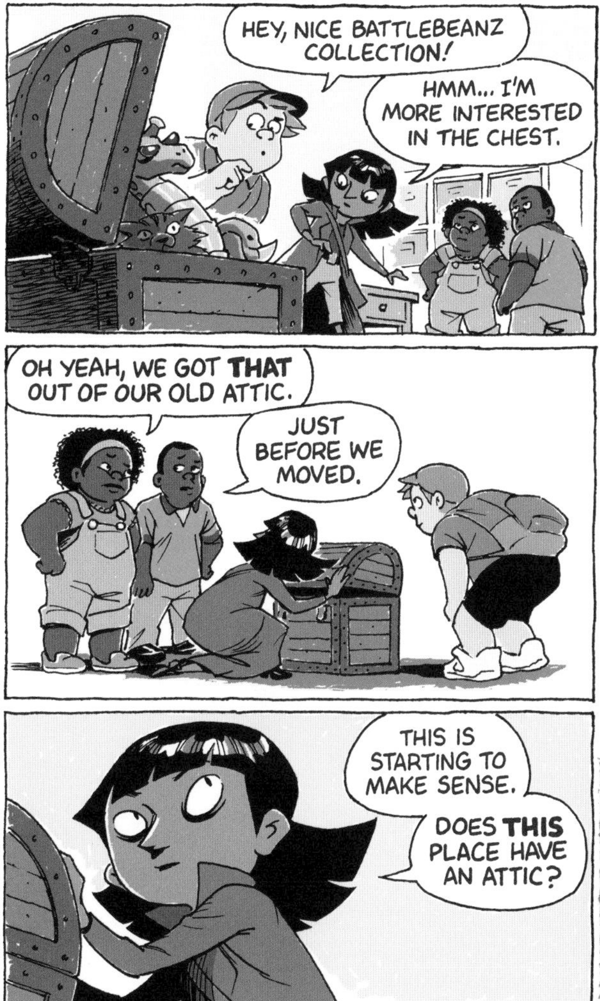
HEY, NICE BATTLEBEANZ COLLECTION!
HMM... I'M MORE INTERESTED IN THE CHEST.
OH YEAH, WE GOT **THAT** OUT OF OUR OLD ATTIC.
JUST BEFORE WE MOVED.
THIS IS STARTING TO MAKE SENSE.
DOES **THIS** PLACE HAVE AN ATTIC?

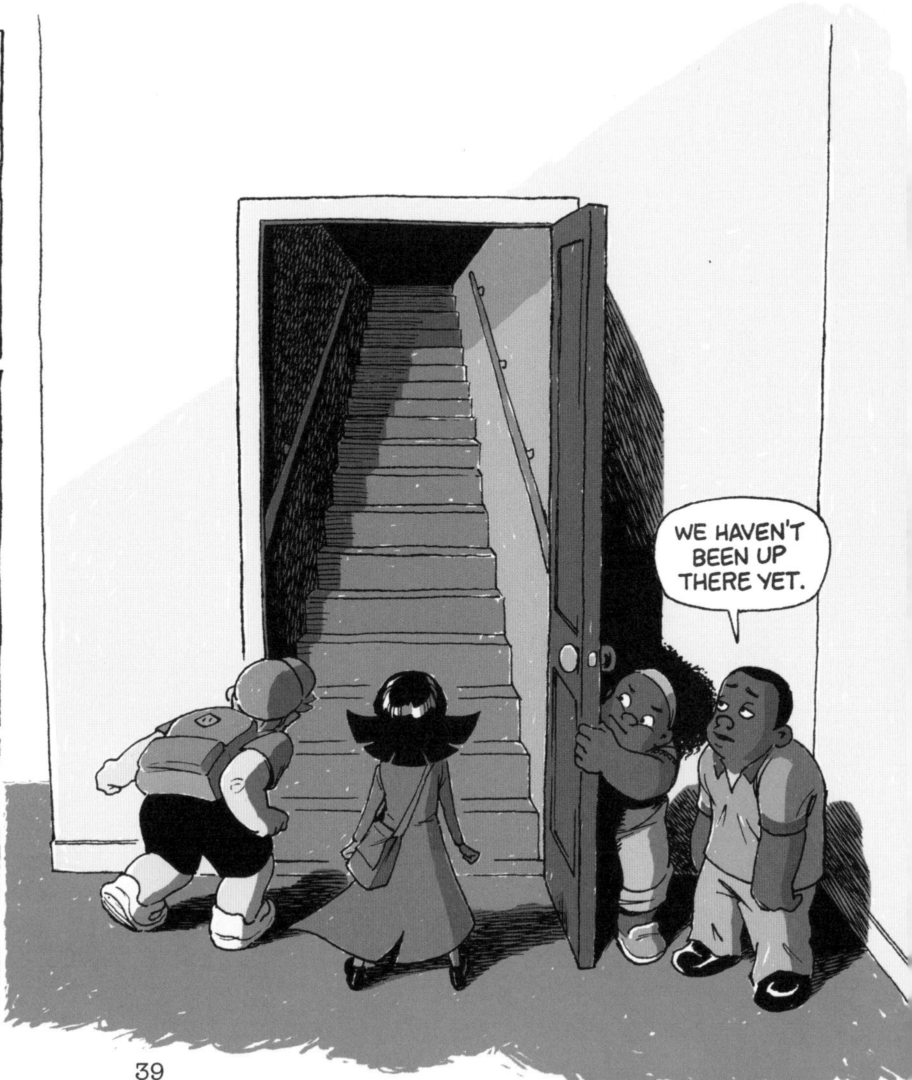
WE HAVEN'T BEEN UP THERE YET.

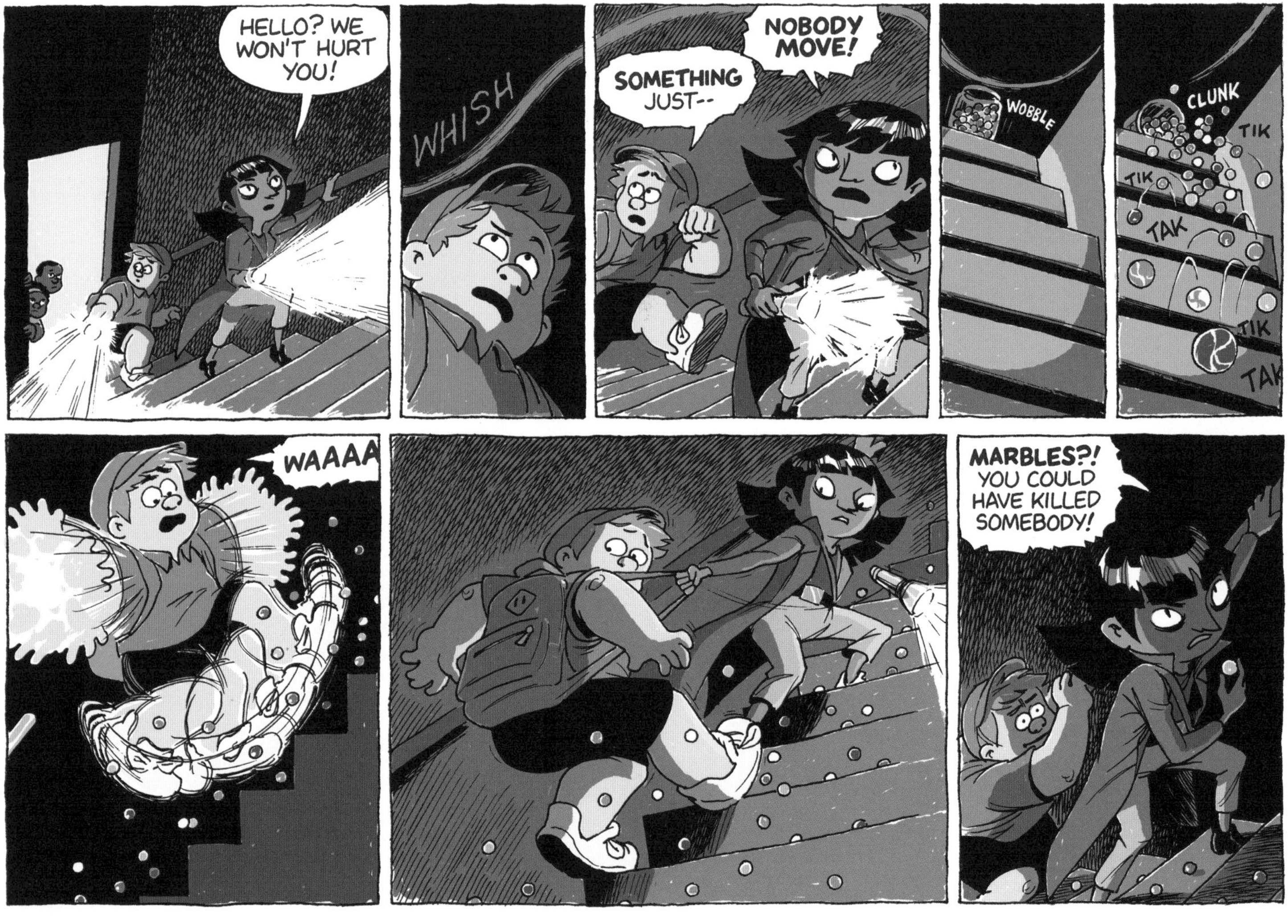
HELLO? WE WON'T HURT YOU!
WHISH
SOMETHING JUST--
NOBODY MOVE!
WOBBLE
CLUNK
TIK
TIK
TAK
TIK
TAK
WAAAA
MARBLES?! YOU COULD HAVE KILLED SOMEBODY!

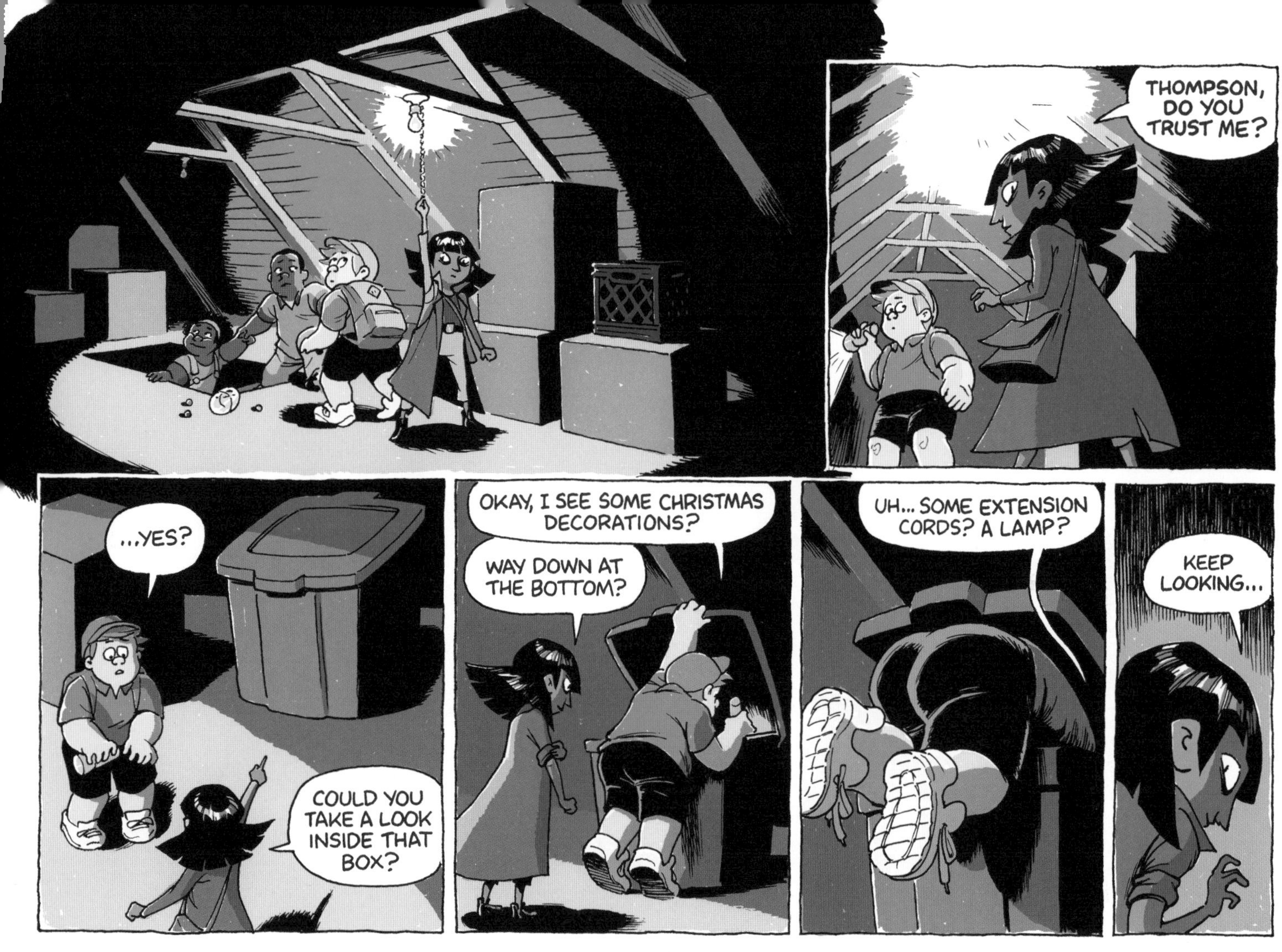
THOMPSON, DO YOU TRUST ME?
...YES?
COULD YOU TAKE A LOOK INSIDE THAT BOX?
OKAY, I SEE SOME CHRISTMAS DECORATIONS?
WAY DOWN AT THE BOTTOM?
UH... SOME EXTENSION CORDS? A LAMP?
KEEP LOOKING...

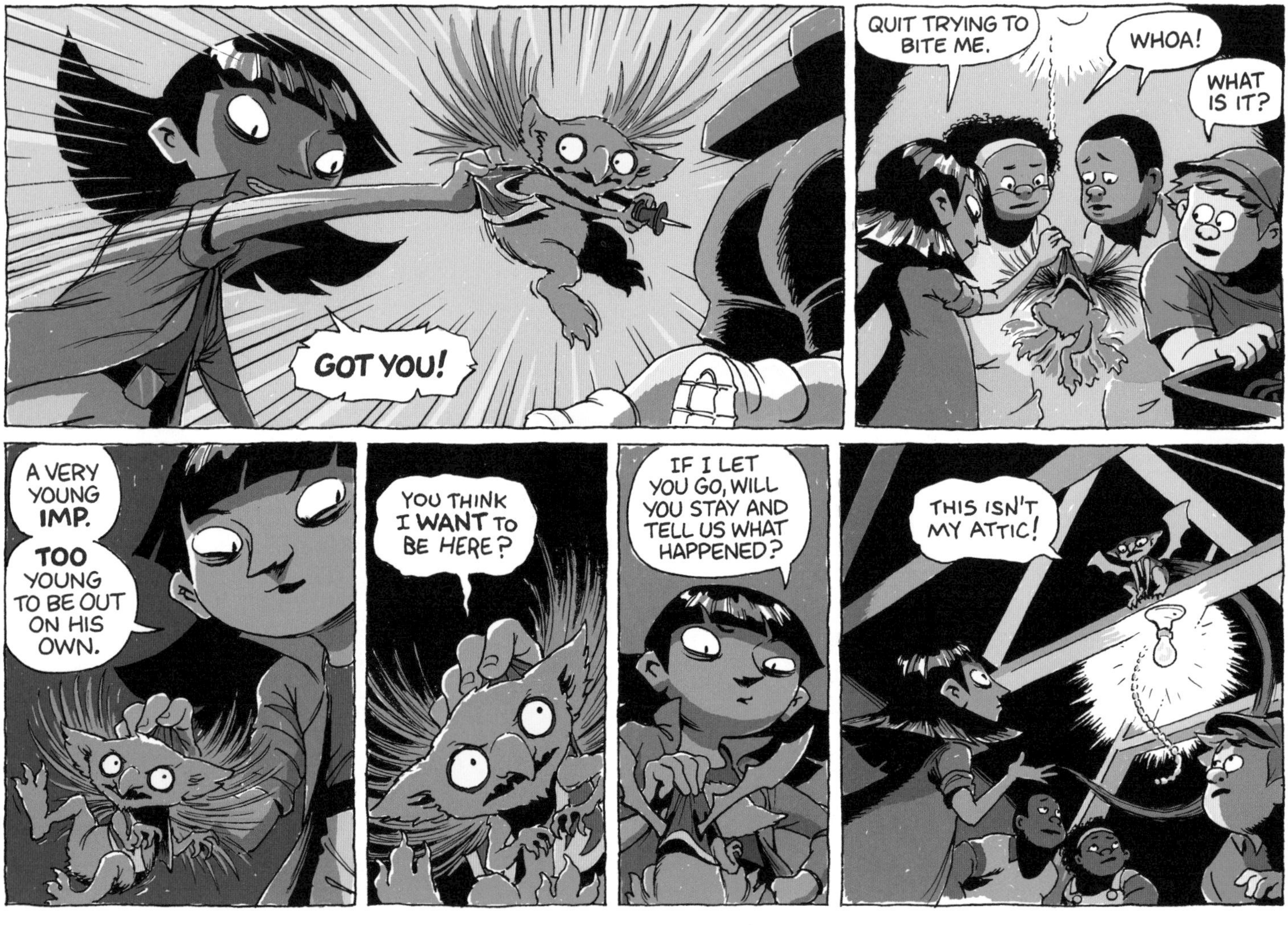
GOT YOU!
QUIT TRYING TO BITE ME.
WHOA!
WHAT IS IT?
A VERY YOUNG IMP.
TOO YOUNG TO BE OUT ON HIS OWN.
YOU THINK I WANT TO BE HERE?
IF I LET YOU GO, WILL YOU STAY AND TELL US WHAT HAPPENED?
THIS ISN'T MY ATTIC!

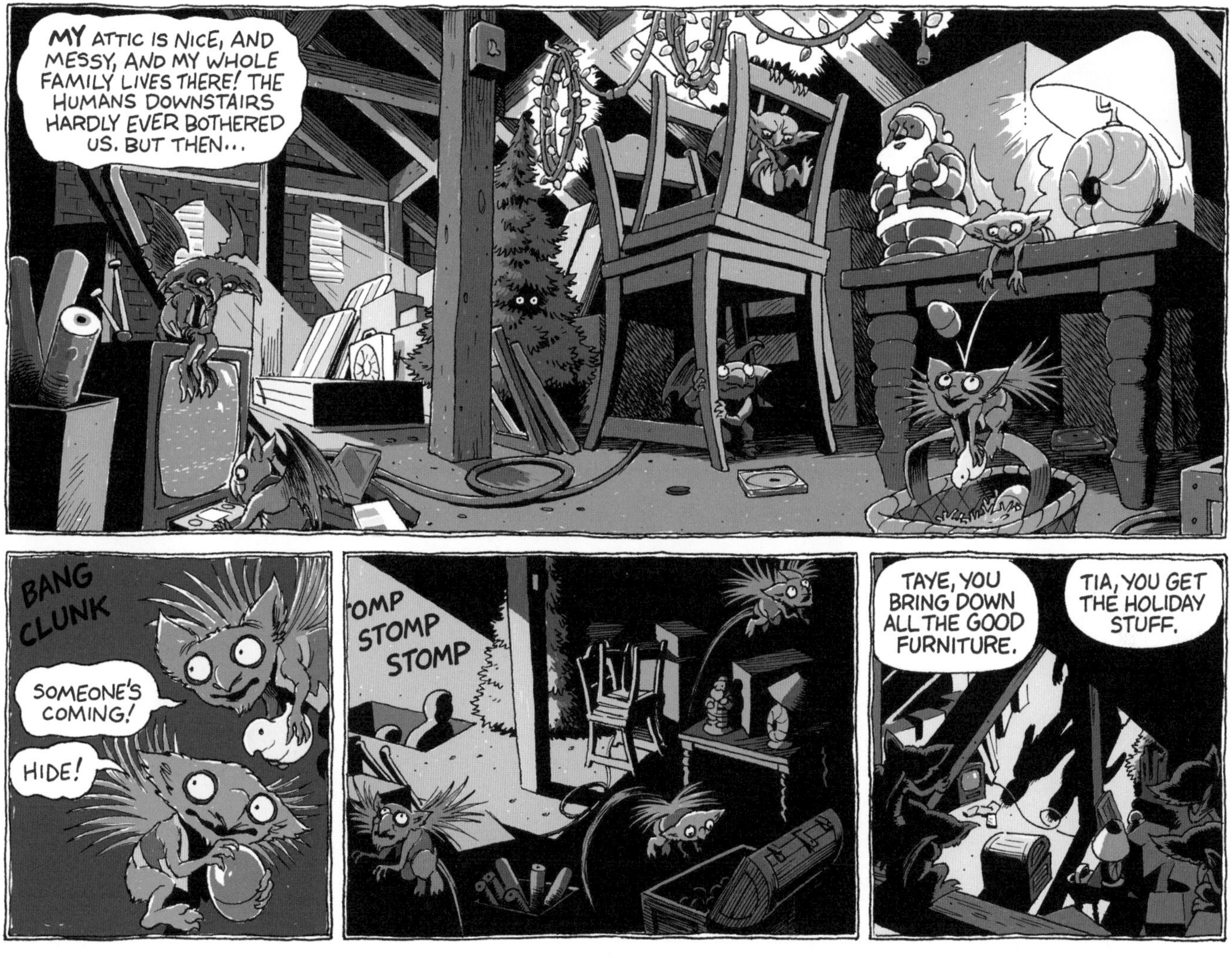
MY ATTIC IS NICE, AND MESSY, AND MY WHOLE FAMILY LIVES THERE! THE HUMANS DOWNSTAIRS HARDLY EVER BOTHERED US. BUT THEN...
BANG
CLUNK
SOMEONE'S COMING!
HIDE!
OMP
STOMP
STOMP
TAYE, YOU BRING DOWN ALL THE GOOD FURNITURE.
TIA, YOU GET THE HOLIDAY STUFF.

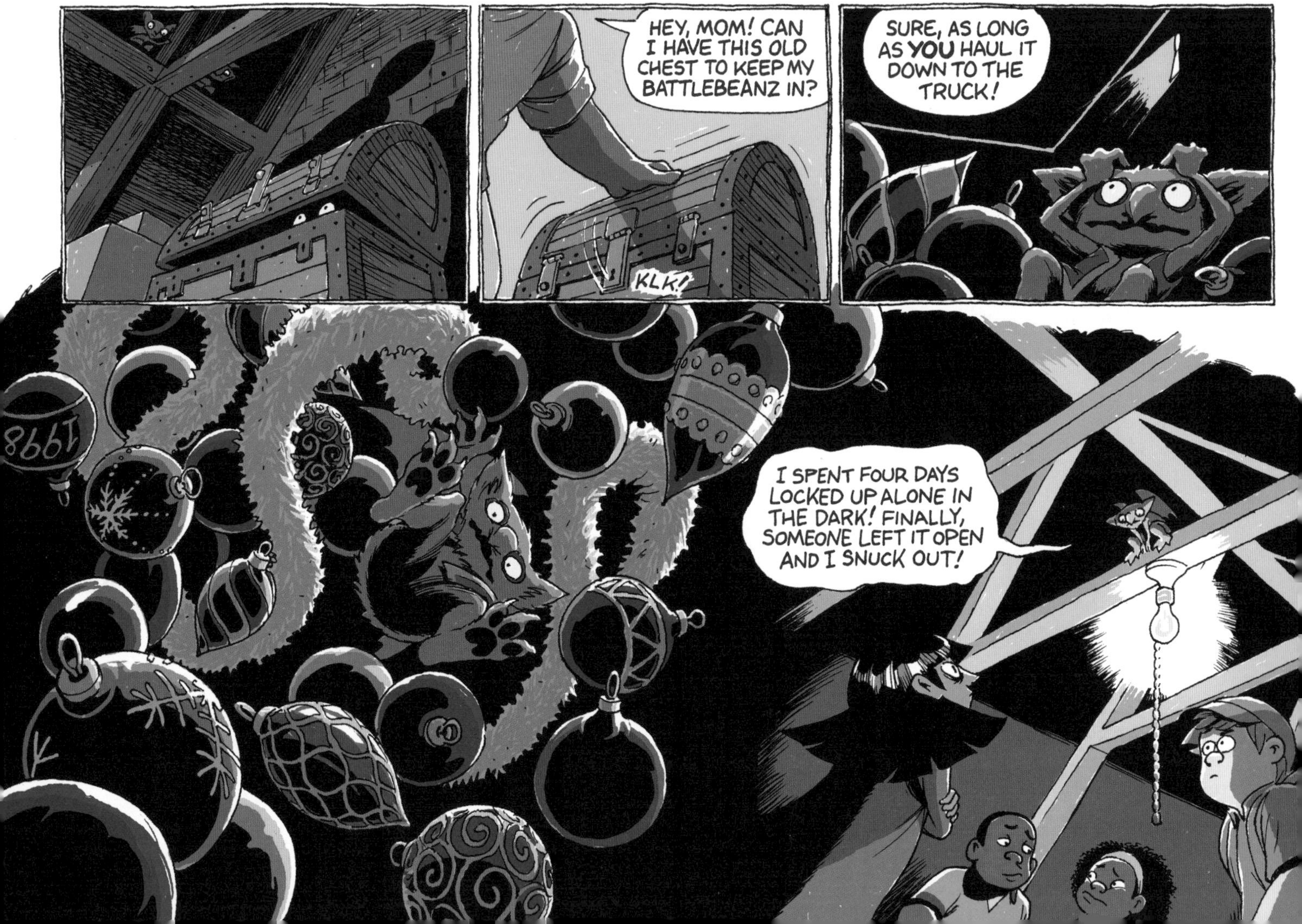
HEY, MOM! CAN I HAVE THIS OLD CHEST TO KEEP MY BATTLEBEANZ IN?
KLK!
SURE, AS LONG AS **YOU** HAUL IT DOWN TO THE TRUCK!
I SPENT FOUR DAYS LOCKED UP ALONE IN THE DARK! FINALLY, SOMEONE LEFT IT OPEN AND I SNUCK OUT!

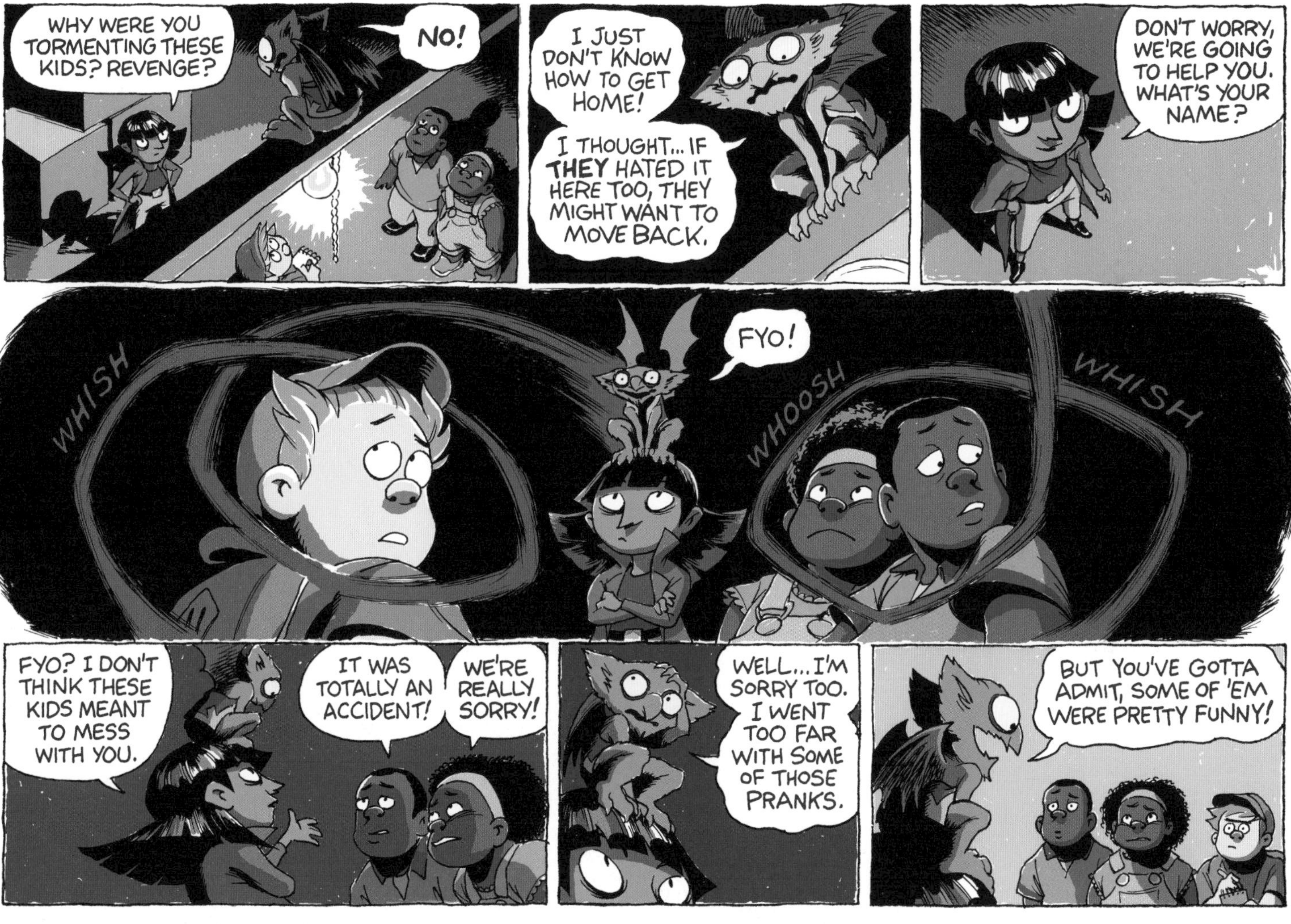

WHY WERE YOU TORMENTING THESE KIDS? REVENGE?
NO!
I JUST DON'T KNOW HOW TO GET HOME!
I THOUGHT... IF **THEY** HATED IT HERE TOO, THEY MIGHT WANT TO MOVE BACK.
DON'T WORRY, WE'RE GOING TO HELP YOU. WHAT'S YOUR NAME?
WHISH
FYO!
WHOOSH
WHISH
FYO? I DON'T THINK THESE KIDS MEANT TO MESS WITH YOU.
IT WAS TOTALLY AN ACCIDENT!
WE'RE REALLY SORRY!
WELL... I'M SORRY TOO. I WENT TOO FAR WITH SOME OF THOSE PRANKS.
BUT YOU'VE GOTTA ADMIT, SOME OF 'EM WERE PRETTY FUNNY!

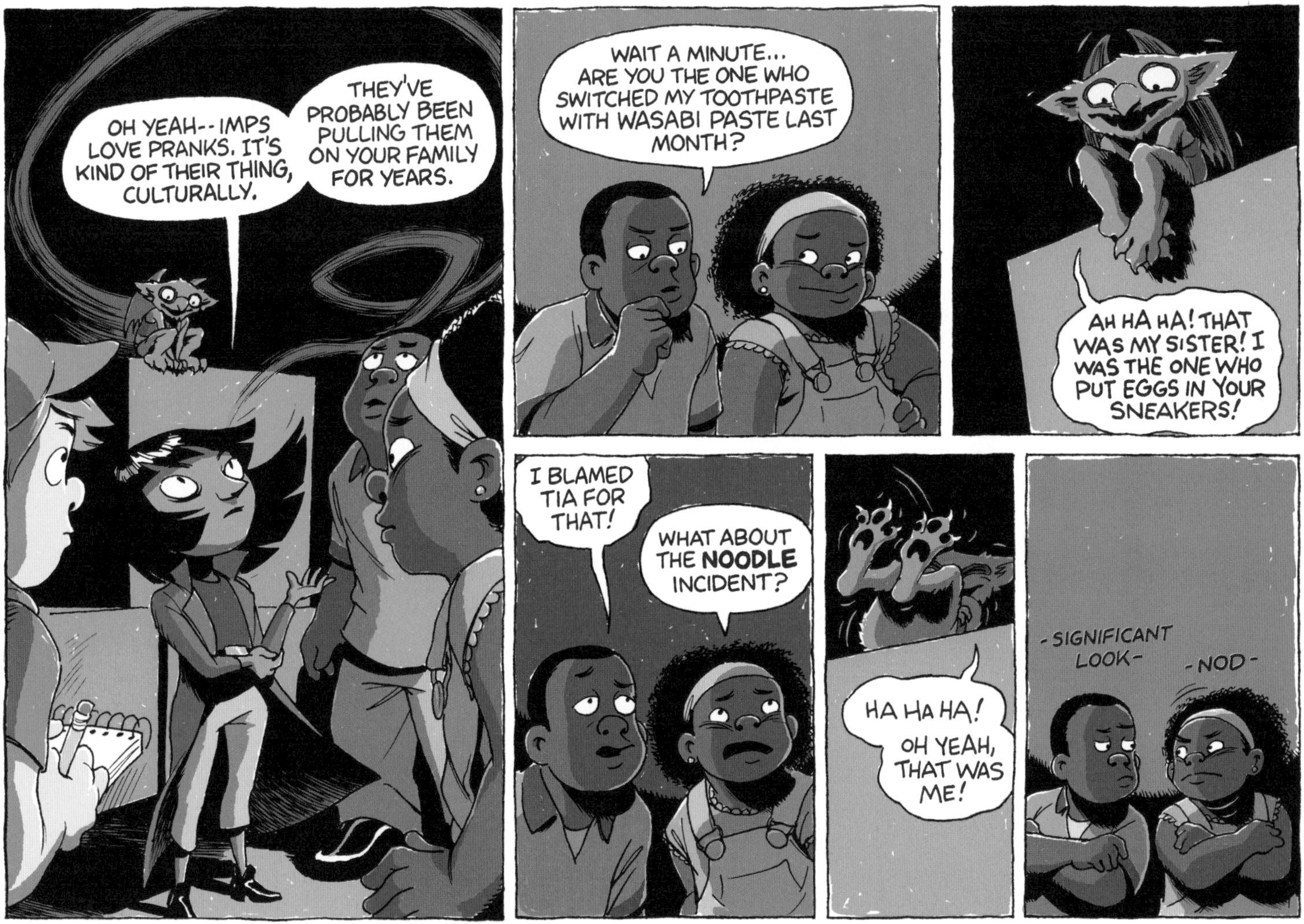
OH YEAH--IMPS LOVE PRANKS. IT'S KIND OF THEIR THING, CULTURALLY.
THEY'VE PROBABLY BEEN PULLING THEM ON YOUR FAMILY FOR YEARS.
WAIT A MINUTE... ARE YOU THE ONE WHO SWITCHED MY TOOTHPASTE WITH WASABI PASTE LAST MONTH?
AH HA HA! THAT WAS MY SISTER! I WAS THE ONE WHO PUT EGGS IN YOUR SNEAKERS!
I BLAMED TIA FOR THAT!
WHAT ABOUT THE **NOODLE** INCIDENT?
HA HA HA!
OH YEAH, THAT WAS ME!
-SIGNIFICANT LOOK-
-NOD-

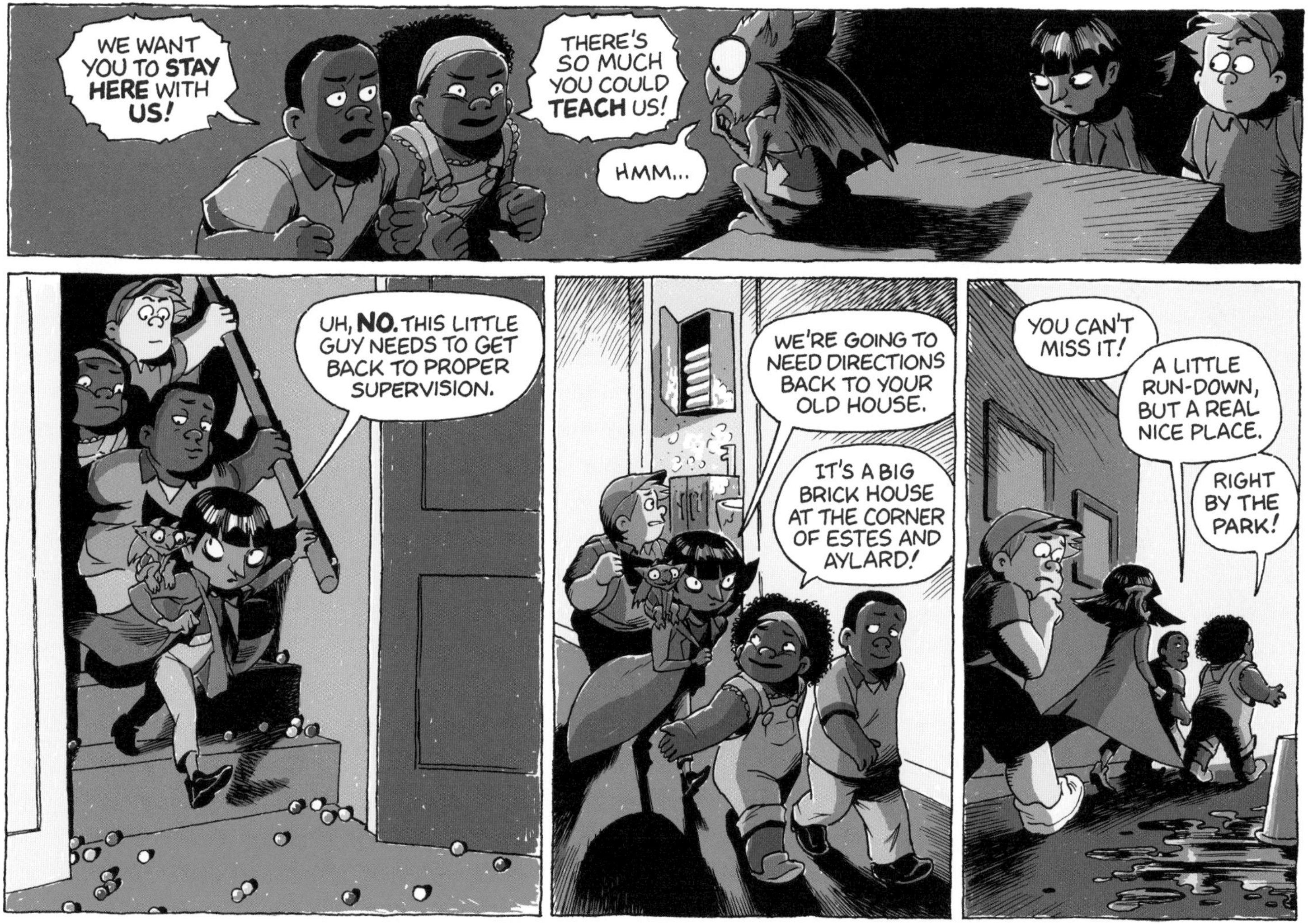
WE WANT YOU TO **STAY HERE** WITH **US**!
THERE'S SO MUCH YOU COULD **TEACH** US!
HMM...
UH, **NO**. THIS LITTLE GUY NEEDS TO GET BACK TO PROPER SUPERVISION.
WE'RE GOING TO NEED DIRECTIONS BACK TO YOUR OLD HOUSE.
IT'S A BIG BRICK HOUSE AT THE CORNER OF ESTES AND AYLARD!
YOU CAN'T MISS IT!
A LITTLE RUN-DOWN, BUT A REAL NICE PLACE.
RIGHT BY THE PARK!

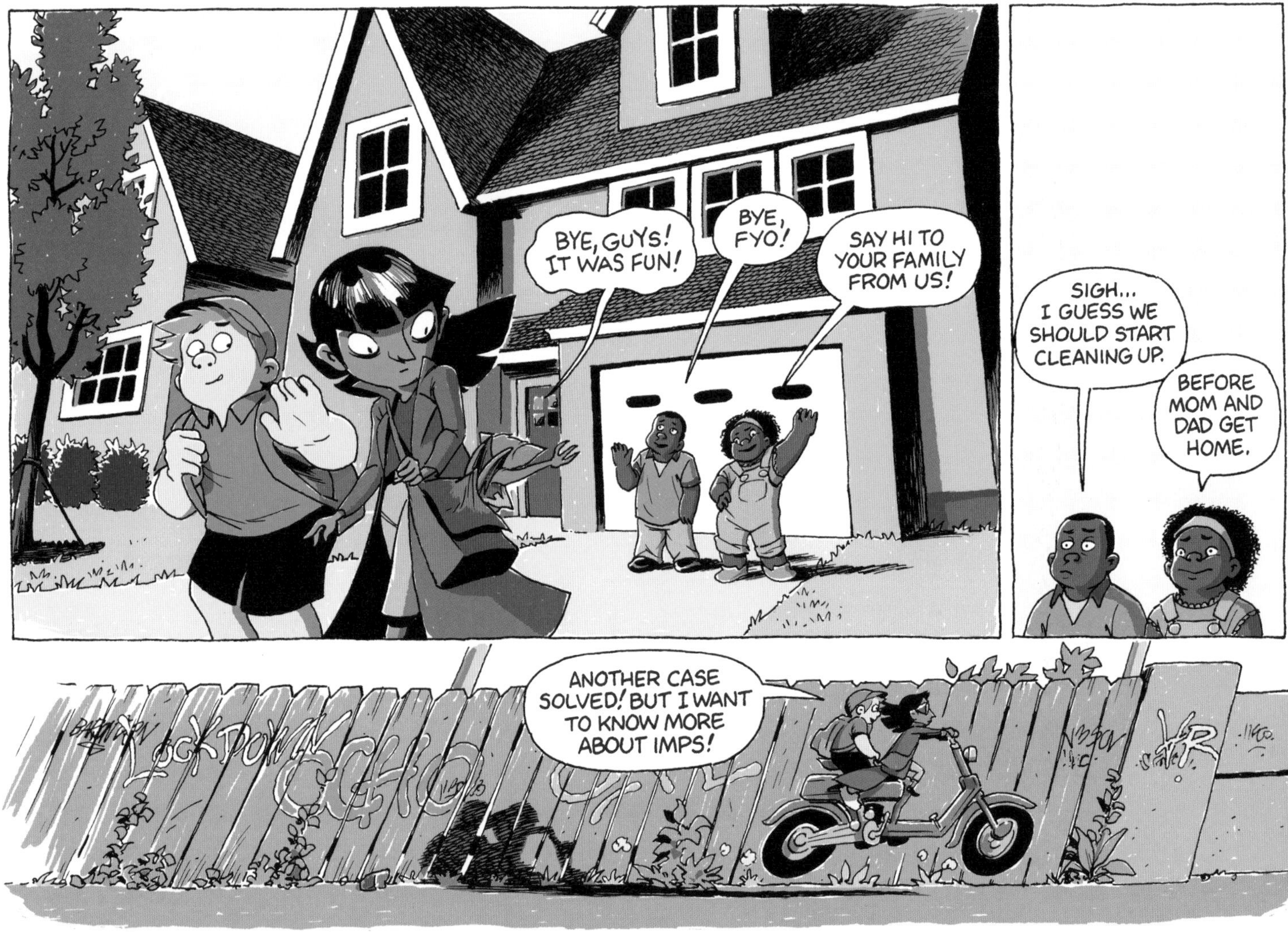
BYE, GUYS! IT WAS FUN!
BYE, FYO!
SAY HI TO YOUR FAMILY FROM US!
SIGH... I GUESS WE SHOULD START CLEANING UP.
BEFORE MOM AND DAD GET HOME.
ANOTHER CASE SOLVED! BUT I WANT TO KNOW MORE ABOUT IMPS!

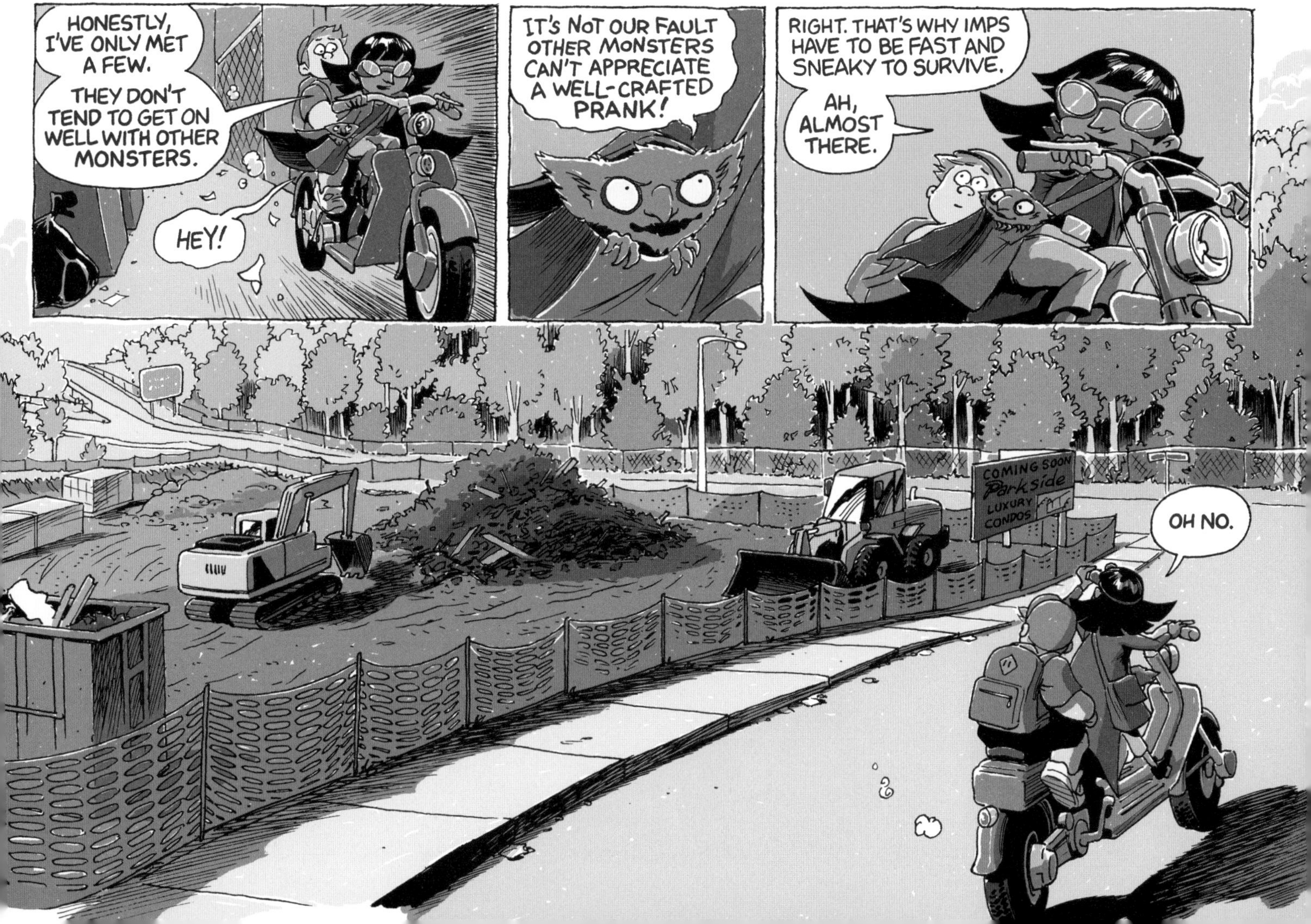
HONESTLY, I'VE ONLY MET A FEW.
THEY DON'T TEND TO GET ON WELL WITH OTHER MONSTERS.
HEY!
IT'S NOT OUR FAULT OTHER MONSTERS CAN'T APPRECIATE A WELL-CRAFTED PRANK!
RIGHT. THAT'S WHY IMPS HAVE TO BE FAST AND SNEAKY TO SURVIVE.
AH, ALMOST THERE.
COMING SOON
Parkside
LUXURY CONDOS
OH NO.

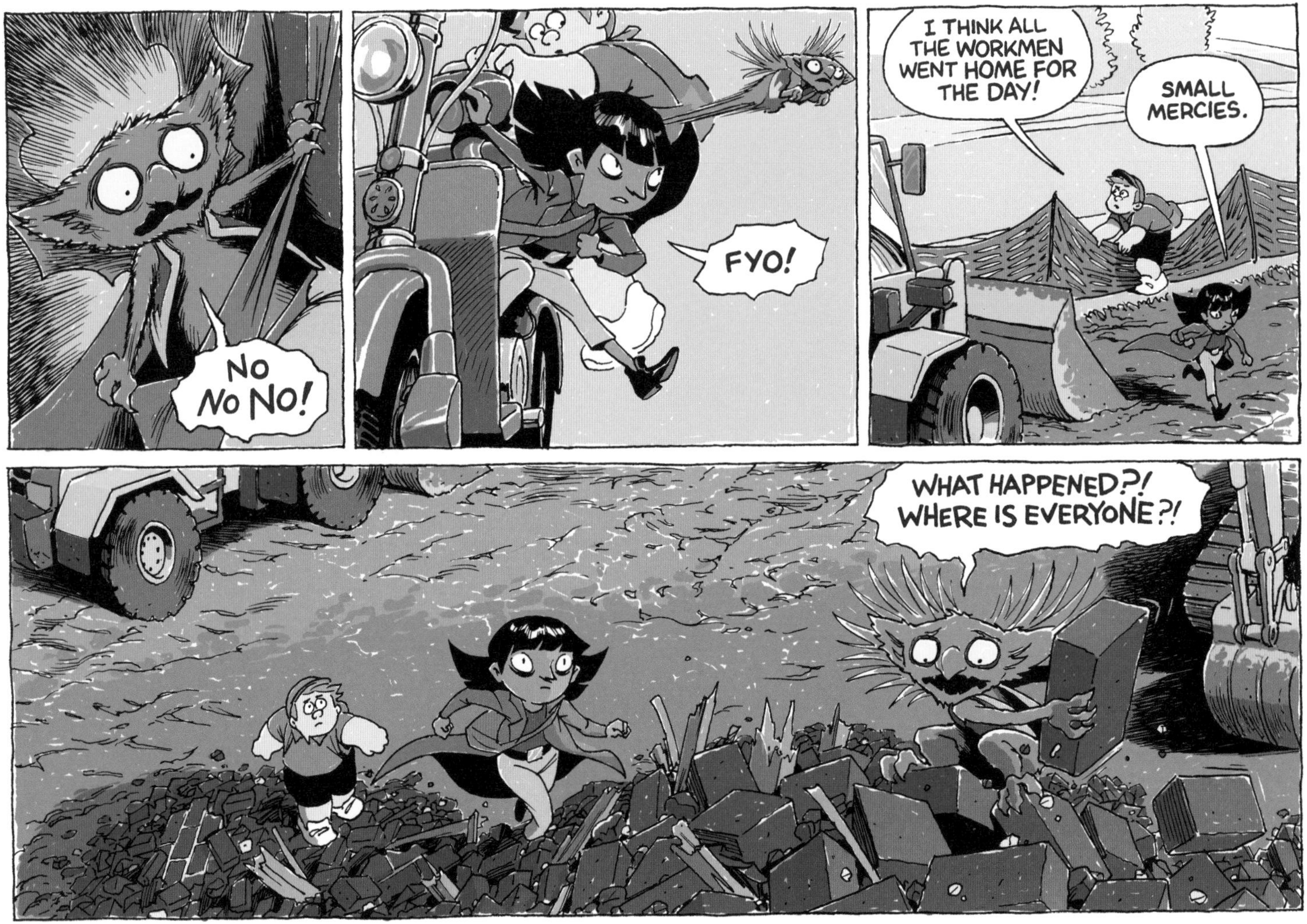
No No No!
FYO!
I THINK ALL THE WORKMEN WENT HOME FOR THE DAY!
SMALL MERCIES.
WHAT HAPPENED?! WHERE IS EVERYONE?!

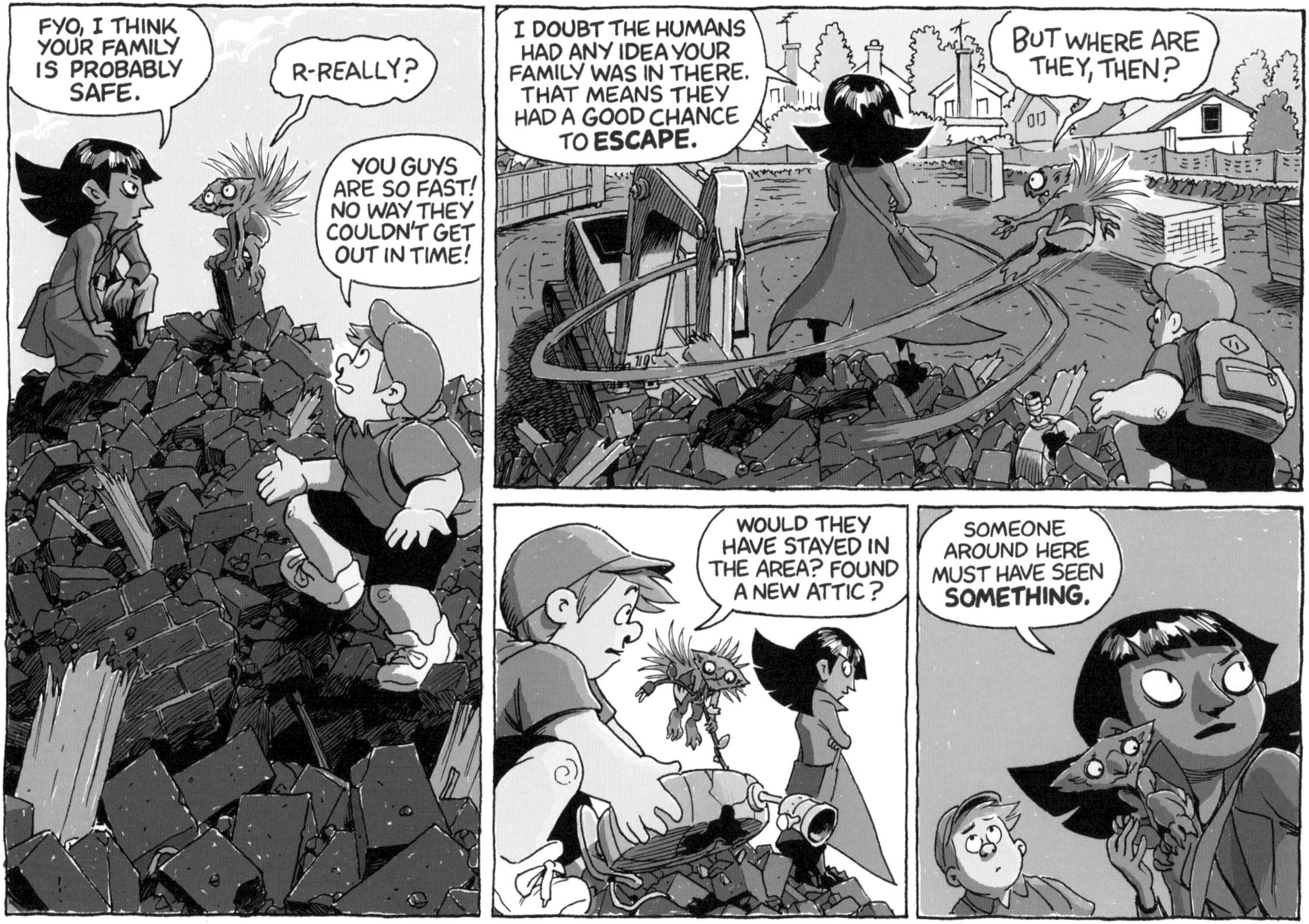
FYO, I THINK YOUR FAMILY IS PROBABLY SAFE.
R-REALLY?
YOU GUYS ARE SO FAST! NO WAY THEY COULDN'T GET OUT IN TIME!
I DOUBT THE HUMANS HAD ANY IDEA YOUR FAMILY WAS IN THERE. THAT MEANS THEY HAD A GOOD CHANCE TO **ESCAPE.**
BUT WHERE ARE THEY, THEN?
WOULD THEY HAVE STAYED IN THE AREA? FOUND A NEW ATTIC?
SOMEONE AROUND HERE MUST HAVE SEEN **SOMETHING.**

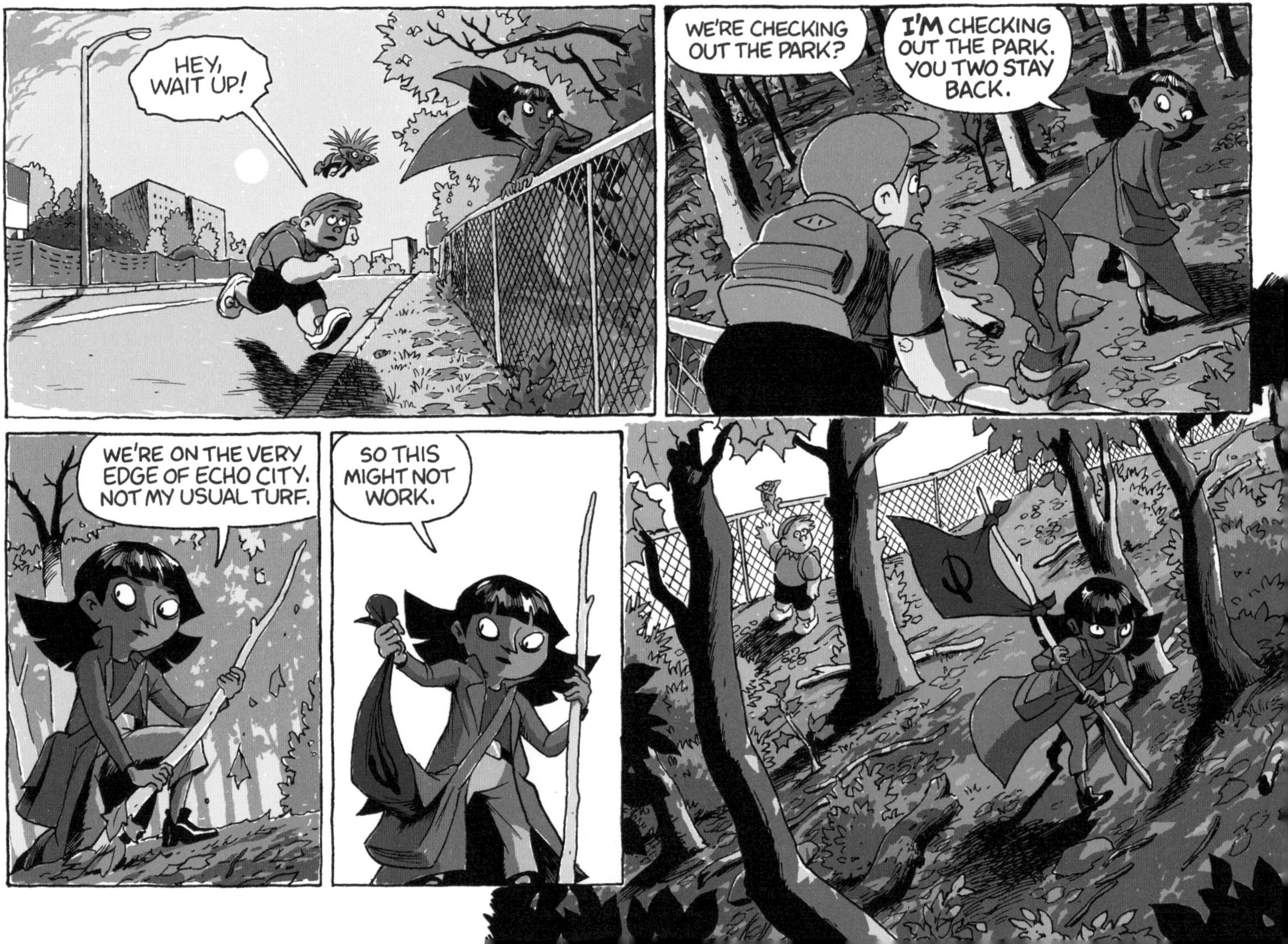
HEY, WAIT UP!
WE'RE CHECKING OUT THE PARK?
I'M CHECKING OUT THE PARK. YOU TWO STAY BACK.
WE'RE ON THE VERY EDGE OF ECHO CITY. NOT MY USUAL TURF.
SO THIS MIGHT NOT WORK.

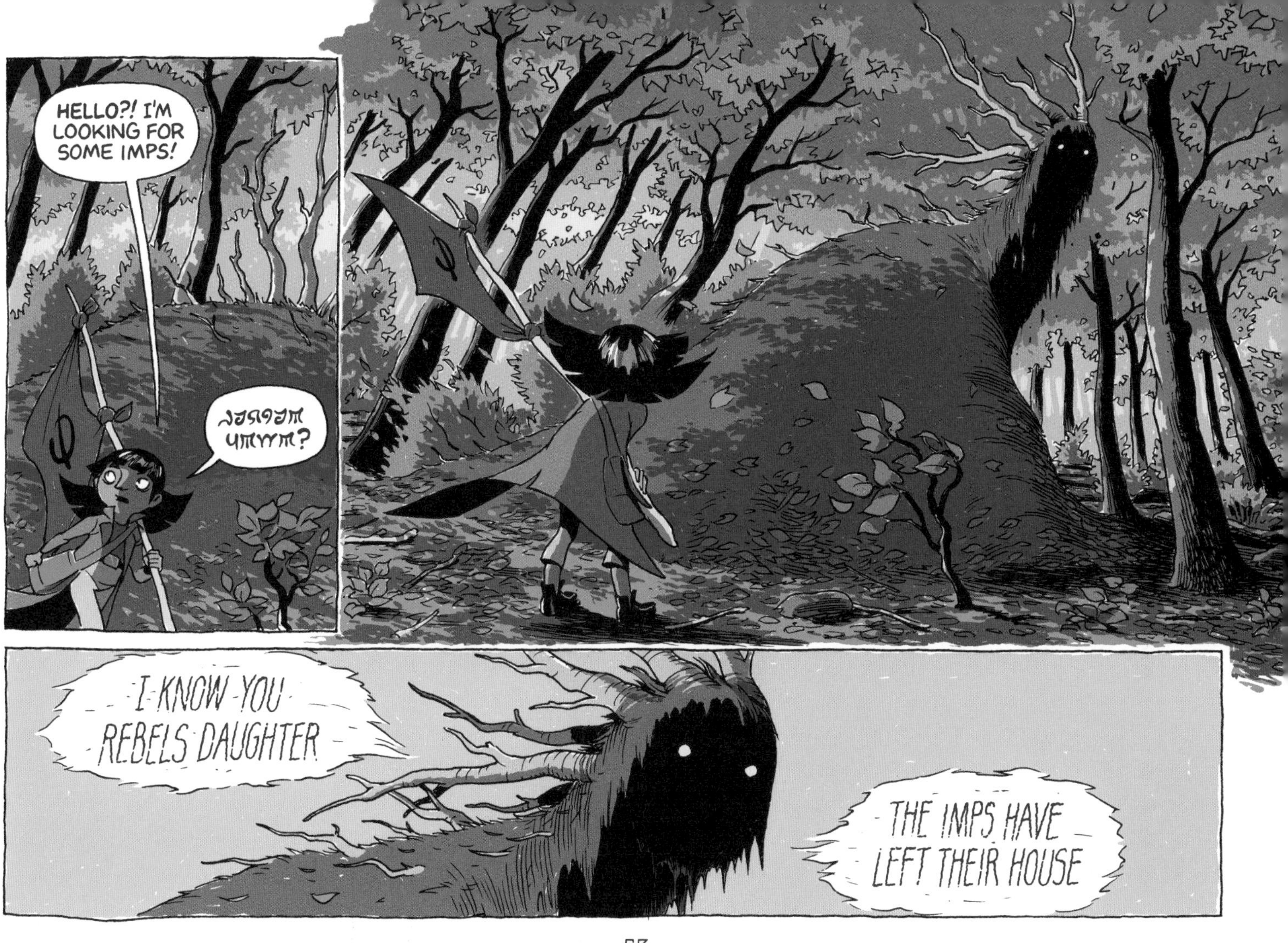
HELLO?! I'M LOOKING FOR SOME IMPS!
I KNOW YOU REBELS DAUGHTER
THE IMPS HAVE LEFT THEIR HOUSE

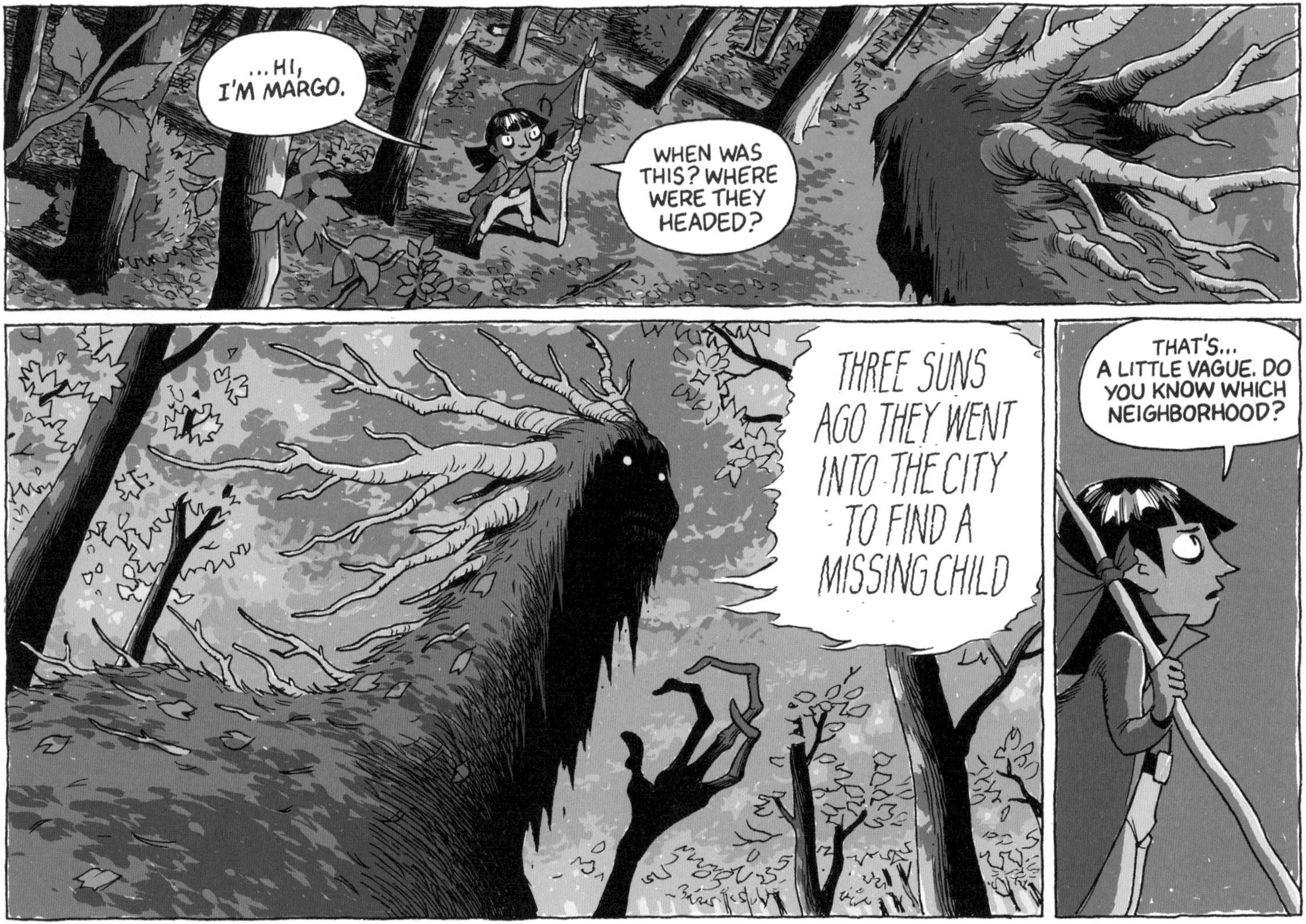
...HI, I'M MARGO.
WHEN WAS THIS? WHERE WERE THEY HEADED?
THREE SUNS AGO THEY WENT INTO THE CITY TO FIND A MISSING CHILD
THAT'S... A LITTLE VAGUE. DO YOU KNOW WHICH NEIGHBORHOOD?

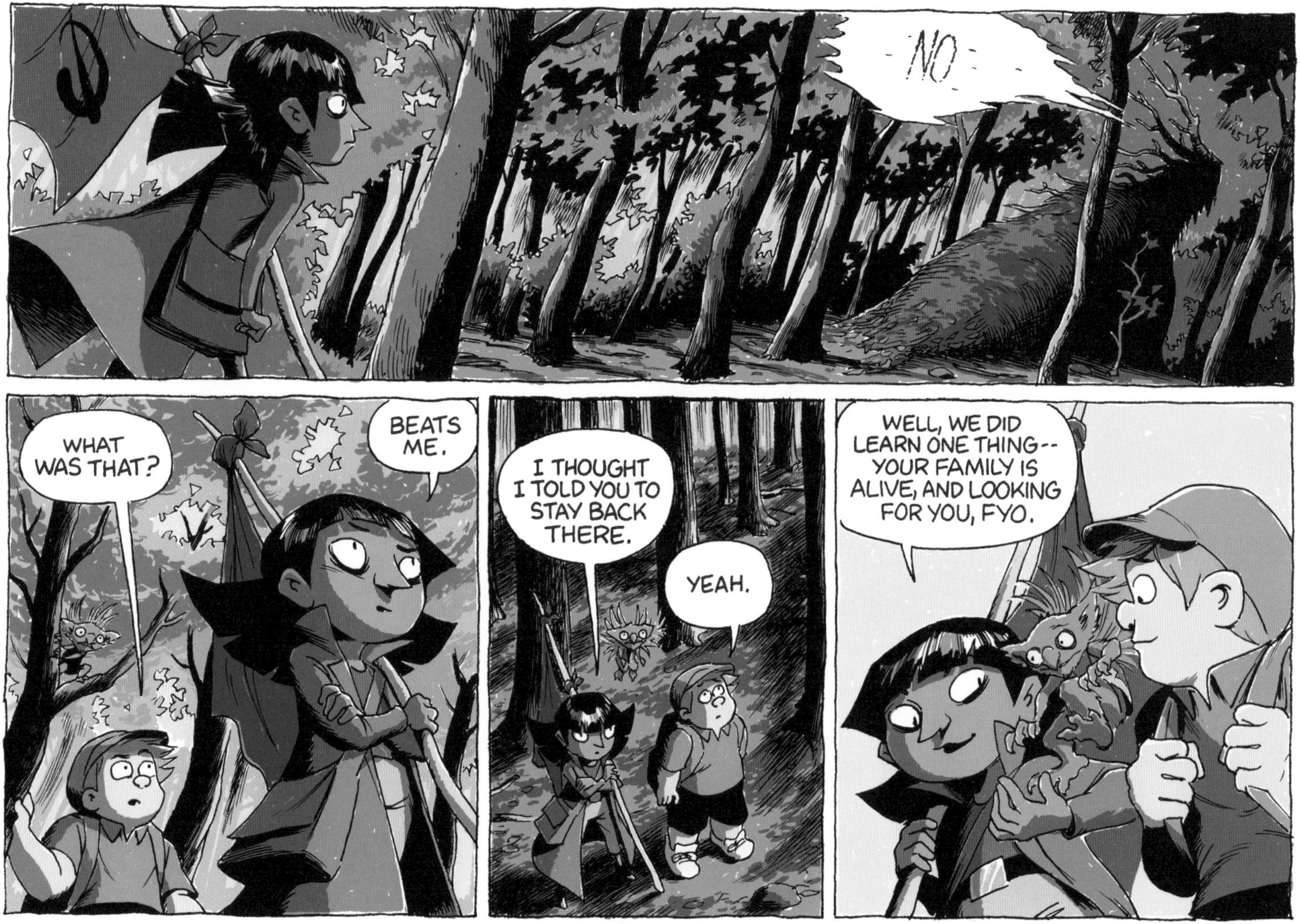
NO
WHAT WAS THAT?
BEATS ME.
I THOUGHT I TOLD YOU TO STAY BACK THERE.
YEAH.
WELL, WE DID LEARN ONE THING-- YOUR FAMILY IS ALIVE, AND LOOKING FOR YOU, FYO.

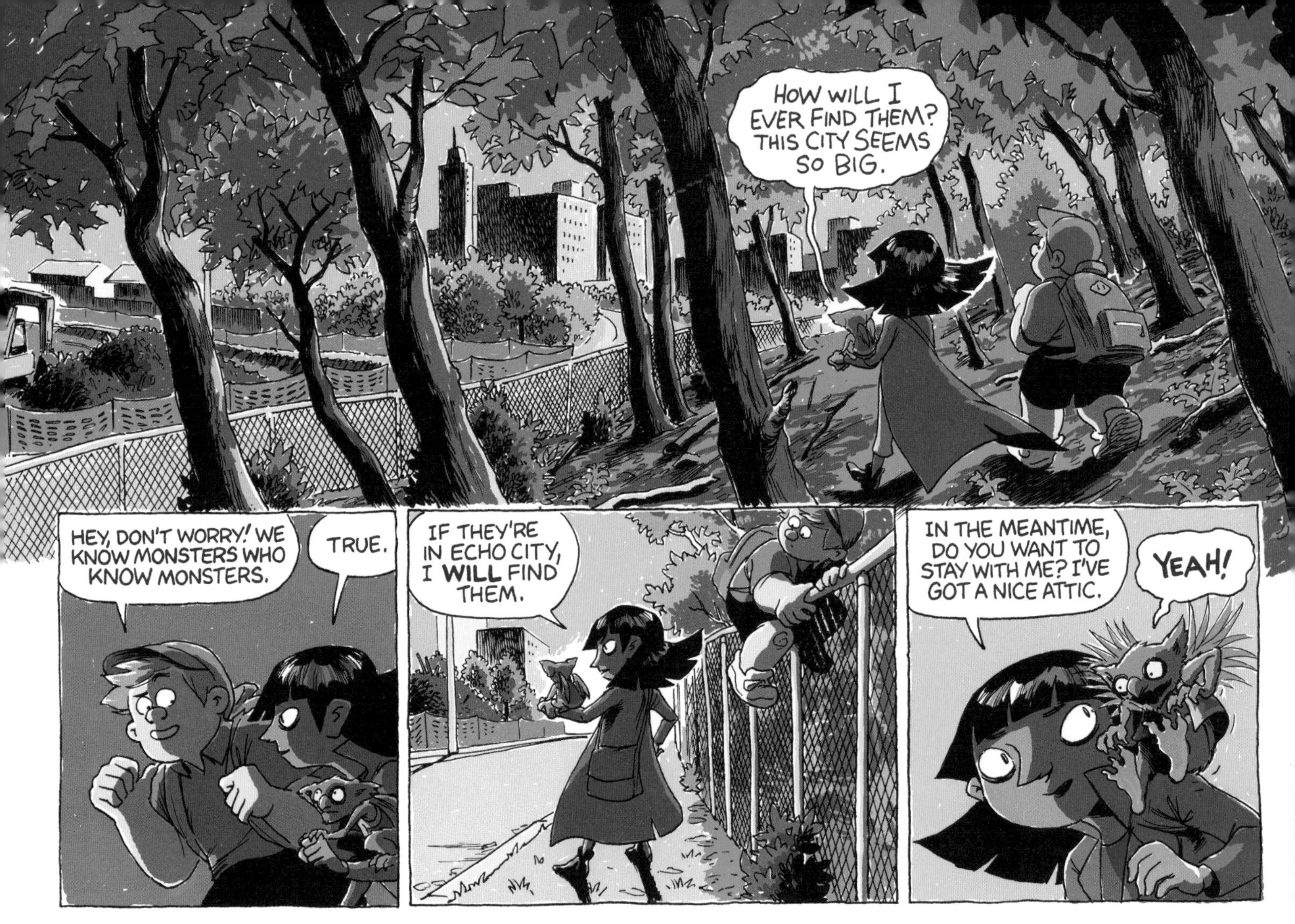
HOW WILL I EVER FIND THEM? THIS CITY SEEMS SO BIG.
HEY, DON'T WORRY! WE KNOW MONSTERS WHO KNOW MONSTERS.
TRUE.
IF THEY'RE IN ECHO CITY, I **WILL** FIND THEM.
IN THE MEANTIME, DO YOU WANT TO STAY WITH ME? I'VE GOT A NICE ATTIC.
YEAH!

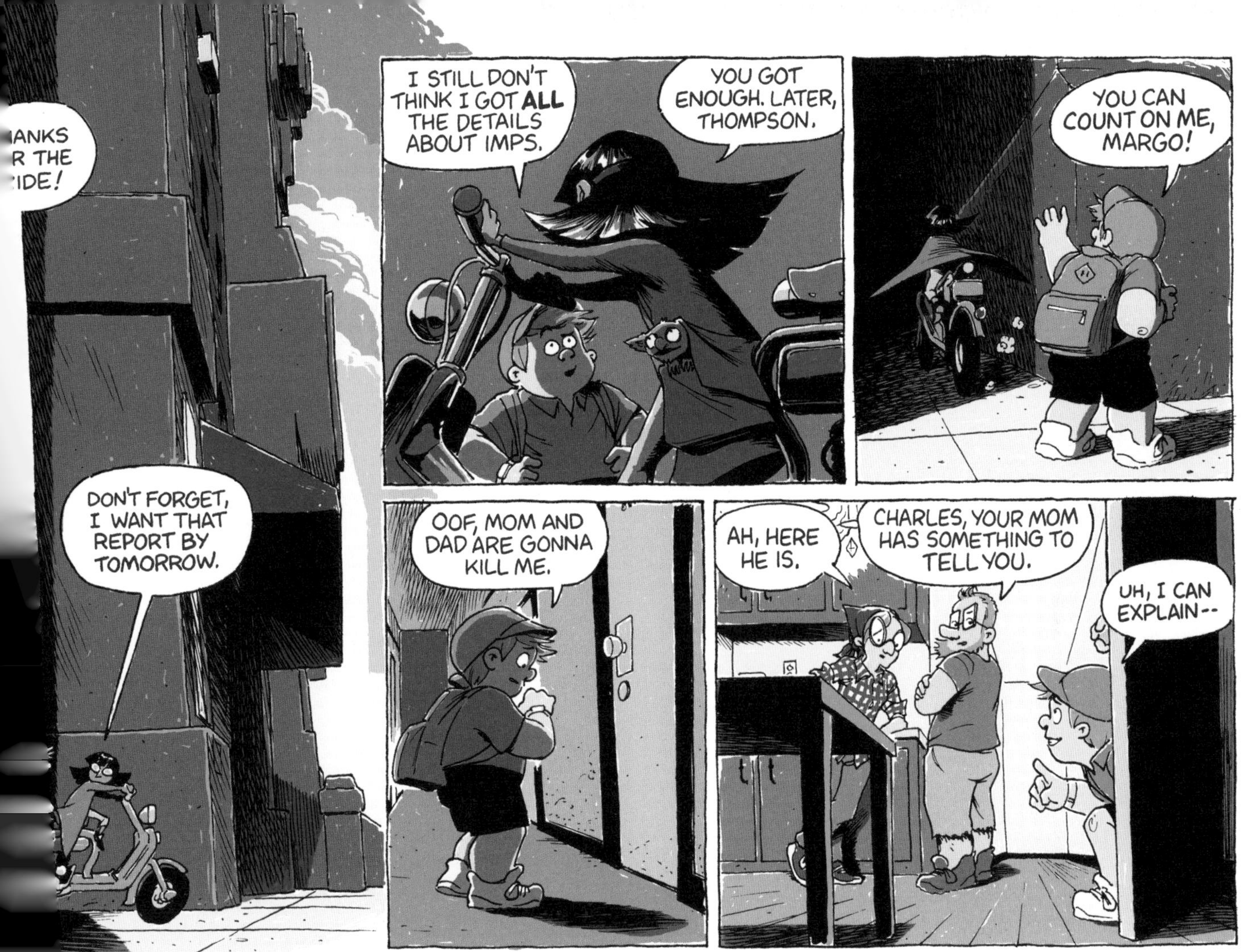
ANKS R THE IDE!
DON'T FORGET, I WANT THAT REPORT BY TOMORROW.
I STILL DON'T THINK I GOT **ALL** THE DETAILS ABOUT IMPS.
YOU GOT ENOUGH. LATER, THOMPSON.
YOU CAN COUNT ON ME, MARGO!
OOF, MOM AND DAD ARE GONNA KILL ME.
AH, HERE HE IS.
CHARLES, YOUR MOM HAS SOMETHING TO TELL YOU.
UH, I CAN EXPLAIN--

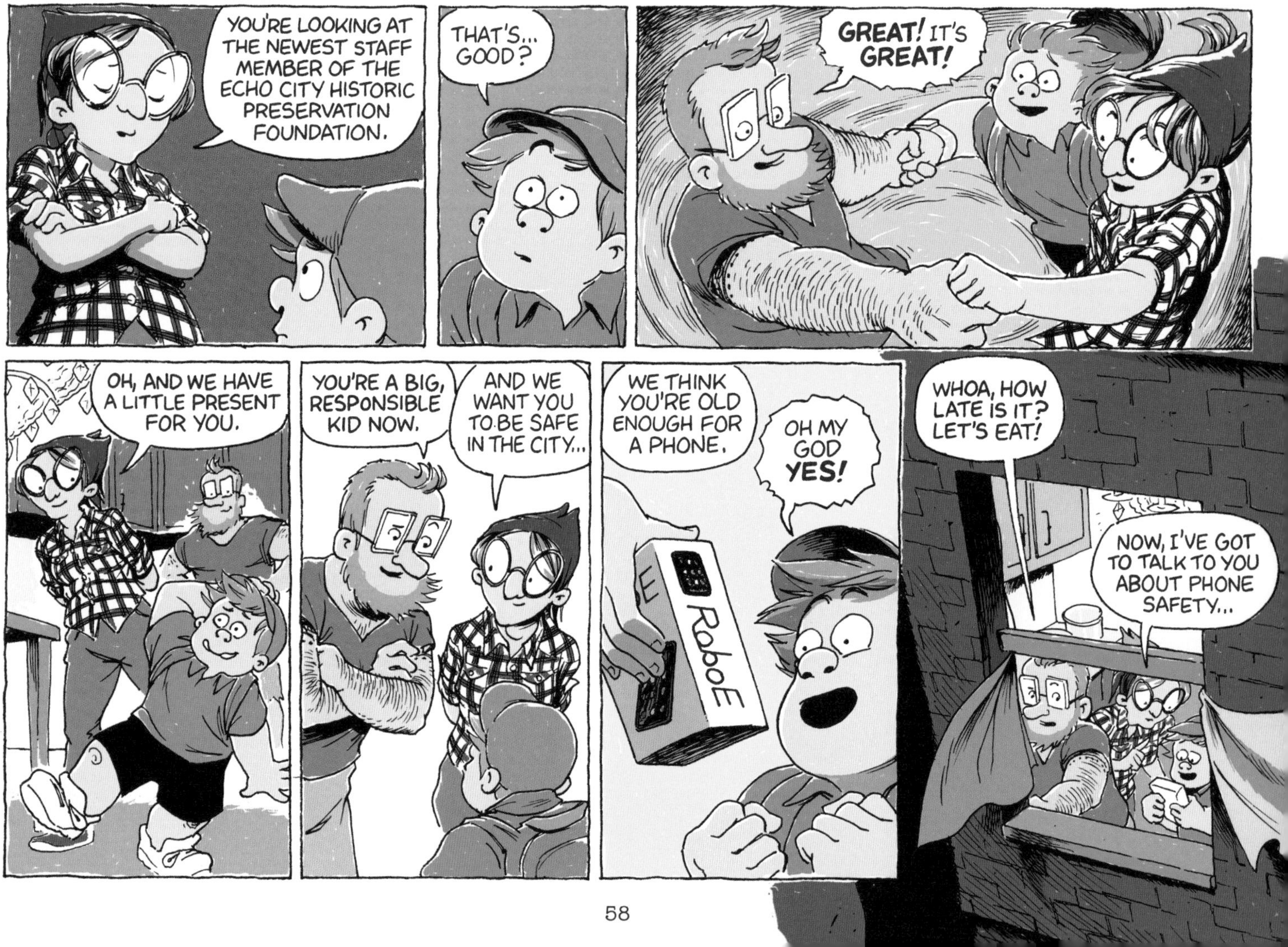
YOU'RE LOOKING AT THE NEWEST STAFF MEMBER OF THE ECHO CITY HISTORIC PRESERVATION FOUNDATION.
THAT'S... GOOD?
GREAT! IT'S GREAT!
OH, AND WE HAVE A LITTLE PRESENT FOR YOU.
YOU'RE A BIG, RESPONSIBLE KID NOW.
AND WE WANT YOU TO BE SAFE IN THE CITY...
WE THINK YOU'RE OLD ENOUGH FOR A PHONE.
RoboE
OH MY GOD YES!
WHOA, HOW LATE IS IT? LET'S EAT!
NOW, I'VE GOT TO TALK TO YOU ABOUT PHONE SAFETY...

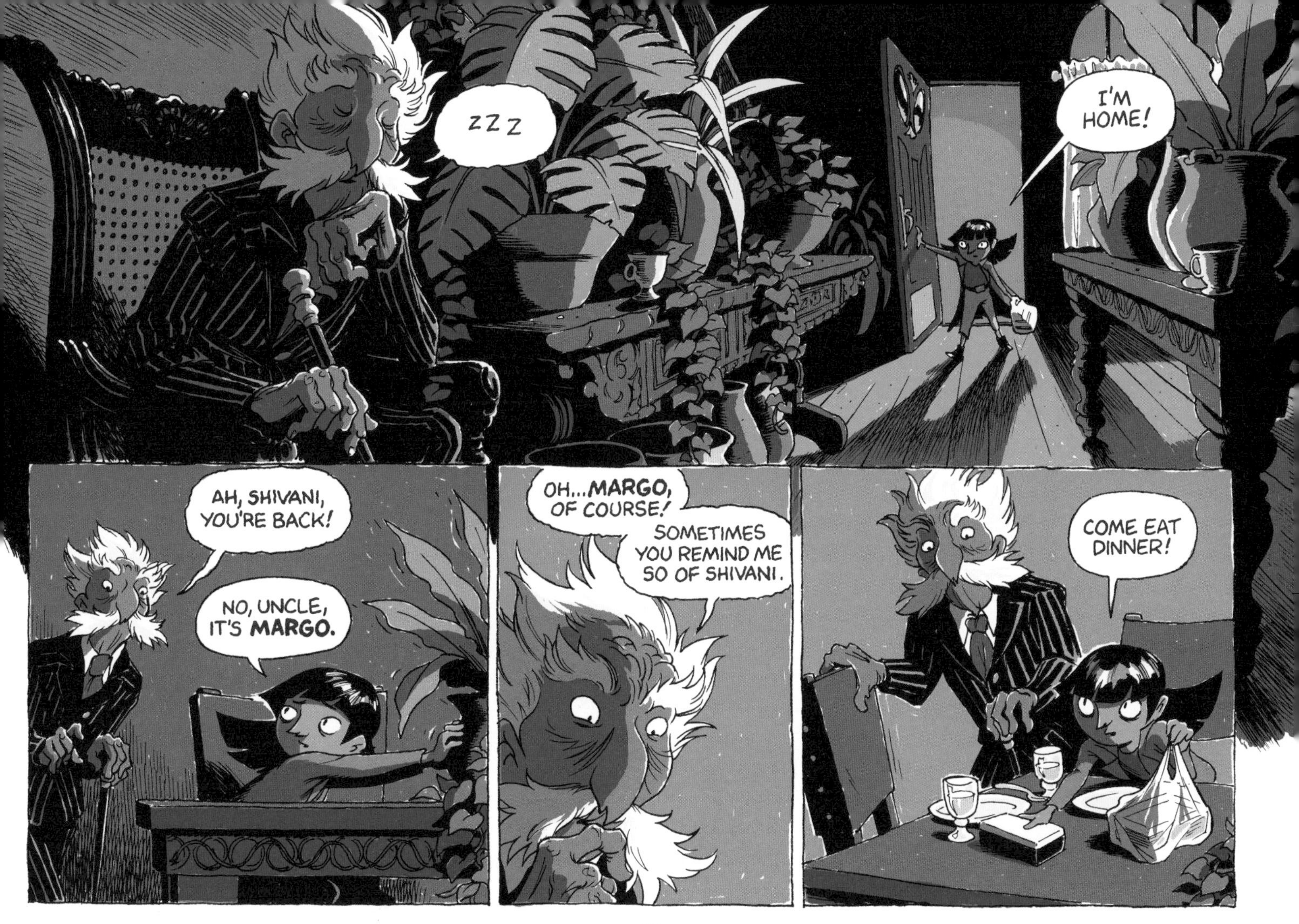
ZZZ
I'M HOME!
AH, SHIVANI, YOU'RE BACK!
NO, UNCLE, IT'S **MARGO.**
OH... **MARGO,** OF COURSE!
SOMETIMES YOU REMIND ME SO OF SHIVANI.
COME EAT DINNER!

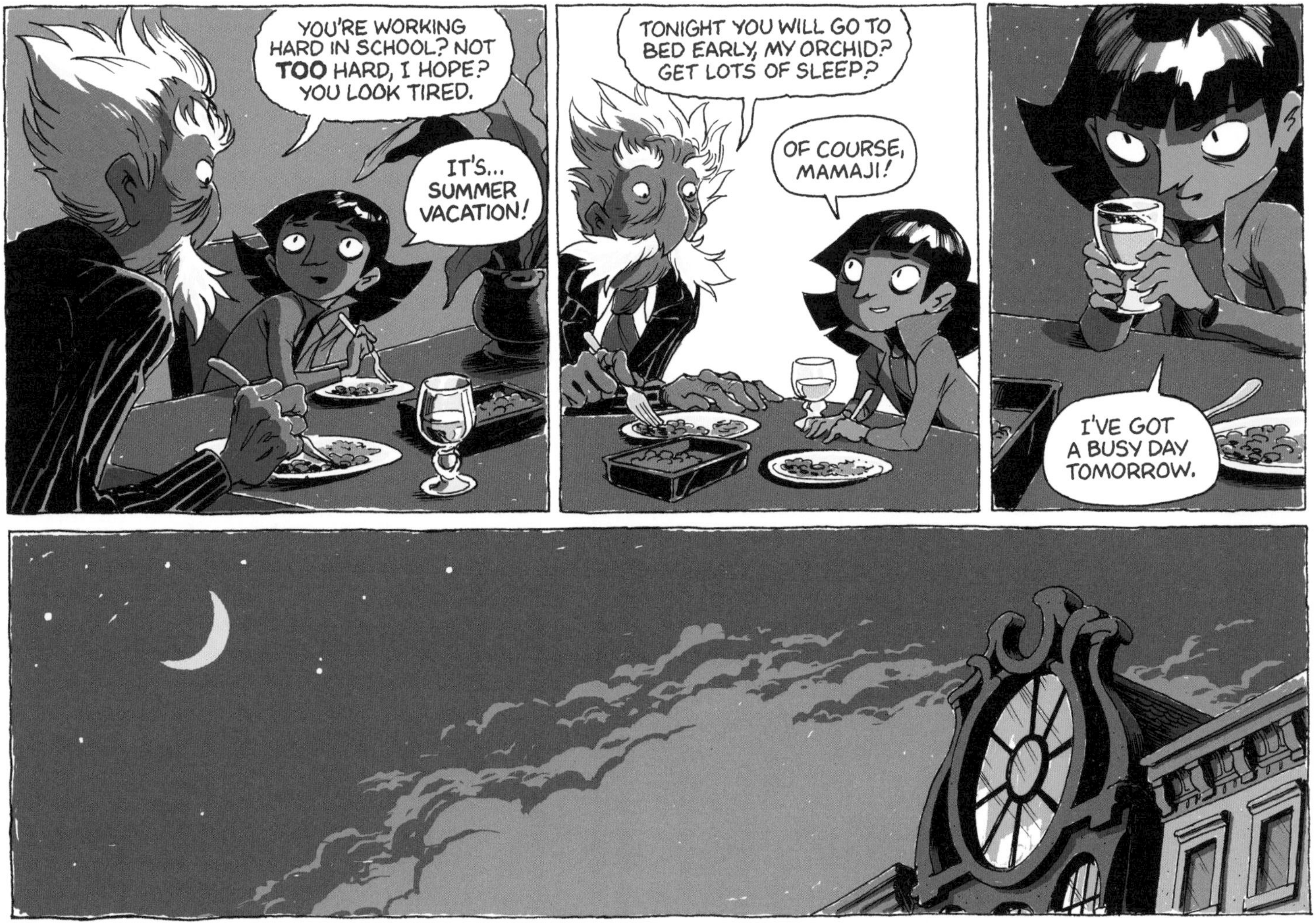
YOU'RE WORKING HARD IN SCHOOL? NOT **TOO** HARD, I HOPE? YOU LOOK TIRED.
IT'S... SUMMER VACATION!
TONIGHT YOU WILL GO TO BED EARLY, MY ORCHID? GET LOTS OF SLEEP?
OF COURSE, MAMAJI!
I'VE GOT A BUSY DAY TOMORROW.

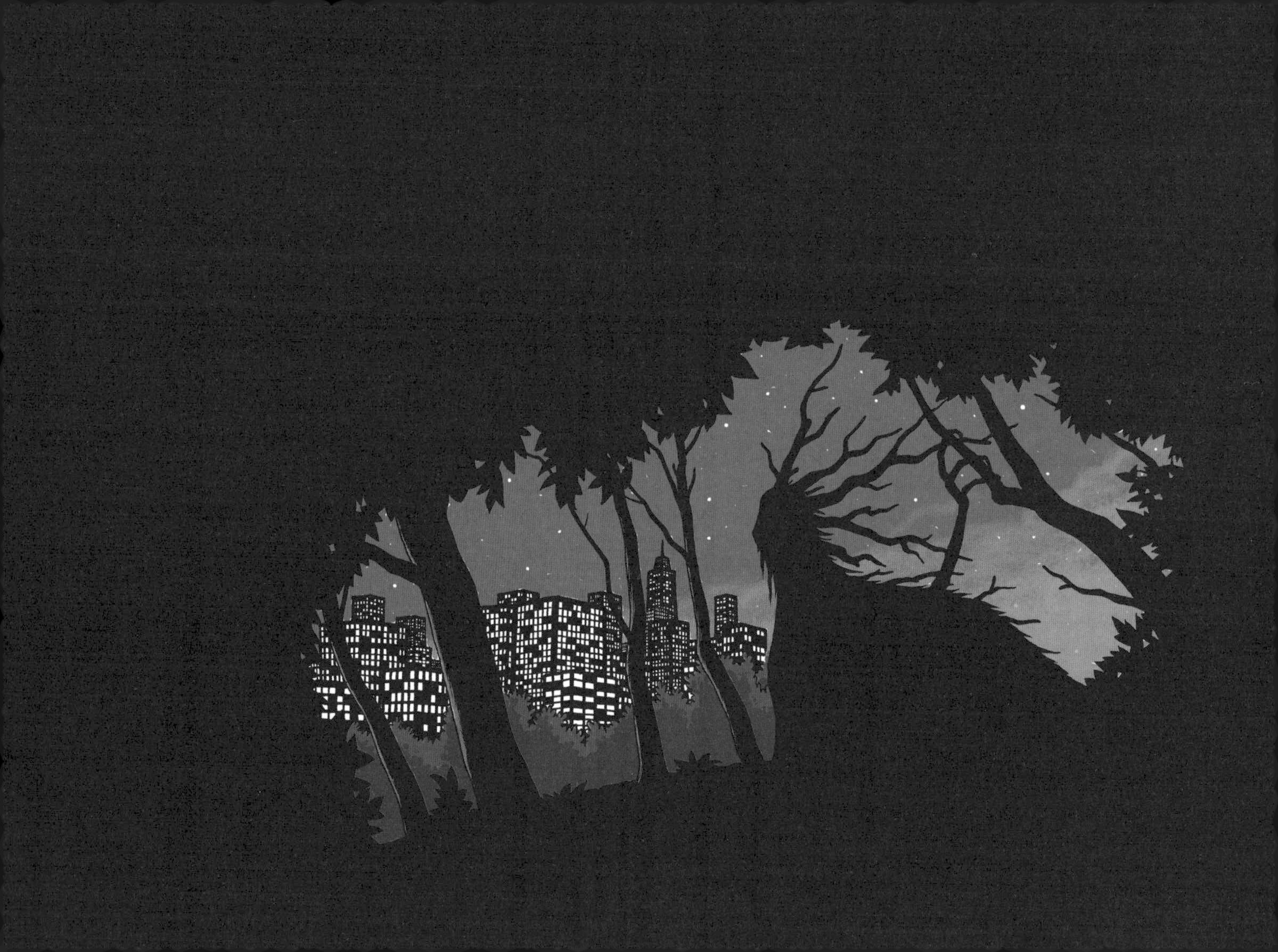

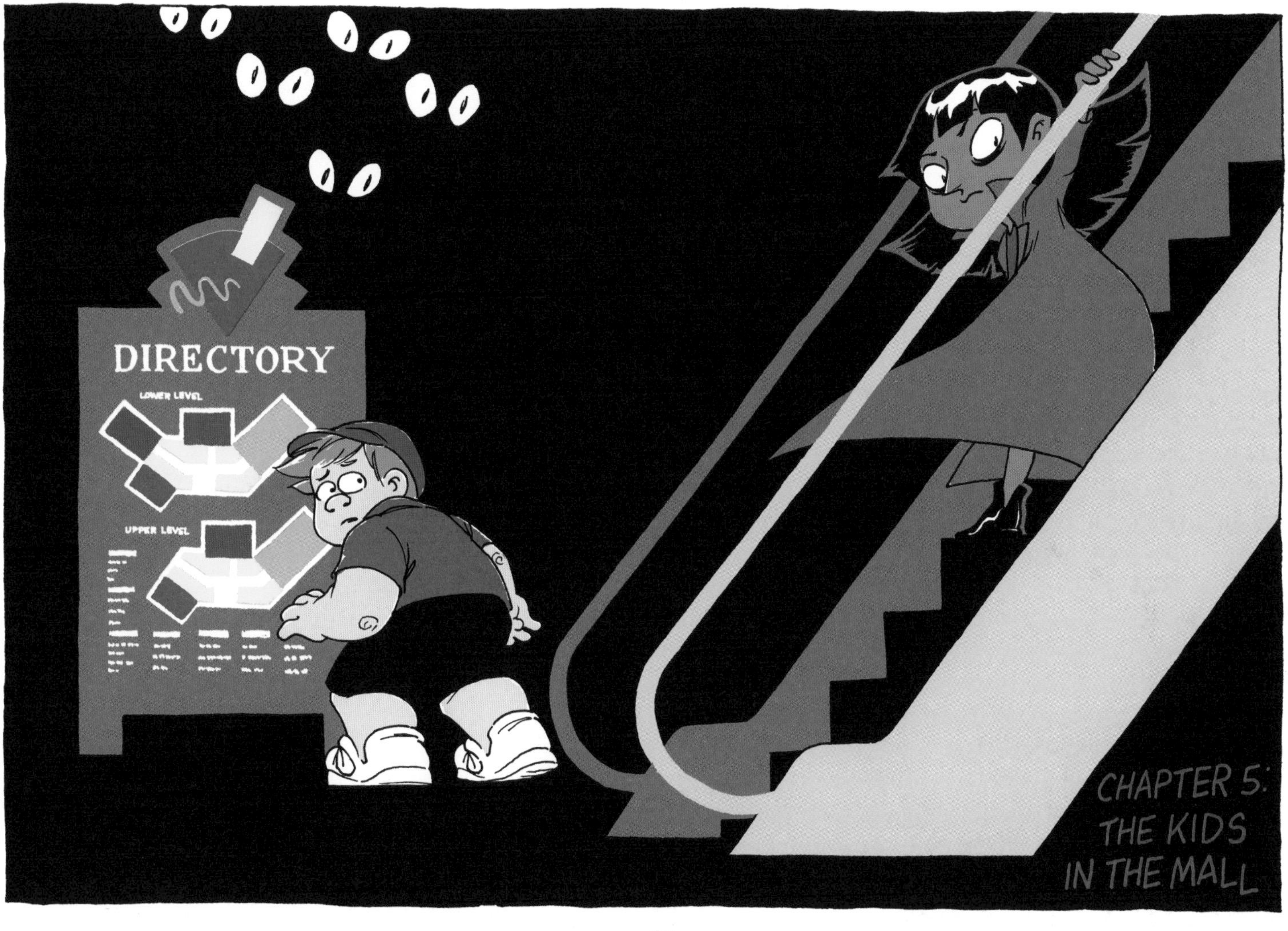
DIRECTORY
LOWER LEVEL
UPPER LEVEL
CHAPTER 5:
THE KIDS
IN THE MALL

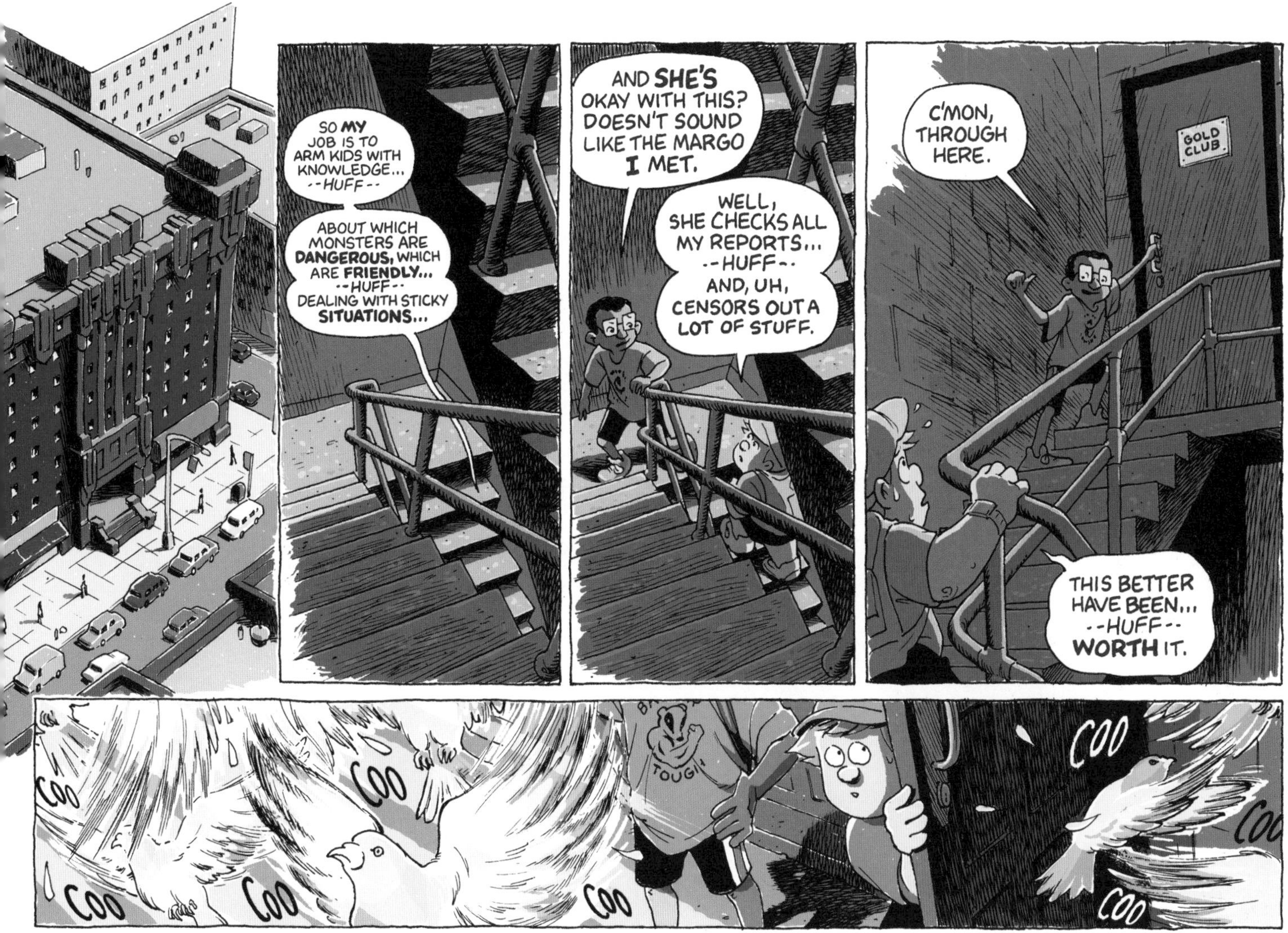
SO MY JOB IS TO ARM KIDS WITH KNOWLEDGE... --HUFF--
ABOUT WHICH MONSTERS ARE DANGEROUS, WHICH ARE FRIENDLY... --HUFF-- DEALING WITH STICKY SITUATIONS...
AND SHE'S OKAY WITH THIS? DOESN'T SOUND LIKE THE MARGO I MET.
WELL, SHE CHECKS ALL MY REPORTS... --HUFF-- AND, UH, CENSORS OUT A LOT OF STUFF.
C'MON, THROUGH HERE.
GOLD CLUB
THIS BETTER HAVE BEEN... --HUFF-- WORTH IT.
COO
COO
COO
COO
COO
COO
COO
COO
TOUGH

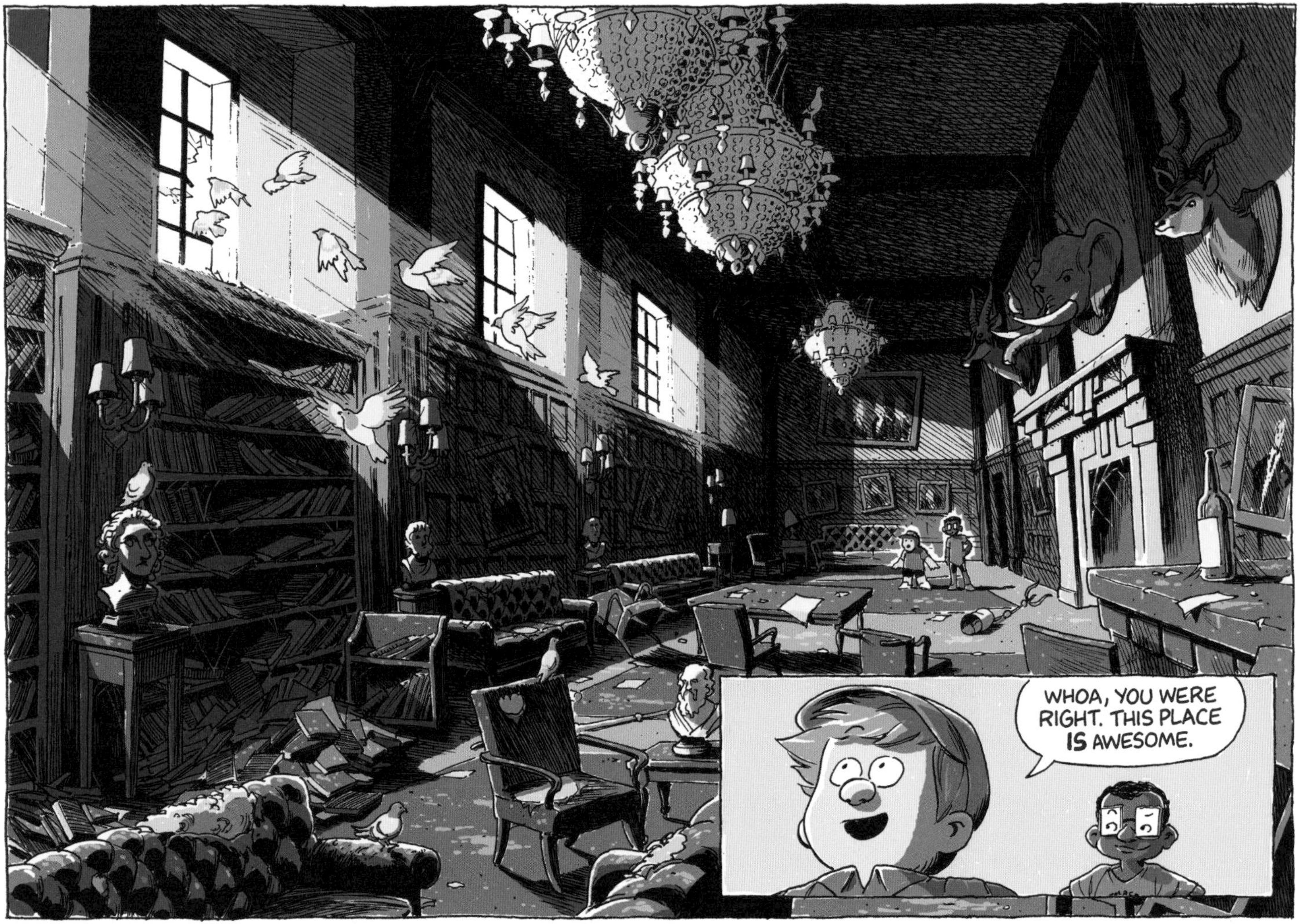
WHOA, YOU WERE RIGHT. THIS PLACE **IS** AWESOME.

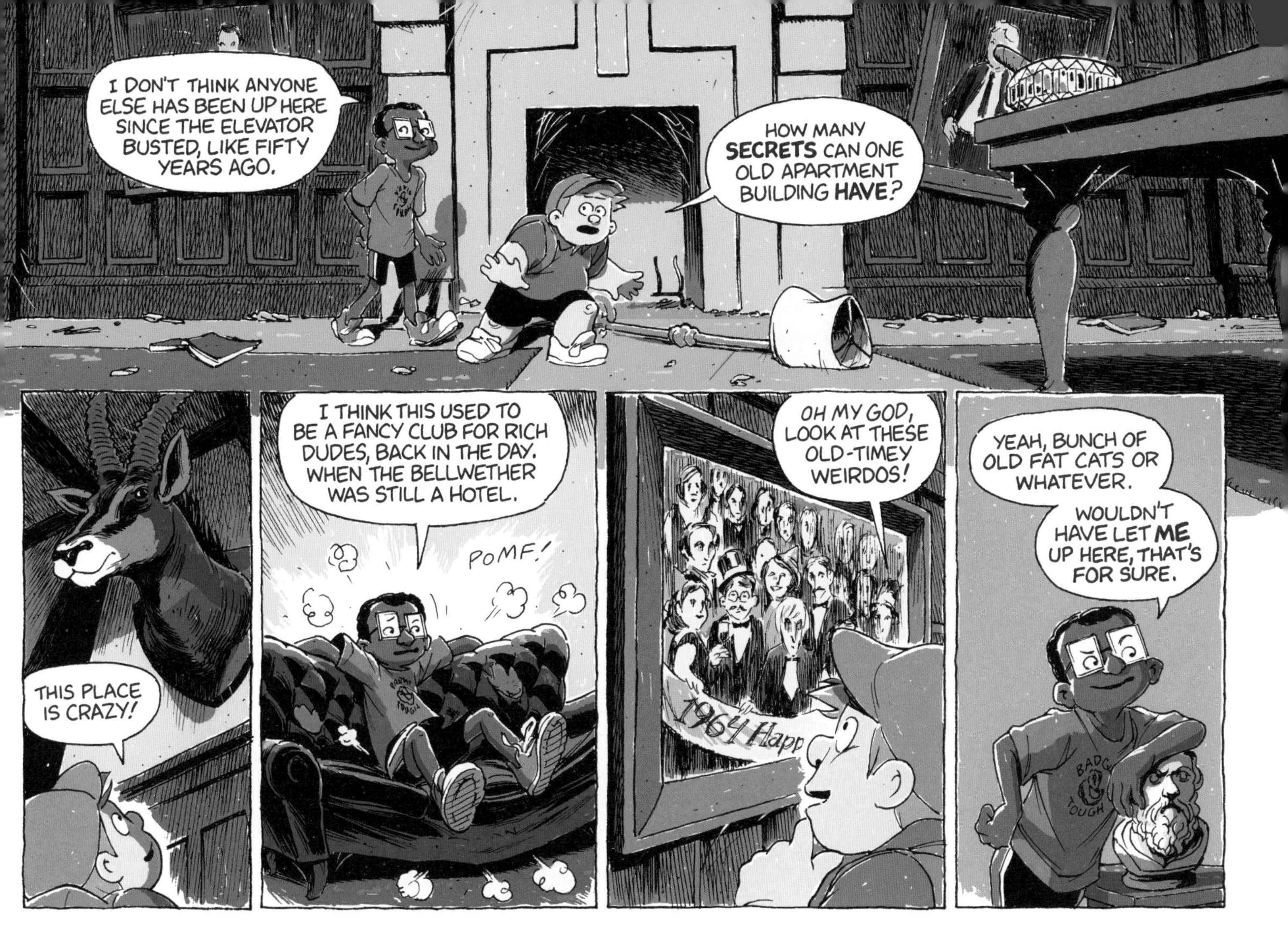
I DON'T THINK ANYONE ELSE HAS BEEN UP HERE SINCE THE ELEVATOR BUSTED, LIKE FIFTY YEARS AGO.
HOW MANY **SECRETS** CAN ONE OLD APARTMENT BUILDING **HAVE**?
THIS PLACE IS CRAZY!
I THINK THIS USED TO BE A FANCY CLUB FOR RICH DUDES, BACK IN THE DAY. WHEN THE BELLWETHER WAS STILL A HOTEL.
POMF!
OH MY GOD, LOOK AT THESE OLD-TIMEY WEIRDOS!
1964 Happ
YEAH, BUNCH OF OLD FAT CATS OR WHATEVER.
WOULDN'T HAVE LET **ME** UP HERE, THAT'S FOR SURE.

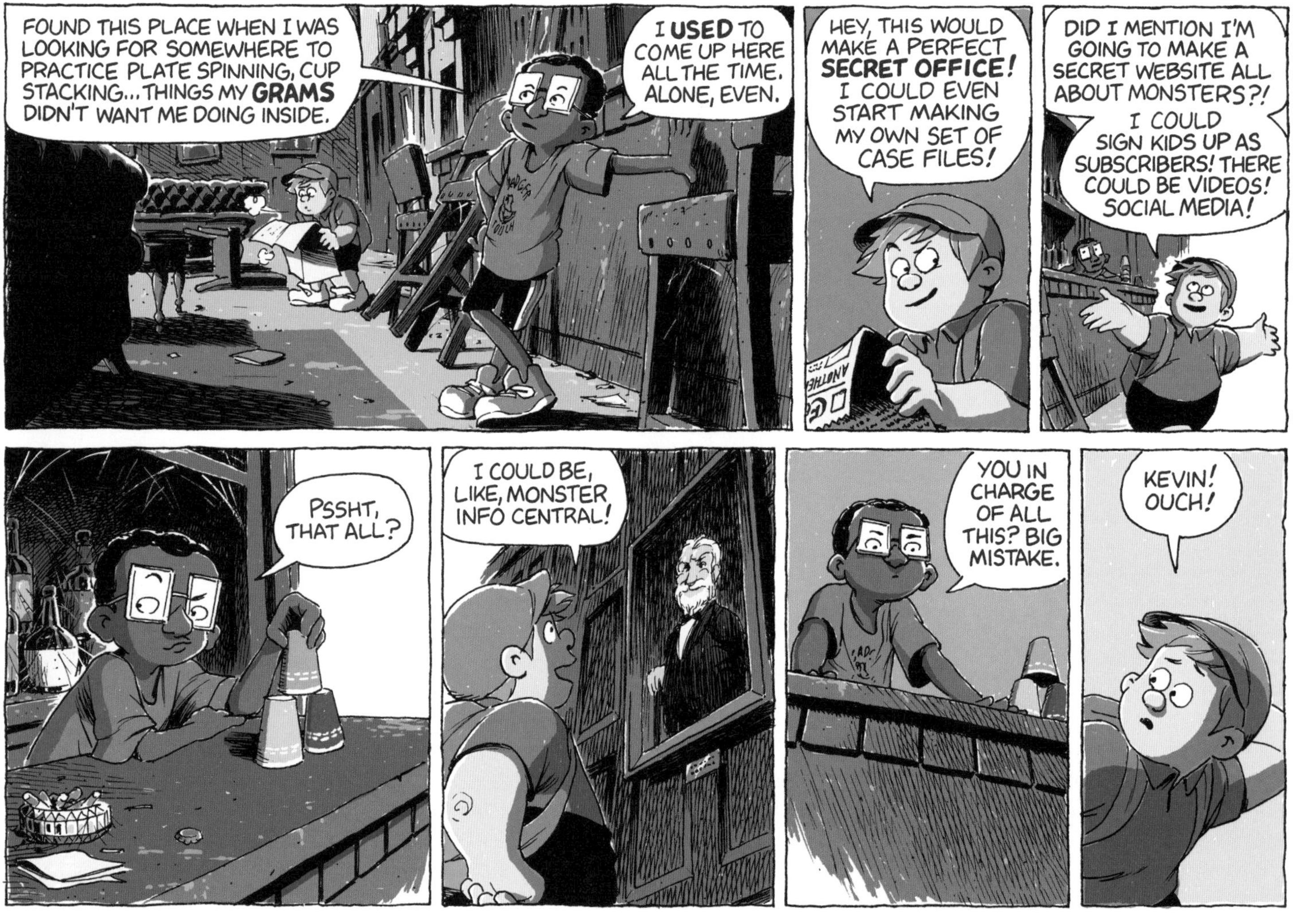
FOUND THIS PLACE WHEN I WAS LOOKING FOR SOMEWHERE TO PRACTICE PLATE SPINNING, CUP STACKING... THINGS MY **GRAMS** DIDN'T WANT ME DOING INSIDE.
I **USED** TO COME UP HERE ALL THE TIME. ALONE, EVEN.
HEY, THIS WOULD MAKE A PERFECT **SECRET OFFICE!** I COULD EVEN START MAKING MY OWN SET OF CASE FILES!
DID I MENTION I'M GOING TO MAKE A SECRET WEBSITE ALL ABOUT MONSTERS?!
I COULD SIGN KIDS UP AS SUBSCRIBERS! THERE COULD BE VIDEOS! SOCIAL MEDIA!
PSSHT, THAT ALL?
I COULD BE, LIKE, MONSTER INFO CENTRAL!
YOU IN CHARGE OF ALL THIS? BIG MISTAKE.
KEVIN! OUCH!

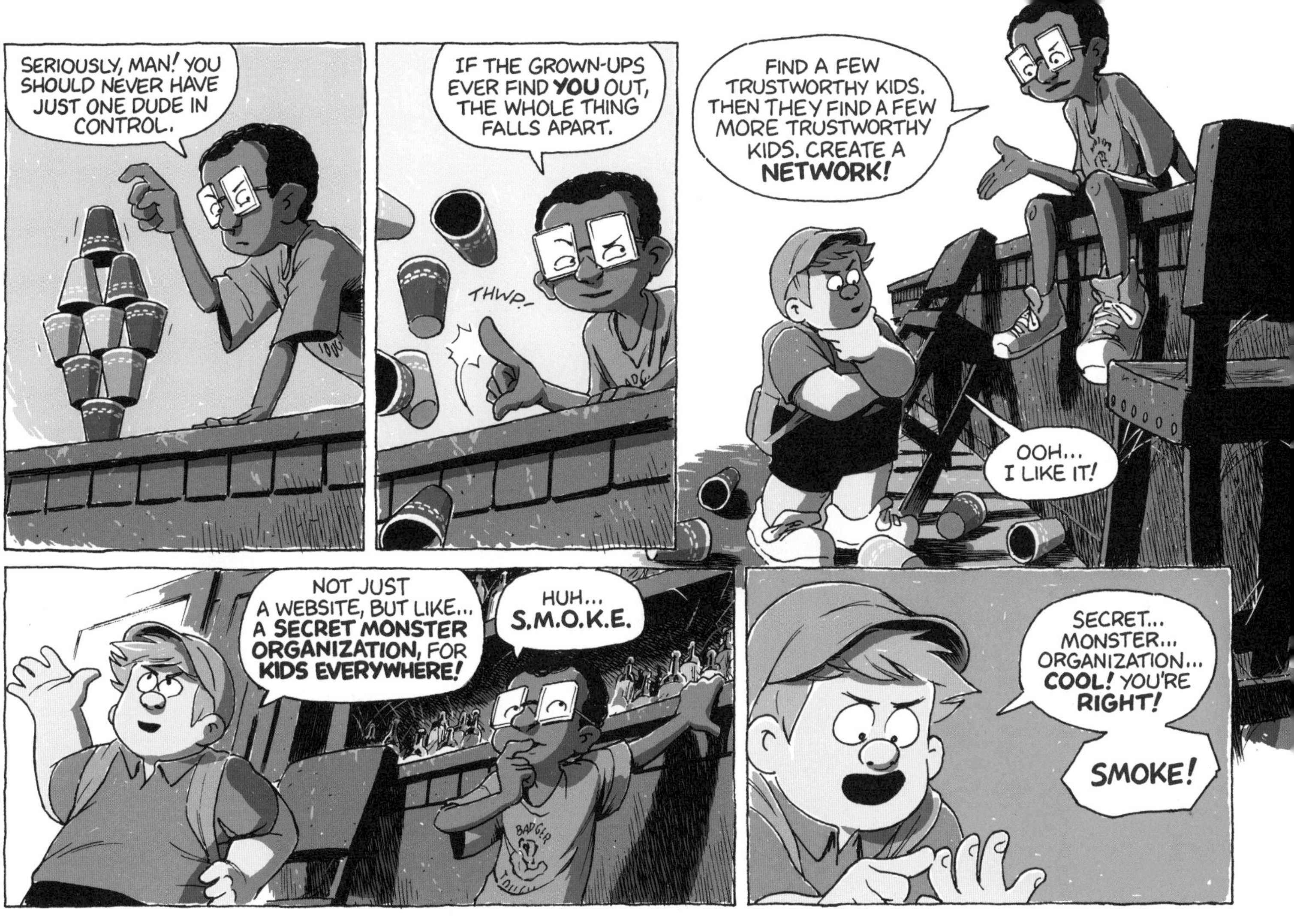
SERIOUSLY, MAN! YOU SHOULD NEVER HAVE JUST ONE DUDE IN CONTROL.
IF THE GROWN-UPS EVER FIND **YOU** OUT, THE WHOLE THING FALLS APART.
THWP!
FIND A FEW TRUSTWORTHY KIDS. THEN THEY FIND A FEW MORE TRUSTWORTHY KIDS. CREATE A **NETWORK!**
OOH... I LIKE IT!
NOT JUST A WEBSITE, BUT LIKE... A **SECRET MONSTER ORGANIZATION,** FOR **KIDS EVERYWHERE!**
HUH... **S.M.O.K.E.**
BADGER
SECRET... MONSTER... ORGANIZATION... **COOL!** YOU'RE **RIGHT!**
SMOKE!

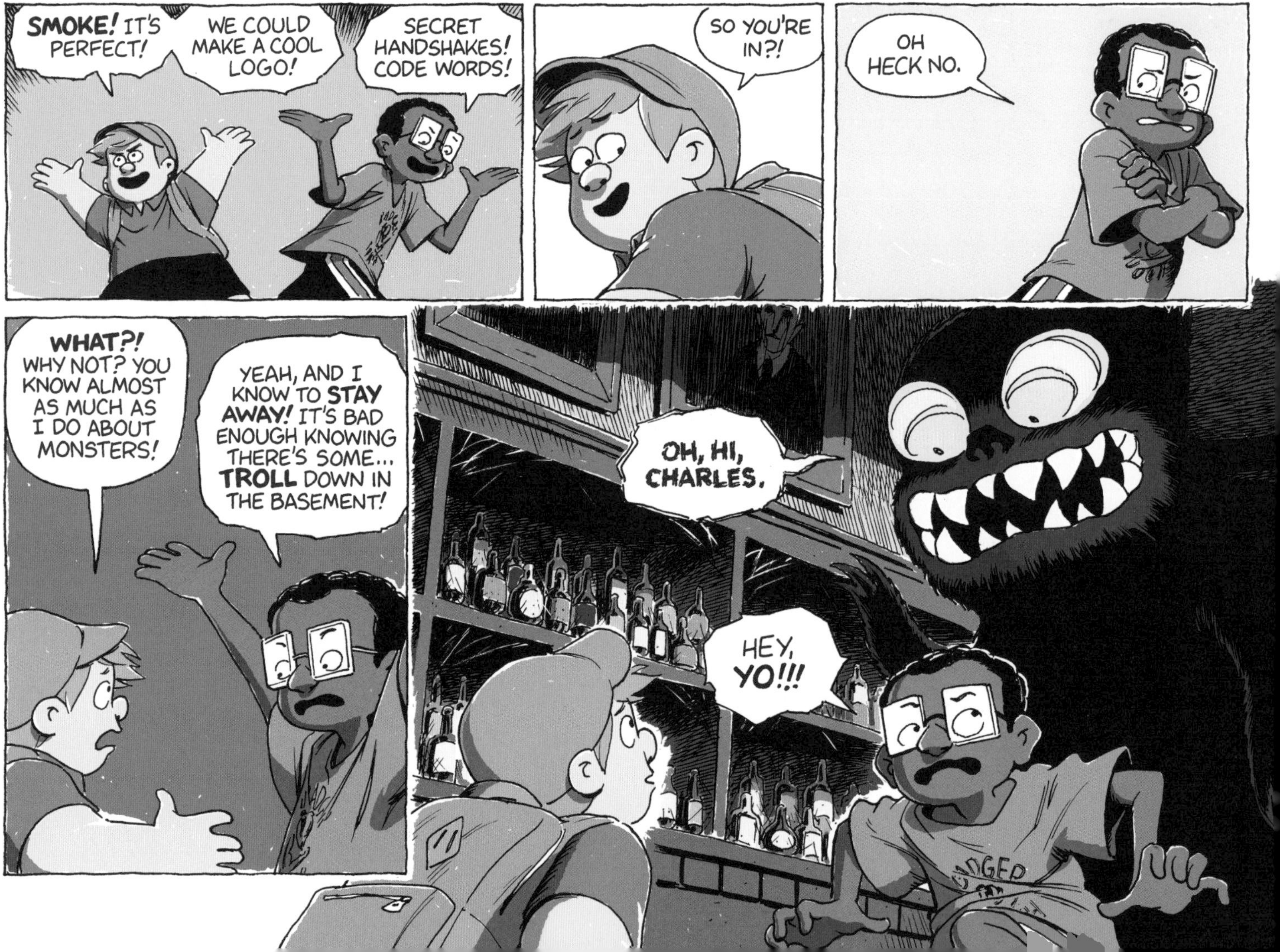
SMOKE! IT'S PERFECT!
WE COULD MAKE A COOL LOGO!
SECRET HANDSHAKES! CODE WORDS!
SO YOU'RE IN?!
OH HECK NO.
WHAT?! WHY NOT? YOU KNOW ALMOST AS MUCH AS I DO ABOUT MONSTERS!
YEAH, AND I KNOW TO STAY AWAY! IT'S BAD ENOUGH KNOWING THERE'S SOME... TROLL DOWN IN THE BASEMENT!
OH, HI, CHARLES.
HEY, YO!!!

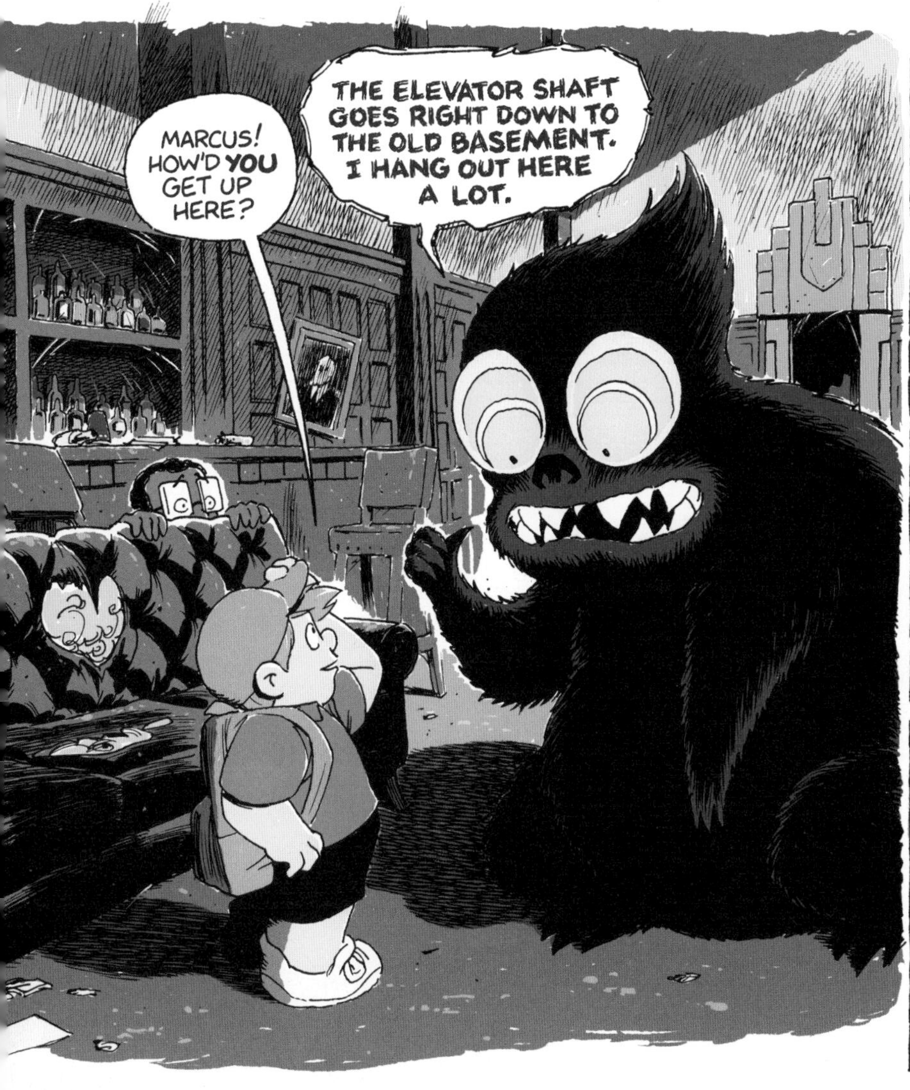
MARCUS! HOW'D YOU GET UP HERE?
THE ELEVATOR SHAFT GOES RIGHT DOWN TO THE OLD BASEMENT. I HANG OUT HERE A LOT.

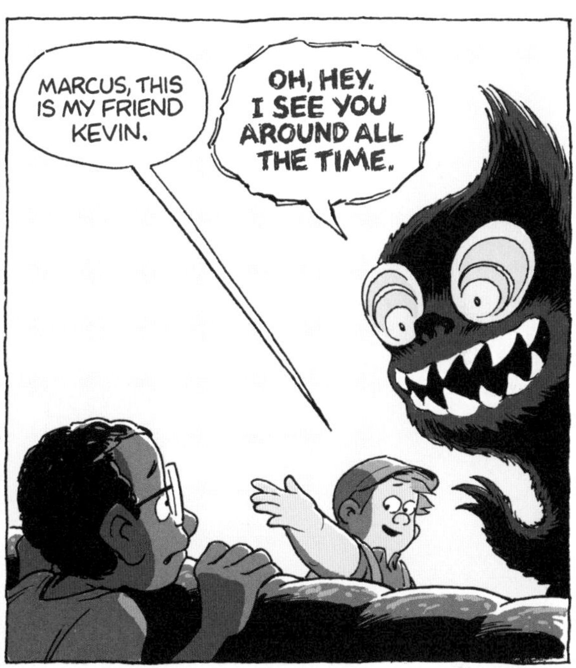
MARCUS, THIS IS MY FRIEND KEVIN.
OH, HEY. I SEE YOU AROUND ALL THE TIME.

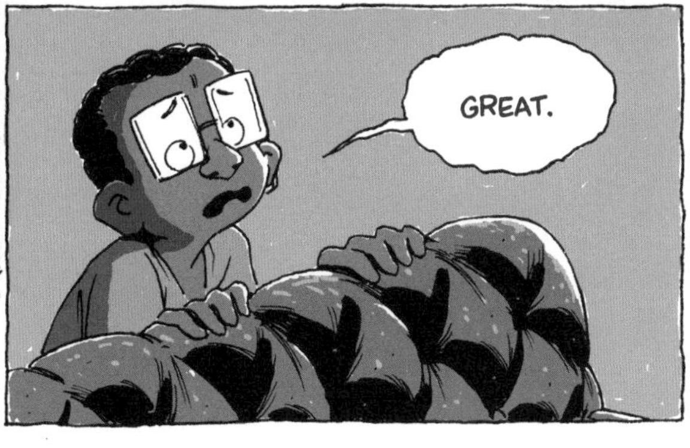
GREAT.

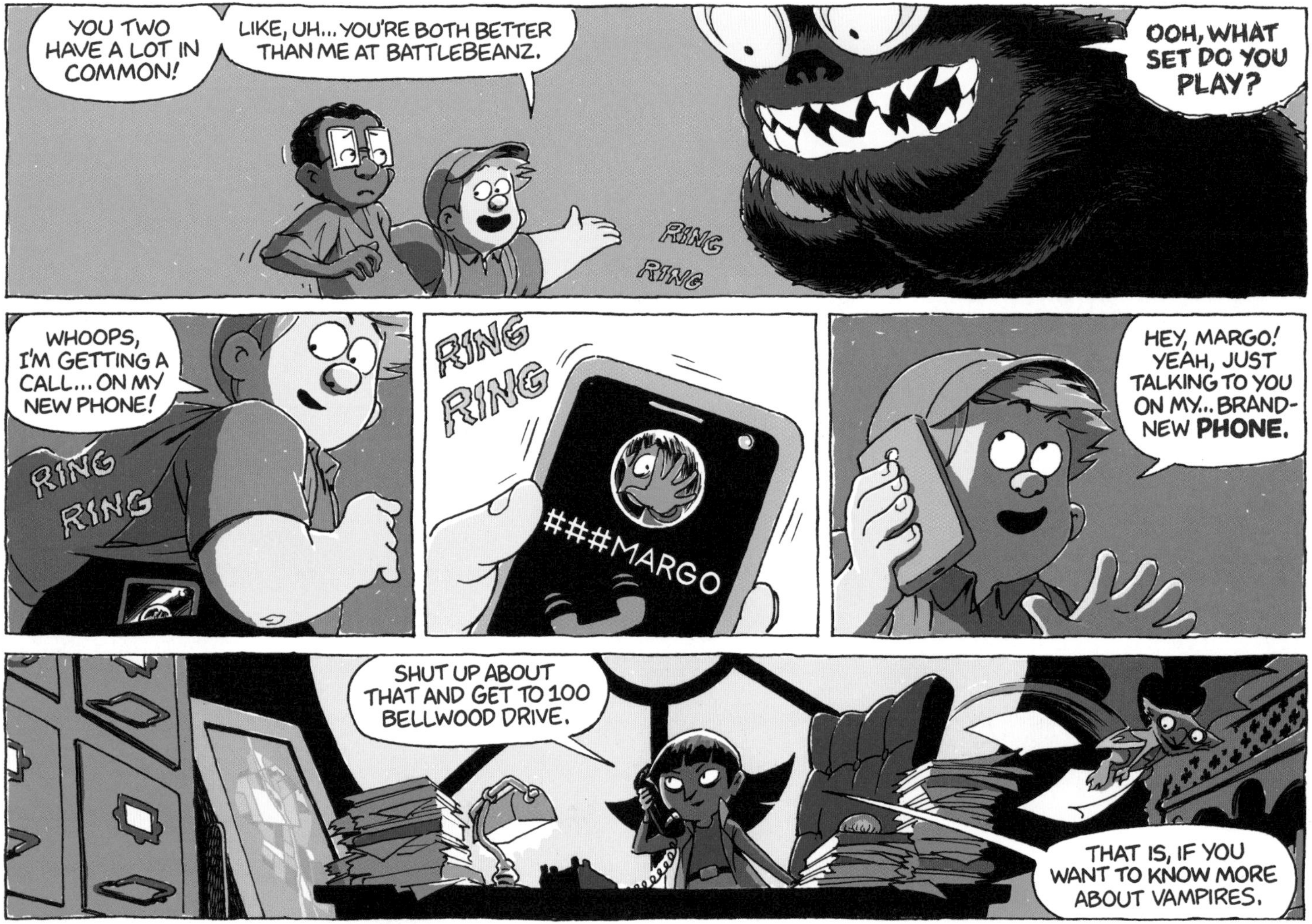
YOU TWO HAVE A LOT IN COMMON!
LIKE, UH... YOU'RE BOTH BETTER THAN ME AT BATTLEBEANZ.
OOH, WHAT SET DO YOU PLAY?
RING
RING
WHOOPS, I'M GETTING A CALL... ON MY NEW PHONE!
RING
RING
RING
RING
###MARGO
HEY, MARGO! YEAH, JUST TALKING TO YOU ON MY... BRAND-NEW **PHONE.**
SHUT UP ABOUT THAT AND GET TO 100 BELLWOOD DRIVE.
THAT IS, IF YOU WANT TO KNOW MORE ABOUT VAMPIRES.

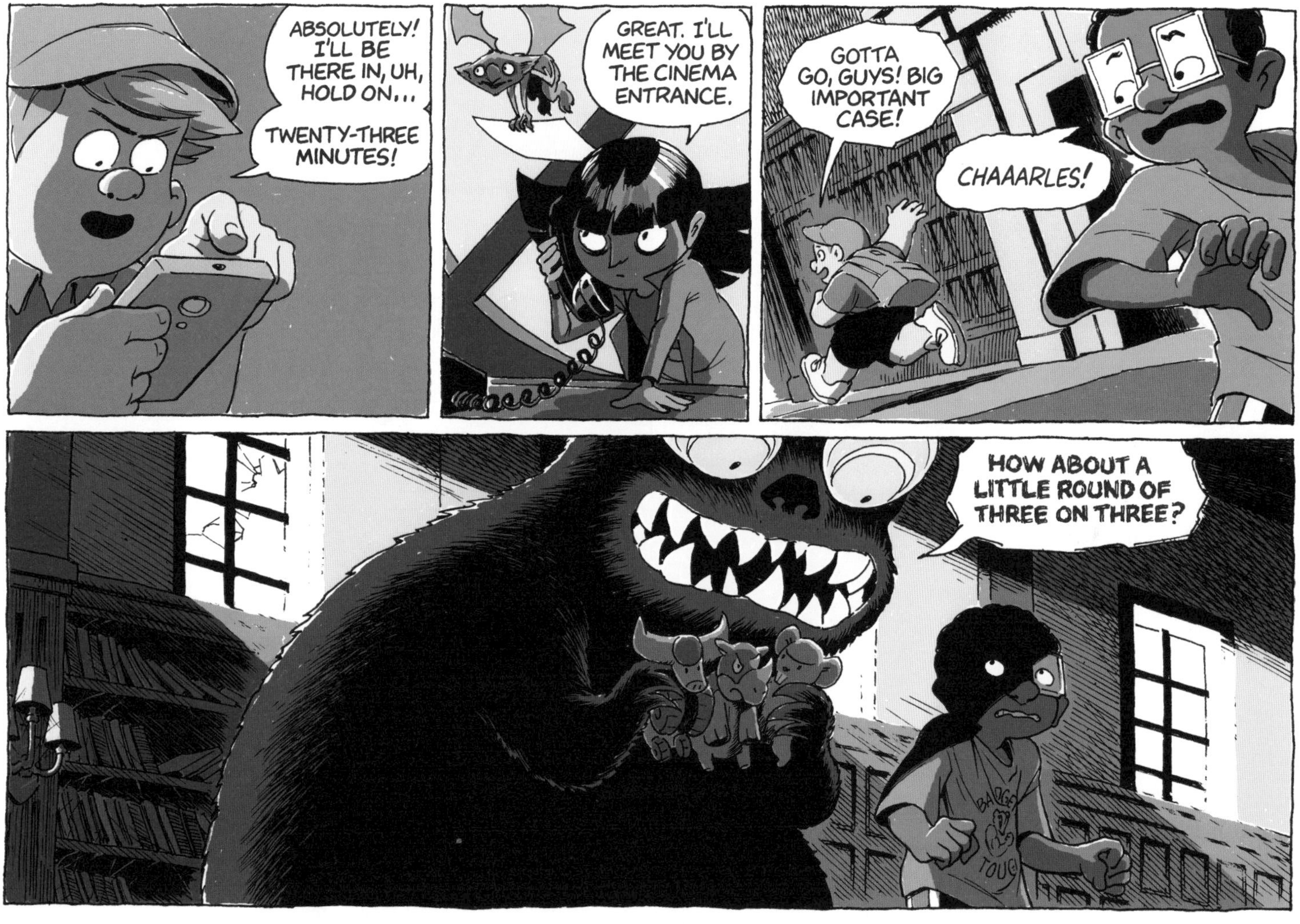
ABSOLUTELY! I'LL BE THERE IN, UH, HOLD ON...
TWENTY-THREE MINUTES!
GREAT. I'LL MEET YOU BY THE CINEMA ENTRANCE.
GOTTA GO, GUYS! BIG IMPORTANT CASE!
CHAAARLES!
HOW ABOUT A LITTLE ROUND OF THREE ON THREE?

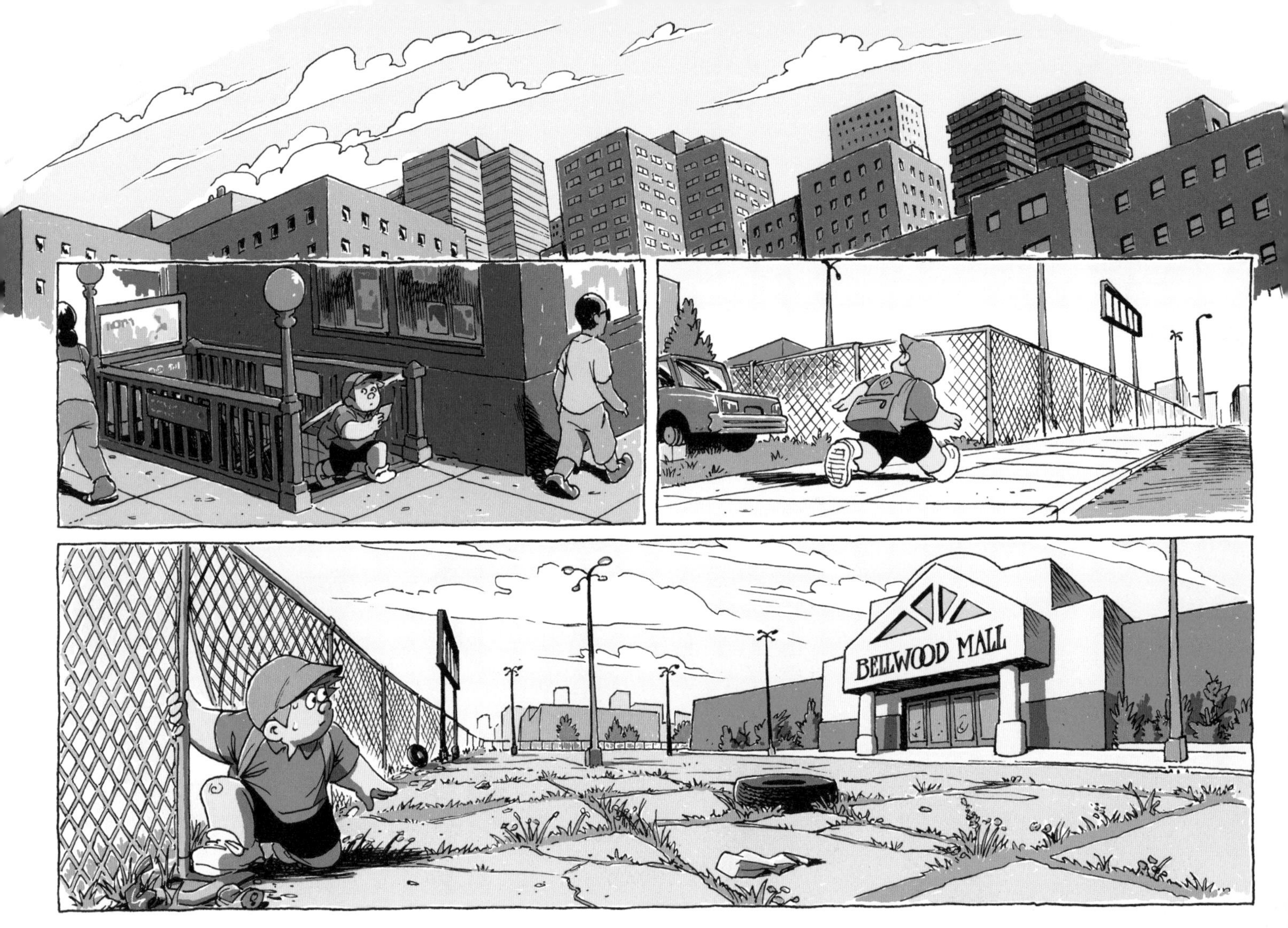
BELLWOOD MALL

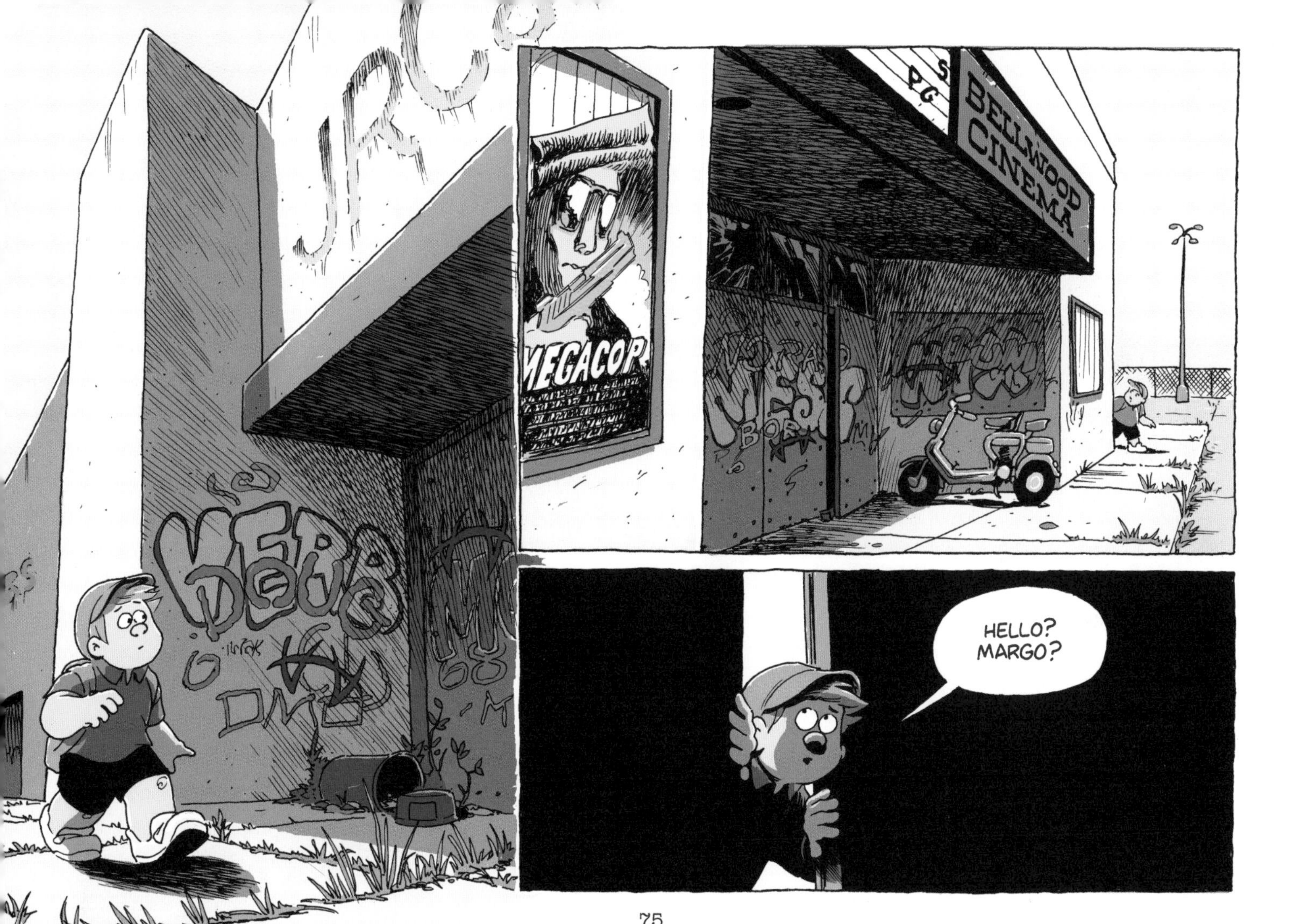
MEGACOP
PG
BELLWOOD CINEMA
HELLO? MARGO?

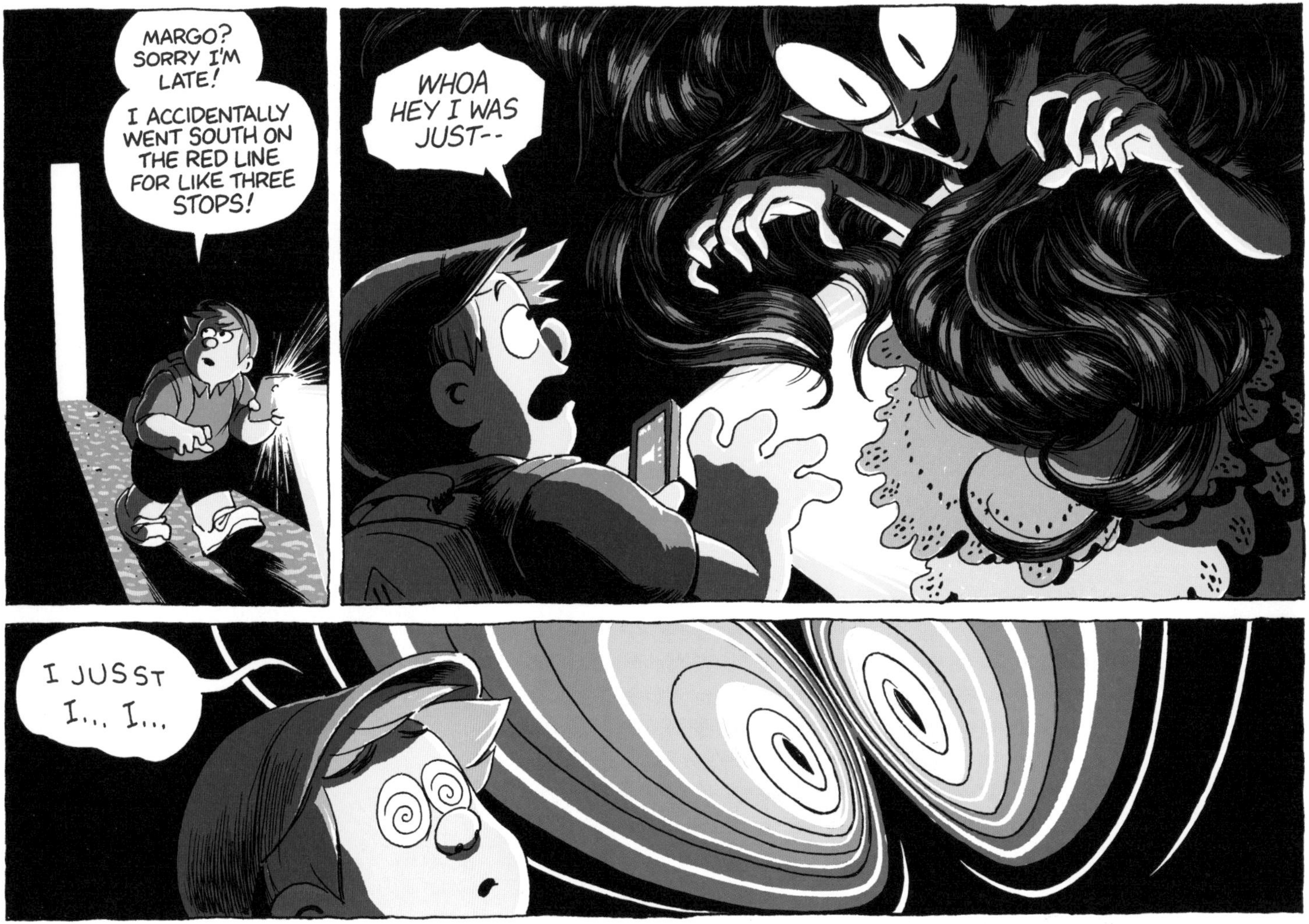
MARGO? SORRY I'M LATE!
I ACCIDENTALLY WENT SOUTH ON THE RED LINE FOR LIKE THREE STOPS!
WHOA HEY I WAS JUST--
I JUSST I... I...

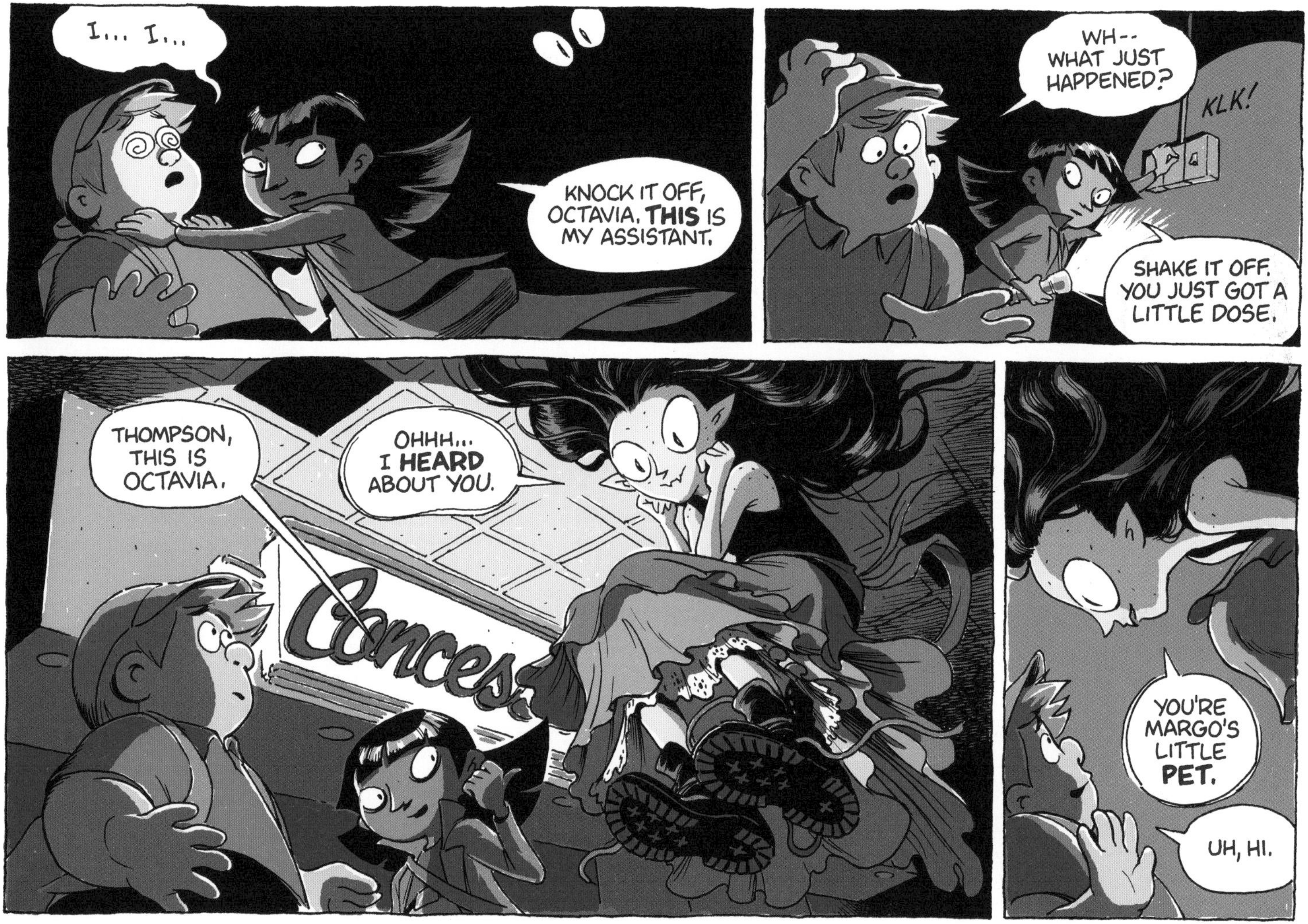
I... I...
KNOCK IT OFF, OCTAVIA. THIS IS MY ASSISTANT.
WH-- WHAT JUST HAPPENED?
KLK!
SHAKE IT OFF. YOU JUST GOT A LITTLE DOSE.
THOMPSON, THIS IS OCTAVIA.
OHHH... I HEARD ABOUT YOU.
Conces
YOU'RE MARGO'S LITTLE PET.
UH, HI.

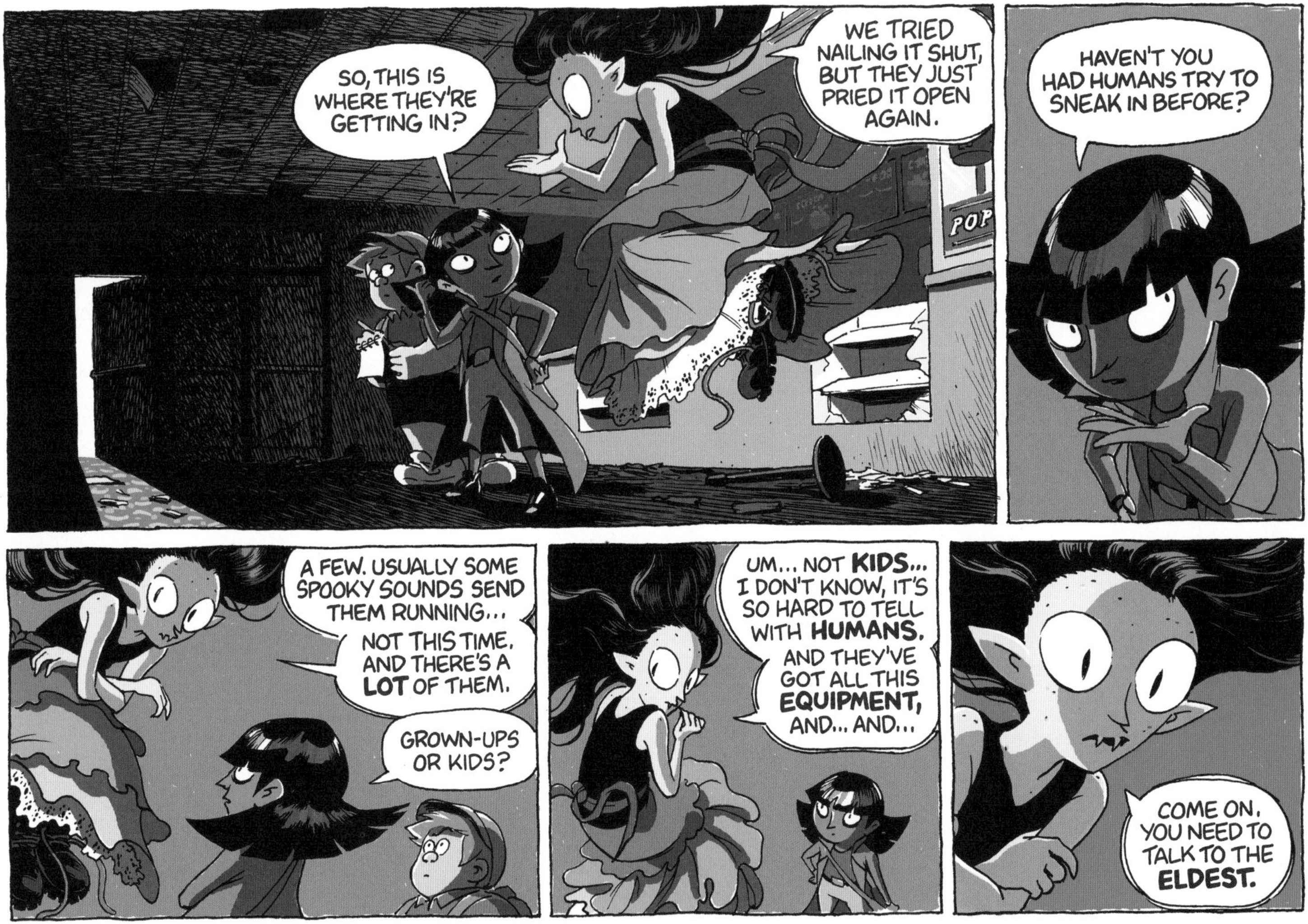
SO, THIS IS WHERE THEY'RE GETTING IN?
WE TRIED NAILING IT SHUT, BUT THEY JUST PRIED IT OPEN AGAIN.
POP
HAVEN'T YOU HAD HUMANS TRY TO SNEAK IN BEFORE?
A FEW. USUALLY SOME SPOOKY SOUNDS SEND THEM RUNNING...
NOT THIS TIME. AND THERE'S A **LOT** OF THEM.
GROWN-UPS OR KIDS?
UM... NOT **KIDS...** I DON'T KNOW, IT'S SO HARD TO TELL WITH **HUMANS.**
AND THEY'VE GOT ALL THIS **EQUIPMENT,** AND... AND...
COME ON, YOU NEED TO TALK TO THE **ELDEST.**

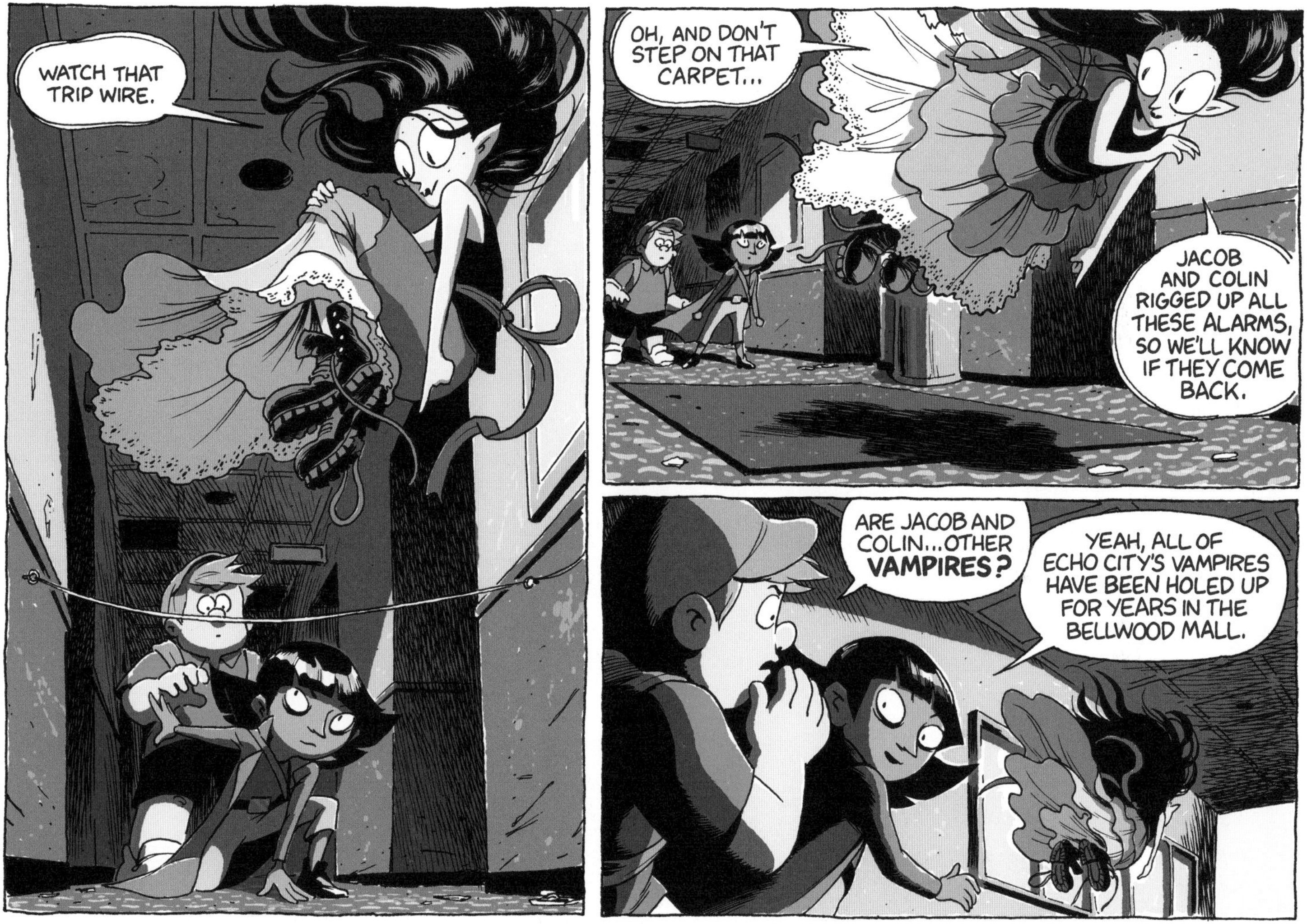
WATCH THAT TRIP WIRE.
OH, AND DON'T STEP ON THAT CARPET...
JACOB AND COLIN RIGGED UP ALL THESE ALARMS, SO WE'LL KNOW IF THEY COME BACK.
ARE JACOB AND COLIN...OTHER **VAMPIRES?**
YEAH, ALL OF ECHO CITY'S VAMPIRES HAVE BEEN HOLED UP FOR YEARS IN THE BELLWOOD MALL.

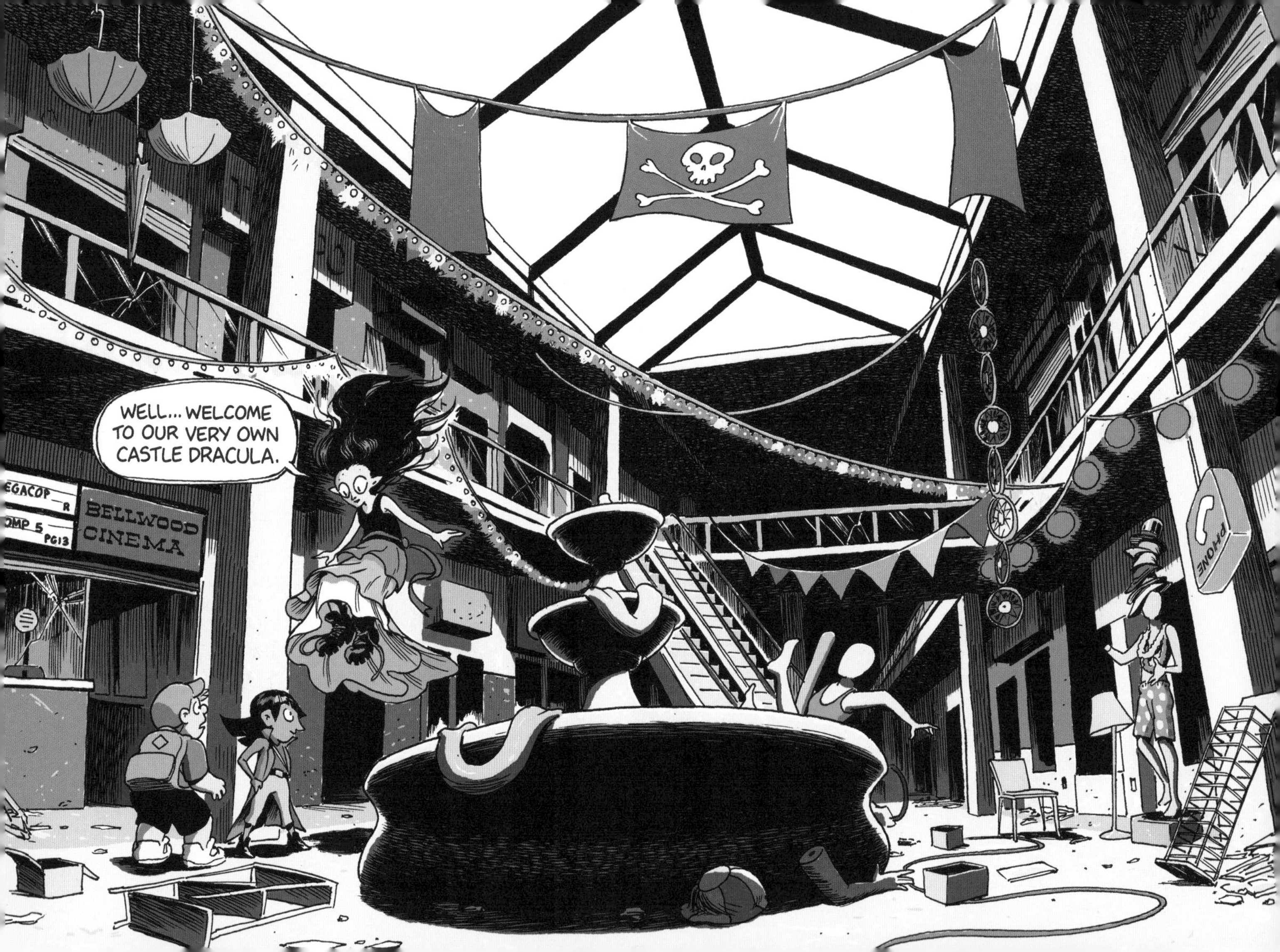
WELL... WELCOME TO OUR VERY OWN CASTLE DRACULA.
EGACOP R
OMP 5 PG13
BELLWOOD CINEMA
PHONE

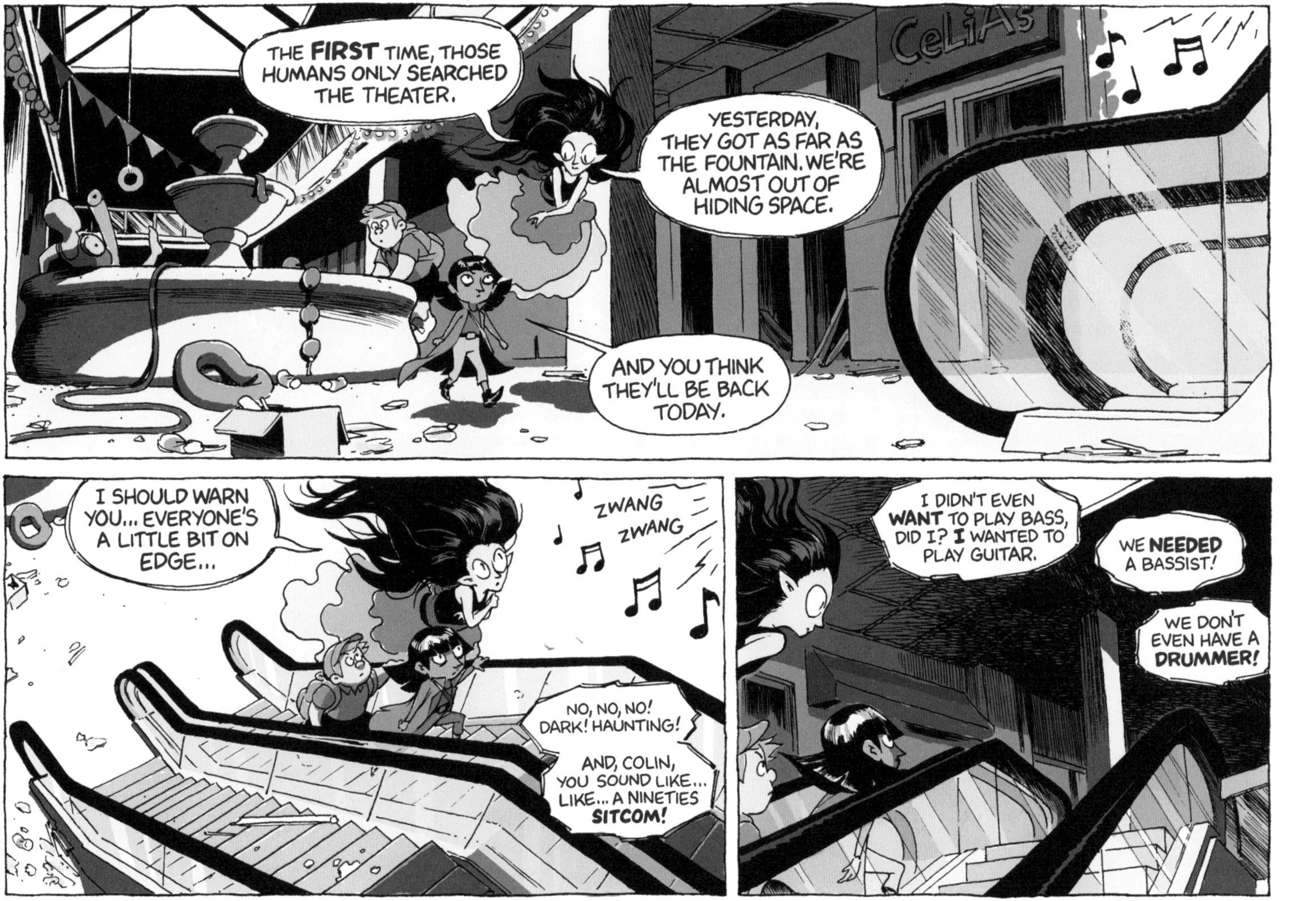
CeLiA's
THE **FIRST** TIME, THOSE HUMANS ONLY SEARCHED THE THEATER.
YESTERDAY, THEY GOT AS FAR AS THE FOUNTAIN. WE'RE ALMOST OUT OF HIDING SPACE.
AND YOU THINK THEY'LL BE BACK TODAY.
I SHOULD WARN YOU... EVERYONE'S A LITTLE BIT ON EDGE...
ZWANG
ZWANG
NO, NO, NO! DARK! HAUNTING!
AND, COLIN, YOU SOUND LIKE... LIKE... A NINETIES **SITCOM!**
I DIDN'T EVEN **WANT** TO PLAY BASS, DID I? **I** WANTED TO PLAY GUITAR.
WE **NEEDED** A BASSIST!
WE DON'T EVEN HAVE A **DRUMMER!**

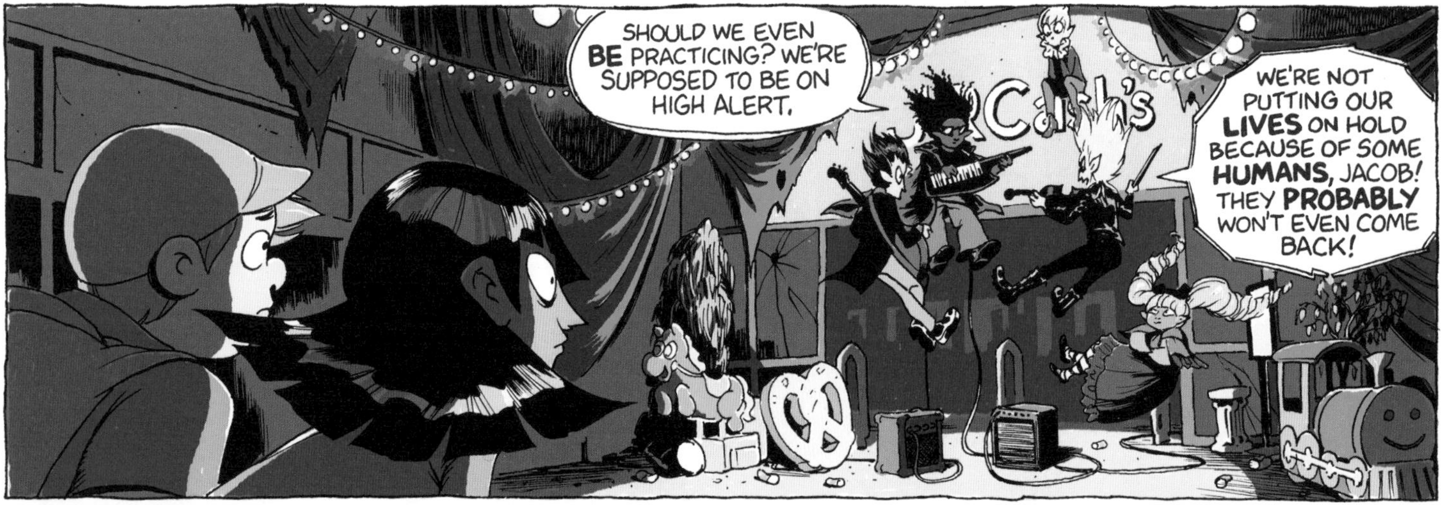
SHOULD WE EVEN **BE** PRACTICING? WE'RE SUPPOSED TO BE ON HIGH ALERT.
WE'RE NOT PUTTING OUR **LIVES** ON HOLD BECAUSE OF SOME **HUMANS,** JACOB! THEY **PROBABLY** WON'T EVEN COME BACK!

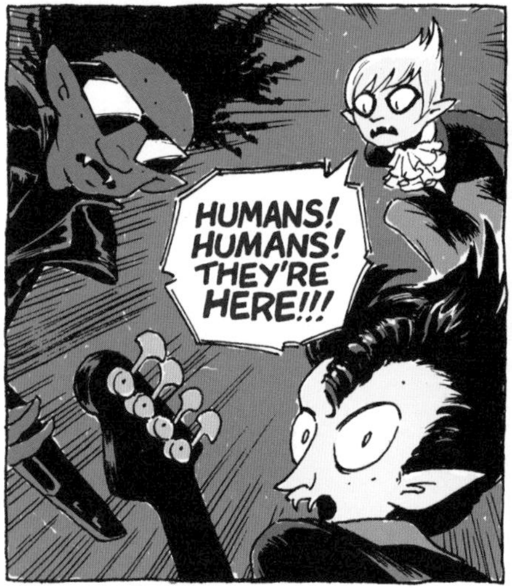
HUMANS! HUMANS! THEY'RE HERE!!!

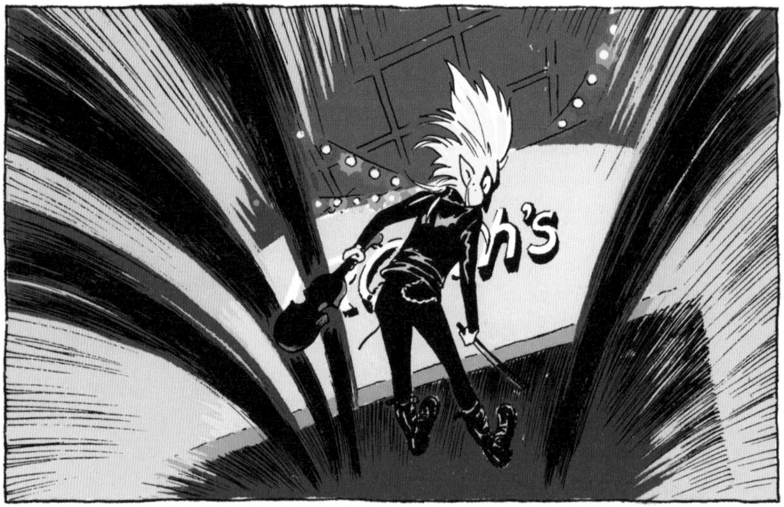

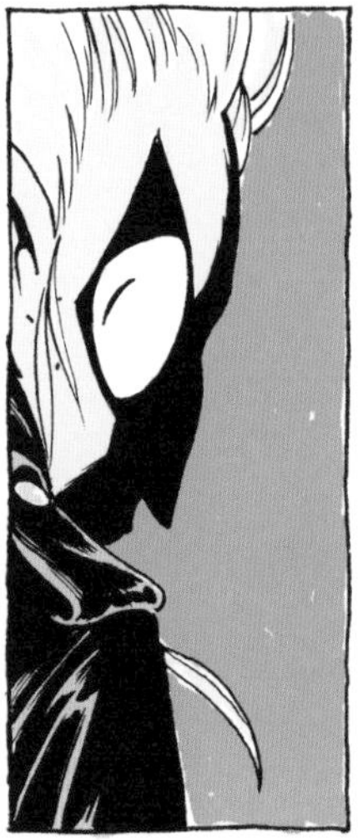

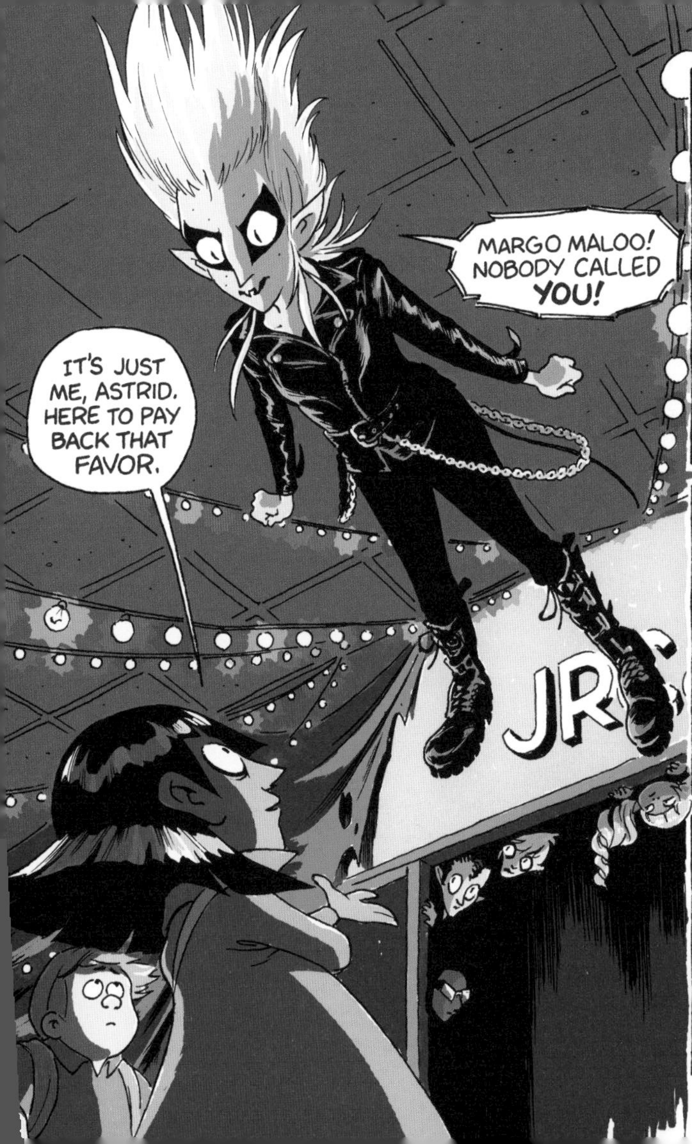
MARGO MALOO! NOBODY CALLED **YOU!**
IT'S JUST ME, ASTRID. HERE TO PAY BACK THAT FAVOR.

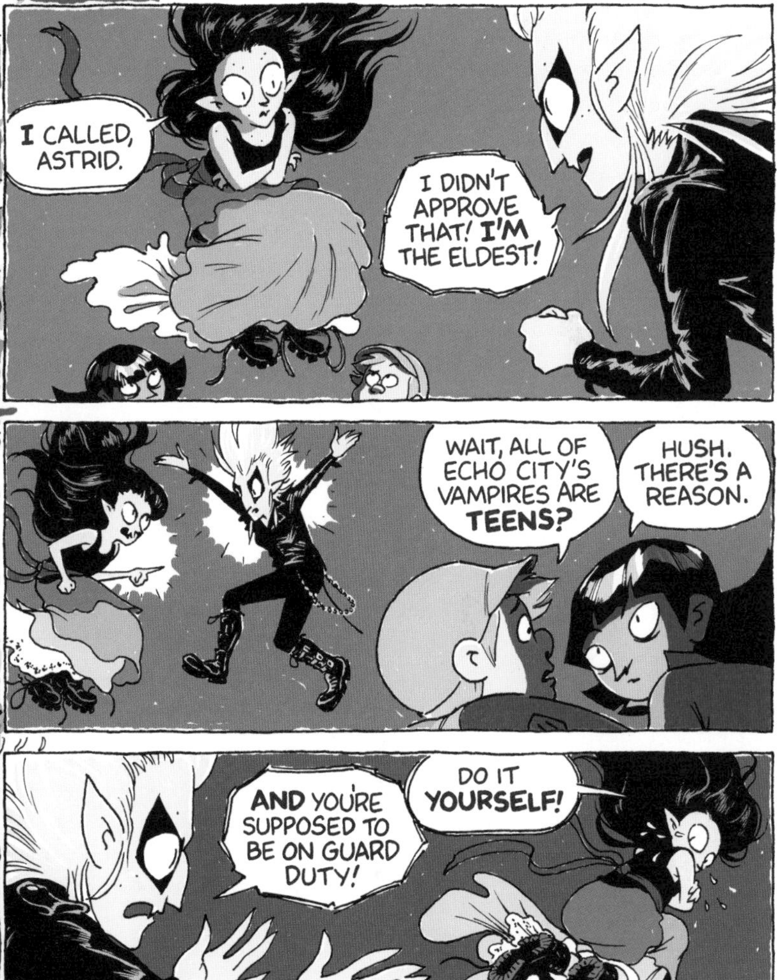
I CALLED, ASTRID.
I DIDN'T APPROVE THAT! **I'M** THE ELDEST!
WAIT, ALL OF ECHO CITY'S VAMPIRES ARE **TEENS?**
HUSH. THERE'S A REASON.
AND YOU'RE SUPPOSED TO BE ON GUARD DUTY!
DO IT **YOURSELF!**

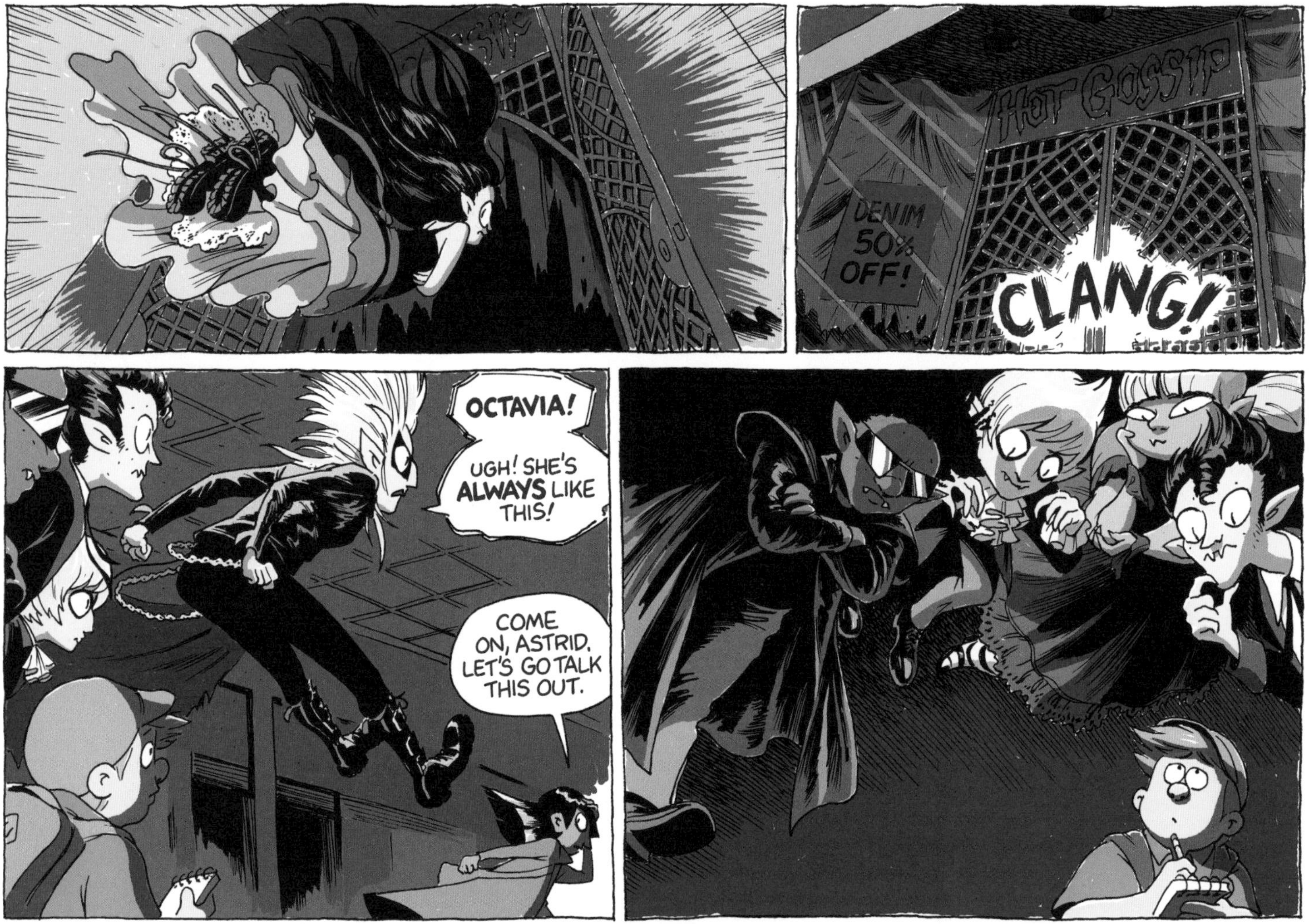
HOT GOSSIP
DENIM 50% OFF!
CLANG!
OCTAVIA!
UGH! SHE'S ALWAYS LIKE THIS!
COME ON, ASTRID. LET'S GO TALK THIS OUT.

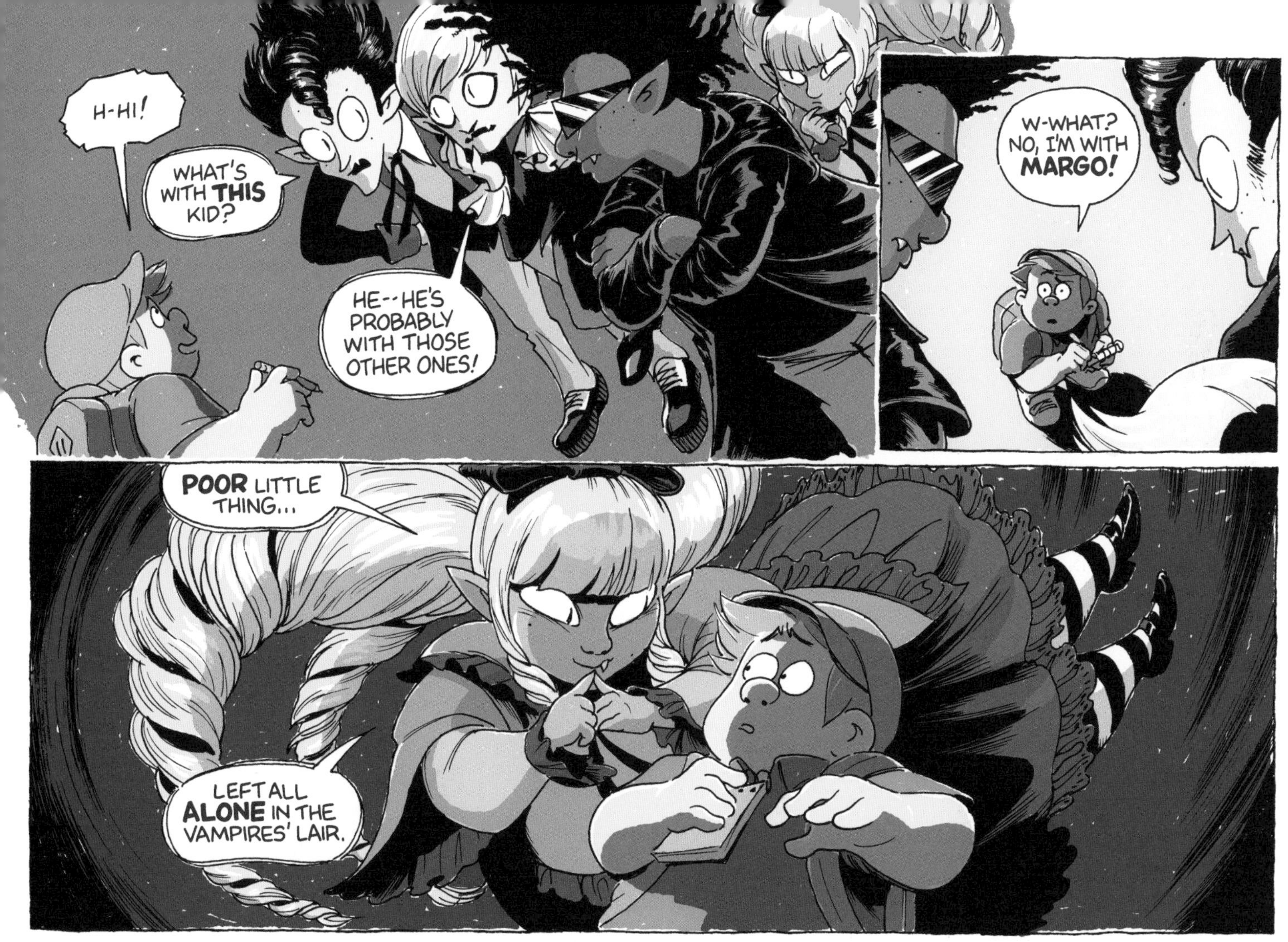
H-HI!
WHAT'S WITH THIS KID?
HE--HE'S PROBABLY WITH THOSE OTHER ONES!
W-WHAT? NO, I'M WITH MARGO!
POOR LITTLE THING...
LEFT ALL ALONE IN THE VAMPIRES' LAIR.

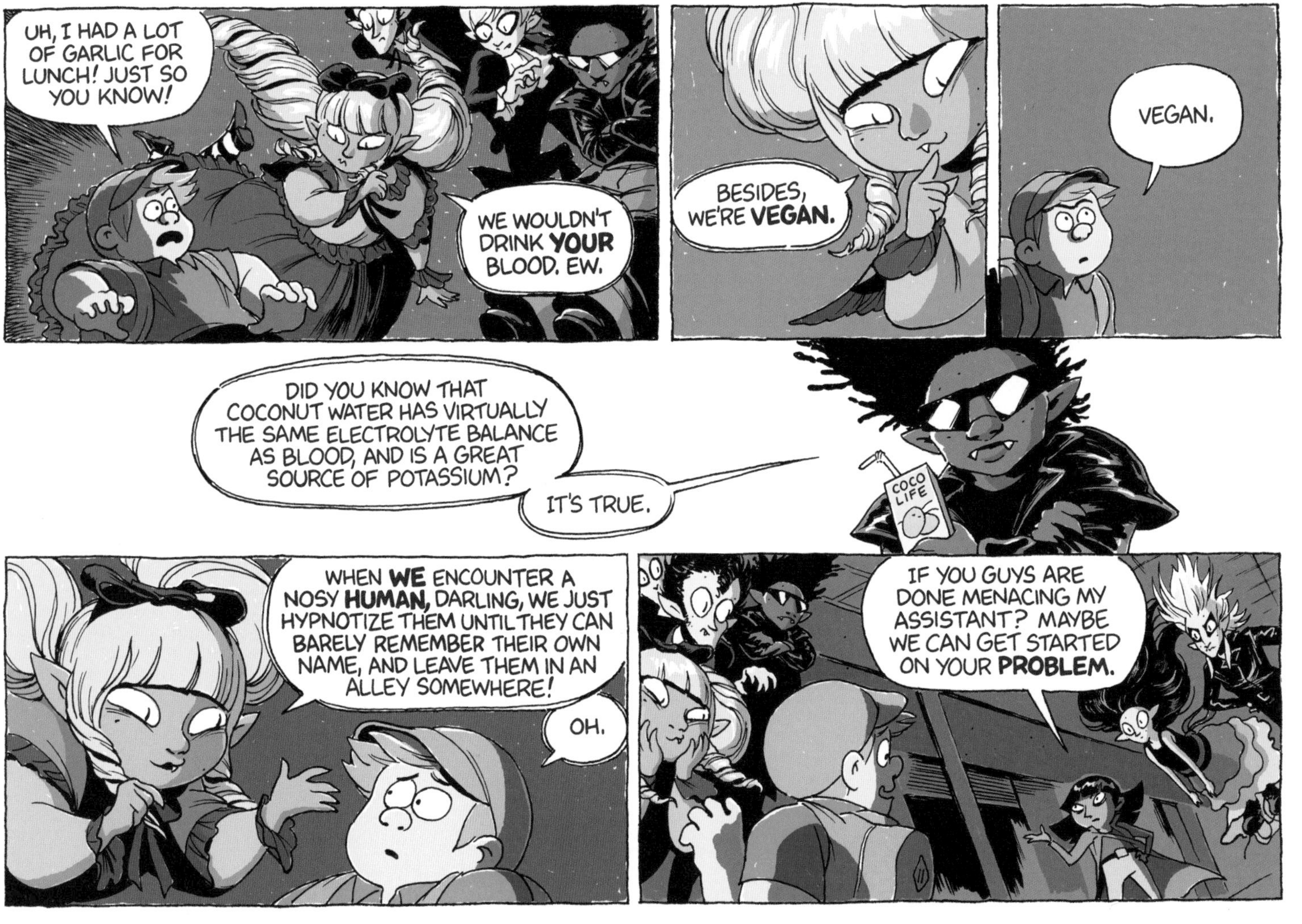
UH, I HAD A LOT OF GARLIC FOR LUNCH! JUST SO YOU KNOW!
WE WOULDN'T DRINK **YOUR** BLOOD. EW.
BESIDES, WE'RE **VEGAN.**
VEGAN.
DID YOU KNOW THAT COCONUT WATER HAS VIRTUALLY THE SAME ELECTROLYTE BALANCE AS BLOOD, AND IS A GREAT SOURCE OF POTASSIUM?
IT'S TRUE.
COCO LIFE
WHEN **WE** ENCOUNTER A NOSY **HUMAN,** DARLING, WE JUST HYPNOTIZE THEM UNTIL THEY CAN BARELY REMEMBER THEIR OWN NAME, AND LEAVE THEM IN AN ALLEY SOMEWHERE!
OH.
IF YOU GUYS ARE DONE MENACING MY ASSISTANT? MAYBE WE CAN GET STARTED ON YOUR **PROBLEM.**

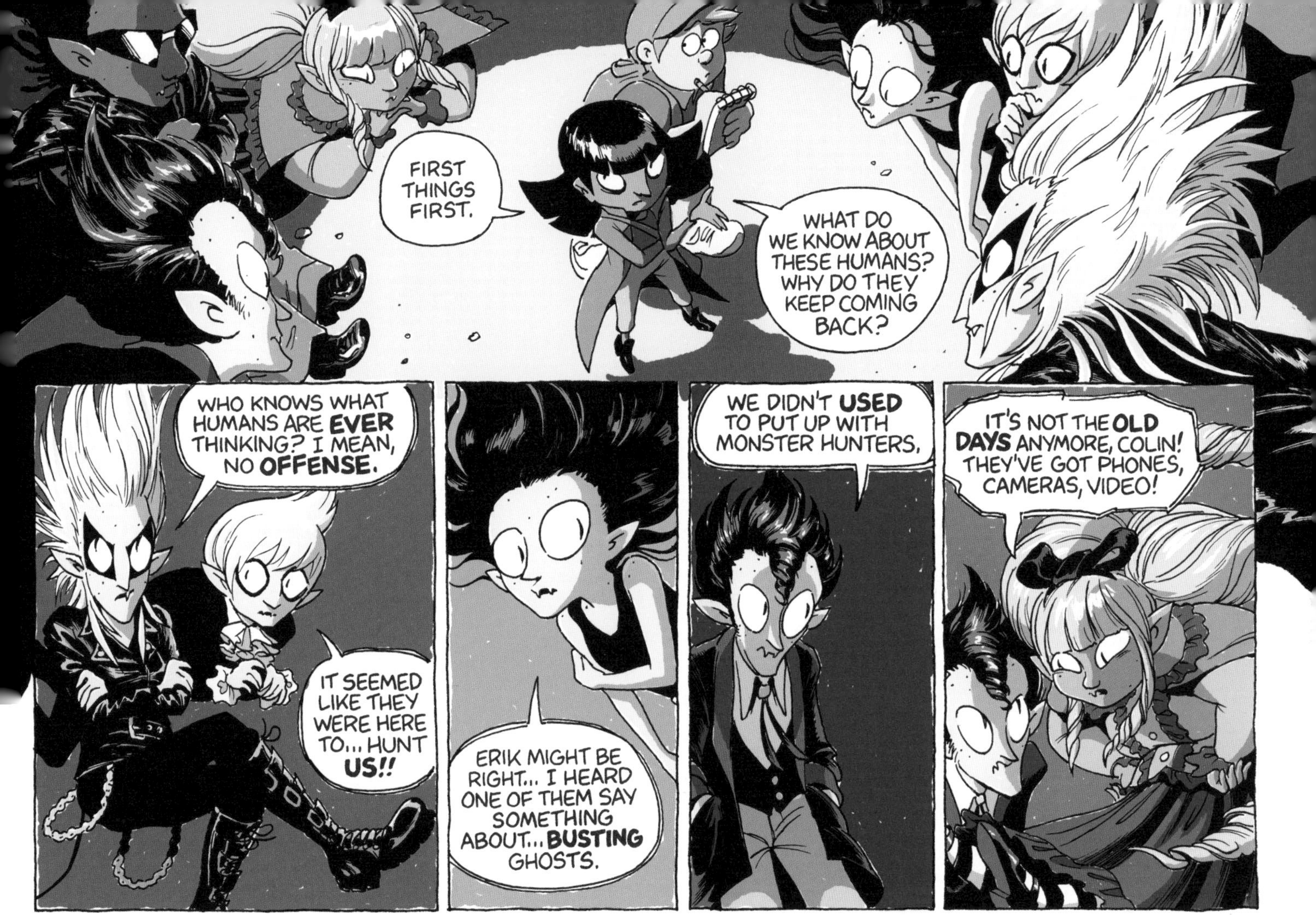
FIRST THINGS FIRST.
WHAT DO WE KNOW ABOUT THESE HUMANS? WHY DO THEY KEEP COMING BACK?
WHO KNOWS WHAT HUMANS ARE **EVER** THINKING? I MEAN, NO **OFFENSE.**
IT SEEMED LIKE THEY WERE HERE TO... HUNT **US!!**
ERIK MIGHT BE RIGHT... I HEARD ONE OF THEM SAY SOMETHING ABOUT... **BUSTING** GHOSTS.
WE DIDN'T **USED** TO PUT UP WITH MONSTER HUNTERS,
IT'S NOT THE **OLD DAYS** ANYMORE, COLIN! THEY'VE GOT PHONES, CAMERAS, VIDEO!

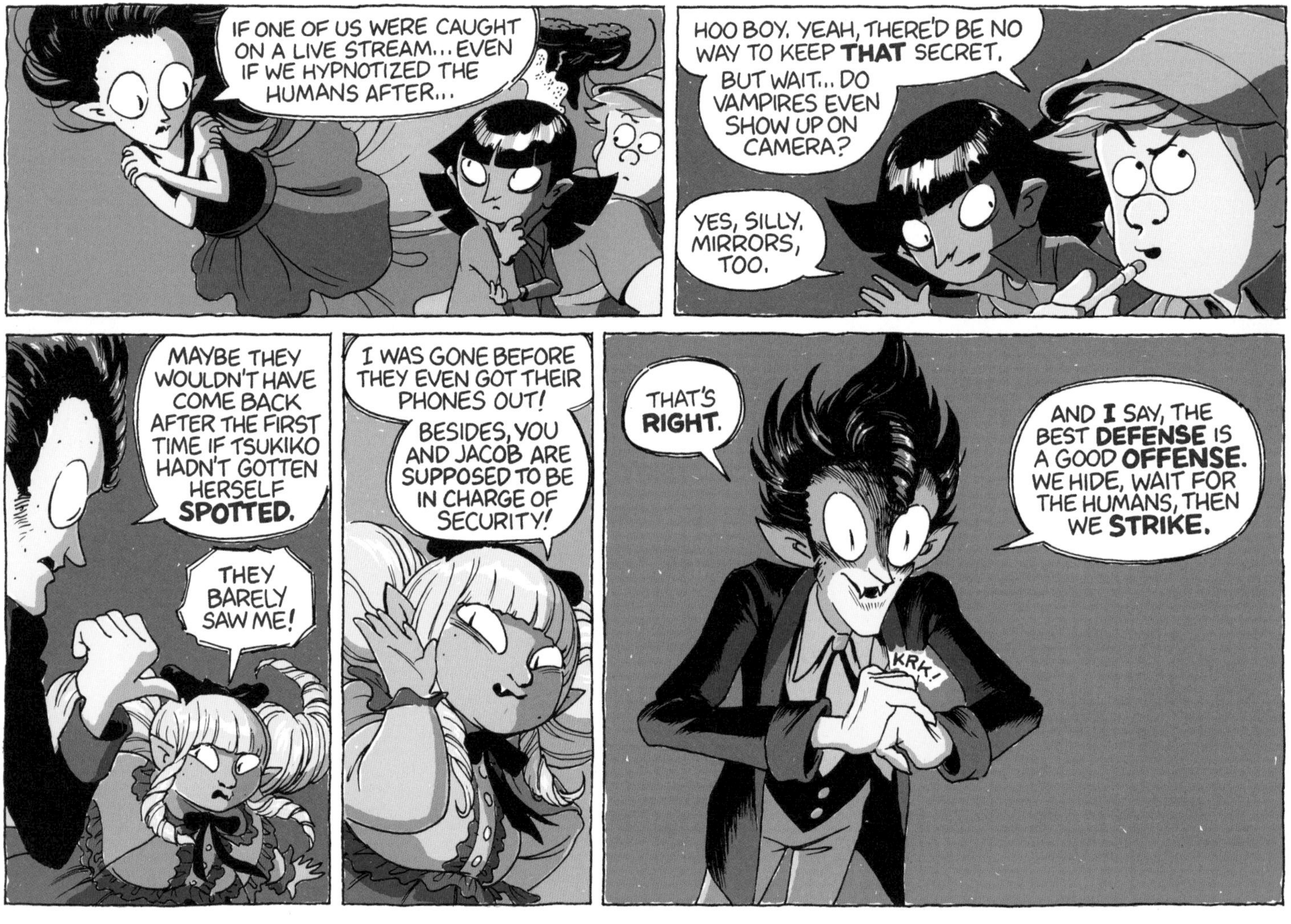
IF ONE OF US WERE CAUGHT ON A LIVE STREAM... EVEN IF WE HYPNOTIZED THE HUMANS AFTER...
HOO BOY. YEAH, THERE'D BE NO WAY TO KEEP **THAT** SECRET.
BUT WAIT... DO VAMPIRES EVEN SHOW UP ON CAMERA?
YES, SILLY. MIRRORS, TOO.
MAYBE THEY WOULDN'T HAVE COME BACK AFTER THE FIRST TIME IF TSUKIKO HADN'T GOTTEN HERSELF **SPOTTED.**
THEY BARELY SAW ME!
I WAS GONE BEFORE THEY EVEN GOT THEIR PHONES OUT!
BESIDES, YOU AND JACOB ARE SUPPOSED TO BE IN CHARGE OF SECURITY!
THAT'S **RIGHT**.
AND **I** SAY, THE BEST **DEFENSE** IS A GOOD **OFFENSE.** WE HIDE, WAIT FOR THE HUMANS, THEN WE **STRIKE.**
KRK!

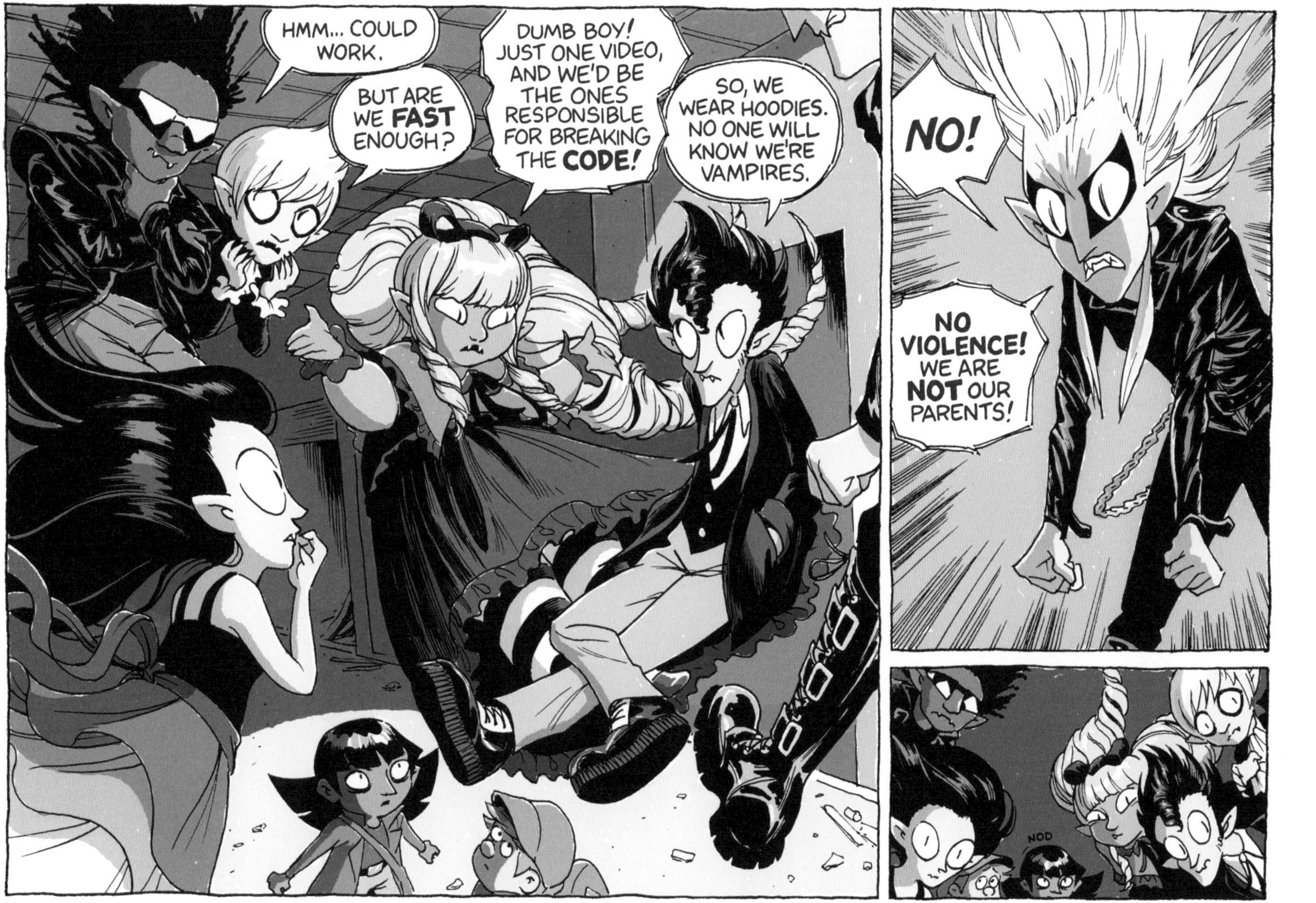
HMM... COULD WORK.
BUT ARE WE **FAST** ENOUGH?
DUMB BOY! JUST ONE VIDEO, AND WE'D BE THE ONES RESPONSIBLE FOR BREAKING THE **CODE**!
SO, WE WEAR HOODIES. NO ONE WILL KNOW WE'RE VAMPIRES.
NO!
NO VIOLENCE! WE ARE **NOT** OUR PARENTS!
NOD

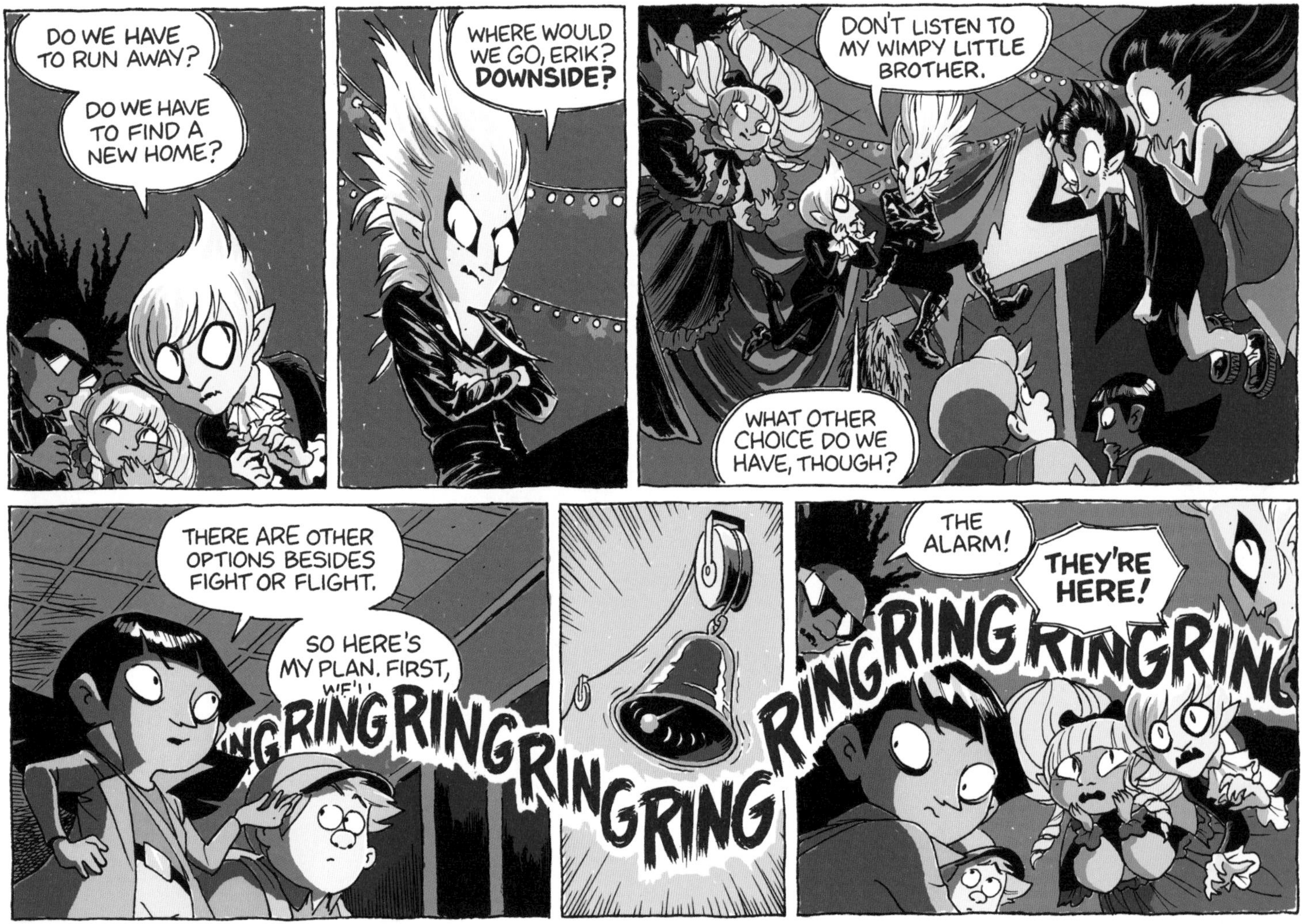
DO WE HAVE TO RUN AWAY?
DO WE HAVE TO FIND A NEW HOME?
WHERE WOULD WE GO, ERIK? **DOWNSIDE?**
DON'T LISTEN TO MY WIMPY LITTLE BROTHER.
WHAT OTHER CHOICE DO WE HAVE, THOUGH?
THERE ARE OTHER OPTIONS BESIDES FIGHT OR FLIGHT.
SO HERE'S MY PLAN. FIRST,
NGRINGRINGRINGRINGRING
RINGRINGRINGRINGRING
THE ALARM!
THEY'RE HERE!

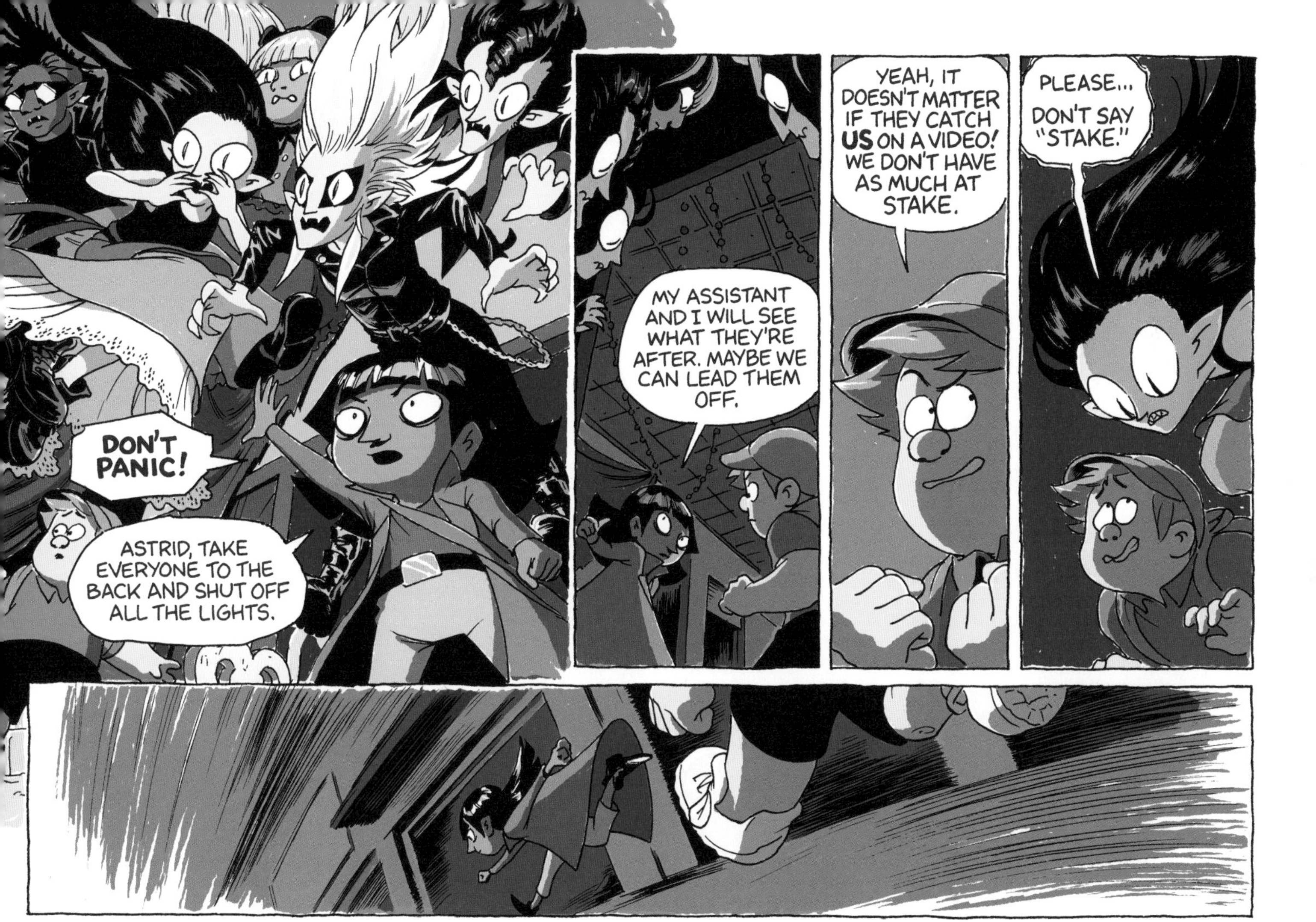
DON'T PANIC!
ASTRID, TAKE EVERYONE TO THE BACK AND SHUT OFF ALL THE LIGHTS.
MY ASSISTANT AND I WILL SEE WHAT THEY'RE AFTER. MAYBE WE CAN LEAD THEM OFF.
YEAH, IT DOESN'T MATTER IF THEY CATCH US ON A VIDEO! WE DON'T HAVE AS MUCH AT STAKE.
PLEASE...
DON'T SAY "STAKE."

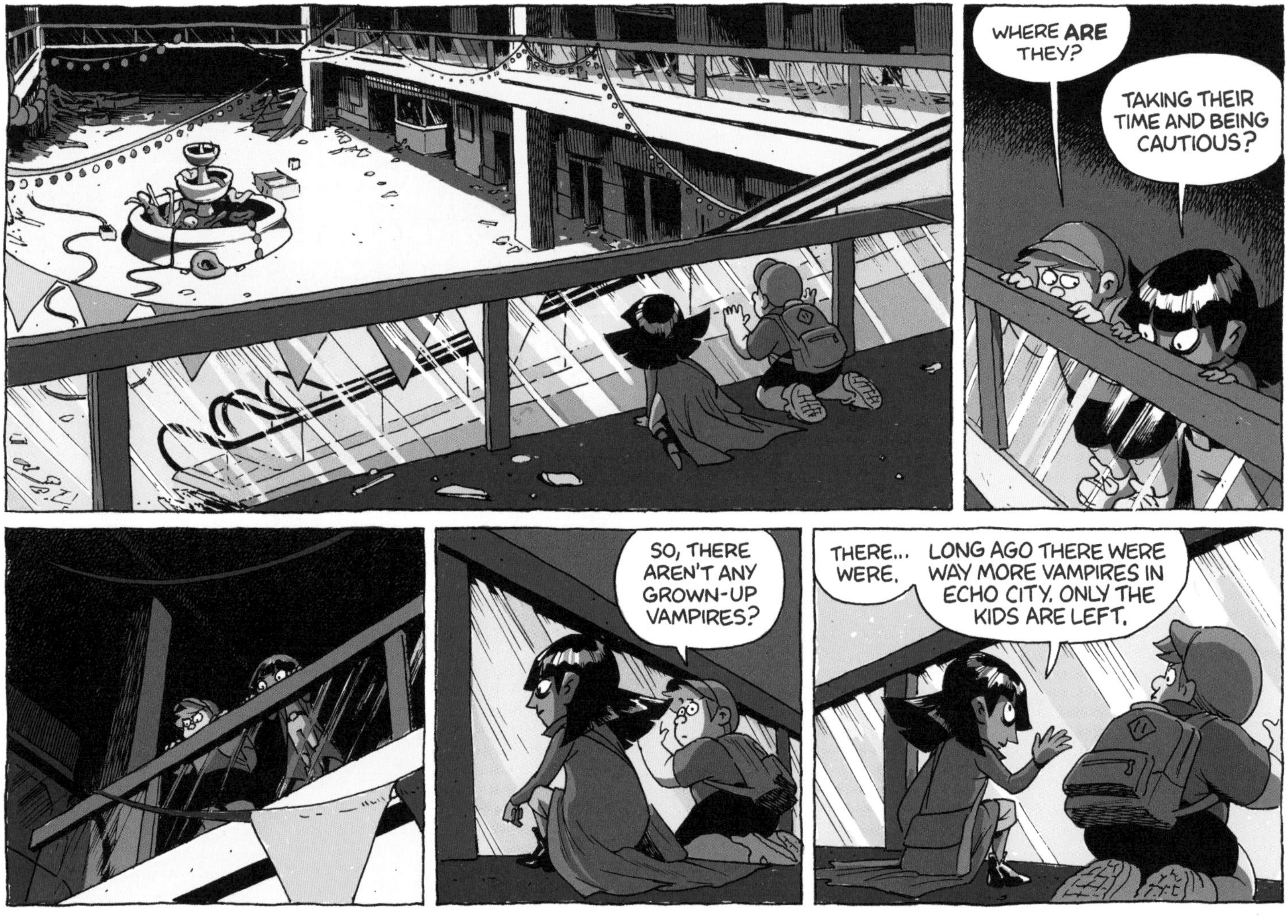
WHERE ARE THEY?
TAKING THEIR TIME AND BEING CAUTIOUS?
SO, THERE AREN'T ANY GROWN-UP VAMPIRES?
THERE... WERE.
LONG AGO THERE WERE WAY MORE VAMPIRES IN ECHO CITY. ONLY THE KIDS ARE LEFT.

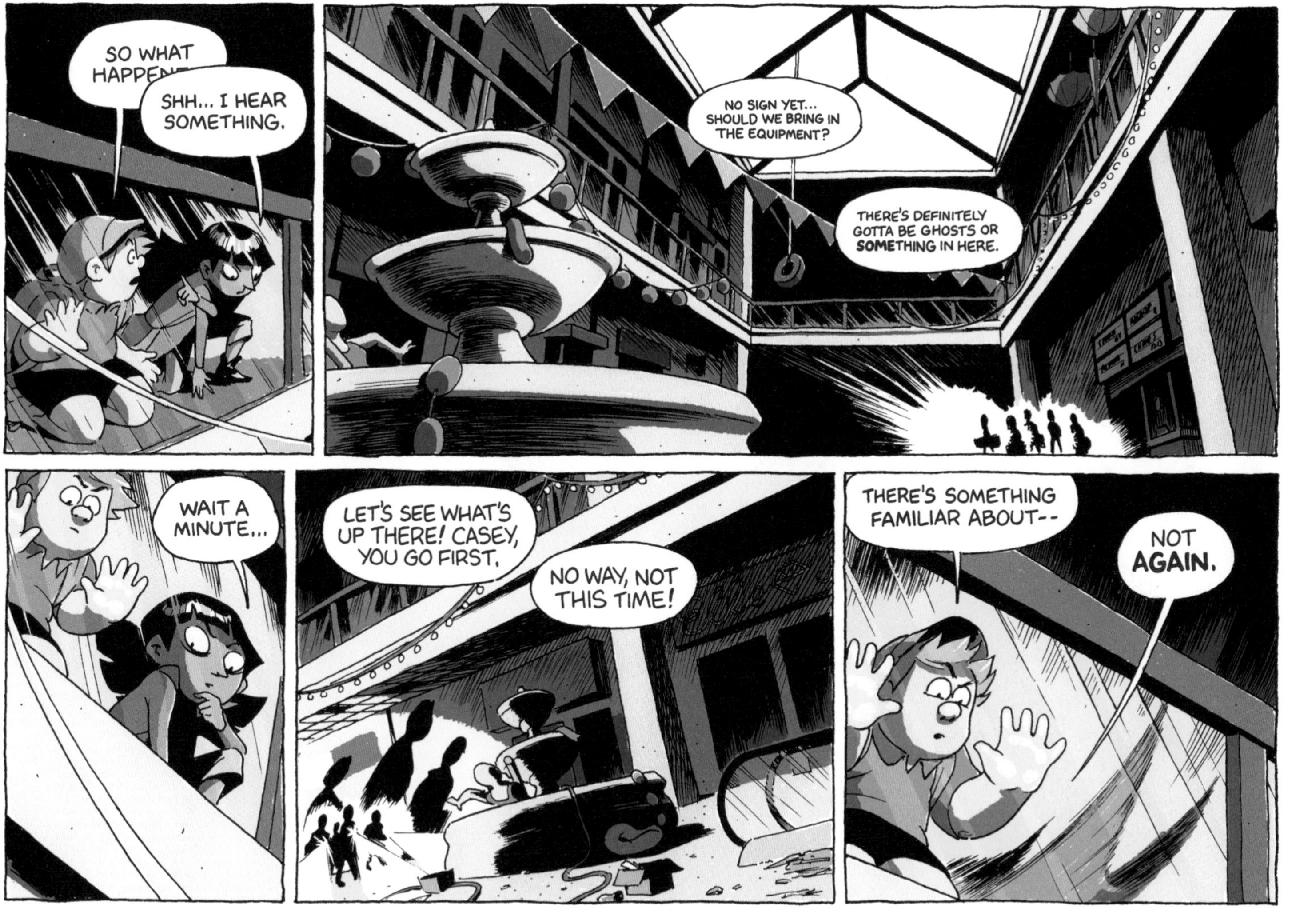
SO WHAT HAPPEN
SHH... I HEAR SOMETHING.
NO SIGN YET... SHOULD WE BRING IN THE EQUIPMENT?
THERE'S DEFINITELY GOTTA BE GHOSTS OR SOMETHING IN HERE.
WAIT A MINUTE...
LET'S SEE WHAT'S UP THERE! CASEY, YOU GO FIRST.
NO WAY, NOT THIS TIME!
THERE'S SOMETHING FAMILIAR ABOUT--
NOT AGAIN.

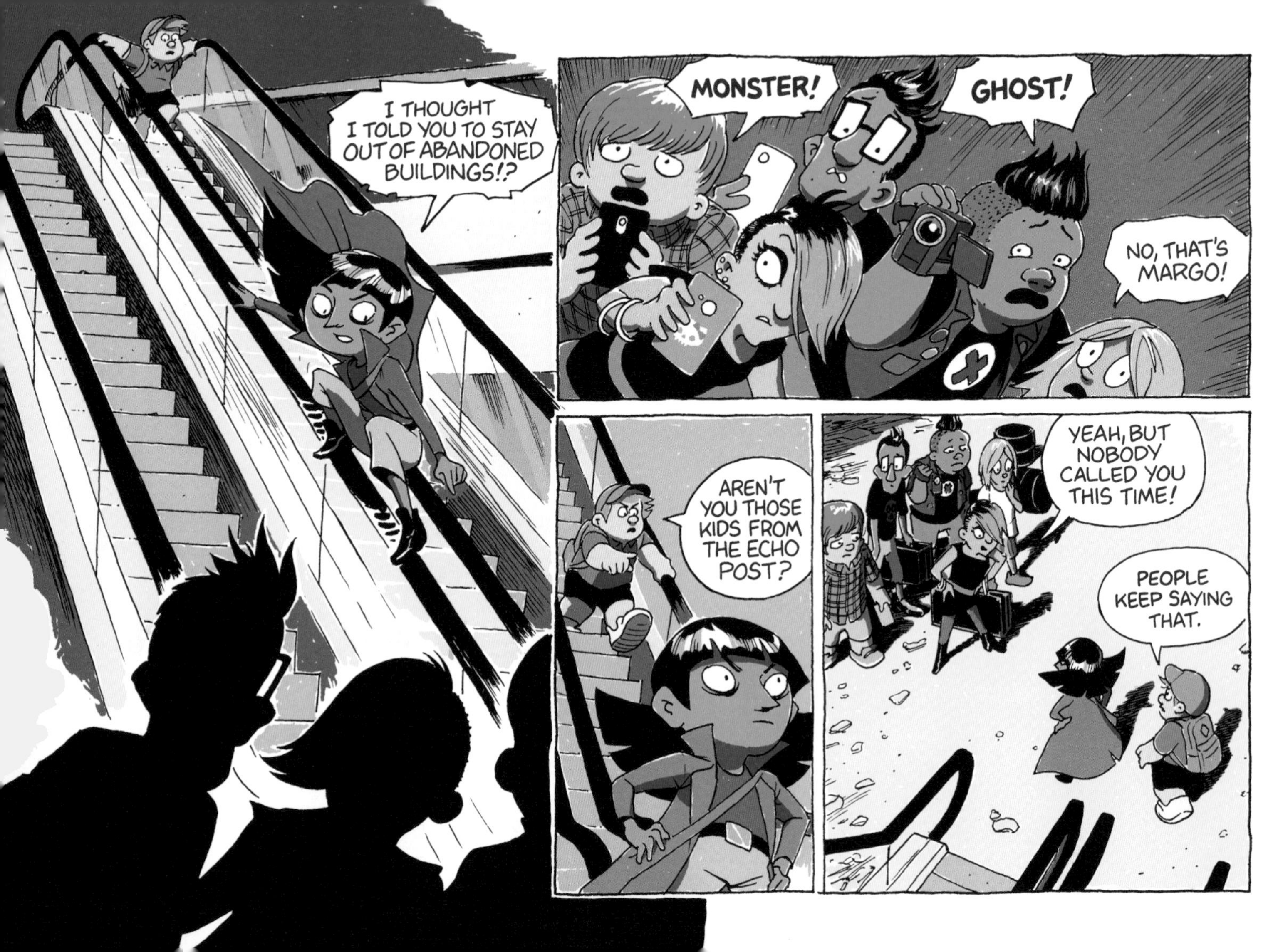
I THOUGHT I TOLD YOU TO STAY OUT OF ABANDONED BUILDINGS!?
MONSTER!
GHOST!
NO, THAT'S MARGO!
AREN'T YOU THOSE KIDS FROM THE ECHO POST?
YEAH, BUT NOBODY CALLED YOU THIS TIME!
PEOPLE KEEP SAYING THAT.

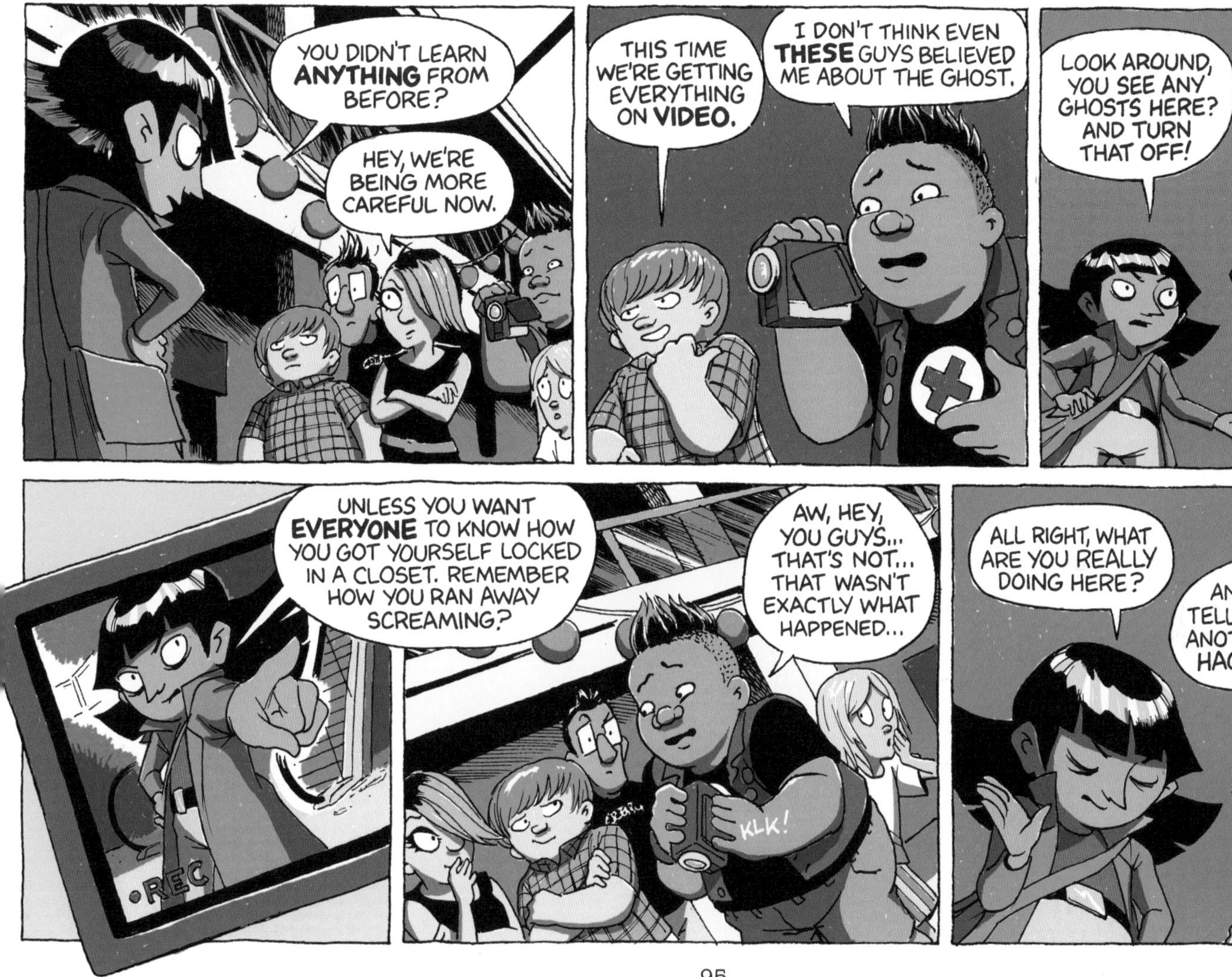
YOU DIDN'T LEARN ANYTHING FROM BEFORE?
HEY, WE'RE BEING MORE CAREFUL NOW.
THIS TIME WE'RE GETTING EVERYTHING ON VIDEO.
I DON'T THINK EVEN THESE GUYS BELIEVED ME ABOUT THE GHOST.
LOOK AROUND, YOU SEE ANY GHOSTS HERE? AND TURN THAT OFF!
REC
UNLESS YOU WANT EVERYONE TO KNOW HOW YOU GOT YOURSELF LOCKED IN A CLOSET. REMEMBER HOW YOU RAN AWAY SCREAMING?
AW, HEY, YOU GUYS... THAT'S NOT... THAT WASN'T EXACTLY WHAT HAPPENED...
KLK!
ALL RIGHT, WHAT ARE YOU REALLY DOING HERE?
AND DON'T TELL US IT WAS ANOTHER LOST HACKY SACK.

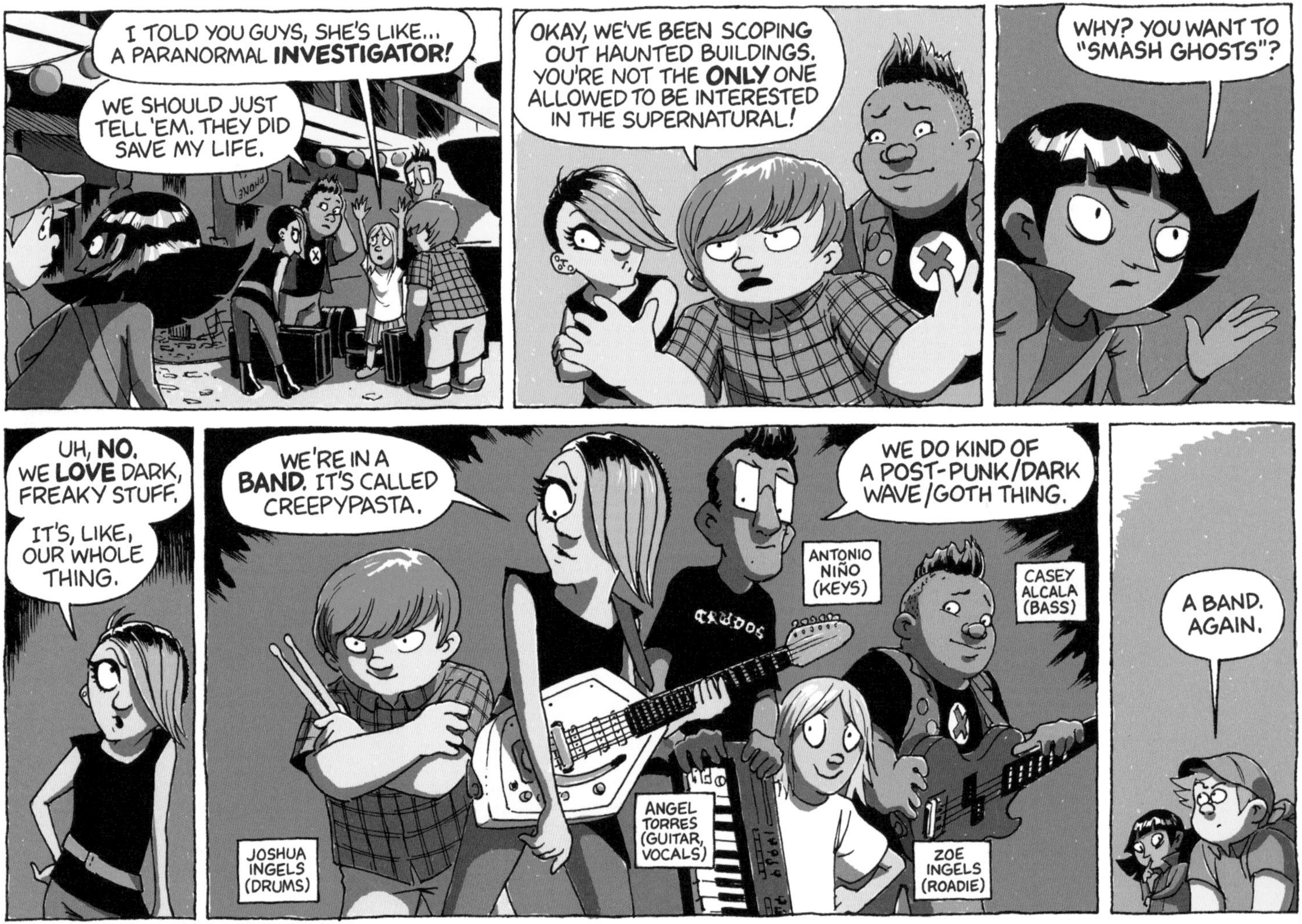
I TOLD YOU GUYS, SHE'S LIKE... A PARANORMAL **INVESTIGATOR!**
WE SHOULD JUST TELL 'EM. THEY DID SAVE MY LIFE.
PHONE
OKAY, WE'VE BEEN SCOPING OUT HAUNTED BUILDINGS. YOU'RE NOT THE **ONLY** ONE ALLOWED TO BE INTERESTED IN THE SUPERNATURAL!
WHY? YOU WANT TO "SMASH GHOSTS"?
UH, **NO.** WE **LOVE** DARK, FREAKY STUFF.
IT'S, LIKE, OUR WHOLE THING.
WE'RE IN A **BAND**. IT'S CALLED CREEPYPASTA.
WE DO KIND OF A POST-PUNK/DARK WAVE/GOTH THING.
ANTONIO NIÑO (KEYS)
CASEY ALCALA (BASS)
JOSHUA INGELS (DRUMS)
ANGEL TORRES (GUITAR, VOCALS)
ZOE INGELS (ROADIE)
A BAND. AGAIN.

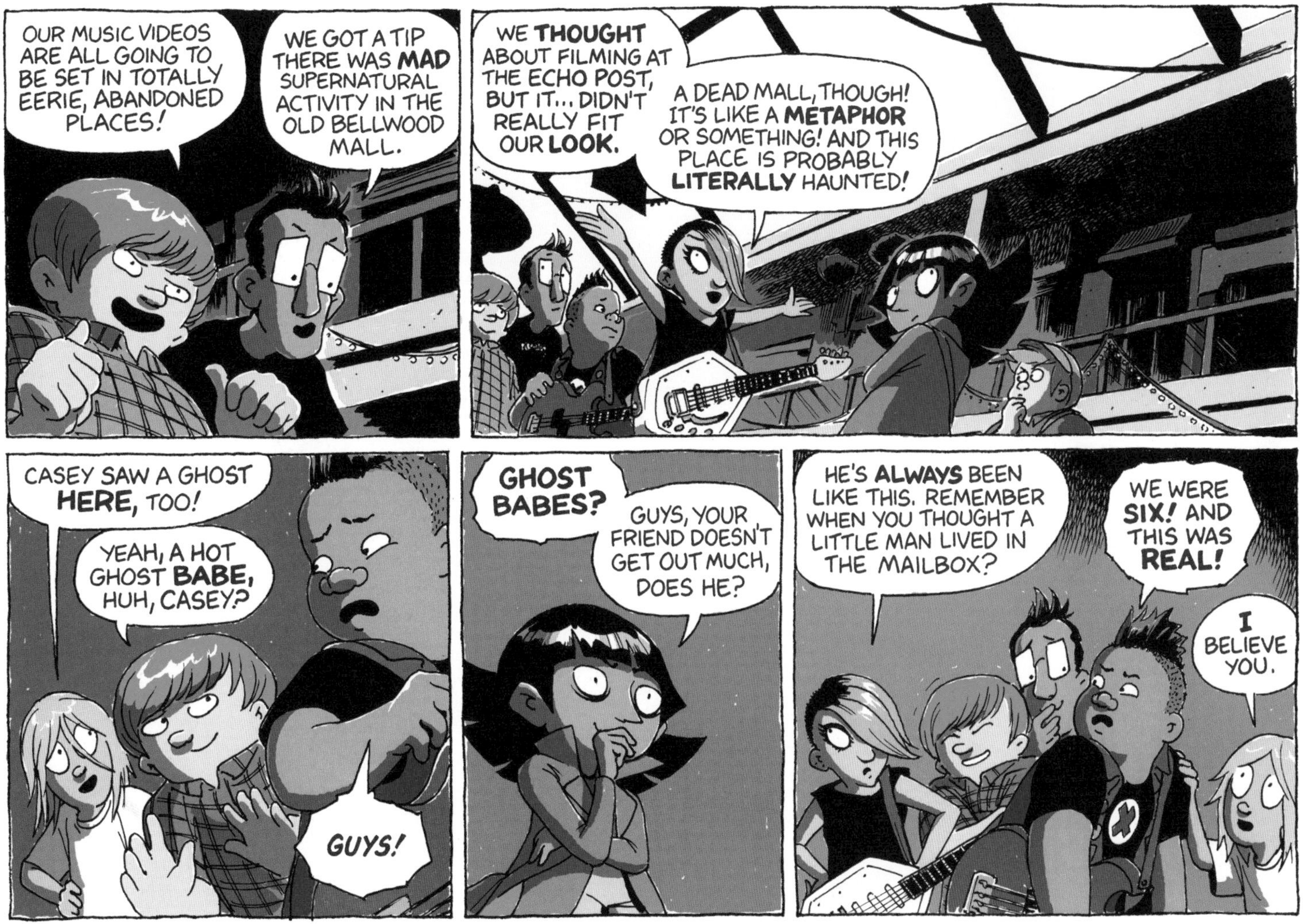
OUR MUSIC VIDEOS ARE ALL GOING TO BE SET IN TOTALLY EERIE, ABANDONED PLACES!
WE GOT A TIP THERE WAS MAD SUPERNATURAL ACTIVITY IN THE OLD BELLWOOD MALL.
WE THOUGHT ABOUT FILMING AT THE ECHO POST, BUT IT... DIDN'T REALLY FIT OUR LOOK.
A DEAD MALL, THOUGH! IT'S LIKE A METAPHOR OR SOMETHING! AND THIS PLACE IS PROBABLY LITERALLY HAUNTED!
CASEY SAW A GHOST HERE, TOO!
YEAH, A HOT GHOST BABE, HUH, CASEY?
GUYS!
GHOST BABES?
GUYS, YOUR FRIEND DOESN'T GET OUT MUCH, DOES HE?
HE'S ALWAYS BEEN LIKE THIS. REMEMBER WHEN YOU THOUGHT A LITTLE MAN LIVED IN THE MAILBOX?
WE WERE SIX! AND THIS WAS REAL!
I BELIEVE YOU.

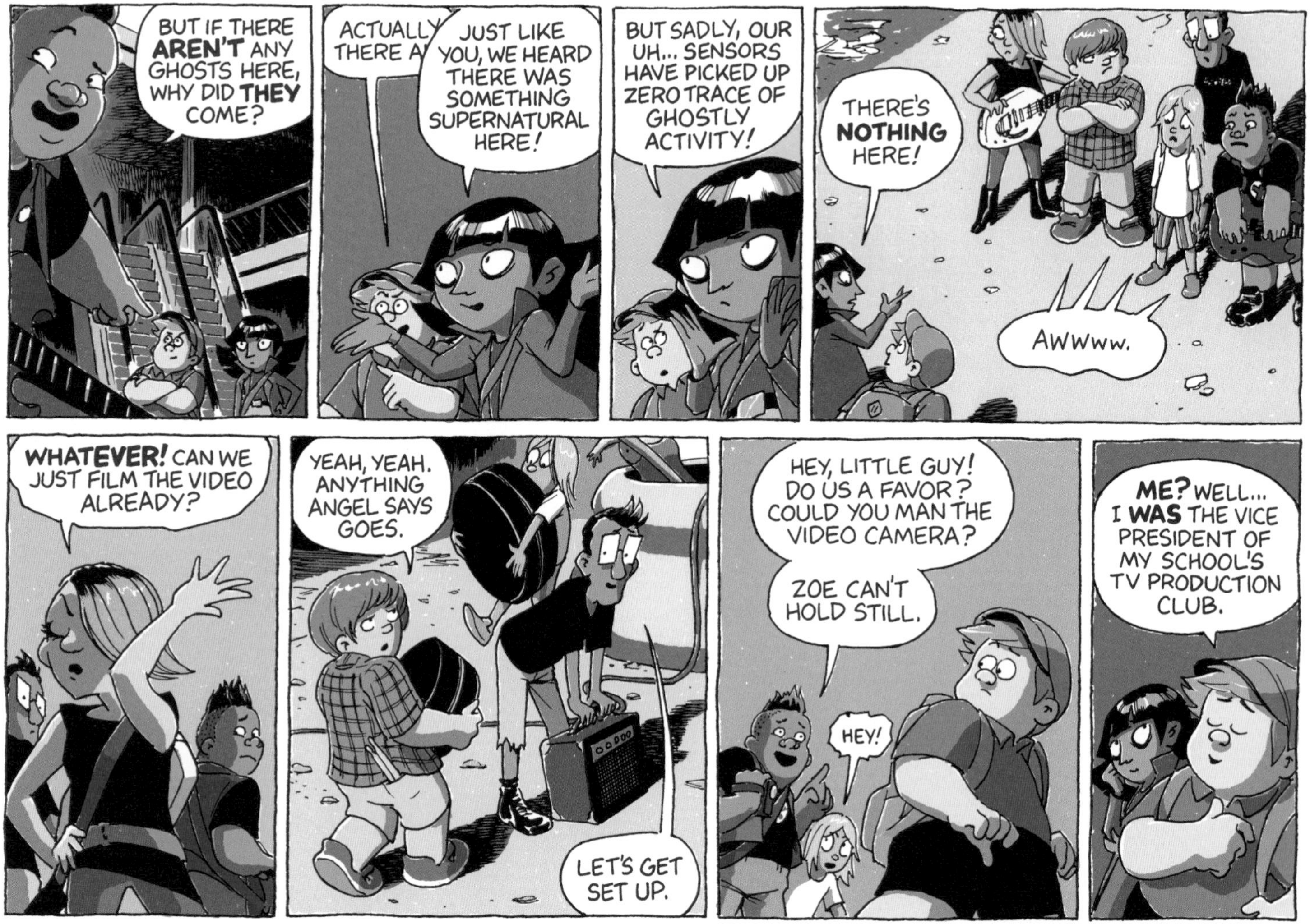
BUT IF THERE **AREN'T** ANY GHOSTS HERE, WHY DID **THEY** COME?
ACTUALLY THERE A
JUST LIKE YOU, WE HEARD THERE WAS SOMETHING SUPERNATURAL HERE!
BUT SADLY, OUR UH... SENSORS HAVE PICKED UP ZERO TRACE OF GHOSTLY ACTIVITY!
THERE'S **NOTHING** HERE!
AWWWW.
WHATEVER! CAN WE JUST FILM THE VIDEO ALREADY?
YEAH, YEAH. ANYTHING ANGEL SAYS GOES.
LET'S GET SET UP.
HEY, LITTLE GUY! DO US A FAVOR? COULD YOU MAN THE VIDEO CAMERA?
ZOE CAN'T HOLD STILL.
HEY!
ME? WELL... I **WAS** THE VICE PRESIDENT OF MY SCHOOL'S TV PRODUCTION CLUB.

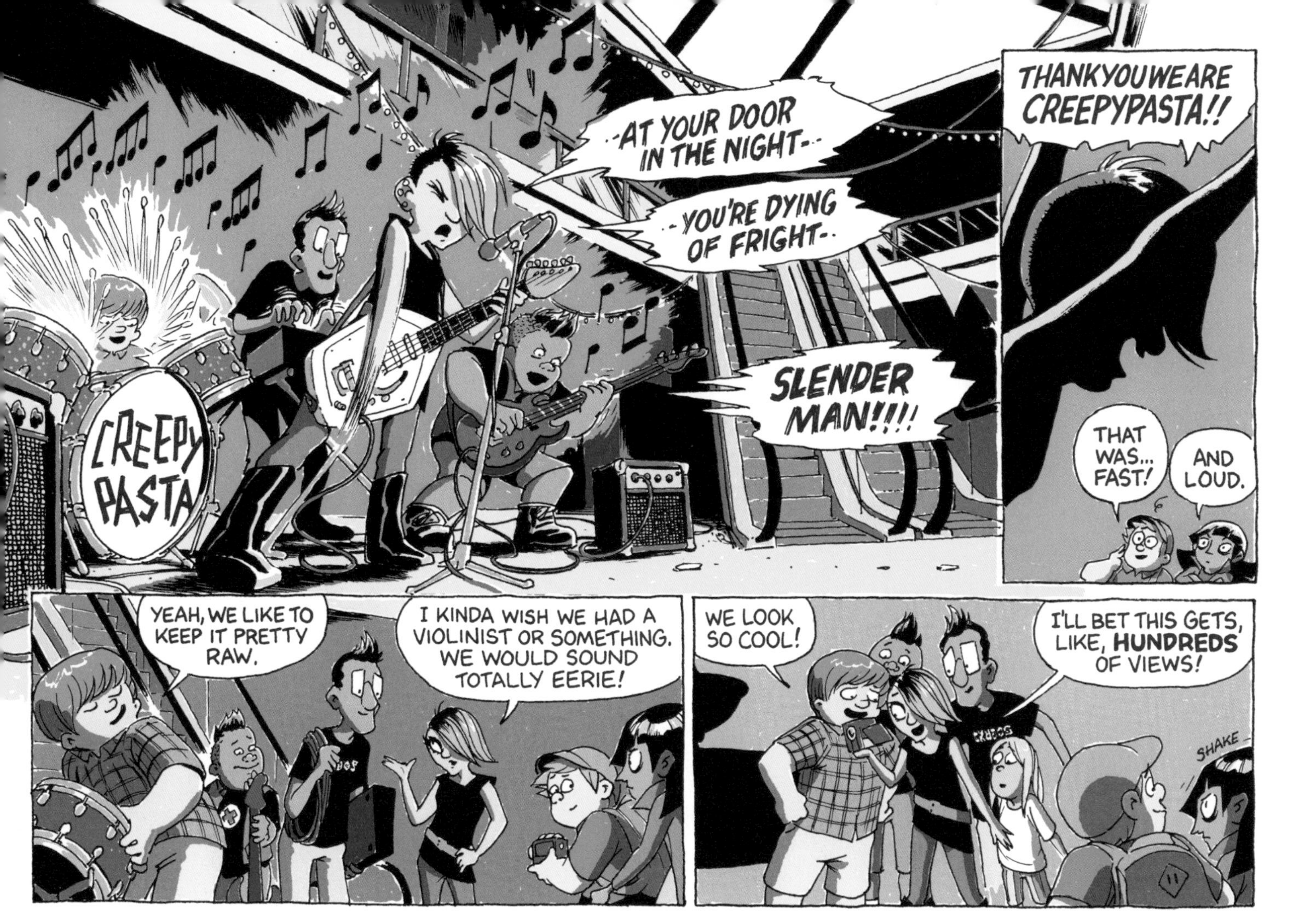
-AT YOUR DOOR IN THE NIGHT-
-YOU'RE DYING OF FRIGHT-
SLENDER MAN!!!!
CREEPY PASTA
THANKYOUWEARE CREEPYPASTA!!
THAT WAS... FAST!
AND LOUD.
YEAH, WE LIKE TO KEEP IT PRETTY RAW.
I KINDA WISH WE HAD A VIOLINIST OR SOMETHING. WE WOULD SOUND TOTALLY EERIE!
WE LOOK SO COOL!
I'LL BET THIS GETS, LIKE, HUNDREDS OF VIEWS!
SHAKE

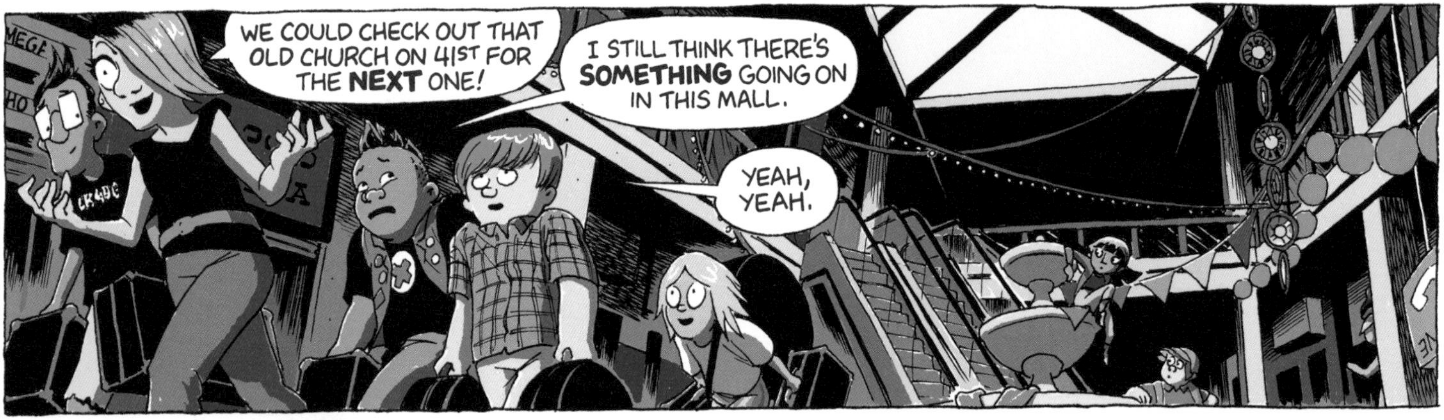
WE COULD CHECK OUT THAT OLD CHURCH ON 41ST FOR THE **NEXT** ONE!
I STILL THINK THERE'S **SOMETHING** GOING ON IN THIS MALL.
YEAH, YEAH.

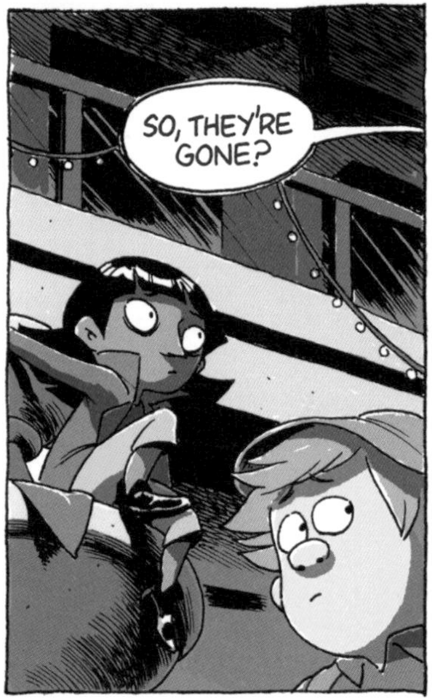
SO, THEY'RE GONE?

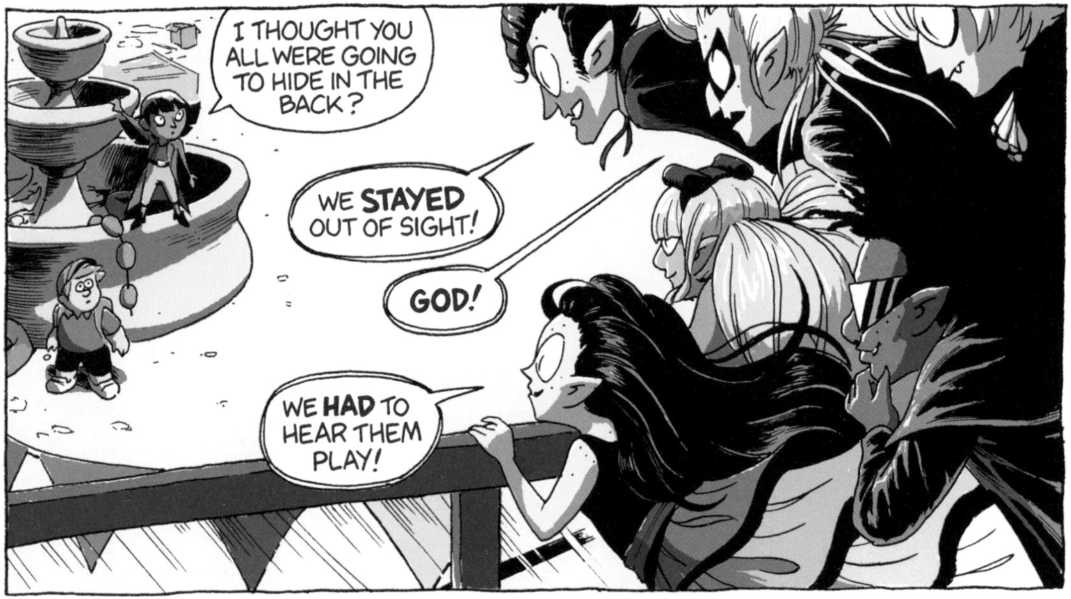
I THOUGHT YOU ALL WERE GOING TO HIDE IN THE BACK?
WE **STAYED** OUT OF SIGHT!
GOD!
WE **HAD** TO HEAR THEM PLAY!

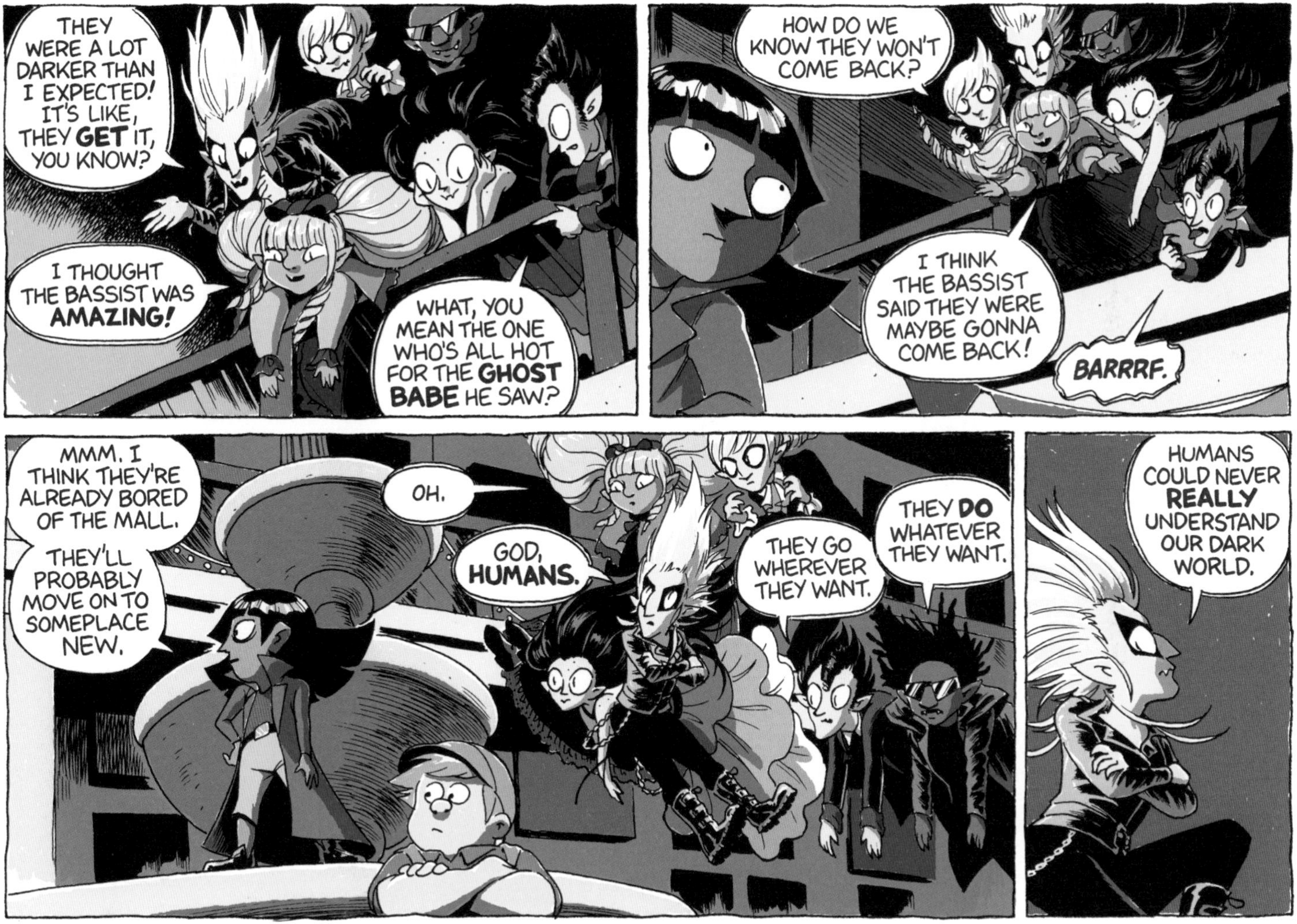
THEY WERE A LOT DARKER THAN I EXPECTED! IT'S LIKE, THEY **GET** IT, YOU KNOW?
I THOUGHT THE BASSIST WAS **AMAZING!**
WHAT, YOU MEAN THE ONE WHO'S ALL HOT FOR THE **GHOST BABE** HE SAW?
HOW DO WE KNOW THEY WON'T COME BACK?
I THINK THE BASSIST SAID THEY WERE MAYBE GONNA COME BACK!
BARRRF.
MMM. I THINK THEY'RE ALREADY BORED OF THE MALL.
THEY'LL PROBABLY MOVE ON TO SOMEPLACE NEW.
OH.
GOD, **HUMANS.**
THEY GO WHEREVER THEY WANT.
THEY **DO** WHATEVER THEY WANT.
HUMANS COULD NEVER **REALLY** UNDERSTAND OUR DARK WORLD.

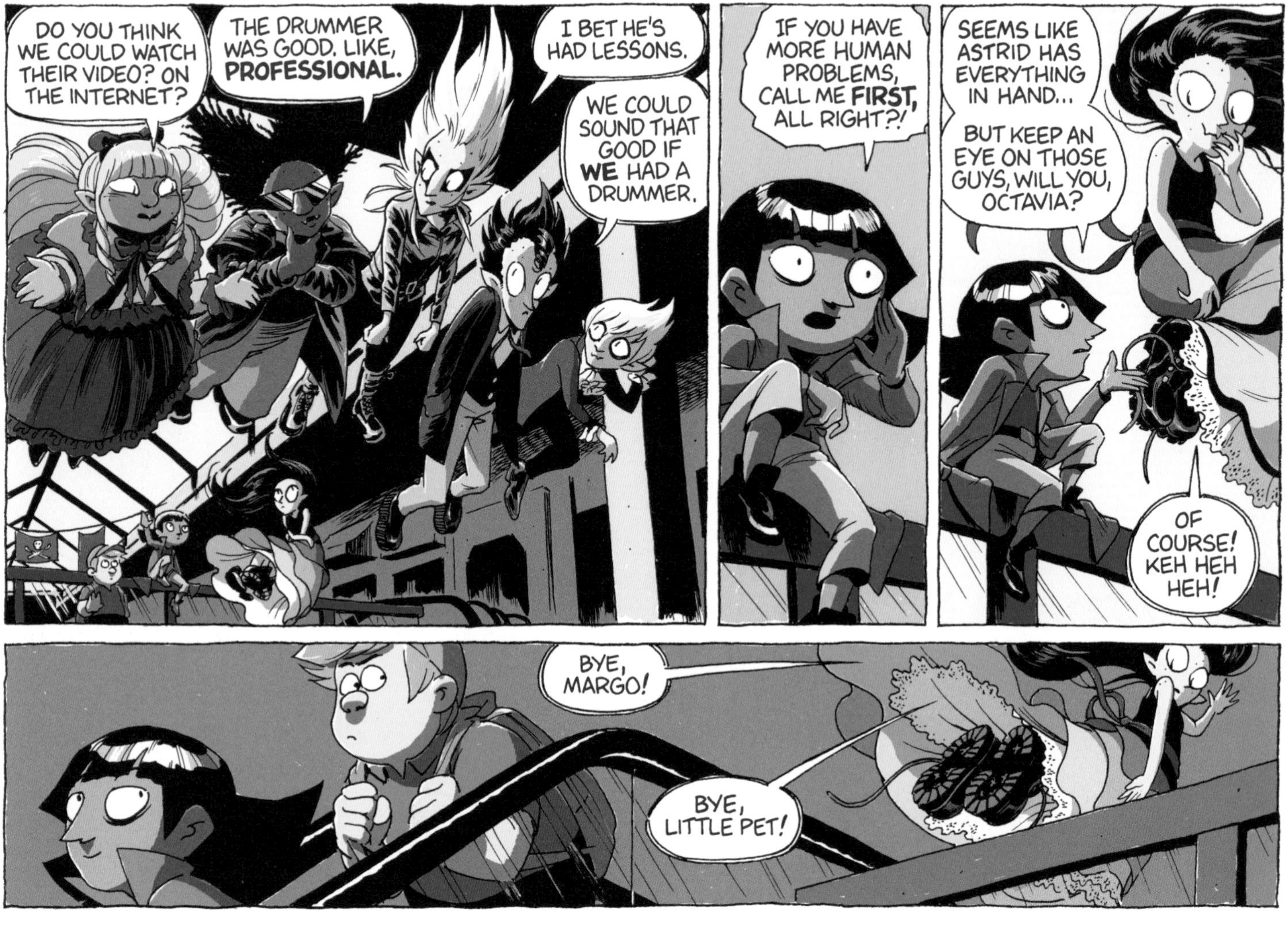
DO YOU THINK WE COULD WATCH THEIR VIDEO? ON THE INTERNET?
THE DRUMMER WAS GOOD. LIKE, **PROFESSIONAL.**
I BET HE'S HAD LESSONS.
WE COULD SOUND THAT GOOD IF **WE** HAD A DRUMMER.
IF YOU HAVE MORE HUMAN PROBLEMS, CALL ME **FIRST,** ALL RIGHT?!
SEEMS LIKE ASTRID HAS EVERYTHING IN HAND...
BUT KEEP AN EYE ON THOSE GUYS, WILL YOU, OCTAVIA?
OF COURSE! KEH HEH HEH!
BYE, MARGO!
BYE, LITTLE PET!

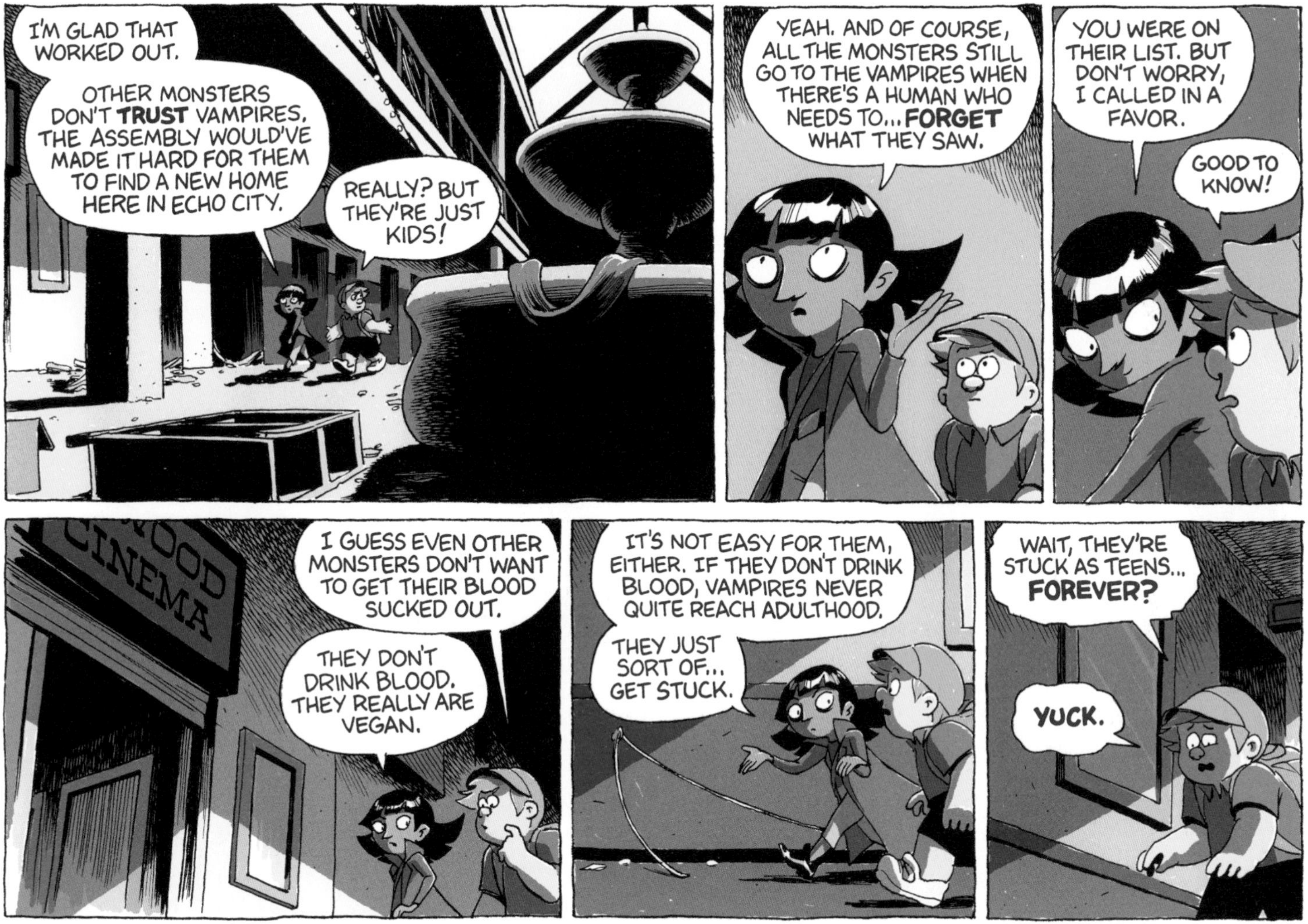
I'M GLAD THAT WORKED OUT.
OTHER MONSTERS DON'T **TRUST** VAMPIRES. THE ASSEMBLY WOULD'VE MADE IT HARD FOR THEM TO FIND A NEW HOME HERE IN ECHO CITY.
REALLY? BUT THEY'RE JUST KIDS!
YEAH. AND OF COURSE, ALL THE MONSTERS STILL GO TO THE VAMPIRES WHEN THERE'S A HUMAN WHO NEEDS TO... **FORGET** WHAT THEY SAW.
YOU WERE ON THEIR LIST. BUT DON'T WORRY, I CALLED IN A FAVOR.
GOOD TO KNOW!
CINEMA
I GUESS EVEN OTHER MONSTERS DON'T WANT TO GET THEIR BLOOD SUCKED OUT.
THEY DON'T DRINK BLOOD. THEY REALLY ARE VEGAN.
IT'S NOT EASY FOR THEM, EITHER. IF THEY DON'T DRINK BLOOD, VAMPIRES NEVER QUITE REACH ADULTHOOD.
THEY JUST SORT OF... GET STUCK.
WAIT, THEY'RE STUCK AS TEENS... **FOREVER?**
YUCK.

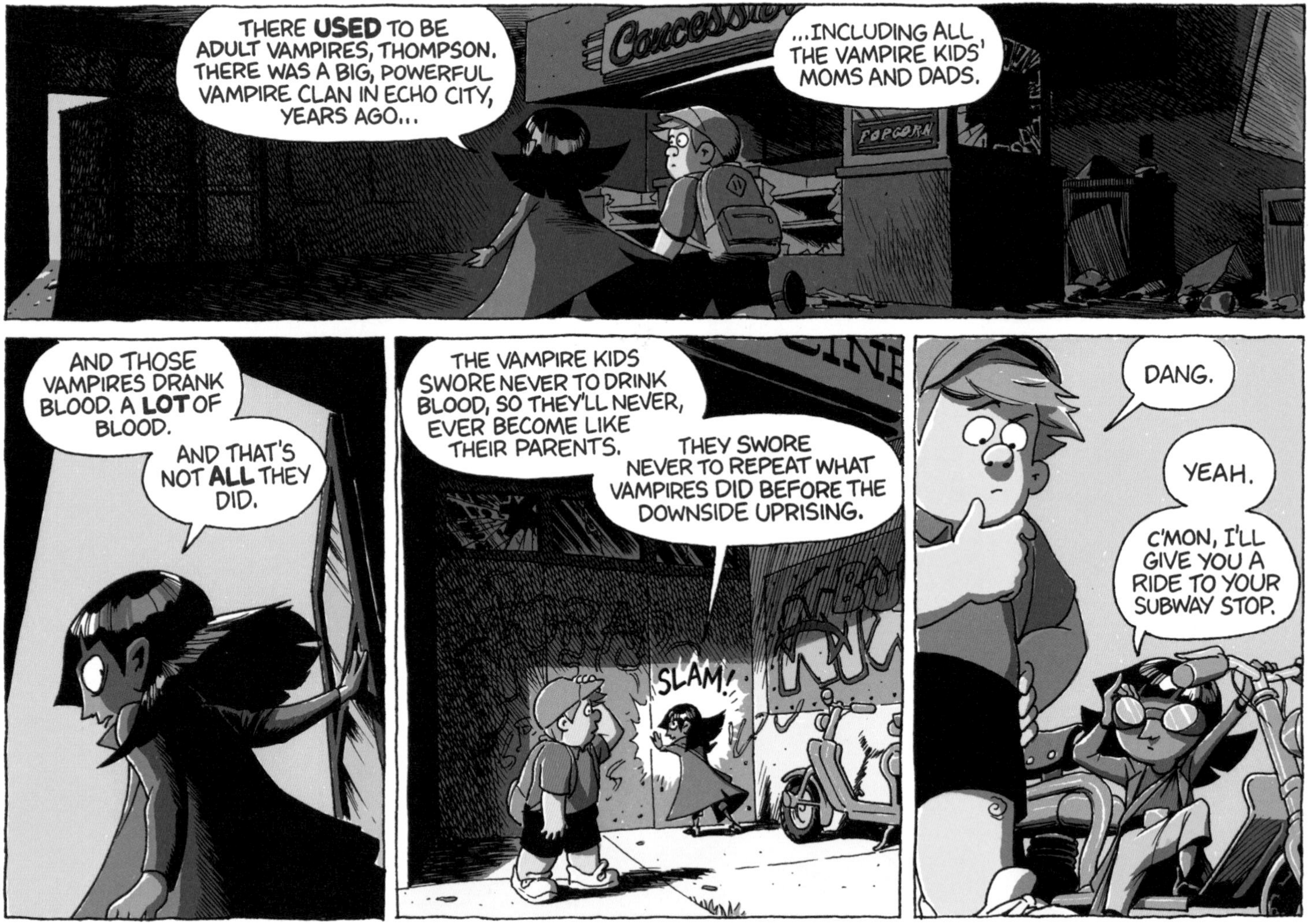
THERE **USED** TO BE ADULT VAMPIRES, THOMPSON. THERE WAS A BIG, POWERFUL VAMPIRE CLAN IN ECHO CITY, YEARS AGO...
...INCLUDING ALL THE VAMPIRE KIDS' MOMS AND DADS.
POPCORN
AND THOSE VAMPIRES DRANK BLOOD. A **LOT** OF BLOOD.
AND THAT'S NOT **ALL** THEY DID.
THE VAMPIRE KIDS SWORE NEVER TO DRINK BLOOD, SO THEY'LL NEVER, EVER BECOME LIKE THEIR PARENTS.
THEY SWORE NEVER TO REPEAT WHAT VAMPIRES DID BEFORE THE DOWNSIDE UPRISING.
SLAM!
DANG.
YEAH.
C'MON, I'LL GIVE YOU A RIDE TO YOUR SUBWAY STOP.

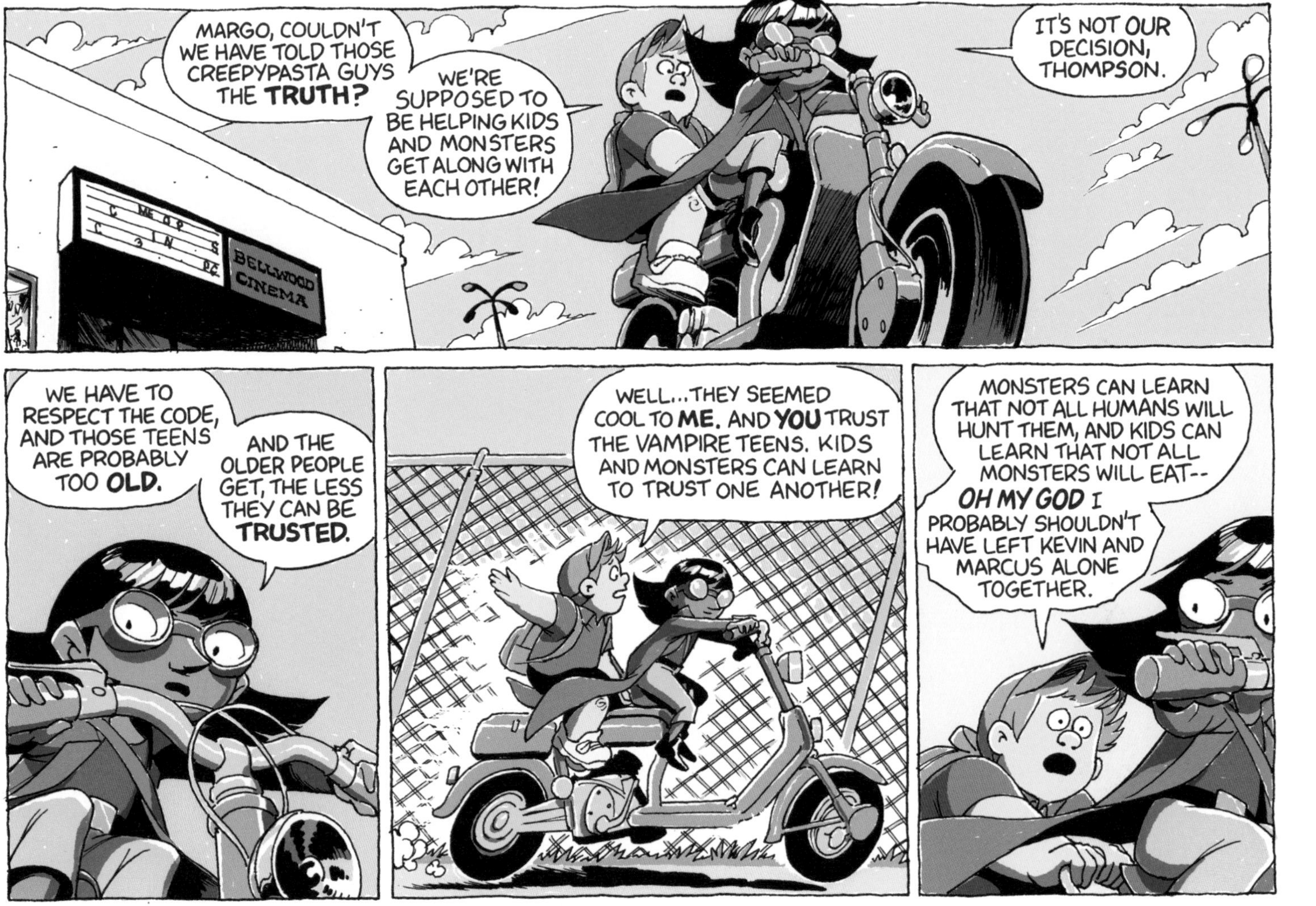
MARGO, COULDN'T WE HAVE TOLD THOSE CREEPYPASTA GUYS THE **TRUTH?**
WE'RE SUPPOSED TO BE HELPING KIDS AND MONSTERS GET ALONG WITH EACH OTHER!
BELLWOOD CINEMA
IT'S NOT **OUR** DECISION, THOMPSON.
WE HAVE TO RESPECT THE CODE, AND THOSE TEENS ARE PROBABLY TOO **OLD.**
AND THE OLDER PEOPLE GET, THE LESS THEY CAN BE **TRUSTED.**
WELL... THEY SEEMED COOL TO **ME.** AND **YOU** TRUST THE VAMPIRE TEENS. KIDS AND MONSTERS CAN LEARN TO TRUST ONE ANOTHER!
MONSTERS CAN LEARN THAT NOT ALL HUMANS WILL HUNT THEM, AND KIDS CAN LEARN THAT NOT ALL MONSTERS WILL EAT--
OH MY GOD I PROBABLY SHOULDN'T HAVE LEFT KEVIN AND MARCUS ALONE TOGETHER.

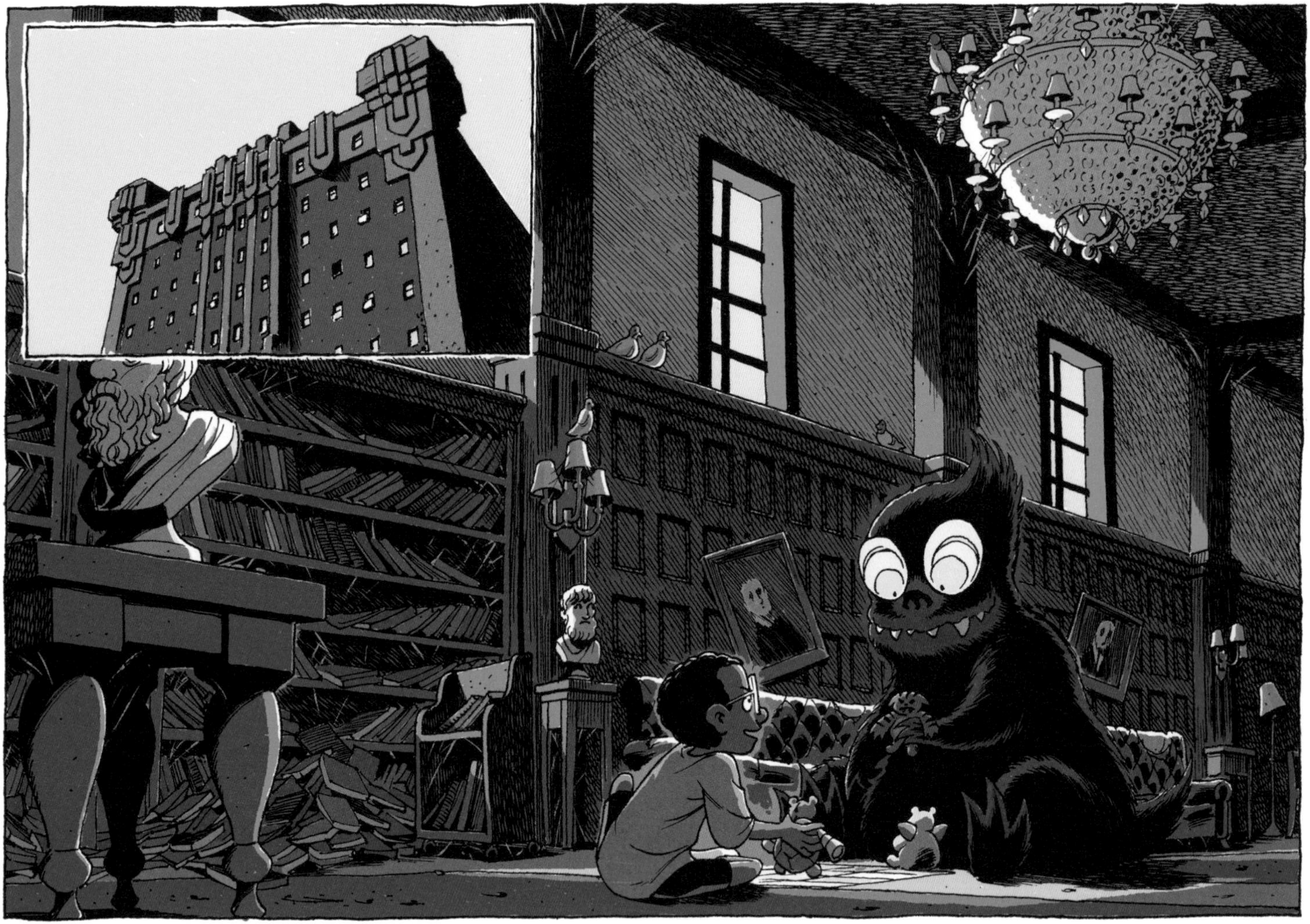

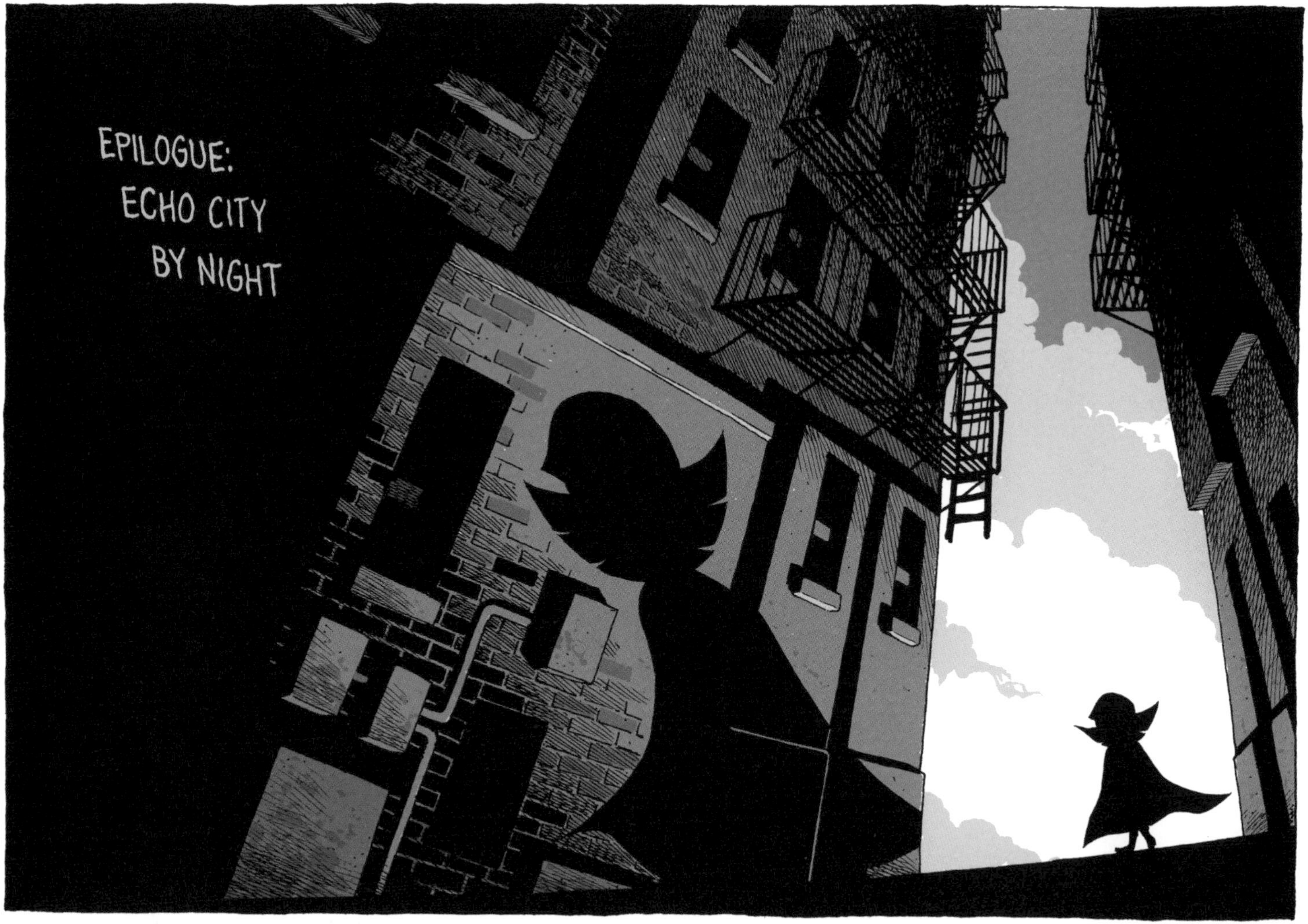
EPILOGUE:
ECHO CITY
BY NIGHT

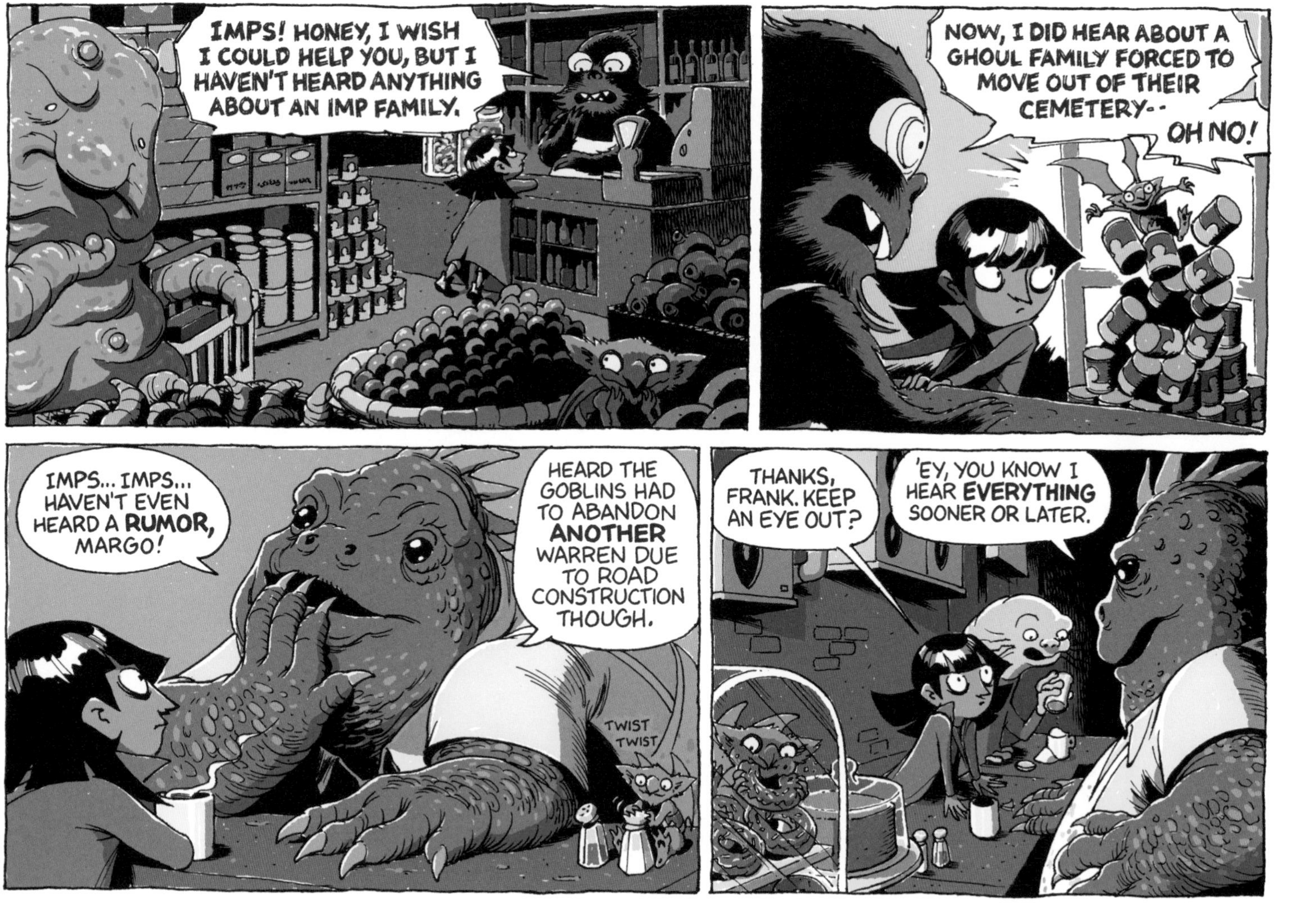
IMPS! HONEY, I WISH I COULD HELP YOU, BUT I HAVEN'T HEARD ANYTHING ABOUT AN IMP FAMILY.
NOW, I DID HEAR ABOUT A GHOUL FAMILY FORCED TO MOVE OUT OF THEIR CEMETERY- -
OH NO!
IMPS... IMPS... HAVEN'T EVEN HEARD A **RUMOR,** MARGO!
HEARD THE GOBLINS HAD TO ABANDON **ANOTHER** WARREN DUE TO ROAD CONSTRUCTION THOUGH.
TWIST TWIST
THANKS, FRANK. KEEP AN EYE OUT?
'EY, YOU KNOW I HEAR **EVERYTHING** SOONER OR LATER.

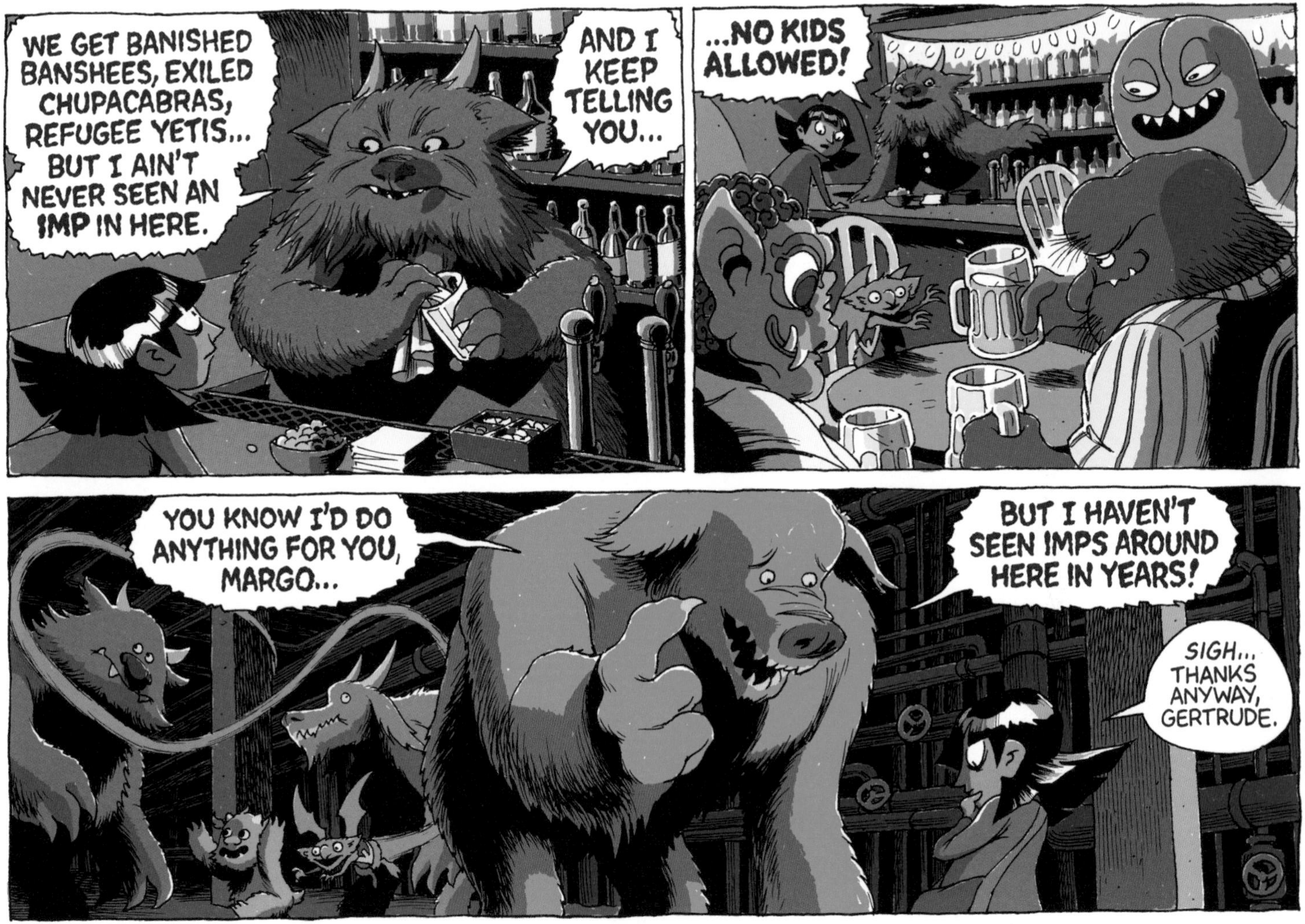
WE GET BANISHED BANSHEES, EXILED CHUPACABRAS, REFUGEE YETIS... BUT I AIN'T NEVER SEEN AN IMP IN HERE.
AND I KEEP TELLING YOU...
...NO KIDS ALLOWED!
YOU KNOW I'D DO ANYTHING FOR YOU, MARGO...
BUT I HAVEN'T SEEN IMPS AROUND HERE IN YEARS!
SIGH... THANKS ANYWAY, GERTRUDE.

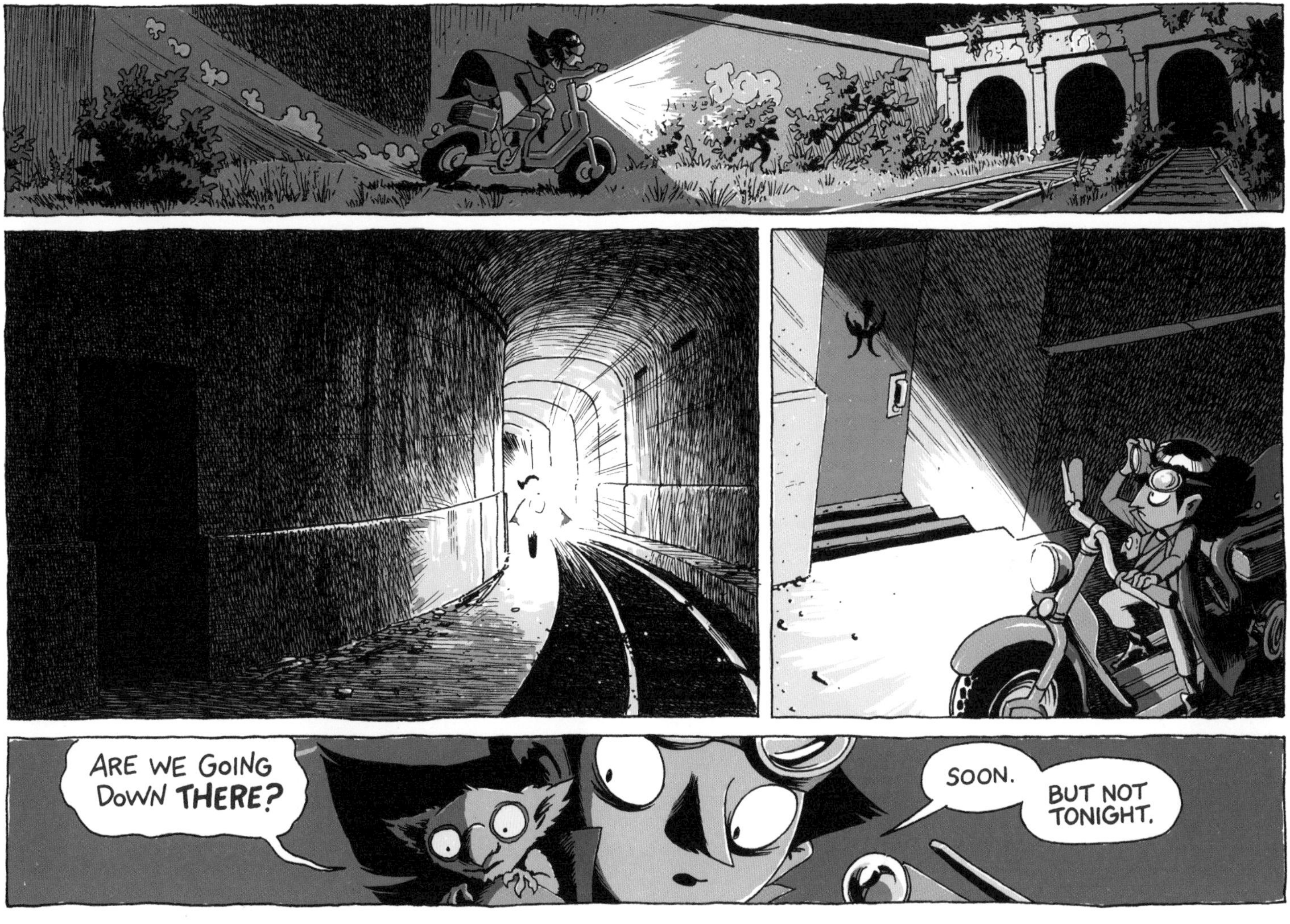
JOB
ARE WE GOING DOWN THERE?
SOON.
BUT NOT TONIGHT.

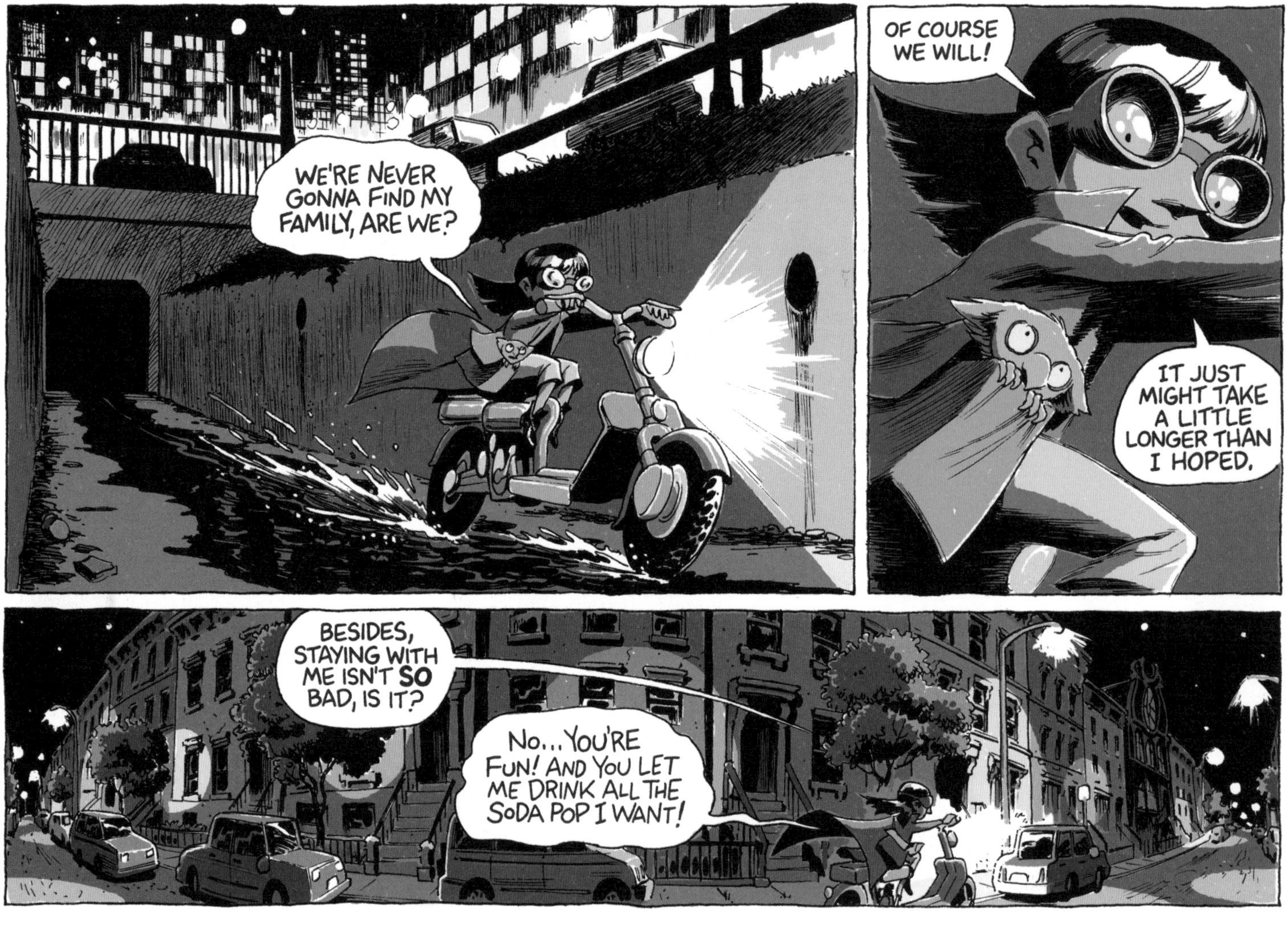
WE'RE NEVER GONNA FIND MY FAMILY, ARE WE?
OF COURSE WE WILL!
IT JUST MIGHT TAKE A LITTLE LONGER THAN I HOPED.
BESIDES, STAYING WITH ME ISN'T **SO** BAD, IS IT?
NO... YOU'RE FUN! AND YOU LET ME DRINK ALL THE SODA POP I WANT!

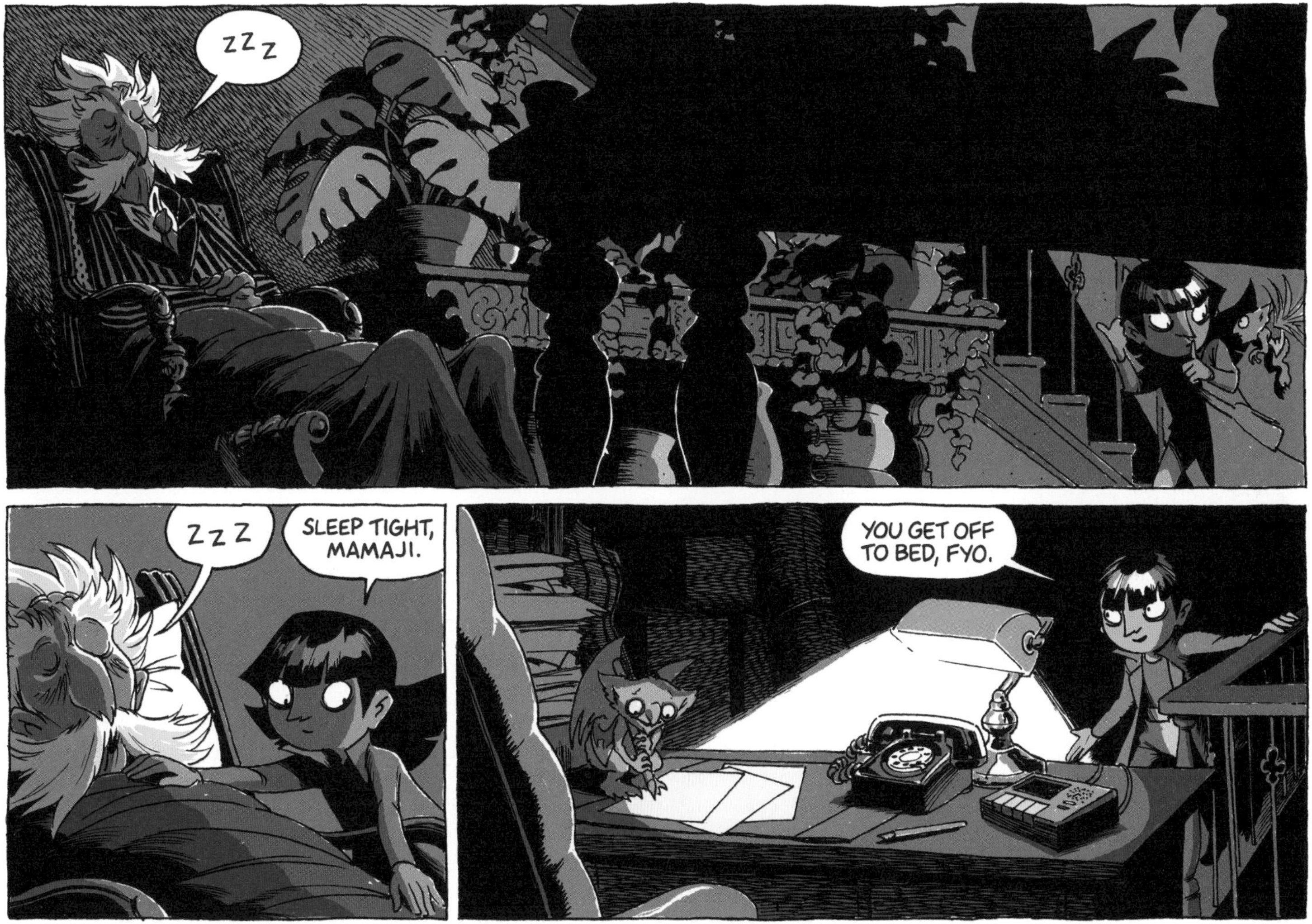
ZZZ
ZZZ
SLEEP TIGHT, MAMAJI.
YOU GET OFF TO BED, FYO.

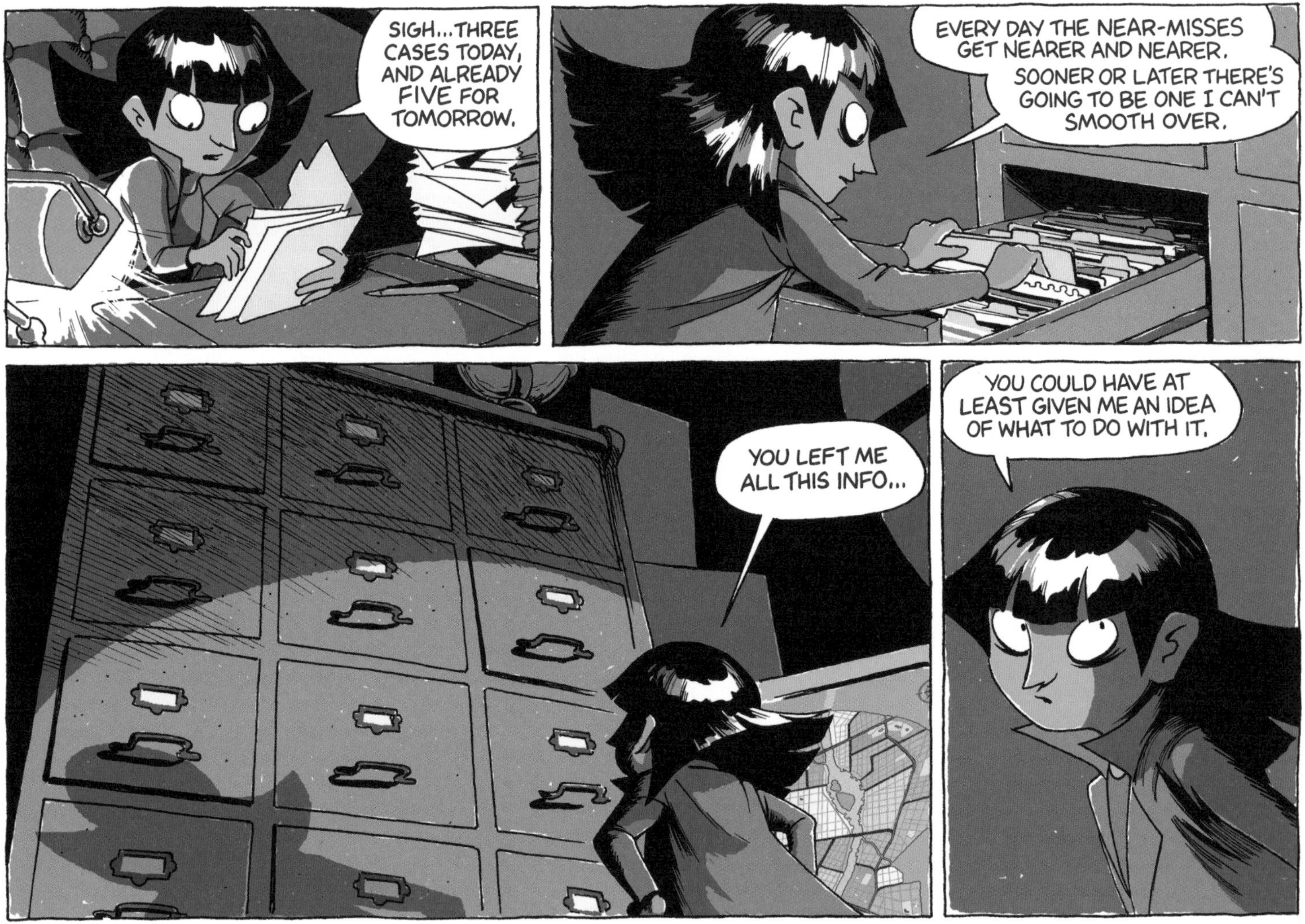
SIGH...THREE CASES TODAY, AND ALREADY FIVE FOR TOMORROW.
EVERY DAY THE NEAR-MISSES GET NEARER AND NEARER.
SOONER OR LATER THERE'S GOING TO BE ONE I CAN'T SMOOTH OVER.
YOU LEFT ME ALL THIS INFO...
YOU COULD HAVE AT LEAST GIVEN ME AN IDEA OF WHAT TO DO WITH IT.

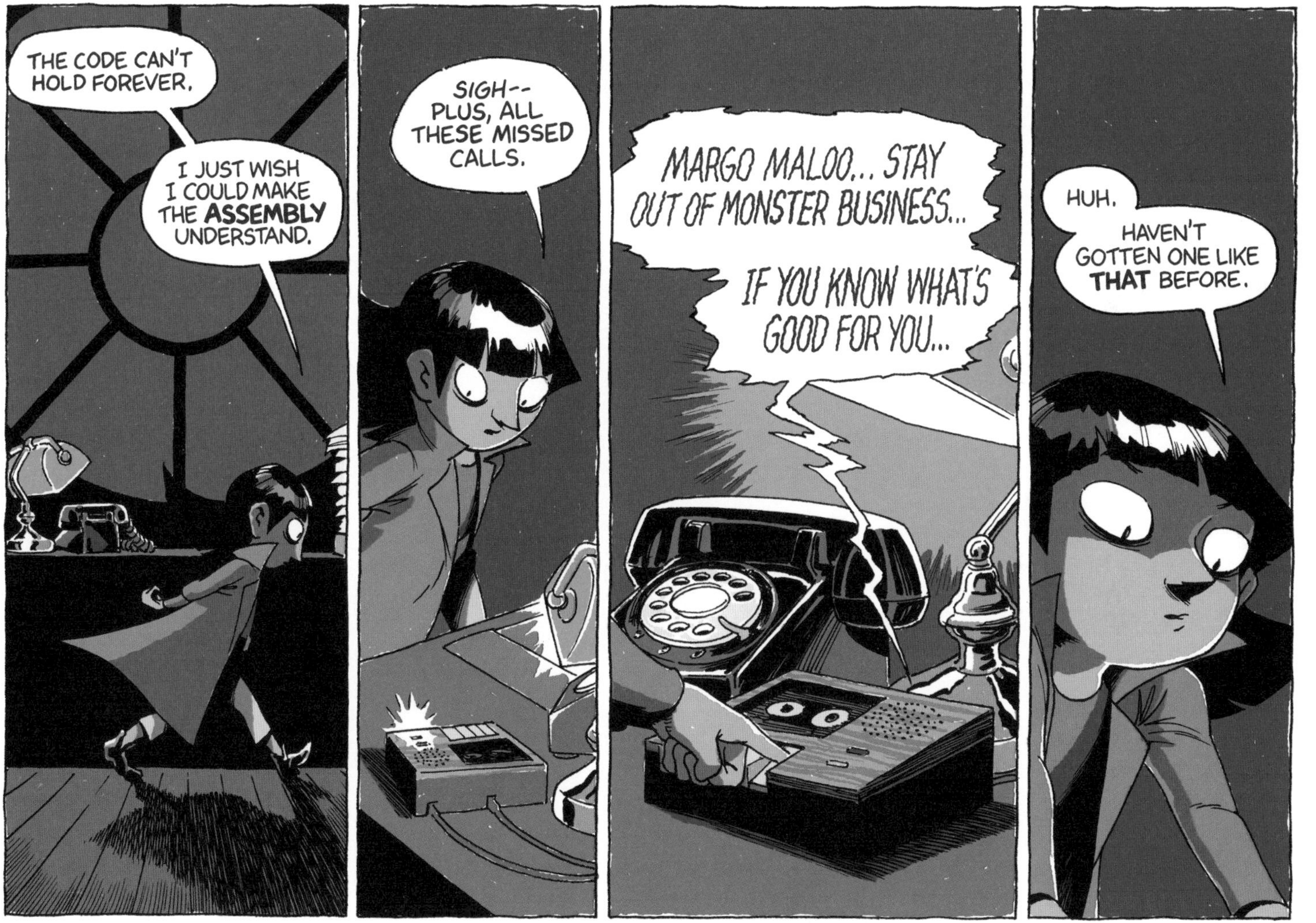
THE CODE CAN'T HOLD FOREVER.
I JUST WISH I COULD MAKE THE **ASSEMBLY** UNDERSTAND.
SIGH-- PLUS, ALL THESE MISSED CALLS.
MARGO MALOO... STAY OUT OF MONSTER BUSINESS...
IF YOU KNOW WHAT'S GOOD FOR YOU...
HUH.
HAVEN'T GOTTEN ONE LIKE **THAT** BEFORE.

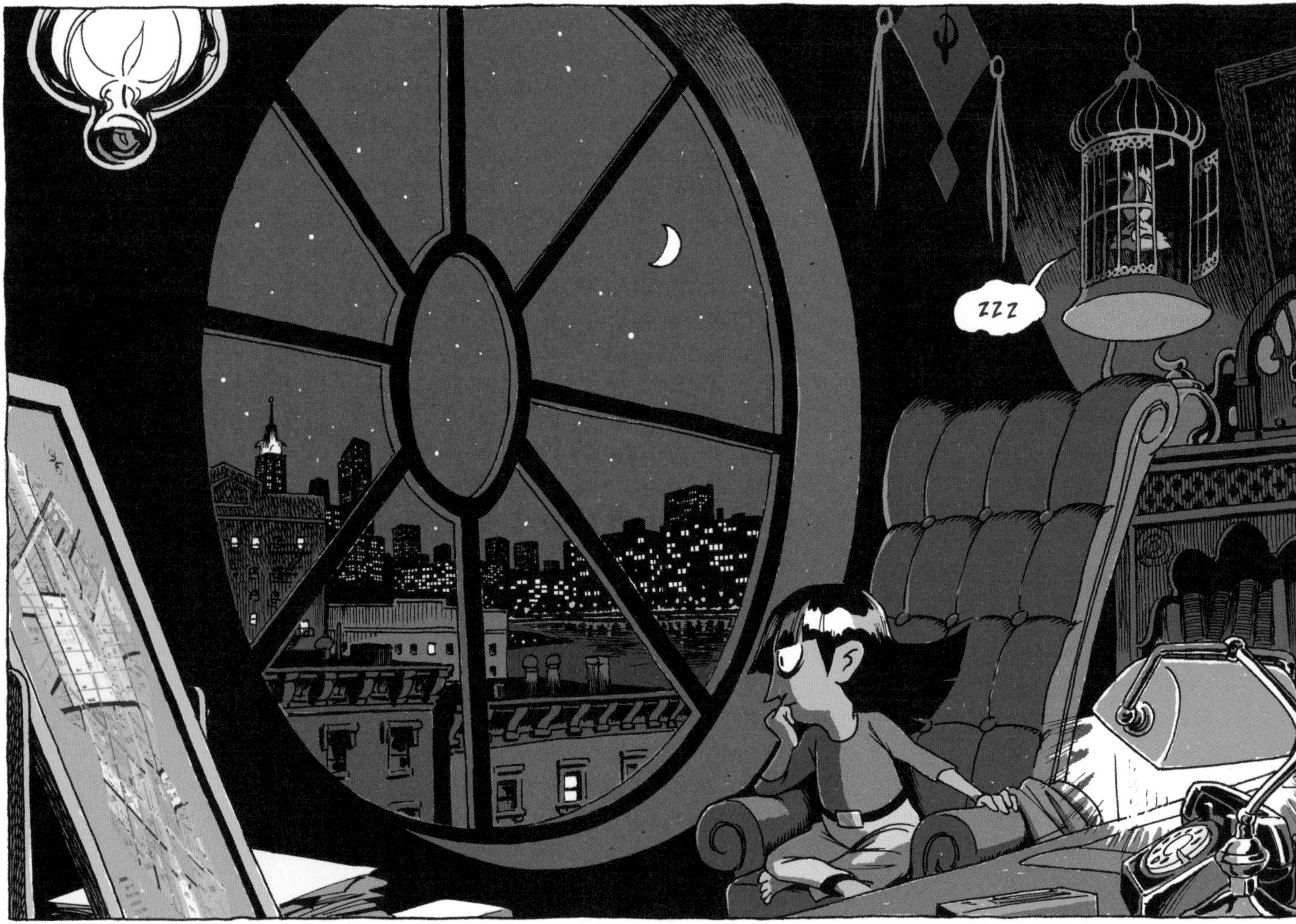
ZZZ

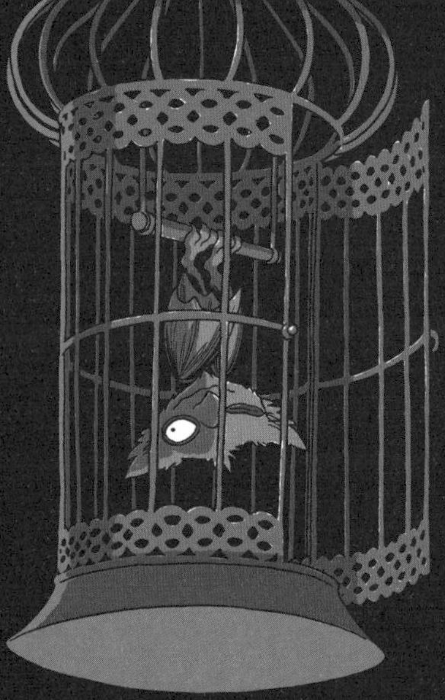

In the last book, I gave my wife, Eleanor Davis, all the thanks in existence, but somehow since then, I've accumulated several truckloads more!

[Backs up truck; dumps thanks all over her.]

Thanks to those patient patrons who support me between books, the crew at First Second, and extra thanks to Katherine Guillen and Joey Weiser for well-timed coloring help.

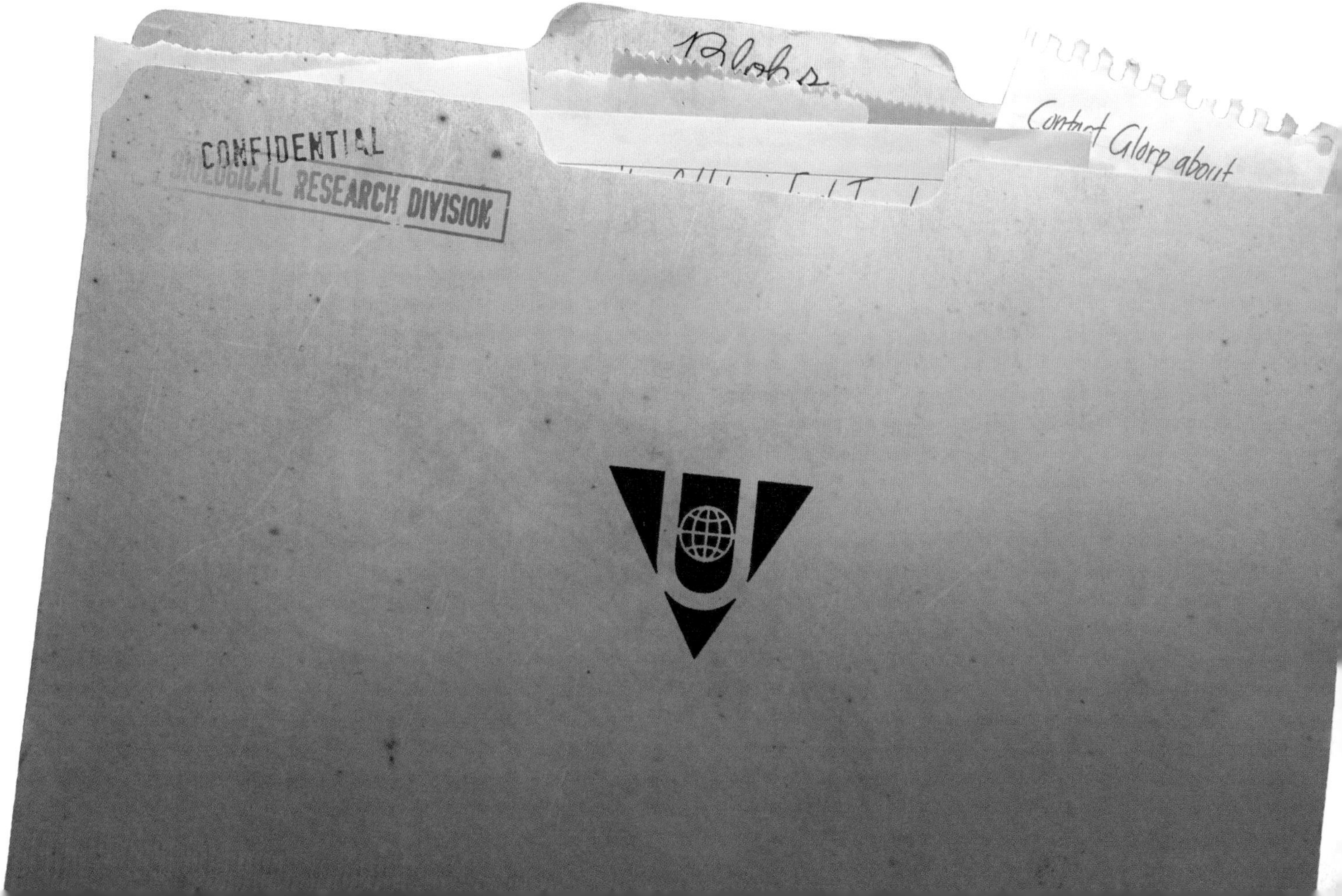
CONFIDENTIAL
RESEARCH DIVISION
Blobs
Contact Glorp about

Blobs

Blobs (Pondus Oblimo) are a species of amoeboid, jelly-like monsters.

<u>Appearance:</u> Blobs' gelatinous bodies can squash and stretch into almost any shape, but they usually take a teardrop-shaped form. They sprout armlike appendages to interact with objects and can form a "mouth" in order to speak, though they don't need it to eat. Their shimmering, translucent bodies range from pink to reddish purple. The maximum size a blob can reach is still unknown - specimens larger than automobiles have been discovered. *They get even larger...*

<u>Behaviour:</u> Blobs are slow and solitary creatures. They favor dark, damp environments, like sewers, and stake out a territory. When blobs reach a large size over many years, they can undergo a process of budding, whereby a new blob splits off from the adult. The adult will raise the young blob for a few decades, until it is large enough to live on its own.

<u>Diet:</u> Blobs can absorb just about any form of organic matter, usually preferring the algae and fungus that can be found growing on the damp walls and floor of their habitat.
Sometimes reputed to be ever-expanding and insatiable threats, in reality they are quite picky about their diet and seldom absorb sentient beings.

<u>Danger Level: Guarded</u>
Blobs are peaceful and slow to anger, preferring to squeeze into a hiding place until a threat has passed. Still, when presented with no other option, they could easily absorb a human.

Blob talisman grows inside the blob's body, like a pearl

Sometimes given as a very special gift

Baby blobs split from their parents
Cute

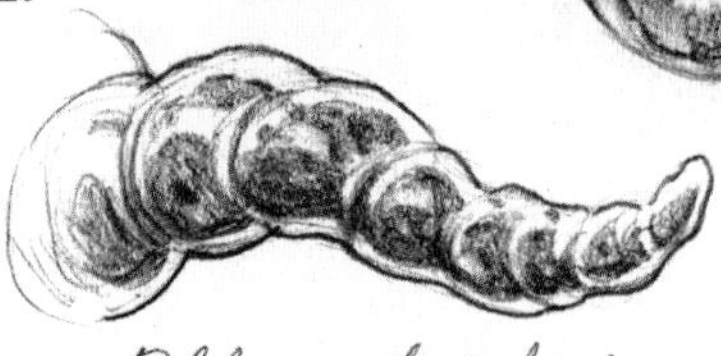

Blob pseudopod, for picking things up

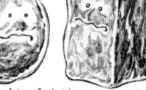

Blobs are capable of taking many shapes

Imps

Imps (Daemon impropulus) are a small, winged, frenetic species of monster, known for troublemaking and pranks.

Appearance: Imps are small and furry, with batlike wings, fringed ears, and distinctive red rings around their eyes. They come in shades of dusky red, pink, and purple. Adult imps are usually a little more than a foot in height, and weigh 1 - 3 lbs.

Behaviour: Imps are very quick, able to hover in place and quickly dart away at blinding speed, like a hummingbird. Their metabolisms run high, and they rarely hold still for long. Imps inhabit dark attics, alcoves, lofts, and other dark, high places. Their family clusters can number anywhere from between six to several dozen. Imps are quite common in Echo City, with thousands roaming the city's attics.

Not anymore... Apparently the vampires didn't care much for the imps' pranks. Only a few survived the vampire era to the present day.

Imp society puts a high value on the "prank," causing as much mischief as possible without getting caught. Imp leaders are expected to excel at pranks, which are thought to indicate high intelligence and strategic thinking.

Diet: Imps feed almost exclusively on fruit juice and other sugary liquids. Their high metabolism means they must consume almost their bodyweight of fruit juice daily. They are quite fond of human soda pop.

Danger Level: Low
Imps rarely pose any sort of actual danger, though their shenanigans can be quite exhausting and occasionally painful.

Imps' pranks can be dangerous when they're feeling truly threatened!

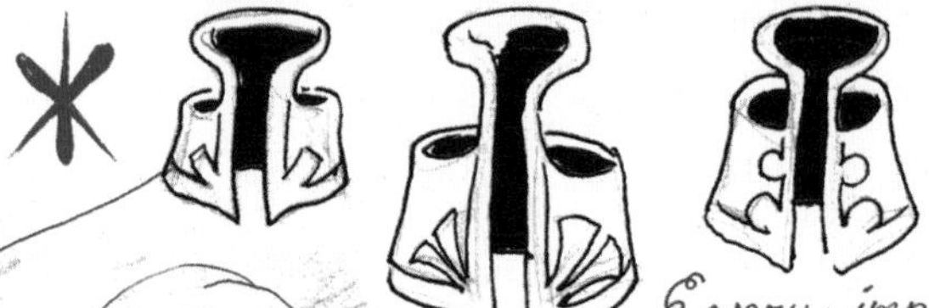

Every imp has a unique pattern on its vest

Patterns are passed down in imp families

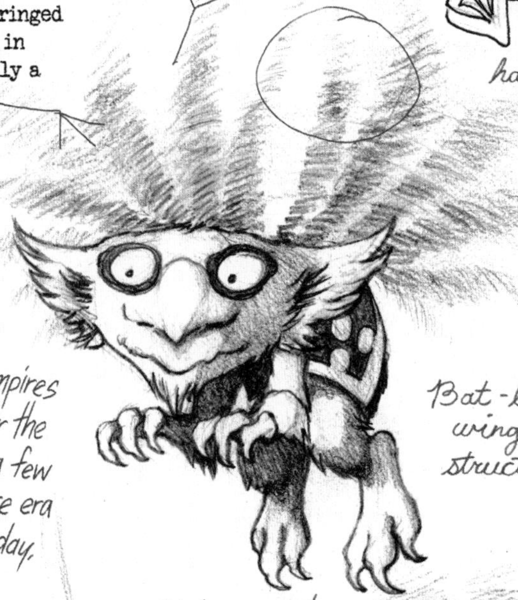

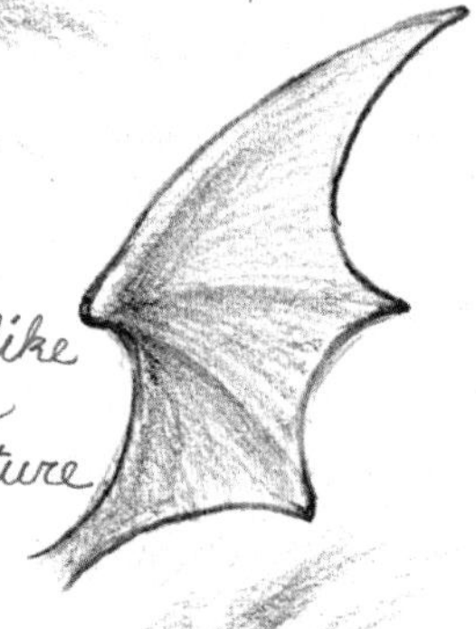

Bat-like wing structure

At top speed, imps move faster than the human eye can follow

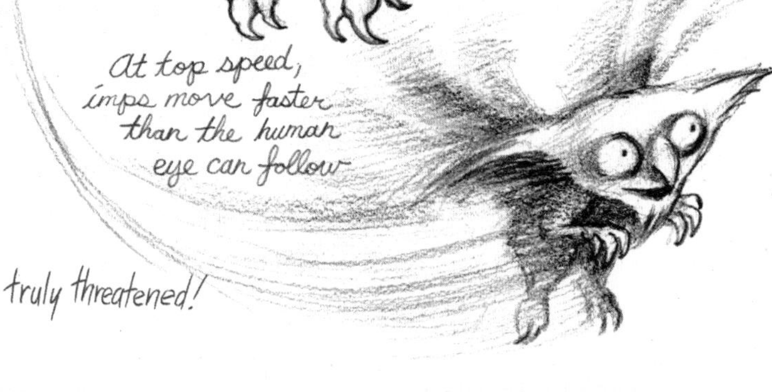

Lizard People

Lizard people (Reptilia anthropomorphus) are a species of large, bipedal, reptilian monsters.

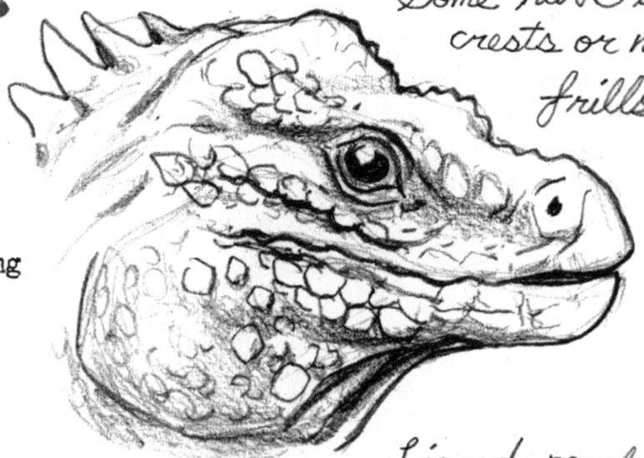

Some have spiny crests or neck frills

Appearance: Lizard people could almost be mistaken for hugely overgrown iguanas or geckos walking on two legs. Most wear some sort of clothing when outside, to help them control their body temperature in colder environs.

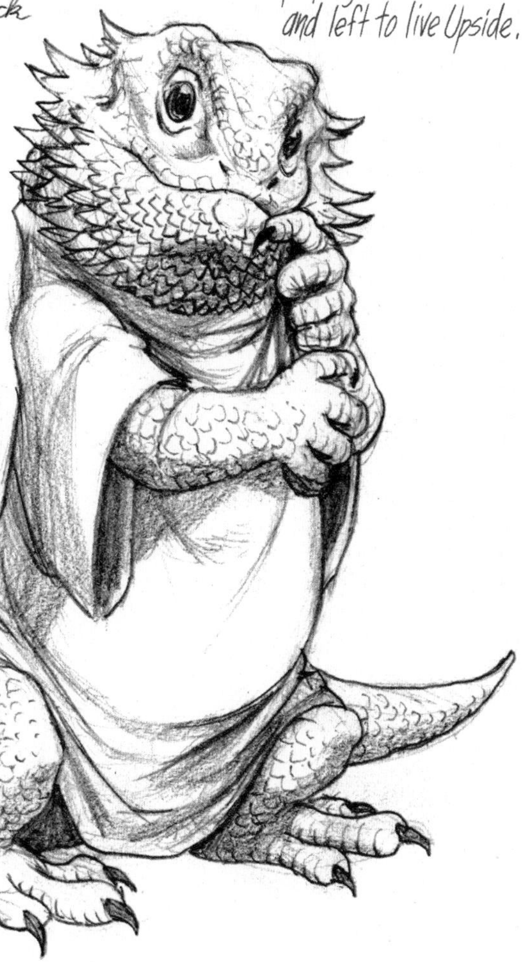

Rebellious young lizard people get kicked out and left to live Upside.

Lizard people have highly developed palettes and enjoy elaborate meals

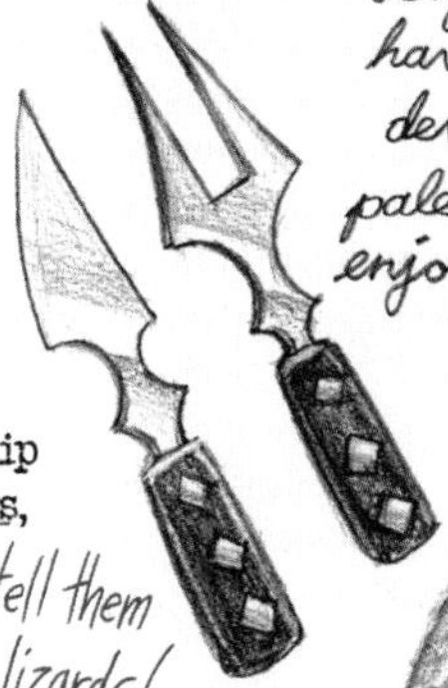

Behaviour: Lizard people live in large, complicated social groups and favor warm, well-lit places. Young lizardlings are raised to place their family above all others. Family rank is important, with the most eminent families getting the best territory, and low-ranking families pushed into the coldest corners. Duels between young lizard people are common. Lizard people worship a pantheon of dinosaurs as venerated ancestors, leaving them gifts of food.

DON'T try to tell them dinosaurs weren't actually lizards!

Diet: Lizard people are mainly carnivorous, but will eat just about anything. A lot of good cooks

Danger Level: Guarded
Lizard people can be good-humored. However, they are easily offended by any slight against their family. Beware an angry hiss - it might be the only warning sign they give before attacking.

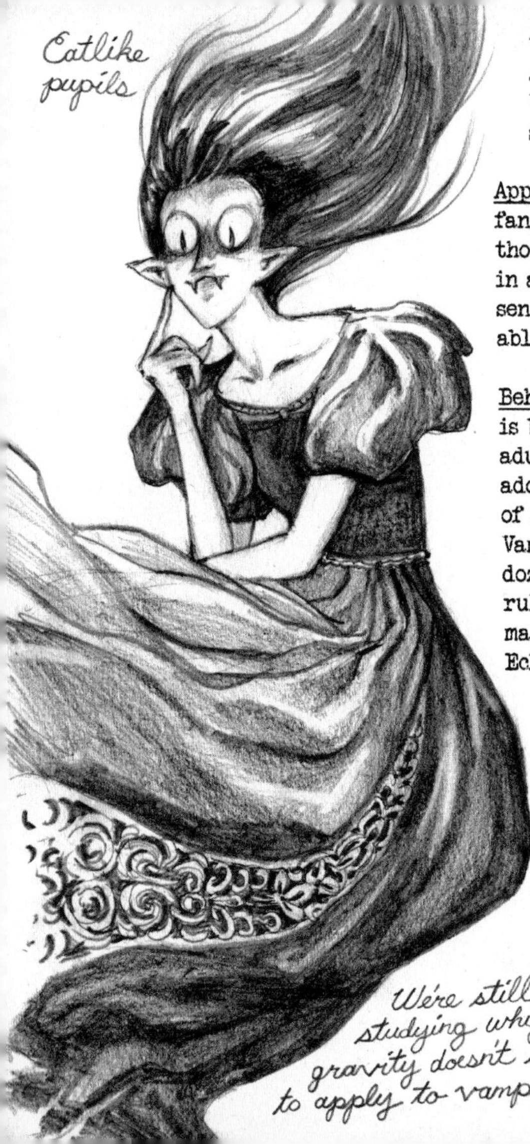
Catlike pupils
We're still studying why gravity doesn't seem to apply to vampires

Vampires

Vampires (Nocturnus sanguinans) are one of the most human-like species of monster, known for their blood-drinking habits.

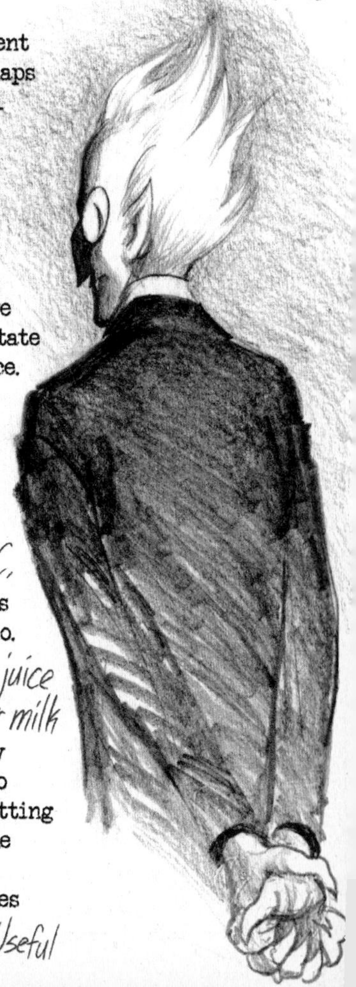
Karl Strix, the Eldest
Yikes

Appearance: Vampires resemble tall, pallid humans, with prominent fangs and very large eyes. They are extremely long-lived - perhaps thousands of years - but even ancient vampires remain youthful in appearance. They tend to be fashionable, though the fashion sense they exhibit may be decades out of date. They are also able to fly, and usually do.

Behaviour: Vampires, of course, are famed blood-drinkers. Blood is biologically necessary for them to develop into full-grown adults. Young vampires grow slowly for centuries, but only leave adolescence with their first blood meal. Vampires can enter a state of hibernation when necessary - for instance, when food is scarce. Vampires are relatively few in number - no more than a few dozen live in Echo City - but quickly became the dominant, ruling class of all monsters. Leadership is based on age, thus making the Eldest Vampire, Karl Strix, the leader of all Echo City's monsters. Not anymore! Current eldest (Astrid Strix) barely has ANY power in E.C.

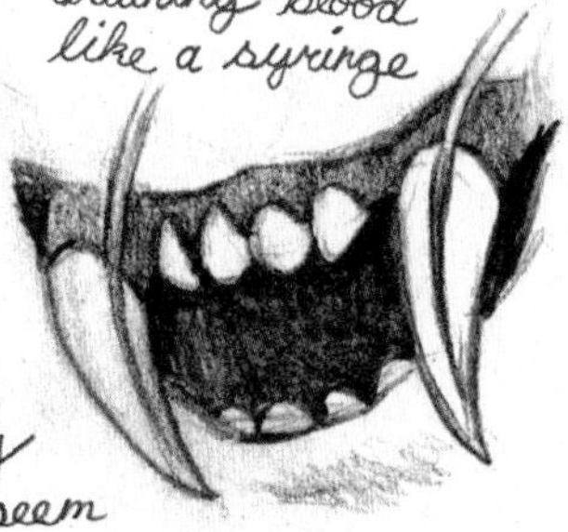
Hollow canals in fangs, for draining blood like a syringe

Diet: Blood, of course - human is preferred, but any kind will do. They CAN survive on fruit juice or milk

Danger Level: High

Adult vampires are incredibly strong and fast. They can also hypnotize via eye contact, putting the victim into an irresistible trance that can take days to shake off (and sometimes leaves permanent memory effects). Useful

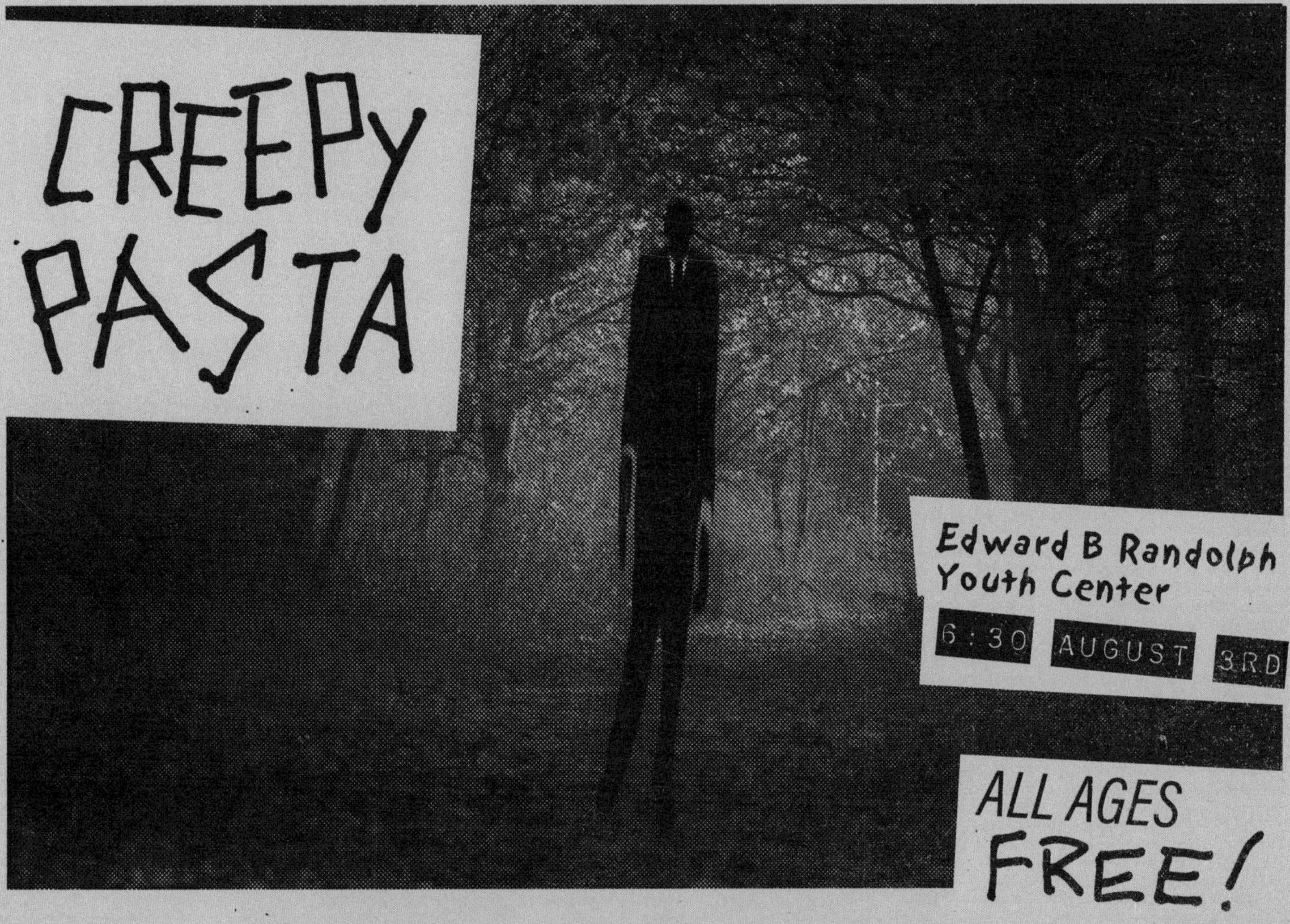
CREEPY PASTA
Edward B Randolph
Youth Center
6:30 AUGUST 3RD
ALL AGES
FREE!

These kids keep
finding monster hiding spots —
look into this

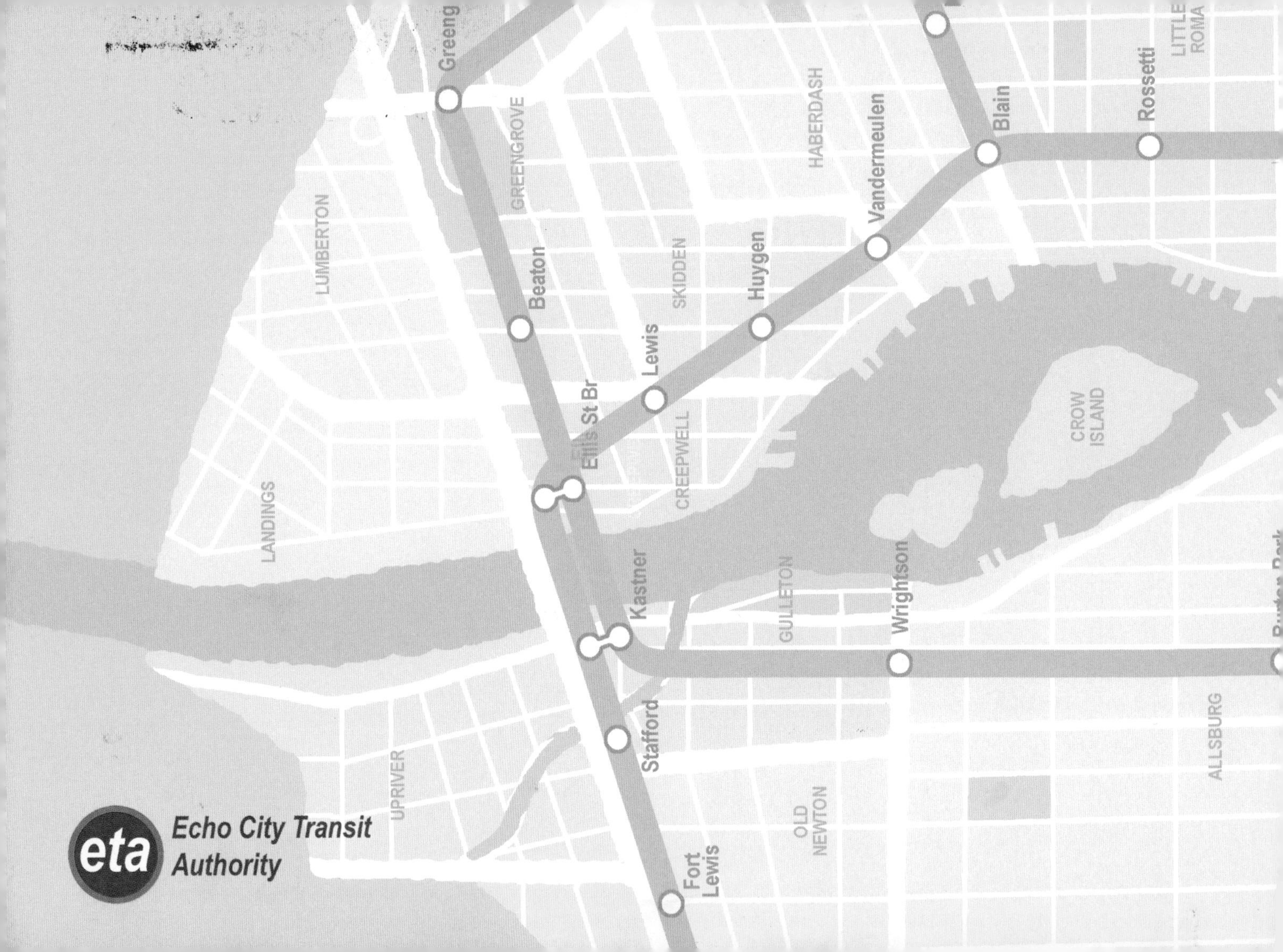
Greeng
GREENGROVE
LUMBERTON
HABERDASH
Vandermeulen
Blain
Rossetti
LITTLE ROMA
Beaton
SKIDDEN
Huygen
Lewis
Ellis St Br
CREEPWELL
CROW ISLAND
LANDINGS
Kastner
GULLETON
Wrightson
Stafford
UPRIVER
OLD NEWTON
Fort Lewis
ALLSBURG
eta
Echo City Transit Authority